SUZANNE BROCKMANN

TALL, DARK AND DEADLY

HQN™

Recycling programs
for this product may
not exist in your area.

ISBN-13: 978-0-373-77619-1

TALL, DARK AND DEADLY

Copyright © 2000 by Harlequin Books S.A.

The publisher acknowledges the copyright holder
of the individual works as follows:

GET LUCKY
Copyright © 2000 by Suzanne Brockmann

TAYLOR'S TEMPTATION
Copyright © 2001 by Suzanne Brockmann

This edition published by arrangement with Harlequin Books S.A.

For questions and comments about the quality of this book
please contact us at Customer_eCare@Harlequin.ca.

® and TM are trademarks of the publisher. Trademarks indicated with
® are registered in the United States Patent and Trademark Office, the
Canadian Trade Marks Office and in other countries.

www.HQNBooks.com

Printed in U.S.A.

CONTENTS

GET LUCKY

For Patricia McMahon

PROLOGUE

IT WAS LIKE BEING HIT by a professional linebacker.

The man barreled down the stairs and bulldozed right into Sydney, nearly knocking her onto her rear end.

To add insult to injury, he mistook her for a man.

"Sorry, bud," he tossed back over his shoulder as he kept going down the stairs.

She heard the front door of the apartment building open and then slam shut.

It was the perfect end to the evening. Girls' night out—plural—had turned into girl's night out—singular. Bette had left a message on Syd's answering machine announcing that she couldn't make it to the movies tonight. Something had come up. Something that was no doubt, six-foot-three, broad-shouldered, wearing a cowboy hat and named Scott or Brad or Wayne.

And Syd had received a call from Hilary on her cell phone as she was pulling into the multiplex parking lot. *Her* excuse for cancelling was a kid with a fever of one hundred and two.

Turning around and going home would have been too depressing. So Syd had gone to the movie alone. And ended up even *more* depressed.

The show had been interminably long and pointless, with buff young actors flexing their way across the screen. She'd alternately been bored by the story and embarrassed, both for the actors and for herself, for being fascinated by the sheer breathtaking perfection of their bodies.

Men like that—or like the football player who'd nearly knocked her over—didn't date women like Sydney Jameson.

It wasn't that she wasn't physically attractive, because she was. Or at least she could be when she bothered to do more than run a quick comb through her hair. Or when she bothered to dress in something other than the baggy shirts and loose-fitting, comfortable jeans that were her standard apparel—and that allowed the average Neanderthal rushing past her down the stairs to mistake her for a man. Of course, she comforted herself, the dimness of the 25-watt bulbs that the landlord, Mr. El Cheap-o Thompkins, had installed in the hallway light fixtures hadn't helped.

Syd trudged up the stairs to the third floor. This old house had been converted to apartments in the late 1950s. The top floor—formerly the attic—had been made into two units, both of which were far more spacious than anyone would have thought from looking at the outside of the building.

She stopped on the landing.

The door to her neighbor's apartment was ajar.

Gina Sokoloski. Syd didn't know her next-door neighbor that well. They'd passed on the stairs now and then, signed for packages when the other wasn't home, had brief conversations about such thrilling topics as the best time of year for cantaloupe.

Gina was young and shy—not yet twenty years old—and a student at the junior college. She was plain and quiet and rarely had visitors, which suited Syd just fine after living for eight months next door to the frat boys from hell.

Gina's mother had come by once or twice—one of

those tidy, quietly rich women who wore a giant diamond ring and drove a car that cost more than Syd could make in three very good years as a freelance journalist.

The he-man who'd barrelled down the stairs wasn't what Syd would have expected a boyfriend of Gina's to look like. He was older than Gina by about ten years, too, but this could well be more proof that opposites did, indeed, attract.

This old building made so many weird noises during the night. Still, she could've sworn she'd heard a distinctly human sound coming from Gina's apartment. Syd stepped closer to the open door and peeked in, but the apartment was completely dark. "Gina?"

She listened harder. There it was again. A definite sob. No doubt the son of a bitch who'd nearly knocked her over had just broken up with Gina. Leave it to a man to be in such a hurry to be gone that he'd leave the door wide open.

"Gina, your door's unlatched. Is everything okay in here?" Syd knocked more loudly as she pushed the door open even farther.

The dim light from the hallway shone into the living room and...

The place was trashed. Furniture knocked over, lamps broken, a bookshelf overturned. Dear God, the man hurrying down the stairs hadn't been Gina's boyfriend. He'd been a burglar.

Or worse...

Hair rising on the back of her neck, Syd dug through her purse for her cell phone. Please God, don't let Gina have been home. Please God, let that funny little sound be the ancient swamp cooler or the pipes or the wind wheezing through the vent in the crawl space between the ceiling and the eaves....

But then she heard it again. It was definitely a muffled whimper.

Syd's fingers closed around her phone as she reached with her other hand for the light switch on the wall by the door. She flipped it on.

And there, huddled in the corner of her living room, her face bruised and bleeding, her clothing torn and bloody, was Gina.

Syd locked the door behind her and dialed 911.

CHAPTER ONE

ALL EARLY-MORNING CONVERSATION in Captain Joe Catalanotto's outer office stopped dead as everyone turned to look at Lucky.

It was a festival of raised eyebrows and opened mouths. The astonishment level wouldn't have been any higher if Lieutenant Luke "Lucky" O'Donlon of SEAL Team Ten's Alpha Squad had announced he was quitting the units to become a monk.

All the guys were staring at him—Jones and Blue and Skelly. A flash of surprise had even crossed Crash Hawken's imperturbable face. Frisco was there, too, having come out of a meeting with Joe and Harvard, the team's senior chief. Lucky had caught them all off guard. It would've been funny—except he wasn't feeling much like laughing.

"Look, it's no big deal," Lucky said with a shrug, wishing that simply saying the words would make it so, wishing he could feel as nonchalant as he sounded.

No one said a word. Even recently promoted Chief Wes Skelly was uncharacteristically silent. But Lucky didn't need to be telepathic to know what his teammates were thinking.

He'd lobbied loud and long for a chance to be included in Alpha Squad's current mission—a covert assignment for which Joe Cat himself didn't even know the details. He'd only been told to ready a five-man team to insert somewhere in Eastern Europe; to prepare to depart at a moment's notice, prepare to be gone for an undetermined amount of time.

It was the kind of assignment guaranteed to get the heart pumping and adrenaline running, the kind of assignment Lucky lived for.

And Lucky had been one of the chosen few. Just yesterday morning he'd done a victory dance when Joe Cat had told him to get his gear ready to go. Yet here he was, barely twenty-four hours later, requesting reassignment, asking the captain to count him out—*and* to call in some old favors to get him temporarily assigned to a not-so-spine-tingling post at the SEAL training base here in Coronado, effective ASAP.

Lucky forced a smile. "It's not like you'll have trouble replacing me, Captain." He glanced at Jones and Skelly who were both practically salivating at the thought of doing just that.

The captain gestured with his head toward his office, completely unfooled by Lucky's pretense at indifference. "You want to step inside and tell me what this is all about?"

Lucky didn't need the privacy. "It's no big secret, Cat. My sister's getting married in a few weeks. If I leave on this assignment, there's a solid chance I won't be back in time."

Wes Skelly couldn't keep his mouth shut a second longer. "I thought you were heading down to San Diego last night to read her the riot act."

Lucky had intended to. He'd gone to visit Ellen and her alleged fiancé, one geeky college professor by the name of Gregory Price, intending to lay down the law; intending to demand that his twenty-two-year-old baby sister wait at least another year before she take such a major step as marriage. He'd gone fully intending to be persuasive. She was impossibly young. How could she be ready to commit to one man—one who wore sweaters to work, at that—when she hadn't had a chance yet to truly live?

But Ellen was Ellen, and Ellen had made up her mind. She was so certain, so unafraid. And as Lucky had watched her smile at the man she was determined to spend the rest of her life with, he'd marveled at the fact that they'd had the same mother. Of course, maybe it was the fact they had different fathers that made them such opposites when it came to commitment. Because, although Ellen was ready to get married at twenty-two, Lucky could imagine feeling too young to be tied down at age eighty-two.

Still, he'd been the one to give in.

It was Greg who had convinced him. It was the way he looked at Ellen, the way the man's love for Lucky's little sister shone in his eyes that had the SEAL giving them both his blessing—and his promise that he'd be at the wedding to give the bride away.

Never mind the fact that he'd have to turn down what was shaping up to be the most exciting assignment of the year.

"I'm the only family she's got," Lucky said quietly. "I've got to be there for her wedding, if I can. At least I've got to *try*."

The Captain nodded. "Okay," he said. That was explanation enough for him. "Jones, ready your gear."

Wes Skelly made a squawk of disappointment that was cut off by one sharp look from the senior chief. He turned away abruptly.

Captain Catalanotto glanced at Frisco, who worked as a classroom instructor when he wasn't busy helping run the SEAL BUD/S training facility. "What do you think about using O'Donlon for your little project?"

Alan "Frisco" Francisco had been Lucky's swim buddy. Years ago, they'd made it through BUD/S training together and had worked side by side on countless assignments—until Desert Storm. Lucky had been ready to ship out to the Middle East with the rest of Alpha Squad when he'd received word that his mother had died. He'd stayed behind and Frisco had gone—and gotten his leg nearly blown off during a rescue mission. Even though Frisco no longer came out into the field, the two men had stayed tight.

In fact, Lucky was going to be the godfather later this year when Frisco and his wife Mia had their first baby.

Frisco now nodded at the Captain. "Yeah," he said. "Definitely. O'Donlon's perfect for the assignment."

"What assignment?" Lucky asked. "If it's training an all-woman SEAL team, then, yes, thank you very much, I'm your man."

There, see? He'd managed to make a joke. He was already starting to feel better. Maybe he wasn't going out into the real world with Alpha Squad, but he was going to get a chance to work with his best friend again. And—his natural optimism returning—he just *knew* there was a Victoria's Secret model in his immediate future. This *was* California, after all. And he wasn't nicknamed Lucky for nothing.

But Frisco didn't laugh. In fact, he looked seriously grim as he tucked a copy of the morning paper beneath his arm. "Not even close. You're going to hate this."

Lucky looked into the eyes of the man he knew better than a brother. And he didn't have to say a word. Frisco knew it didn't really matter what his buddy did over the next few weeks. Everything would pale beside the lost opportunity of the assignment he'd passed up.

Frisco gestured for him to come outside.

Lucky took one last look around Alpha Squad's office. Harvard was already handling the paperwork that would put him temporarily under Frisco's command. Joe Cat was deep in discussion with Wes Skelly, who still looked unhappy that he'd been passed over yet again. Blue McCoy, Alpha Squad's executive officer, was on the phone, his voice lowered—probably talking to Lucy. He had on that telltale frown of concern he wore so often these days when he spoke to his wife. She was a San Felipe police detective, involved with some big secret case that had the usually unflappable Blue on edge.

Crash sat communing with his computer. Jones had left in a rush, but now he returned, his gear already organized. No doubt the dweeb had already packed last night, just in case, like a good little Boy Scout. Ever since the man had gotten married, he hurried home whenever he had the chance, instead of partying hard with Lucky and Bob and Wes. Jones's nickname was Cowboy, but his wild and woolly days of drinking and chasing women were long gone. Lucky had always considered the smooth-talking, good-looking Jones to be something of a rival both in love and war, but he was completely agreeable these days, walking around with a permanent smile on his face, as if he knew something Lucky didn't.

Even when Lucky had won the spot on the current team—the spot he'd just given up—Jones had smiled and shaken his hand.

The truth was, Lucky resented Cowboy Jones. By all rights, he should be miserable—a man like that—roped into marriage, tied down with a drooling kid in diapers.

Yeah, he resented Cowboy, no doubt about it.

Resented, and envied him his complete happiness.

Frisco was waiting impatiently by the door, but Lucky took his time. "Stay cool, guys."

He knew when Joe Cat got the order to go, the team would simply vanish. There would be no time spent on farewells.

"God, I hate it when they leave without me," he said to Frisco as he followed his friend into the bright sunshine. "So, what's this about?"

"You haven't seen today's paper, have you?" Frisco asked.

Lucky shook his head. "No, why?"

Frisco silently handed him the newspaper he'd been holding.

The headline said it all—Serial Rapist Linked to Coronado SEALs?

Lucky swore pungently. "Serial *rapist?* This is the first I've heard of this."

"It's the first any of us have heard of this," Frisco said grimly. "But apparently there's been a series of rapes in Coronado and San Felipe over the past few weeks. And with the latest—it happened two nights ago—the police now believe there's some kind of connection linking the attacks. Or so they say."

Lucky quickly skimmed the article. There were very few facts about the attacks—seven—or about the victims. The only mention of the women who'd been attacked was of the latest—an unnamed 19-year-old college student. In all cases, the rapist wore a feature-distorting pair of panty hose on his head, but he was described as a Caucasian man with a crew cut, with either brown or dark blond hair, approximately six feet tall, muscularly built and about thirty years of age.

The article focused on ways in which women in both towns could ensure their safety. One of the tips recommended was to stay away—far away—from the U.S. Navy base.

The article ended with the nebulous statement, "When

asked about the rumored connection of the serial rapist to the Coronado naval base, and in particular to the teams of SEALs stationed there, the police spokesman replied, 'Our investigation will be thorough, and the military base is a good place to start.'

"Known for their unconventional fighting techniques as well as their lack of discipline, the SEALs have had their presence felt in the towns of Coronado and San Felipe many times in the past, with late-night and early-morning explosions often startling the guests at the famed Hotel del Coronado. Lieutenant Commander Alan Francisco of the SEALs could not be reached for comment."

Lucky swore again. "Way to make us look like the spawn of Satan. And let me guess just how hard—" he looked at the top of the article for the reporter's name "—this S. Jameson guy tried to reach you for comment."

"Oh, the reporter tried," Frisco countered as he began moving toward the jeep that would take him across the base to his office. Lucky could tell from the way he leaned on his cane that his knee was hurting today. "But I stayed hidden. I didn't want to say anything to alienate the police until I had the chance to talk to Admiral Forrest. And he agreed with my plan."

"Which is…?"

"There's a task force being formed to catch this son of a bitch," Frisco told him. "Both the Coronado and San Felipe police are part of it—as well as the state police, and a special unit from FInCOM. The admiral pulled some strings, and got us included. That's why I went to see Cat and Harvard. I need an officer I can count on to be part of this task force. Someone I can trust."

Someone exactly like Lucky. He nodded. "When do I start?"

"There's a meeting in the San Felipe police station

at 0900 hours. Meet me in my office—we'll go down there together. Wear your whites and every ribbon you've got." Frisco climbed behind the wheel of the jeep, tossing his cane into the back. "There's more, too. I want you to handpick a team, and I want you to catch this bastard. As quickly as possible. If the perp *is* a spec-warrior, we're going to need more than a task force to nail him."

Lucky held on to the side of the jeep. "Do you really think this guy could be one of us?"

Frisco shook his head. "I don't know. I hope to hell he's not."

The rapist had attacked seven women—one of them a girl just a little bit younger than his sister. And Lucky knew that it didn't matter who this bastard was. It only mattered that they stop him before he struck again.

"Whoever he is," he promised his best friend and commanding officer, "I'll find him. And after I do, he's going to be sorry he was born."

SYDNEY WAS RELIEVED TO find she wasn't the only woman in the room. She was glad to see that Police Detective Lucy McCoy was part of the task force being set up this morning, its single goal: to catch the San Felipe Rapist.

Out of the seven attacks, five had taken place in the lower-rent town of San Felipe. And although the two towns were high-school sports-team rivals, this was one case in which Coronado was more than happy to let San Felipe take the title.

They'd gathered here at the San Felipe police station ready to work together to apprehend the rapist.

Syd had first met Detective Lucy McCoy last Saturday night. The detective had arrived on the scene at Gina Sokoloski's apartment clearly pulled out of bed, her face clean of makeup, her shirt buttoned wrong—and spitting mad that she hadn't been called sooner.

Syd had been fiercely guarding Gina, who was frighteningly glassy-eyed and silent after the trauma of her attack.

The male detectives had tried to be gentle, but even gentle couldn't cut it at a time like this. *Can you tell us what happened, miss?*

Sheesh. As if Gina would be able to look up at these men and tell them how she'd turned to find a man in her living room, how he'd grabbed her before she could run, slapped his hand across her mouth before she could scream, and then...

And then that Neanderthal who had nearly run Syd down on the stairs had raped this girl. Brutally. Violently. Syd would've bet good money that she had been a virgin, poor shy little thing. What an awful way to be introduced to sex.

Syd had wrapped her arms tightly around the girl, and told the detectives in no uncertain terms that they had better get a woman down here, pronto. After what Gina had been through, she didn't need to suffer the embarrassment of having to talk about it with a man.

But Gina had told Detective Lucy McCoy all of it, in a voice that was completely devoid of emotion—as if she were reporting facts that had happened to someone else, not herself.

She'd tried to hide. She'd cowered in the corner, and he hit her. And hit her. And then he was on top of her, tearing her clothing and forcing himself between her legs. With his hands around her throat, she'd struggled even just to breathe, and he'd...

Lucy had quietly explained about the rape kit, explained about the doctor's examination that Gina still had to endure, explained that as much as Gina wanted to, she couldn't take a shower. Not yet.

Lucy had explained that the more Gina could tell her about the man who'd attacked her, the better their chances were of catching him. If there was anything more she could report about the words he'd spoken, any little detail she may have left out....

Syd had described the man who nearly knocked her over on the stairs. The lighting was bad. She hadn't gotten a good look at him. In fact, she couldn't even be sure that he wasn't still wearing the nylon stocking over his face that Gina had described. But she could guess at his height—taller than she was, and his build—powerful—and she could say for a fact that he was a white male, somewhere between twenty-five and thirty-five years of age, with very short, crew-cut hair.

And he spoke in a low-pitched, accentless voice. *Sorry, bud.*

It was weird and creepy to think that a man who'd brutalized Gina would have taken the time to apologize for bumping into Syd. It was also weird and creepy to think that if Syd had been home, she might have heard the noise of the struggle, heard Gina's muffled cries and might've been able to help.

Or, perhaps Syd might've been the victim herself.

Before they'd headed over to the hospital, Gina had loosened her grip on the torn front of her shirt and showed Lucy and Syd a burn. The son of a bitch had branded the girl on her breast, in what looked like the shape of a bird.

Lucy had stiffened, clearly recognizing the marking. She'd excused herself, and found the other detectives. And although she'd spoken in a lowered voice, Syd had moved to the door so she could hear.

"It's our guy again," Lucy McCoy had grimly told the other detectives. "Gina's been burned with a Budweiser, too."

Our guy *again*. When Syd asked if there had been other similar attacks, Lucy had bluntly told her that she wasn't at liberty to discuss that.

Syd had gone to the hospital with the girl, staying with her until her mother arrived.

But then, despite the fact that it was three o'clock in the morning, there were too many unanswered questions for Syd to go home and go to sleep. As a former investigative reporter, she knew a thing or two about finding answers to unanswered questions. A few well-placed phone calls connected her to Silva Fontaine, a woman on the late-night shift at the hospital's Rape Counseling Center. Silva had informed Syd that six women had come in in half as many weeks. Six women who hadn't been attacked by husbands or boyfriends or relatives or co-workers. Six women who had been attacked in their own homes by an unknown assailant. Same as Gina.

A little research on the Internet had turned up the fact that a *budweiser* wasn't just a bottle of beer. U.S. Navy personnel who went through the rigorous Basic Underwater Demolition Training over at the SEAL facility in nearby Coronado were given a pin in the shape of a flying eagle carrying a trident and a stylized gun, upon their entrance into the SEAL units.

This pin was nicknamed a budweiser.

Every U.S. Navy SEAL had one. It represented the SEAL acronym of sea, air and land, the three environments in which the commando-like men expertly operated. In other words, they jumped out of planes, soaring through the air with specially designed parachutes as easily as they crawled through jungle, desert or city, as easily as they swam through the deep waters of the sea.

They had a near-endless list of warrior qualifications—everything from hand-to-hand combat to high-tech computer warfare, underwater demolition to sniper-quality marksmanship. They could pilot planes or boats, operate tanks and land vehicles.

Although it wasn't listed, they could also, no doubt, leap tall buildings with a single bound.

Yeah, the list was impressive. It was kind of like looking at Superman's resume.

But it was also alarming.

Because *this* superhero had turned bad. For weeks, some psycho Navy SEAL had been stalking the women of San Felipe. Seven women had been brutally attacked, yet there had been no warnings issued, no news reports telling women to take caution.

Syd had been furious.

She'd spent the rest of the night writing.

And in the morning, she'd gone to the police station, the freelance article she'd written for the *San Felipe Journal* in hand.

She'd been shown into Chief Zale's office and negotiations had started. The San Felipe police didn't want any information about the attacks to be publicized. When Zale found out Syd was a freelance reporter, and that she'd been there at the crime scene for hours last night, he'd nearly had an aneurysm. He was convinced that if this story broke, the rapist would go into deep hiding and they'd never apprehend him. The chief told Syd flatly that the police didn't know for certain if all seven of the attacks had been made by the same man—the branding of the victim with the budweiser pin had only been done to Gina and one other woman.

Zale had demanded Syd hold all the detailed information about the recent attacks. Syd had countered with a request to write the exclusive story after the rapist was caught, to sit in with the task force being formed to apprehend the rapist—provided she could write a series of police-approved articles for the local papers, now warning women of the threat.

Zale had had a cow.

Syd had stood firm despite being blustered at for several hours, and eventually Zale had conceded. But, wow, had he been ticked off.

Still, here she was. Sitting in with the task force.

She recognized the police chief and several detectives from Coronado, as well as several representatives from the California State Police. And although no one introduced her, she caught the names of a trio of FInCOM Agents, as well. Huang, Sudenberg and Novak—she jotted their names in her notebook.

It was funny to watch them interact. Coronado didn't think much of San Felipe, and vice versa. However, both groups preferred each other over the state troopers. The Finks simply remained aloof. Yet solidarity was formed—at least in part—when the U.S. Navy made the scene.

"Sorry, I'm late." The man in the doorway was blindingly handsome—the blinding due in part to the bright white of his naval uniform and the dazzling rows of colorful ribbons on his chest. But only in part. His face was that of a movie star, with an elegantly thin nose that hinted of aristocracy, and eyes that redefined the word *blue*. His hair was sunstreaked and stylishly long in front. Right now it was combed neatly back, but with one puff of wind, or even a brief blast of humidity, it would be dancing around his face, waving tendrils of spun gold. His skin was perfectly tanned—the better to show off the white flash of his teeth as he smiled.

He was, without a doubt, the sheer perfection of a Ken doll come to life.

Syd wasn't sure, but she thought the braids on his sleeves meant he was some sort of officer.

The living Ken—with all of his U.S. Navy accessories—somehow managed to squeeze his extremely broad shoulders through the door. He stepped into the room. "Lieutenant Commander Francisco asked me to convey his regrets." His voice was a melodic baritone, slightly husky with just a trace of Southern California, dude. "There's been a serious training accident on the base, and he was unable to leave."

San Felipe Detective Lucy McCoy leaned forward. "Is everyone all right?"

"Hey, Lucy." He bestowed a brief but special smile upon the female detective. It didn't surprise Syd one bit that he should know the pretty brunette by name. "We got a SEAL candidate in a DDC—a deck decompression chamber. Frisco—Lieutenant Commander Francisco— had to fly out to the site with some of the doctors from the naval hospital. It was a routine dive, everything was done completely by the book—until one of the candidates started showing symptoms of the bends—*while* he was in the water. They still don't know what the hell went wrong. Bobby got him out and back on board, and popped him in the DDC, but from his description, it sounds like this guy's already had a CNS hit—a central nervous system hit," he translated. "You know, when a nitrogen bubble expands in the brain." He shook his head, his blue eyes somber, his pretty mouth grim. "Even if this man survives, he could be seriously brain damaged."

U.S. Navy Ken sat down in the only unoccupied chair

at the table, directly across from Sydney, as he glanced around the room. "I'm sure you all understand Lieutenant Commander Francisco's need to look into this situation immediately."

Syd tried not to stare, but it was hard. At three feet away, she should have been able to see this man's imperfections—if not quite a wart, then maybe a chipped tooth. Some nose hair at least.

But at three feet away, he was even more gorgeous. *And* he smelled good, too.

Chief Zale gave him a baleful look. "And you are...?"

Navy Ken half stood up again. "I'm sorry. Of course, I should have introduced myself." His smile was sheepish. Gosh darn it, it said, I plumb forgot that not everybody here knows who I am, wonderful though I may be. "Lieutenant Luke O'Donlon, of the U.S. Navy SEALs."

Syd didn't have to be an expert at reading body language to know that everyone in the room—at least everyone male—hated the Navy. And if they hadn't before, they sure did now. The jealousy in the room was practically palpable. Lieutenant Luke O'Donlon gleamed. He shone. He was all white and gold and sunlight and sky-blue eyes.

He was a god. The mighty king of all Ken dolls.

And he knew it.

His glance touched Syd only briefly as he looked around the room, taking inventory of the police and FInCOM personnel. But as Zale's assistant passed out manila files, Navy Ken's gaze settled back on Syd. He smiled, and it was such a perfect, slightly puzzled smile, Syd nearly laughed aloud. Any second now and he was going to ask her who she was.

"Are you FInCOM?" he mouthed to her, taking the file

that was passed to him and warmly nodding his thanks to the Coronado detective who was sitting beside him.

Syd shook her head, no.

"From the Coronado PD?" he asked silently.

Zale had begun to speak, and Syd shook her head again, then pointedly turned her attention to the head of the table.

The San Felipe police chief spoke at length about stepping up patrol cars in the areas where the rapes had taken place. He spoke of a team that would be working around the clock, attempting to find a pattern in the locations of the attacks, or among the seven victims. He talked about semen samples and DNA. He glared at Syd as he spoke of the need to keep the details of the crimes, of the rapist's MO—method of operation—from leaking to the public. He brought up the nasty little matter of the SEAL pin, heated by the flame from a cigarette lighter and used to burn a mark onto the bodies of the last two victims.

Navy Ken cleared his throat and interrupted. "I'm sure it's occurred to you that if this guy *were* a SEAL, he'd have to be pretty stupid to advertise it this way. Isn't it much more likely that he's trying to make you believe he's a SEAL?"

"Absolutely," Zale responded. "Which is why we implied that we thought he was a SEAL in the article that came out in this morning's paper. We want him to think he's winning, to become careless."

"So you *don't* think he's a SEAL," the SEAL tried to clarify.

"Maybe," Syd volunteered, "he's a SEAL who wants to be caught."

Navy Ken's eyes narrowed slightly as he gazed at her, clearly thinking hard. "I'm sorry," he said. "I know just about everyone else here, but we haven't been introduced. Are you a police psychologist?"

Zale didn't let Syd reply. "Ms. Jameson is going to be working very closely with you, Lieutenant."

Ms. not Doctor. Syd saw that information register in the SEAL's eyes.

But then she realized what Zale had said and sat back in her chair. "I am?"

O'Donlon leaned forward. "Excuse me?"

Zale looked a little too pleased with himself. "Lieutenant Commander Francisco put in an official request to have a SEAL team be part of this task force. Detective McCoy convinced me that it might be a good idea. If our man is or was a SEAL, you may have better luck finding him."

"I assure you, luck won't be part of it, sir."

Syd couldn't believe O'Donlon's audacity. The amazing part was that he spoke with such conviction. He actually believed himself.

"That remains to be seen," Zale countered. "I've decided to give you permission to form this team, provided you keep Detective McCoy informed of your whereabouts and progress."

"I can manage that." O'Donlon flashed another of his smiles at Lucy McCoy. "In fact, it'll be a pleasure."

"Oh, ack." Syd didn't realize she'd spoken aloud until Navy Ken glanced at her in surprise.

"And provided," Zale continued, "you agree to include Ms. Jameson in your team."

The SEAL laughed. Yes, his teeth *were* perfect. "No," he said, "Chief. You don't understand. A SEAL team is a team of *SEALs*. Only SEALs. Ms. Jameson will—no offense, ma'am—only get in the way."

"That's something you're just going to have to deal

with," Zale told him a little too happily. He didn't like the Navy, and he didn't like Syd. This was his way of getting back at them both. "I'm in charge of this task force. You do it my way, or your men don't leave the naval base. There are other details to deal with, but Detective McCoy will review them with you."

Syd's brain was moving at warp speed. Zale thought he was getting away with something here—by casting her off on to the SEALs. But *this* was the real story—the one that would be unfolding *within* the confines of the naval base as well as without. She'd done enough research on the SEAL units over the past forty-odd hours to know that these unconventional spec-warriors would be eager to stop the bad press and find the San Felipe Rapist on their own. She was curious to find out what would happen if the rapist *did* turn out to be one of them. Would they try to hide it? Would they try to deal with punishment on their own terms?

The story she was going to write could be an in-depth look at one of America's elite military organizations. And it could well be exactly what she needed to get herself noticed, to get that magazine editor position, back in New York City, that she wanted so desperately.

"I'm sorry." O'Donlon started an awful lot of his sentences with an apology. "But there's just no way a police social worker could keep up with—"

"I'm not a social worker," Syd interrupted.

"Ms. Jameson is one of our chief eyewitnesses," Zale said. "She's been face to face with our man."

O'Donlon faltered. His face actually got pale, and he dropped all friendly, easygoing pretense. And as Syd gazed into his eyes, she got a glimpse of his horror and shock.

"My God," he whispered. "I didn't...I'm sorry—I had no idea...."

He was ashamed. And embarrassed. Honestly shaken. "I feel like I should apologize for all men, everywhere."

Amazing. Navy Ken wasn't all plastic. He was at least part human. Go figure.

Obviously, he thought she had been one of the rapist's victims.

"No," she said quickly. "I mean, thanks, but I'm an eyewitness because my neighbor was attacked. I was coming up the stairs as the man who raped her was coming down. And I'm afraid I didn't even get that good a look at him."

"God," O'Donlon said. "*Thank* God. When Chief Zale said...I thought..." He drew in a deep breath and let it out forcefully. "I'm sorry. I just can't imagine..." He recovered quickly, then leaned forward slightly, his face speculative. "So...you've actually *seen* this guy."

Syd nodded. "Like I said, I didn't—"

O'Donlon turned to Zale. "And you're giving her to *me?*"

Syd laughed in disbelief. "Excuse me, I would appreciate it if you could rephrase that...."

Zale stood up. Meeting over. "Yeah. She's all yours."

CHAPTER TWO

"HAVE YOU EVER BEEN HYPNOTIZED?" Lucky glanced over at the woman sitting beside him as he pulled his pickup truck onto the main drag that led to the naval base.

She turned to give him a disbelieving look.

She was good at that look. He wondered if it came naturally or if she'd worked to perfect it, practicing for hours in front of her bathroom mirror. The thought made him smile, which only made her glower even harder.

She was pretty enough—if you went for women who hid every one of their curves beneath androgynous clothes, women who never let themselves smile.

No, he mused, looking at her more closely as he stopped at a red light. He'd once dated a woman who'd never smiled. Jacqui Fontaine. She'd been a beautiful young woman who was so terrified of getting wrinkles she kept her face carefully devoid of all expression. In fact, she'd gotten angry with him for making her laugh. At first he'd thought she was joking, but she'd been serious. She'd asked him back to her apartment after they'd seen a movie, but he'd declined. Sex would have been positively bizarre. It would have been like making love to a mannequin. The thought still made him shudder.

This woman, however, had laugh lines around her eyes. Proof that she did smile. Probably frequently, in fact.

She just had no intention of smiling at *him*.

Her hair was thick and dark, curling around her face, unstyled and casual—cut short enough so that she probably could get away with little more than raking her fingers through it after climbing out of bed.

Her eyes were dark brown and impossibly large in a face that could only be called pixielike.

Provided, of course, that pixies had a solid dose of unresolved resentment. She didn't like him. She hadn't liked him from the moment he'd walked into the San Felipe police-station conference room.

"Cindy, wasn't it?" He knew damn well that her name was Sydney. But what kind of woman was named *Sydney?* If he was going to have to baby-sit the woman who could potentially ID the San Felipe Rapist, why couldn't she be named Crystal or Mellisande—and dress accordingly?

"No," she said tightly, in a voice that was deceptively low and husky, unfairly sexy considering she clearly didn't want anyone looking at her to think even remotely about sex, "it wasn't. And no, I've never been hypnotized."

"Great," he said, trying to sound as enthusiastic as possible as he parked in the lot near Frisco's office. *His* office now, too, at least temporarily. "Then we're going to have some fun. A real adventure. Uncharted territory. Boldly going, etcetera."

Now Sydney was looking at him with something akin to horror in her eyes. "You can't be serious."

Lucky took the keys out of the ignition and opened the truck's door. "Of course not. Not completely. Who'd ever want to be completely serious about anything?" He climbed out and looked back inside at her. "But the part I'm not completely serious about is whether it's going to be fun. In fact, I suspect it's going to be pretty low key. Probably dull. Unless while you're under, I can convince the hypnotist to make you quack like a duck."

If she *were* a Crystal or a Mellisande, Lucky would've winked at her, but he knew, without a doubt, that winking at Sydney would result in her trying to melt him into unidentifiable goo with her death-ray glare.

Most women liked to be winked at. Most women could be softened up with an appreciative look and a compliment. Most women responded to his "hey, baby" body language and subtle flirting with a little "hey, baby" body language and subtle flirting in return. With most women, he didn't have to wait long for an invitation to move from subtle flirting to flat-out seduction.

Sydney, however, was not most women.

"Thanks, but I don't want to be hypnotized," she told him as she climbed awkwardly down from the cab of his truck. "I've read that some people are less susceptible to hypnotism—that they just can't be hypnotized. I'm pretty sure I'm one of them."

"How do you know," Lucky reasoned, "if you've never tried?"

His best smile bounced right off her. "It's a waste of time," she said sternly.

"Well, I'm afraid I don't think so." Lucky tried his apologetic smile as he led the way into the building, but that one didn't work either. "I guess you'll have an opportunity to prove me wrong."

Sydney stood still. "Do you *ever* not get your way?"

Lucky pretended to think about that for a moment. "No," he finally said. He smiled. "I always get my way, and I'm never completely serious. You keep that in mind, and we'll get along just fine."

SYDNEY STOOD IN THE building's lobby watching as Lieutenant Luke O'Donlon greeted a lovely, dark-haired, very pregnant woman with a stunner from his vast repertoire of smiles.

"Hey, gorgeous—what are you doing here?" He wrapped his arms around her and planted a kiss full on her lips.

His wife. Had to be.

It was funny, Syd wouldn't have believed this man capable of marriage. And it still didn't make sense. He didn't walk like a married man. He certainly didn't talk like a married man. Everything about him, from the way he sat as he drove his truck to the way he smiled at anything and everything even remotely female, screamed bachelor. *Terminal* bachelor.

Yet as Syd watched, he crouched down and pressed his face against the woman's burgeoning belly. "Hello in there!"

Whoever she was, she *was* gorgeous. Long, straight, dark hair cascaded down her back. Her delicately featured face held a hint of the Far East. She rolled her beautiful, exotic eyes as she laughed.

"This is why I don't come out here that often," she said to Syd over the top of O'Donlon's head as he pressed his ear to her stomach, listening now. "I'm Mia Francisco, by the way."

Francisco. The Lieutenant Commander's wife.

"He's singing that Shania Twain song," O'Donlon reported, looking past Syd and grinning. "The one Frisco says never leaves your CD player?"

Syd turned to see a teenaged girl standing behind her— all long legs and skinny arms, surrounded by an amazing cloud of curly red hair.

The girl smiled, but it was decidedly half-hearted. "Ha, ha, Lucky," she said. "Very funny."

"We heard about the diving accident," Mia explained

as O'Donlon straightened up. "They weren't releasing any names, and we couldn't reach Alan, so Tasha talked me into driving out to make sure Thomas was okay."

"Thomas?"

"King," Mia said. "Former student of mine? You remember him, don't you? He's going through BUD/S training with this class."

"Yeah." O'Donlon snapped his fingers. "Right. Black kid, serious attitude."

"It wasn't Thomas," the red-haired girl—Tasha—informed him. "It was someone else who got hurt."

"An ensign named Marc Riley. They've got him stabilized. He's in a lot of pain, but it's not as bad as they first thought." Mia smiled at Syd again, friendly but curious, taking in her shapeless linen jacket, her baggy khaki pants, her cloddish boots and the mannish blouse she wore buttoned all the way to her neck.

Syd had no doubt that she looked extremely different from the usual sort of women who followed Lieutenant O'Donlon around.

"I'm sorry," Mia continued. "We didn't mean to shanghai Lucky this way."

Lucky. The girl had referred to O'Donlon by that name, too. It was too perfect. Syd tried her best not to smirk.

"It's not a problem," she said. "I'm Syd Jameson."

"We're working together on a special project," the man who was actually nicknamed *Lucky* interjected, as if he were afraid Mia might assume they were together socially. Yeah, as if.

"Is that the same project Lucy McCoy kicked us out of Alan's office to talk to him about?" Mia asked.

Lucky started to speak, then put his hands over Tasha's ears and swore. The girl giggled, and he winked at her before looking at Mia. "Lucy's already here?"

"Tell Alan it's my fault you're late."

"Yeah, great." Lucky laughed as he waved good-bye, leading Syd down one of the corridors. "I'll tell him I'm delayed because I stopped to flirt with his wife. *That'll* go over just swell."

Syd had to run to keep up. She had no doubt that whatever excuse O'Donlon gave for being late, he would be instantly forgiven. Grown men didn't keep nicknames like Lucky well past adolescence for no reason.

Lucky.

Sheesh.

Back in seventh grade, Syd had had a nickname.

Stinky.

She'd forgotten to wear deodorant one day. Just one *day,* and she was Stinky until the end of the school year.

Speaking of stinky, she'd have dressed differently if she'd known she was going to be running a marathon today. Lieutenant Lucky O'Donlon was well out in front of her and showed no sign of slowing down. How big was this place, anyway?

Not content to wait for an elevator, he led the way into a stairwell and headed up.

Syd was already out of breath, but she pushed herself to keep up, afraid if she let him out of her sight, she'd lose him. She tried to keep her eyes glued to his broad back, but it was hard, particularly since his perfect rear end was directly in her line of sight.

Of course he had a perfect rear end—trim and tiny, about one one-hundredth the size of hers, and a perfect match for his narrow hips. She shouldn't have expected anything less from a man named Lucky.

She followed his microbutt back out into the hallway and into an empty outer office and...

Syd caught her breath as he knocked on a closed door.

The SEAL wasn't even slightly winded, damn him, and here she was, all but bent over, hands on her knees, puffing and wheezing.

"Smoker?" he asked, almost apologetically. Almost, but not quite. He was just a little too amused to be truly sorry.

"No," she said. She was more out of shape than she'd realized. She'd always enjoyed running, but this spring and summer she hadn't quite managed to get started again.

The door opened, and standing in the inner office was a man who could have been a mirror reflection of Lucky. His hair was a slightly different color, and his face was more craggy than pretty, but the widths of the two men's shoulders were close to exact.

"I have a meeting with Admirals Forrest and Stonegate," the man said in a way of greeting. "Lucy's already here. Hear her out, and do whatever you've got to do to catch this guy. Preferably before the end of this week."

He looked from Lucky to Syd. His eyes were different from Lucky's and not just in color. He seemed capable of looking past the unruly hair that was falling into her own eyes, past the high neck of her shirt, past her near-permanent expression of slightly bored, slightly raised-eyebrow disbelief that she'd adopted after too many years of being given nicknames like Stinky.

Whatever he saw when he looked at her made him smile.

And it wasn't a condescending smile, or a "wow, you are such a freak" smile, either.

It was warm and welcoming. He held out his hand. "I'm Alan Francisco." His grip was as pleasantly solid as his smile. "Welcome to Coronado. If there's anything you need while you're here, I'm sure Lieutenant O'Donlon will be more than happy to provide it for you."

And just like that, he was gone. It wasn't until he was out the far door that Syd realized he'd moved stiffly, leaning heavily on a cane.

With a jolt, she realized she was standing there gazing after Alan Francisco. Lucky had already gone into the lieutenant commander's office, and she followed, shutting the door behind her.

Surprise, surprise—Lucky had his arms wrapped around Detective McCoy. As Syd watched, he gave her a hello kiss.

"I didn't get to say hello properly before," he murmured. "You are looking too good for words, babe." Keeping his arm looped around her shoulders, he turned to Syd. "Lucy's husband, Blue, is XO of SEAL Team Ten's Alpha Squad."

Lucy's husband. Syd blinked. Lucy had a husband, who was also a SEAL. And presumably the two men were acquaintances, if not friends. This guy was too much.

"XO means executive officer," Lucy explained, giving Lucky a quick hug before slipping free from his grasp, reaching up to adjust the long brown hair that had slipped free from her ponytail holder. She really did have remarkably pretty eyes. "Blue's second in command of Alpha Squad."

"Blue," Syd repeated. "His name's really *Blue?*"

"It's a nickname," Lucy told her with a smile. "SEALs tend to get nicknames when they first go through BUD/S training. Let's see, we've got Cat, Cowboy, Frisco—" she ticked the names off on her fingers "—Blue, Lucky, Harvard, Crow, Fingers, Snakefoot, Wizard, Elmer, the Priest, Doc, Spaceman, Crash..."

"So your husband works here on the Navy base," Syd clarified.

"Some of the time," Lucy said. She glanced at Lucky and

what that look meant, Syd couldn't begin to guess. "Alpha Squad went wheels up while we were downtown."

Syd couldn't guess the meaning of Lucy's words, either. "Wheels up?" She was starting to sound like a parrot.

"They've shipped out," Lucky explained. He leaned back casually, half sitting on Lieutenant Commander Francisco's desk. "The expression refers to a plane's wheels leaving the ground. Alpha Squad is outta town."

Again, Lucy and Lucky seemed to be communicating with no words—only a long, meaningful look. Was it possible that this blue-eyed blond god was having an affair with the wife of a superior officer? Anything was possible, but that seemed a little too sordid.

"What you've done," Lucy said quietly, breaking the silence, "is going to mean everything to Ellen. Looking back, you *know* it's going to be worth it."

"I could still be shipped out myself," he countered. "If something big came up, and I was needed, I wouldn't even be able to attend my *own* wedding."

Syd cleared her throat. She didn't know what they were talking about, didn't *want* to know. She wasn't interested in Ellen—whoever she was—or what Lucky and Lucy McCoy did behind her husband's back. She just wanted to help catch the rapist, get her story and be off to New York.

"I'm okay, you know," Lucky told the detective. "And I'll be even more okay if you'll meet me for dinner one of these nights."

Lucy gave him a quick smile, glancing at Syd, obviously aware that the two of them weren't alone. "You've got my number," she said. She sat down at the conference table that was over by the window. "Right now, we need to go over some task-force rules, talk about your team."

Lucky sat at the head of the table. "Great. Let's start

with *my* rules. You let me form a team of SEALs, you don't
hammer me with a lot of useless rules and hamper me with
unqualified people who will only slow us down—" he shot
Syd an apologetic version of his smile "—no offense—and
then we'll catch your guy."

Lucy didn't blink. "The members of your team have to
meet Chief Zale's approval."

"Oh, no way!"

"He—and *I*—believe that since we don't know who
we're dealing with, and since you have plenty of alter-
natives for personnel, you should construct your team
from SEALs or SEAL candidates who *absolutely*—no
question—do not fit the rapist's description."

Syd sat down across from Lucky. "So in other words,
no one white, powerfully built, with a crew cut."

Lucky sputtered. "That eliminates the majority of the
men stationed in Coronado."

Lucy nodded serenely. "That's right. And the majority
of the men are all potential suspects."

"You honestly think a real SEAL could have raped
those women?"

"I think until we know more, we need to be conservative as to whom we allow into our information loop," she
told him. "You'd be a suspect yourself, Luke, but your
hair's too long."

"Gee, thanks for the vote of confidence."

"The second rule is about weapons," Lucy continued.
"We don't want you running around town armed to the
teeth. And that means knives as well as sidearms."

"Sure," he said. "Great. And when we apprehend this
guy, we'll throw spoons at him."

"You won't apprehend him," she countered. "The task
force will. Your team's job is to help locate him. Track him
down. Try to think like this son of a bitch and anticipate

his next move, so we—the police and FInCOM—can be there, waiting for him."

"Okay," Lucky said. He pointed across the table at Sydney. "I'll follow your rules—if you take her off my hands. After we do the hypnotist thing tomorrow afternoon, all she's going to do is get in the way." He looked at Syd. "No offense."

"Too bad," she said, "because I *am* offended."

Lucky looked at her again. "I don't know what Zale has against you, but it's obvious he doesn't like *me*. He's trying to make it close to impossible for my team to operate by assigning me…"

"I'm a reporter," Syd told him.

"…what amounts to little more than baby-sitting duty and…" His impossibly blue eyes widened. "A reporter." Now he was the parrot. His eyes narrowed. "Sydney Jameson. S. Jameson. Ah, jeez, you're not just a reporter, you're *that* reporter." He glared at her. "Where the hell do you get off making us all sound like psychotic killers?"

He was serious. He'd taken offense to the one part of her story the police had actually requested she include. "Cool your jets, Ken," she told him. "The police wanted me to make it sound as if they actually believed the rapist was a SEAL."

"It's entirely likely our man is a SEAL wannabe," Lucy interjected. "We were hoping the news story would feed his ego, maybe make him careless."

"Ken?" Lucky asked Syd. "My name's Luke."

Oops, had she actually called him that? "Right. Sorry." Syd gave him the least sorry smile she could manage.

Lucky looked at her hard before he turned to Lucy. "How the hell did a reporter get involved?"

"Her neighbor was attacked. Sydney stayed with the girl—and this *was* just a girl. She wasn't more than nineteen years old, Luke. Sydney was there when I arrived, and oddly enough, I didn't think to inquire as to whether she was with UPI or Associated Press."

"So what did you do?" Lucky turned back to Syd. "Blackmail your way onto the task force?"

"Damn straight." Syd lifted her chin. "Seven rapes and not a single word of warning in any of the papers. It was a story that needed to be written—desperately. I figured I'd write it—*and* I'll write the exclusive behind-the-scenes story about tracking and catching the rapist, too."

He shook his head, obviously in disgust, and Syd's temper flared. "You know, if I were a man," she snapped, "you'd be impressed by my assertive behavior."

"So did you actually see this guy, or did you just make that part up?" he asked.

Syd refused to let him see how completely annoyed he made her feel. She forced her voice to sound even, controlled. "He nearly knocked me over coming down the stairs. But like I told the police, the light's bad in the hallways. I didn't get a real clear look at him."

"Is there a chance it was good enough for you to look at a lineup of my men and eliminate them as potential suspects?" he demanded.

Lucy sighed. "Lucky, I don't—"

"I want Bobby Taylor and Wes Skelly on my team."

"Bobby's fine. He's Native American," she told Syd. "Long dark hair, about eight feet tall and seven feet wide—definitely not our man. But Wes…"

"Wes shouldn't be a suspect," Lucky argued.

"Police investigations don't work that way," Lucy argued in response. "Yes, he *shouldn't* be a suspect. But Chief Zale wants every individual on your team to be completely, obviously not the man we're looking for."

"This is a man who's put his life on the line for me—for

your husband—more times than you want to know. If Sydney could look at Skelly and—"

"I really don't remember much about the man's face," Syd interrupted. "He came flying down the stairs, nearly wiped me out, stopped a few steps down. I'm not even sure he turned all the way around. He apologized, and was gone."

Lucky leaned forward. "He *spoke* to you?"

God, he was good-looking. Syd forced away the little flutter she felt in her stomach every time he gazed at her. She really was pathetic. She didn't like this man. In fact, she was well on her way to disliking him intensely, and yet simply looking into his eyes was enough to make her knees grow weak.

Obviously, it had been way too long since she'd last had sex. Not that her situation was likely to change any time in the near future.

"What did he say?" Lucky asked. "His exact words?"

Syd shrugged, hating to tell him what the man had said, but knowing he wouldn't let up until she did.

Just do it. She took a deep breath. "He said, 'Sorry, bud.'"

"Sorry...*bud?*"

Syd felt her face flush. "Like I said. The light was bad in there. He must've thought I was, you know, a man."

Lucky O'Donlon didn't say anything aloud, but as he sat back in his seat, the expression on his face spoke volumes. His gaze traveled over her, taking in her unfeminine clothes, her lack of makeup. An understandable mistake for any man to make, he telegraphed with his eyes.

He finally looked over at Lucy. "The fact remains that I can't possibly work with a reporter following me around."

"Neither can I," she countered.

"I've worked for years as an investigative reporter," Syd told them both. "Hasn't it occurred to either one of you that I might actually be able to help?"

CHAPTER THREE

THIS SHOULDN'T BE TOO HARD.

Lucky was a people person—charming, charismatic, likeable. He knew that about himself. It was one of his strengths.

He could go damn near anywhere and be best friends with damn near anyone within a matter of hours.

And that was what he had to do right here, right now with Sydney Jameson. He had to become her best friend and thus win the power to manipulate her neatly to the sidelines. Come on, Syd, help out your old pal Lucky by staying out of the way.

His soon-to-be-old-pal Syd sat in stony silence beside him in his pickup truck, arms folded tightly across her chest, as he drove her back to her car which was parked in the police-station lot.

Step one. Get a friendly conversation going. Find some common ground. Family. Most people could relate to family.

"So my kid sister's getting married in a few weeks." Lucky shot Syd a friendly smile as well, but he would've gotten a bigger change of expression from the Lincoln head at Mount Rushmore. "It's kind of hard to believe. You know, it feels like she just turned twelve. But she's twenty-two, and in most states that's old enough for her to do what she wants."

"In *every* state it's old enough," Syd said. What do you know? She was actually listening. At least partly.

"Yeah," Lucky said. "I know. That was a joke."

"Oh," she said and looked back out the window.

O-kay.

Lucky kept on talking, filling the cab of the truck with friendly noise. "I went into San Diego to see her, intending to tell her no way. I was planning at least to talk her into waiting a year, and you know what she tells me? I bet you can't guess in a million years."

"Oh, I bet I can't either," Syd said. Her words had a faintly hostile ring, but at least she was talking to him.

"She said, we can't wait a year." Lucky laughed. "And I'm thinking murder, right? I'm thinking where's my gun, I'm going to at the very least scare the hell out of this guy for getting my kid sister pregnant, and then Ellen tells me that if they wait a year, this guy Greg's sperm will expire."

He had Syd's full attention now.

"Apparently, Greg had leukemia as a teenager, years and years ago. And before he started the treatment that would save him but pretty much sterilize him, he made a few deposits in a sperm bank. The technology's much better now and frozen sperm has a longer, um, shelf life, so to speak, but Ellen's chances of having a baby with the sperm that Greg banked back when he was fifteen is already dropping."

Lucky glanced at Syd, and she looked away. Come on, he silently implored her. Play nice. Be friends. I'm a nice guy.

"Ellen really loves this guy," he continued, "and you should see the way he looks at her. He's too old for her by about seventeen years, but it's so damn obvious that he loves her. So how could I do anything but wish them luck and happiness?"

Syd actually graced him with a glance. "How are your parents taking this?"

Lucky shook his head, glad at the perfect opportunity to segue into poor-little-orphaned-me. This *always* won him sympathy points when talking to a woman. "No parents. Just me and Ellen. Mom had a heart attack years ago. You know, you really don't hear much about it, but women are at just as much risk for heart disease as men and—" He cut himself off. "Sorry—I've kind of turned into a walking public service announcement about the topic. I mean, she was so young, and then she was so gone."

"I'm sorry," Syd murmured.

"Thanks. It was roughest on Ellen, though," he continued. "She was still just a kid. Her dad died when she was really young. We had different fathers and I'm not really sure what happened to mine. I think he might've become a Tibetan monk and taken a vow of silence to protest Jefferson Airplane's breakup." He flashed her a smile. "Yeah, I know what you're thinking. With a name like Lucky, I should have rich parents living in Bel Air. I actually went to Bel Air a few years ago and tried to talk this old couple into adopting me, but no go."

Syd actually smiled at that one. Bingo. He *knew* she was hiding a sense of humor in there somewhere.

"Now that you know far too much about me," he said, "it's your turn. You're from New York, right?"

Her eyes narrowed suspiciously. "How did you know that? I don't have an accent."

"But you don't need an accent when you come from New York," Lucky said with a grin. "The fact that you do everything in hyperspeed gives you away. Those of us from southern California can spot a New Yorker a mile away. It's a survival instinct. If we can't learn to ID you, we can't know to take cover or brace for impact when you make the scene."

Sydney might've actually laughed at that. But he wasn't sure. Her smile had widened though, and he'd been dead right about it. It was a good one. It lit her up completely, and made her extremely attractive—at least in a small, dark, non-blond-beauty-queen sort of way.

And as Lucky smiled back into Sydney's eyes, the answer to all his problems became crystal clear.

Boyfriend.

It was highly likely that he could get further faster if he managed to become Sydney Jameson's boyfriend. Sex could be quite a powerful weapon. And he knew she was attracted to him, despite her attempts to hide it. He'd caught her checking him out more than once when she thought he wasn't paying attention.

This was definitely an option that was entirely appealing on more than one level. He didn't have to think twice.

"Do you have plans for tonight?" he asked, slipping smoothly out of best-friend mode and into low-scale, friendly seduction. The difference was subtle, but there *was* a difference. "Because I don't have any plans for tonight and I'm starving. What do you say we go grab some dinner? I know this great seafood place right on the water in San Felipe. You can tell me about growing up in New York over grilled swordfish."

"Oh," she said, "I don't think—"

"Do you have other plans?"

"No," she said, "but—"

"This is perfect," he bulldozed cheerfully right over her. "If we're going to work together, we need to get to know each other better. *Much* better. I just need to stop at home and pick up my wallet. Can you believe I've been walking around all day without any cash?"

Hoo-yah, this was perfect. They were literally four blocks from his house. And what better location to initiate a friendly, low-key seduction than home sweet home?

Syd had to hold on with both hands as Lucky quickly cut across two lanes of traffic to make a right turn into a side street.

"Don't you live on the base?" she asked.

"Nope. Officer's privilege. This won't take long, I promise. We're right in my neighborhood."

Now, *that* was a surprise. This neighborhood consisted of modestly sized, impeccably kept little houses with neat little yards. Syd hadn't given much thought to the lieutenant's living quarters, but if she had, she wouldn't have imagined this.

Sure enough, he pulled into the driveway of a cheery little yellow adobe house. A neatly covered motorcycle was parked at the back of an attached carport. Flowers grew in window boxes. The grass had been recently, pristinely mowed.

"Why don't you come in for a second?" Lucky asked. "I've got some lemonade in the fridge."

Of course he did. A house like this *had* to have lemonade in the refrigerator. Bemused and curious, Syd climbed down from the cab of his shiny red truck.

It was entirely possible that once inside she would be in the land of leather upholstery and art deco and waterbeds and all the things she associated with a glaringly obvious bachelor pad. And instead of lemonade, he'd find— surprise, surprise—a bottle of expensive wine in the back of the refrigerator.

Syd mentally rolled her eyes at herself. Yeah, right. As if this guy would even consider *her* a good candidate for seduction. That wasn't going to happen. Not in a million years. Who did she think she was, anyway? Barbie to his Ken? Not even close. She wouldn't even qualify for Skipper's weird cousin.

Lucky held the door for her, smiling. It was a self-confident smile, a warm smile...an *interested* smile?

No, she had to be imagining that.

But she didn't have time for a double take, because, again, his living room completely surprised her. The furniture was neat but definitely aging. Nothing matched, some of the upholstery was positively flowery. There was nothing even remotely art deco in the entire room. It was homey and warm and just plain comfortable.

And instead of Ansel Adams prints on the wall, there were family photographs. Lucky as a flaxen-haired child, holding a chubby toddler as dark as he was fair. Lucky with a laughing blonde who had to be his mother. Lucky as an already too-handsome thirteen-year-old, caught in the warm, wrestling embrace of a swarthy, dark-haired man.

"Hey, you know, I've got an open bottle of white wine," Lucky called from the kitchen, "if you'd like a glass of that instead of lemonade...?"

What? Syd wasn't aware she had spoken aloud until he repeated himself, dangling both the bottle in question and an extremely friendly smile from the kitchen doorway.

The interest in his smile was *not* her imagination. Nor was the warmth in his eyes.

God, Navy Ken was an outrageously handsome man. And when he looked at her like that, it was very, very hard to look away.

He must've seen the effect he had on her in her eyes. Or maybe it was the fact that she was drooling that gave her away. Because the heat in *his* eyes went up a notch.

"I've got a couple of steaks in the freezer," he said, his rich baritone wrapping as enticingly around her as the slightly pink late-afternoon light coming in through the front blinds. "I could light the grill out back and we could have dinner here. It would be nice not to have to fight the traffic and the crowds."

"Um," Syd said. She hadn't even agreed to go to dinner with him.

"Let's do it. I'll grab a couple of glasses, we can sit on the deck," he decided.

He vanished back into the kitchen, as if her declining his rather presumptuous invitation was an impossibility.

Syd shook her head in disbelief. This was too much. She had absolutely no doubt about it now. Lieutenant Lucky O'Donlon was hitting on her.

His motive was frightfully obvious. He was attempting to win her over. He was trying to make her an ally instead of an adversary in this task-force-coupling from hell. And, in typical alpha male fashion, he'd come to the conclusion that the best way to win her support involved full-naked-body contact. Or at least the promise of it.

Sheesh.

Syd followed him into the kitchen, intending to set him straight. "Look, Lieutenant—"

He handed her a delicate tulip-shaped glass of wine. "Please, call me Lucky." He lifted his own glass, touching it gently to hers, as he shot her a smile loaded with meaning. "And right now I *am* feeling particularly lucky."

Syd laughed. Oh, dear God. And instead of telling him flat out that she had to go and she had to go *now,* she kept her mouth shut. She *didn't* have any plans for tonight, and—God help her—she wanted to see just how far this clown was willing to go.

He continued to gaze at her as he took a sip of his wine.

His eyes were a shade of blue she'd never seen before. It was impossible to gaze back at him and not get just a little bit lost. But that was okay, she decided, as long as she realized that this was a game, as long as she was playing, too, and not merely being played.

He set his wineglass down on the counter. "I've got to change out of my Good Humor man costume. Excuse me for a minute, will you? Dress whites and grilling dinner aren't a good mix. Go on out to the deck—I'll be there in a flash."

He was so confident. He walked out of the kitchen without looking back, assuming she'd obediently do as he commanded.

Syd took a sip of the wine as she leaned back against the counter. It was shockingly delicious. Didn't it figure?

She could hear Lucky sing a few bars of something that sounded suspiciously like an old Beach Boys tune. Didn't that figure also? We'll have fun, fun, fun indeed.

He stopped singing as he pushed the button on his answering machine. There were two calls from a breathy-voiced woman named Heather, a third from an equally vapid-sounding Vareena, a brief "call me at home," from an unidentified man, and then a cheerful female voice.

"Hi, Luke, it's Lucy McCoy. I just spoke to Alan Francisco, and he told me about Admiral Stonegate's little bomb. I honestly don't think this is going to be a problem for you—I've met the candidates he's targeted and they're good men. Anyway, the reason I'm calling is I've found out a few more details about this case that I think you should know, and it's occurred to me that it might be a good idea for the grown-ups—assuming Bobby's part of your team—to meet tonight. I'm on duty until late, so why don't we say eleven o'clock—2300 hours—at Skippy's Harborside? Leave a message on my machine if this works for you. Later, dude."

There was one more call—the pool cleaner wanted to reschedule her visit for later in the week—but then the answering machine gave a final-sounding beep. There was silence for a moment, and then Syd heard Lucky's lowered voice.

"Hey, Luce. S'me. 2300 sounds peachy keen. I haven't talked to Frisco yet—did you actually use the word *candidates*? Why do I hate this already, before I even know what the hell's going on?" He swore softly and laughed. "I guess I just have a good imagination. See you at Skip's."

He hung up the phone without making any noise, then whistled his way into the bathroom.

Syd quietly opened the screen door and tiptoed onto the deck. She stood there, leaning against the railing, looking down into the crystal blueness of his swimming pool and the brilliantly lush flower gardens as he made his grand entrance.

He had changed, indeed. The crisp uniform had been replaced by a pair of baggy cargo shorts and a Hawaiian shirt, worn open to reveal the hard planes of his muscular, tanned chest. Navy Ken had magically become Malibu Ken. He'd run his fingers through his hair, loosening the gel that had glued it down into some semblance of a conservative military style. It now tumbled over his forehead and into his eyes, waving tendrils of sun-bleached gold, some of it long enough to tickle his nose. His feet were bare and even his toes were beautiful. All he needed was a surfboard and twenty-four hours' worth of stubble on his chin, and he'd be ready for the Hunks of the Pacific calendar photo shoot.

And he knew it, too.

Syd took little sips of her wine as Lucky gave a running discourse on his decision four years ago to build this deck, the hummingbird feeders he'd put in the garden, and the fact that they'd had far too little rain this year.

As he lit the grill, he oh-so-casually pointed out that the fence around the backyard made his swimming pool completely private from the eyes of his neighbors, and how—wink, wink—that helped him maintain his all-over tan.

Syd was willing to bet it wouldn't take much to get him to drop his pants and show off the tan in question. Lord, this guy was too much.

And she had absolutely no intention of skinny dipping with him. Not now, not ever, thanks.

"Have you tried it recently?" he asked.

Syd blinked at him, trying to remember his last conversational bounce. Massage. He'd just mentioned some really terrific massage therapy he'd had a few months ago, after a particularly strenuous SEAL mission. She wasn't sure exactly what he'd just asked, but it didn't matter. He didn't wait for her to answer.

"Here, let me show you." He set his glass on the railing of the deck and turned her so that she was facing away from him.

It didn't occur to him that she might not want him to touch her. His grip was firm, his hands warm through the thin cotton of her shirt and jacket as he massaged her shoulders. He touched her firmly at first, then harder, applying pressure with his thumbs.

"Man, you're tense." His hands moved up her neck, to the back of her head, his fingers against her skin, in her hair.

Oh. My. God.

Whatever he was doing felt impossibly good. Fabulously good. *Sinfully* good. Syd closed her eyes.

"It's been a stressful few days, hasn't it?" he murmured, his mouth dangerously close to her ear. "I'm glad we've got this chance to, you know, start over. Get to know each other. I'm…looking forward to…being friends."

God, he was good. She almost believed him.

His hands kept working their magic, and Syd waited to see what he'd do or say next, hoping he'd take his time before he crossed the line of propriety, yet knowing that it wasn't going to be long.

He seemed to be waiting for some sort of response from her, so she made a vague noise of agreement that came out sounding far too much like a moan of intense pleasure as he touched a muscle in her shoulders that no doubt had been tightly, tensely flexed for the past fifteen years, at least.

"Oh, yeah," he breathed into her ear. "You know, I feel it, too. It's crazy, isn't it? We hardly know each other and yet…" In one smooth move he turned her to face him. "I'm telling you, Sydney, I've been dying to do this from the moment we first met."

It was amazing. It was like something out of a movie. Syd didn't have time to step back, to move away. His neon-blue gaze dropped to her mouth, flashed back to her eyes, and then, whammo.

He was kissing her.

Syd had read in her massive research on Navy SEALs that each member of a team had individual strengths and skills. Each member was a specialist in a variety of fields. And Lieutenant Lucky O'Donlon, aka Navy Ken, was clearly a specialist when it came to kissing.

She meant to pull away nanoseconds after his lips

touched hers. She meant to step back and freeze him with a single, disbelieving, uncomprehending look.

Instead, she melted completely in his arms. The bones in her body completely turned to mush.

He tasted like the wine, sweet and strong. He smelled like sunblock and fresh ocean air. He felt so solid beneath her hands—all those muscles underneath the silk of his shirt, shoulders wider than she'd ever imagined. He was all power, all male.

And she lost her mind. There was no other explanation. Insanity temporarily took a tight hold. Because she kissed him back. Fiercely, yes. Possessively, absolutely. Ravenously, no doubt about it. She didn't just kiss him, she inhaled the man.

She slanted her head to give him better access to her mouth as he pulled her more tightly against him.

It was crazy. It was impossibly exciting—he was undeniably even more delicious than that excellent wine. His hands skimmed her back, cupping the curve of her rear end, pressing her against his arousal and—

And sanity returned with a crash. Syd pulled back, breathing hard, furious with him, even more furious with herself.

This man was willing to take her to bed, to be physically intimate with her—all simply to control her. Sex meant so little to him that he could cheerfully use himself as a means to an end.

And as for herself—her body had betrayed her, damn it. She'd been hiding it, denying it, but the awful truth was, this man was hot. She'd never been up close to a man as completely sexy and breathtakingly handsome as Lucky O'Donlon. He was physical perfection, pure dazzling masculine beauty. His looks were movie-star quality, his body a work of art, his eyes a completely new and unique shade of blue.

No, he wasn't just hot, he was white-hot. Unfortunately, he was also insensitive, narrow-minded, egocentric and conniving. Sydney didn't like him—a fact she conveniently seemed to have forgotten when he kissed her.

The hunger in his perfect eyes was nearly mesmerizing as he reached for her again.

"Thanks but no thanks," she managed to spit out as she sidestepped him. "And while I'm at it, I'll pass on dinner, too."

He was completely thrown. If she'd felt much like being amused, she could have had a good laugh at the expression on his face as he struggled to regroup. "But—"

"Look, Ken, I'm not an idiot. I know damn well what this is about. You figure you can keep me happy by throwing me a sexual bone—no pun intended. And yes, your kisses are quite masterful, but just the same—no thanks."

He tried to feign innocence and then indignation. "You think that…? Wait, no, I would never try to—"

"What?" she interrupted. "I'm supposed to believe that crap about 'isn't it crazy? This attraction—you feel it, too?'" She laughed in disbelief. "Sorry, I don't buy it, pal. Guys like you hit on women like me for only two reasons. It's either because you want something—"

"I'm telling you right now that you're wrong—"

"Or you're desperate."

"Whoa." It was his turn to laugh. "You don't think very highly of yourself, do you?"

"Look me in the eye," she said tightly, "and tell me honestly that your last girlfriend wasn't blond, five-foot-ten and built like a supermodel. Look me in the eye and tell me you've always had a thing for flat-chested women with big hips." Syd didn't let him answer. She went back into the house, raising her voice so he could hear her. "I'll catch a cab back to the police-station parking lot."

She heard him turn off the grill, but then he followed her. "Don't be ridiculous. I'll give you a ride to your car."

Syd pushed her way out the front door. "Do you think you can manage to do that without embarrassing us both again?"

He locked it behind him. "I'm sorry if I embarrassed you or offended you or—"

"You did both, Lieutenant. How about we just not say anything else right now, all right?"

He stiffly opened the passenger-side door to his truck and stood aside so that she could get in. He was dying to speak, and Syd gave him about four seconds before he gave in to the urge to keep the conversation going.

"I happen to find you very attractive," Luke said as he climbed behind the wheel.

Two and a half seconds. She knew he'd give in. She should have pointedly ignored him, but she, too, couldn't keep herself from countering.

"Yeah," she said. "Right. Next you'll tell me it's my delicate and ladylike disposition that turns you on."

"You have no idea what's going on in my head." He started his truck with a roar. "Maybe it is."

Syd uttered a very non-ladylike word.

The lieutenant glanced at her several times, and cranked the air-conditioning up a notch as Syd sat and stewed. God, the next few weeks were going to be dreadful. Even if he didn't hit on her again, she was going to have to live with the memory of that kiss.

That amazing kiss.

Her knees still felt a little weak.

He pulled into the police-station parking lot a little too fast and the truck bounced. But he remembered which car was hers and pulled up behind it, his tires skidding slightly in the gravel as he came to a too-swift stop.

Syd turned and looked at him.

He stared straight ahead. It was probably the first time he'd ever been turned down, and he was embarrassed. She could see a faint tinge of pink on his cheeks.

She almost felt sorry for him. Almost.

After she didn't move for several seconds, he turned and looked at her. "This *is* your car, right?"

She nodded, traces of feeling sorry turning into hot anger. "Well?"

"Well, what?" He laughed ruefully. "Something tells me you're not waiting for a good-night kiss."

He wasn't going to tell her. He'd had no intention of telling her, the son of a bitch.

Syd glared at him.

"What?" he said again. "Jeez, what did I do now?"

"Eleven o'clock," she reminded him as sweetly as she could manage. "Skippy's Harborside?"

Guilt and something else flickered in his eyes. Disappointment that she'd found out, no doubt. Certainly not remorse for keeping the meeting a secret. He swore softly.

"Don't make me go over your head, Lieutenant," Syd warned him. "I'm part of your team, part of this task force."

He shook his head. "That doesn't mean you need to participate in every meeting."

"Yes, it does."

He laughed. "Lucy McCoy and I are friends. This meeting is just an excuse to—"

"Exchange information about the case," she finished for him. "I heard her phone message. I would have thought it was just a lovers' tryst myself, but she mentioned what's-his-name, Bobby, would be there."

"Lovers' tryst…?" He actually looked affronted. "If you're implying that there's something improper between Lucy and me—"

Syd rolled her eyes. "Oh, come on. It's a little obvious there's something going on. I wonder if she knows what you were trying to do with me. I suppose she couldn't complain because she's married to—"

"How dare you?"

"Your…what did you call it? XO? She's married to your XO."

"Lucy and I are *friends*." His face was a thundercloud—his self-righteous outrage wasn't an act. "She loves her husband. And Blue…he's…he's the best."

His anger had faded, replaced by something quiet, something distant. "I'd follow Blue McCoy into hell if he asked me to," Luke said softly. "I'd never dishonor him by fooling around with his wife. Never."

"I'm sorry," Syd told him. "I guess… You just… You told me you never take anything too seriously, so I thought—"

"Yeah, well, you were wrong." He stared out the front windshield, holding tightly to the steering wheel with both hands. "Imagine that."

Syd nodded. And then she dug through her purse, coming up with a small spiral notebook and a pen. She flipped to a blank page and wrote down the date.

Luke glanced at her, frowning slightly. "What…?"

"I'm so rarely wrong," she told him. "When I am, it's worth taking note of."

She carefully kept her face expressionless as he studied her for several long moments.

Then he laughed slightly, curling one corner of his mouth up into an almost-smile. "You're making a joke."

"No," she said. "I'm not." But she smiled and gave herself away. She climbed out of the truck. "See you tonight."

"No," he said.

"Yes." She closed the door and dug in her purse for her car keys.

He leaned across the cab to roll down the passenger-side window. "No," he said. "Really. Syd, I need to be able to talk to Lucy and Bob without—"

"Eleven o'clock," she said. "Skippy's. I'll be there."

As she got into her car and drove away, she glanced back and saw Luke's face through the windshield.

No, this meeting wasn't going to happen at Skippy's at eleven. But the time couldn't be changed—Lucy McCoy had said she was on duty until late.

But if she were Navy Ken, she'd call Lucy and Bobby what's-his-name and move the location—leaving Syd alone and fuming at Skipper's Harborside at eleven o'clock.

Bobby what's-his-name.

Syd pulled up to a red light and flipped through her notebook, looking for the man's full name. Chief Robert Taylor. *Yes.* Bobby Taylor. Described as an enormous SEAL, at least part Native American. She hadn't yet met the man, but maybe that was a good thing.

Yeah, this could definitely work.

CHAPTER FOUR

LUCKY HADN'T REALLY EXPECTED to win, so he wasn't surprised when he followed Heather into La Cantina and saw Sydney already sitting at one of the little tables with Lucy McCoy.

He'd more than half expected the reporter to second-guess his decision to change the meeting's location and track them down, and she hadn't disappointed him. That was part of the reason he'd called Heather for dinner and then dragged her here, to this just-short-of-seedy San Felipe bar.

Syd had accused him of being desperate as she'd completely and brutally rejected his advances. The fact that she was right—that he had had a motive when he lowered his mouth to kiss her—only somehow served to make it all that much worse.

Even though he knew it was foolish, he wanted to make sure she knew just how completely non-desperate he was, and how little her rejection had mattered to him, by casually showing up with a drop-dead gorgeous, blond beauty queen on his arm.

He also wanted to make sure there was no doubt left lingering in her nosy reporter's brain that there was something going on between him and Blue McCoy's wife.

Just the thought of such a betrayal made him feel ill.

Of course, maybe it was Heather's constant, mindless

prattle that was making the tuna steak he'd had for dinner do a queasy somersault in his stomach.

Still he got a brief moment of satisfaction as Syd turned and saw him. As she saw Heather.

For a fraction of a second, her eyes widened. He was glad he'd been watching her, because she quickly covered her surprise with that slightly bored, single-raised-eyebrow half-smirk she had down pat.

The smirk had stretched into a bonafide half smile of lofty amusement by the time Lucky and Heather reached their table.

Lucy's smile was far more genuine. "Right on time."

"You're early," he countered. He met Syd's gaze. "And you're here."

"I got off work thirty minutes early," Lucy told him. "I tried calling you, but I guess you'd already left."

Syd silently stirred the ice in her drink with a straw. She was wearing the same baggy pants she'd had on that afternoon, but she'd exchanged the man-size, long-sleeved, button-down shirt for a plain white T-shirt, her single concession to the relentless heat. She hadn't put on any makeup for the occasion, and her short dark hair looked as if she'd done little more than run her fingers through it.

She looked tired. And nineteen times more real and warm than perfect, plastic Heather.

As Lucky watched, Syd lifted her drink and took a sip through the straw. With lips like that, she didn't need makeup. They were moist and soft and warm and perfect. He knew that firsthand after kissing her.

That one kiss they'd shared had been far more real and meaningful than Lucky's entire six month off-and-on, whenever-he-was-in-town, non-relationship with Heather.

And yet, after kissing him as if the world were coming to an end, Syd had pushed him away.

"Heather and I had dinner at Smokey Joe's," Lucky told them. "Heather Seeley, this is Lucy McCoy and Sydney Jameson."

But Heather was already looking away, her MTV-length attention span caught by the mirrors on the wall and her distant but gorgeous reflection...

Syd finally spoke. "Gee, I had no idea we could bring a date to a task-force meeting."

"Heather's got some phone calls to make," Lucky explained. "I figured this wasn't going to take too long, and after..." He shrugged.

After, he could return to his evening with Heather, bring her home, go for a swim in the moonlight, lose himself in her perfect body. "You don't mind giving us some privacy, right, babe?" He pulled Heather close and brushed her silicone-enhanced lips with his. Her perfect, *plastic* body...

Sydney sharply looked away from them, suddenly completely absorbed by the circles of moisture her glass had made on the table.

And Lucky felt stupid. As Heather headed for the bar, already dialing her cell phone, he sat down next to Lucy and across from Syd and felt like a complete jackass.

He'd brought Heather here tonight to show Syd...what? That he was a jackass? Mission accomplished.

Okay, yes, he *had* taken Syd into his arms on his deck earlier this evening in an effort to win her alliance. But somehow, some way, in the middle of that giddy, free-fall-inducing kiss, his strictly business motives had changed. He thought it had probably happened when her mouth had opened so warmly and willingly beneath his.

Or it might've been before that. It might've been the very instant his lips touched hers.

Whenever it had happened, all at once it had become very, *very* clear to him that he kept on kissing her purely because he wanted to.

Desperately.

Yes, there was that word again. As he ordered a beer from the bored cocktail waitress, as he pointed out Heather and told the waitress to get her whatever she wanted— on him—he tried desperately not to sound as if he were reeling from his own ego-induced stupidity in bringing Heather here. He knew Syd was listening. She was still pretending to be enthralled with the condensation on the table, but she *was* listening, so he referred to Heather as "that gorgeous blonde by the bar, with the body to die for."

Message sent: *I don't need you to want to kiss me ever again.*

Except he was lying. He needed. Maybe not quite desperately, but it was getting pretty damn close. Jeez, this entire situation was growing stupider and stupider with every breath he took.

Syd was so completely not Lucky's type. And he was forced to work with her to boot, although he was still working on ways to shake her permanently after tomorrow's session with the hypnotist.

She was opinionated, aggressive, impatient and far too intelligent—a know-it-all who made damn sure the rest of the world knew that she knew it all, too.

If she tried, even just a little bit, she'd be pretty. In a very less-endowed-than-most-women way.

Truth was, if life were a wet T-shirt contest and Heather and Syd were the contestants, Heather would win, hands down. Standing side by side, Syd would be rendered invisible, outshone by Heather's golden glory. Standing side by side, there should have been no contest.

Except, one of the two women made Lucky feel completely alive. And it wasn't Heather.

"Hey, Lucy. Lieutenant." U.S. Navy SEAL Chief Bobby Taylor smiled at Sydney as he slipped into the fourth seat at the table. "You must be Sydney. Were my directions okay?" he asked her.

Syd nodded. She looked up at Lucky almost challengingly. "I wasn't sure exactly where the bar was," she told him, "so I called Chief Taylor and asked for directions."

So that's how she found him. Well, wasn't she proud of herself? Lucky made a mental note to beat Bobby to death later.

"Call me Bob. Please." The enormous SEAL smiled at Syd again, and she smiled happily back at him, ignoring Lucky completely.

"No nickname?" she teased. "Like Hawk or Cyclops or Panther?"

And Lucky felt it. Jealousy. Stabbing and hot, like a lightning bolt to his already churning stomach. My God. Was it possible Sydney Jameson found Bob Taylor attractive? More attractive than she found Lucky?

Bobby laughed. "Just Bobby. Some guys during BUD/S tried to call me Tonto, which I objected to somewhat... forcefully." He flexed his fists meaningfully.

Bobby *was* a good-looking man despite the fact that his nose had been broken four or five too many times. He was darkly handsome, with high cheekbones, craggy features, and deep-brown eyes that broadcast his mother's Native American heritage. He had a quiet calmness to him, a Zen-like quality that *was* very attractive.

And then there was his size. Massive was the word for the man. Some women really went for that. Of course, if

Bobby wasn't careful to keep up his PT and his diet, he'd quickly run to fat.

"I considered Tonto politically incorrect," Bobby said mildly. "So I made sure the name didn't stick."

Bobby's fists were the size of canned hams. No doubt he'd been extremely persuasive in his objections.

"These days the Lieutenant here is fond of calling me Stimpy," Bob continued, "which is the name of a really stupid cartoon cat." He looked down at his hands and flexed his hot-dog-sized fingers again. "I've yet to object, but it's getting old."

"No," Lucky said. "It's because Wes—" he turned to Syd. "Bobby's swim buddy is this little wiry guy named Wes Skelly, and visually, well, Ren and Stimpy just seems to fit. It's that really nasty cartoon that—"

"Wes isn't little," Lucy interrupted. "He's as tall as Blue, you know."

"Yeah, but next to Gigantor here—"

"I *like* Gigantor," Bobby decided.

Syd was laughing, and Lucky knew from the way the chief was smiling at her that he was completely charmed, too. Maybe that was the way to win Syd's alliance. Maybe she could be Bobby's girlfriend.

The thought was not a pleasant one, and he dismissed it out of hand. Charming women was *his* strength, damn it, and he was going to charm Sydney Jameson if it was the last thing he did.

Lucy got down to business. "You talk to Frisco?" she asked him.

Lucky nodded grimly. "I did. Do you think it's possible Stonegate doesn't really want us to apprehend the rapist?"

"Why? What happened?" Syd demanded.

"Lieutenant Commander Francisco got called in to

meet with Admiral Stonegate," Lucy explained. "Ron Stonegate's not exactly a big fan of the SEAL teams."

"What'd Stonehead do this time?" Bobby asked.

"Easy on the insults," Lucky murmured. He glanced at Syd, wishing she weren't a reporter, knowing that anything they said could conceivably end up in a news story. "We've been ordered by the…admiral to use this assignment as a special training operation," he said, choosing his words carefully, leaving out all the expletives and less-than-flattering adjectives he would have used had she not been there, "for a trio of SEAL candidates who are just about to finish up their second phase of BUD/S."

"King, Lee and Rosetti," Bobby said, nodding his approval.

Lucky nodded. Bobby had been working as an instructor with this particular group of candidates right from the start of phase one. He wasn't surprised the chief should know the men in question.

"Tell me about them," Lucky commanded. He'd made a quick stop at the base and had pulled the three candidates' files after he'd talked to Frisco and before he'd picked up Heather. But you could only tell so much about a man from words on a piece of paper. He wanted to hear Bobby's opinion.

"They were all part of the same boat team during phase one," Bobby told him. "Mike Lee's the oldest and a lieutenant, Junior Grade, and he was buddied up with Ensign Thomas King—a local kid, much younger. African American. Both have IQs that are off the chart, and both have enough smarts to recognize each other's strengths and weaknesses. It was a good match. Petty Officer Rio Rosetti, on the other hand, is barely twenty-one, barely graduated from high school, struggles to spell his own name, but he can build anything out of nothing. He's magic. He was out in a skiff and the propeller snagged a line and one of the blades snapped. He took it apart, built a new propeller out of the junk that was on board. They couldn't move fast, but they could move. It was impressive.

"Rosetti's swim buddy bailed during the second day of Hell Week," Bobby continued, "and Lee and King took him in. He returned the favor a few days later, when Lee started hallucinating. He was seeing evil spirits and not taking it well, and King and Rosetti took turns sitting on him. The three of them have been tight ever since. King and Lee spend nearly all their off time tutoring Rosetti. With their help, he's managed to stay with the classroom program." He paused. "They're good men, Lieutenant."

It was good to hear that.

Still. "Turning a mission this serious into a training op makes about as much sense as sticking the team with Lois Lane, here," Lucky said.

"Twelve hours, seventeen minutes," Syd said. "Hah."

He blinked at her, temporarily distracted. "Hah? What hah?"

"I knew when you found out that I was a reporter it was only a matter of time before you used the old Lois Lane cliché," she told him. Her attitude wasn't quite smug, but it was a touch too gleeful to be merely matter-of-fact. "I figured twenty-four, but you managed in nearly half the time. Congratulations, Lieutenant."

"Lois Lane," Bobby mused. "Shoot, it's almost as bad as Tonto."

"It's not very original," even Lucy agreed.

"Can we talk about this case please?" Lucky said desperately.

"Absolutely," Lucy said. "Here's *my* late-breaking news. Four more women have come forward since Sydney's article appeared in the paper this morning. *Four*." She shook her head in frustration. "I don't know why some women don't report sexual assault when it happens."

"Is it our guy?" Syd asked. "Same MO?"

"Three of the women were branded with the budweiser. Those three attacks took place within the past four weeks. The fourth was earlier. I'm certain the same perp was responsible for all four attacks," Lucy told them. "And frankly, it's a little alarming that the severity of the beatings he gives his victims seems to be increasing."

"Any pattern among the victims as to location, physical appearance, anything?" Lucky asked.

"If there is, we can't find anything other than that the victims are all females between the ages of eighteen and forty-three, and the attacks all took place in either San Felipe or Coronado," the detective replied. "I'll get you the complete files first thing in the morning. You might as well try searching for a pattern, too. I don't think you're going to find one, but it sure beats sitting around waiting for this guy to strike again."

Bobby's pager went off. He glanced at it as he shut it off, then stood. "If that's all for now, Lieutenant..."

Lucky gestured with his head toward the pager. "Anything I should know about?"

"Just Wes," the bigger man said. "It's been a rough tour for him. Coronado's the last place he wanted to be, and he's been here for nearly three months now." He nodded at Sydney. "Nice meeting you. See you later, Luce." He turned back. "Do me a favor and lock your windows tonight, ladies."

"And every night until we catch this guy," Lucky added as the chief headed for the door. He stood up. "I'm going to take off, too."

"See you tomorrow." Syd barely even looked at him as she turned to Lucy. "Are you in a hurry to get home, detective? Because I have some questions I was hoping you could answer."

Lucky lingered, but aside from a quick wave from Lucy, neither woman gave him a second glance.

"I did some research on sex crimes and serial rapists and serial *murderers*," Syd continued, "and—"

"And you're thinking about what I said about the level of violence escalating," Lucy finished for her. "You want to know if I think this guy's going to cross the line into rape-homicide."

Oh, God, Lucky hadn't even considered *that*. Rape alone was bad enough.

Lucy sighed. "Considering the abuse the perp seems to enjoy dishing out, in my opinion, it could be just a matter of time before he—"

"Heads up," Syd said in a low voice. "Barbie's coming this way."

Barbie?

Lucky looked up to see Heather heading toward them. Her body in motion made heads turn throughout the entire room.

She *was* gorgeous, but she was plastic. Kind of like a Barbie doll. Yeah, the name fit.

He wanted to stay, wanted to hear what Lucy and Syd had to say, but he'd saddled himself with Heather, and now he had to pay the price.

He had to take her home.

With Heather, there was always a fifty-fifty chance she'd invite him up to her place and tear off his clothes. Tonight she'd made a few suggestive comments at dinner that led him to believe it was, indeed, going to be one of those nights where they engaged in a little pleasure gymnastics.

"Ready to go home?" Heather smiled at him, a smile

loaded with promise. A smile he knew that Syd had not missed.

Good. Let her know that he was going to get some tonight. Let her know he didn't need her to make fireworks.

"Absolutely." Lucky put his arm around her waist.

He glanced at Syd, but she was already back to her discussion with Lucy, and she didn't look up.

As Heather dragged him to the door, Lucky knew he was the envy of every man in the bar. He was going home with a beautiful woman who wanted to have wild sex with him.

He should have been running for his car. He should have been in a hurry to get her naked.

But as he reached the door, he couldn't stop himself from hesitating, from looking back at Syd.

She glanced up at that exact moment, and their eyes met and held. The connection was instantaneous. It was cracklingly powerful, burningly intense.

He didn't look away, and neither did she.

It was far more intimate than he'd ever been with Heather, and they'd spent days together naked.

Heather tugged at his arm, pressed her body against him, pulled his head down for a kiss.

Lucky responded instinctively, and when he looked back at Syd, she had turned away.

"Come on, baby," Heather murmured. "I'm in a hurry."

Lucky let her pull him out the door.

THE PICKUP TRUCK WAS following her.

Syd had first noticed the headlights in her rearview mirror as she'd pulled out of La Cantina's parking lot.

The truck had stayed several car lengths behind her as

she'd headed west on Arizona Avenue. And when she'd made a left turn onto Draper, he'd turned, too.

She knew for sure when she did a series of right and left turns, taking the shortcut to her neighborhood. It couldn't be a coincidence. He was definitely following her.

Syd and Lucy had talked briefly after Navy Ken had taken his inflatable Barbie home. She'd stayed in the bar after Lucy had left as well, having a glass of beer as she wrote her latest women's safety article on her laptop. It was far easier to write in the noisy bar than it would have been in her too-quiet apartment. She missed the chaos of the newsroom. *And* being home alone would only have served to remind her that Lucky O'Donlon wasn't.

Miss Vapid USA was, no doubt, his soul mate. Syd wondered rather viciously if they spent all their time together gazing into mirrors. Blond and Blonder.

Lucy had volunteered the information that Heather was typical of the type of women the SEAL fraternized with. He went for beauty queens who were usually in their late teens, with an IQ not much higher than their age.

Syd didn't know why she was surprised. God forbid a man like Luke O'Donlon should ever become involved with a woman who actually *meant* something to him. A woman who talked back to him, offering a differing opinion and a challenging, vivacious honest-to-God relationship....

Who was she kidding? Did she really imagine she tasted integrity in his kisses?

It was true that he'd protested admirably when she'd accused him of trying to steal his XO's wife, but all that meant was that he had a line in his debauchery that he would not cross.

He was hot, he was smooth, he could kiss like a dream, but his passion was empty. For indeed, what was passion without emotion? A balloon that, when popped, revealed nothing but slightly foul-smelling air.

She was glad she'd seen Luke O'Donlon with his Barbie doll. It was healthy, it was realistic and just maybe it would keep her damned subconscious from dreaming erotic dreams about him tonight.

Syd took a right turn onto Pacific, pulling into the right lane and slowing down enough so that anyone in their right mind would pass her, but the truck stayed behind her.

Think. She had to think. Or rather, she had to stop thinking about Luke O'Donlon and his perfect butt and focus on the fact that a sociopathic serial rapist could well be following her through the nearly deserted streets of San Felipe.

She'd written an article dealing with this very subject just minutes ago.

If you think someone is following you, she'd said, do not go home. Drive directly to the police station. If you have a cell phone, use it to call for help.

Syd fumbled in her shoulder bag for her cell phone, hesitating only slightly before she pushed the speed-dial button she'd programmed with Lucky O'Donlon's home phone number. It would serve him right if she interrupted him.

His machine picked up after only two rings, and she skipped over his sexy-voiced message.

"O'Donlon, it's Syd. If you're there, pick up." Nothing. "Lieutenant, I know my voice is the last thing you probably want to hear right now, but I'm being followed." Oh, crud, her voice cracked slightly, and her fear and apprehension peeked through. She took a deep breath, hoping to sound calm and collected, but only managing to sound very small and pitiful. "Are you there?"

No response. The answering machine beeped, cutting her off.

Okay. Okay. As long as she kept moving, she'd be okay.

And chances were, if she pulled into the brightly lit police-station parking lot, whoever was following her would drive away.

But what a missed opportunity *that* would be. If this *were* the rapist behind her, they could catch him. Right now. Tonight.

She pressed one of the other speed-dial numbers she'd programmed into her phone. Detective Lucy McCoy's home number.

One ring. Two rings. Three...

"'Lo?" Lucy sounded as if she'd already been asleep.

"Lucy, it's Syd." She gave a quick rundown of the situation, and Lucy snapped instantly awake.

"Stay on Pacific," Lucy ordered. "What's your license plate number?"

"God, I don't know. My car's a little black Civic. The truck's one of those full-size ones—I haven't been able to see what color—something dark. And he's hanging too far back for me to see his plate number."

"Just keep driving," Lucy said. "Slow and steady. I'm calling in as many cars as possible to intercept."

Slow and steady.

Syd used her cell phone and tried calling Lucky one more time.

Nothing.

Slow and steady.

She was heading north on Pacific. She could just follow the road all the way up to San Francisco, slowly and steadily. Provided the truck behind her let her stop for gas. She was running low. Of course a little car like this could go for miles on a sixteenth of a tank. She had no reason to be afraid. At any minute, the San Felipe police were going to come to the rescue.

Any minute. Any. Minute.

She heard it then—sirens in the distance, getting louder and deafeningly louder as the police cars moved closer.

Three of them came from behind. She watched in her rear-view mirror as they surrounded the truck, their lights flashing.

She slowed to a stop at the side of the road as the truck did the same, twisting to look back through her rear window as the police officers approached, their weapons drawn, bright searchlights aimed at the truck.

She could see the shadow of the man in the cab. He had both hands on his head in a position of surrender. The police pulled open the truck's door, pulled him out alongside the truck where he braced himself, assuming the position for a full-body search.

Syd turned off the ignition and got out, wanting to get closer now that she knew the man following her wasn't armed, wanting to hear what he was saying, wanting to get a good look at him—see if he was the same man who'd nearly knocked her down the stairs after attacking her neighbor.

The man was talking. She could see from the police officers standing around him that he was keeping up a steady stream of conversation. Explanation, no doubt, for why he was out driving around so late at night. Following someone? Officer, that was just an unfortunate coincidence. I was going to the supermarket to pick up some ice cream.

Yeah, right.

As Syd moved closer, one of the police officers approached her.

"Sydney Jameson?" he called.

"Yes," she said. "Thank you for responding so quickly to Detective McCoy's call. Does this guy have identification?"

"He does," the officer said. "He also says he knows you—and that you know him."

What? Sydney moved closer, but the man who'd been following her was still surrounded by the police and she couldn't see his face.

The police officer continued. "He also claims you're both part of a working police task force...?"

Sydney could see in the dim streetlights that the truck was red. *Red.*

As if on cue, the police officers parted, the man turned his face toward her and...

It was. Luke O'Donlon.

"Why the *hell* were you following me?" All of her emotions sparked into anger. "You scared me to death, damn it!"

He himself wasn't too happy about having been frisked by six unfriendly policemen. He was still standing in the undignified search position—legs spread, palms against the side of his truck, and he sounded just as indignant as she did. Maybe even more indignant. "I was following you home. You were supposed to go home, not halfway across the state. Jeez, I was just trying to make sure you were safe."

"What about Heather?" The words popped out before Sydney could stop herself.

But Luke didn't even seem to hear her question. He had turned back to the police officers. "Are you guys satisfied? I'm who I say I am, all right? Can I please stand up?"

The police officer who seemed to be in charge looked to Syd.

"No," she said, nodding yes. "I think you should make him stay like that for about two hours as punishment."

"Punishment?" Luke let out a stream of sailor's language as he straightened up. "For doing something *nice?* For worrying so much about you and Lucy going home from that bar alone that I dropped Heather off at her apartment and came straight back to make sure you'd be okay?"

He hadn't gone home with Miss Ventura County. He'd given up a night of steamy, mindless, emotionless sex because he had been worried about her.

Syd didn't know whether to laugh or hit him.

"Heather wasn't happy," he told her. "That's your answer for 'what about Heather?'" He smiled ruefully. "I don't think she's ever been turned down before."

He *had* heard her question.

She'd spent most of the past hour trying her hardest not to imagine his long, muscular legs entangled with Heather's, his skin slick and his hair damp with perspiration as he...

She'd tried her hardest, but she'd always had a very good imagination.

It was stupid. She'd told herself that it didn't matter, that *he* didn't matter. She didn't even like him. But now here he was, standing in front of her, gazing at her with those impossibly blue eyes, with that twenty-four-carat sun-gilded hair curling in his face from the ocean's humidity.

"You scared me," she said again.

"You?" He laughed. "Something tells me you're un-scareable." He looked around them at the three police cars, lights still spinning, the officers talking on their radios. He shook his head with what looked an awful lot like admiration. "You actually had the presence of mind to call the police from your cell phone, huh? That was good, Jameson. I'm impressed."

Syd shrugged. "It wasn't that big a deal. But I guess you just don't spend that much time with smart women."

Lucky laughed. "Ouch. Poor Heather. She's not even here to defend herself. She's not that bad, you know. A little heartless and consumed by her career, but that's not so different from most people."

"How could you be willing to settle for 'not that bad?'" Syd countered. "You could have just about anyone you wanted. Why not choose someone with a heart?"

"That assumes," he said, "that I'd even *want* someone's heart."

"Ah," she said, turning back to her car. "My mistake."

"Syd."

She turned back to face him.

"I'm sorry I scared you."

"Don't let it happen again," she said. "Warn me in advance all right?" She turned away.

"Syd."

She sighed and turned to face him again. "Quickly, Ken," she begged. "We've got a seven o'clock meeting scheduled at the police station. I'm not a morning person, and I'm even less of a morning person when I get fewer than six hours of sleep."

"I'm going to follow you home," he told her. "When you go up to your apartment, flash your light a few times so I know everything's okay, all right?"

Syd didn't get it. "You don't even like me. Why the concern?"

Lucky smiled. "I never said I didn't like you. I just don't want you on my team. Those are two very different things."

CHAPTER FIVE

"SIT ON THE COUCH—or in the chair," Dr. Lana Quinn directed Sydney. "Wherever you think you'll be more comfortable."

"I appreciate your finding the time to do this on such short notice," Lucky said.

"You got lucky," Lana told him with a smile. "Wes called right after my regular one o'clock cancelled. I was a little surprised actually—it's been a while since I've heard from him."

Lucky didn't know the pretty young psychologist very well. She was married to a SEAL named Wizard with whom he'd never worked. But Wizard had been in the same BUD/S class with Bobby and Wes, and the three men had remained close. And when Lucky had stopped Wes in the hall to inquire jokingly if he knew a hypnotist, Wes had surprised him by saying, yes, as a matter of fact, he did.

"How is Wes?" Lana asked.

Lucky was no shrink himself, but the question was just a little too casual.

She must have realized the way her words had sounded and hastened to explain. "He was in such a rush when he called, I didn't even have time to ask. We used to talk on the phone all the time back when my husband was in Team Six, you know, when he was gone more often than not—I think it was because Wes and I both missed Quinn. And after he transferred back to California, back to Team Ten, Wes kind of dropped out of touch."

"Wes is doing good—just made chief," Lucky told her.

"That's great," Lana enthused—again just a little too enthusiastically. "Congratulate him for me, will you?"

Lucky was not an expert by any means, but he didn't have to be an expert to know there was more to that story than Lana was telling. Not that he believed for one minute that Wes would've had an affair with the wife of one of his best friends. No, Wes Skelly was a caveman in a lot of ways, but his code of honor was among the most solid Lucky had ever known.

It *did* make perfect sense, though, for Wes to have done something truly stupid, like fall in love with his good friend's wife. And if that had happened, Wes *would* have dropped out of Lana's life like a stone. And Lucky suspected she knew that, psychologist that she was.

God, life was complicated. And it was complicated enough without throwing marriage and its restrictions into the picture. He was never getting married, thank you very much.

It was a rare day that went by without Lucky reminding himself of that—in fact, it was his mantra. Never getting married. Never getting married.

Yet lately—particularly as he watched Frisco with his wife, Mia, and Blue with Lucy, and even the captain, Joe Cat, who'd been married to *his* wife, Veronica, longer than any of the other guys in Alpha Squad, Lucky had felt...

Envy.

God, he hated to admit it, but he *was* a little jealous. When Frisco draped his arm around Mia's shoulder, or when she came up behind him and rubbed his shoulders after a long day. When Lucy stopped in at the crowded, busy Alpha Squad office and Blue would look across the room and smile, and she'd smile back. Or Joe Cat. Calling Veronica every chance he got, from a pay phone in downtown Paris, from the Australian outback after a training op. He'd lower his voice, but Lucky had overheard far more than once. *Hey babe, ya miss me? God, I miss you....*

Lucky had come embarrassingly close to getting a lump in his throat more than once.

Despite his rather desperate-sounding mantra, Joe and Blue and Frisco and all of the other married SEALs made the perils of commitment look too damn good.

As Lucky watched, across the room Sydney perched on the very edge of the couch, arms folded tightly across her chest as she looked around Lana's homey office. She didn't want to be here, didn't want to be hypnotized. Her body language couldn't be any more clear.

He settled into the chair across from her. "Thanks for agreeing to this."

He could see her trepidation in the tightness of her mouth as she shook her head. "I don't think it's going to work."

"Yeah, well, maybe it will."

"Don't be too disappointed if it doesn't."

She was afraid of failing. Lucky could understand that. Failure was something he feared as well.

"Why don't you take off your jacket," Lana suggested to Sydney. "Get loose—unbutton your shirt a little, roll up your sleeves. I want you to try to get as comfortable as possible. Kick off your boots, try to relax."

"I don't think this is going to work," Sydney said again, this time to Lana, as she slipped her arms out of her jacket.

"Don't worry about that," Lana told her, sitting down in the chair closest to Sydney. "Before we go any further,

I want to tell you that my methods are somewhat unconventional. But I have had some degree of success working with victims of crimes, helping them clarify the order and details of certain traumatic or frightening events, so bear with me. And again, there's no guarantee that this *will* work, but we've got a better shot at it if you try to be open-minded."

Syd nodded tightly. "I'm trying."

She was. Lucky had to give her that. She didn't want to be here, didn't *have* to be here, yet here she was.

"Let's start with you telling me what you felt when you encountered the man on the stairs," Lana said. "Did you see him coming, or were you startled by him?"

"I heard the clatter of his footsteps," Syd told her as she unfastened first one, then two, then three buttons on her shirt.

Lucky looked away, aware that he was watching her, aware that he didn't want her to stop at three, remembering with a sudden alarming clarity the way she had felt when he'd held her in his arms. She'd tasted so sweet and hot and...

Lucky was dressed in his summer uniform, and he resisted the urge to loosen his own collar. He was overheating far too often these days. He *should* have called Heather after following Syd home last night. He should have called and groveled. Chances are she would have let him in.

But he'd gone home instead. He'd swum about four hundred laps in his pool, trying to curb his restlessness, blaming it on the fact that Alpha Squad was out there, in the real world, while he'd been left behind.

"He was moving fast," Syd continued. "He clearly didn't see me, and I couldn't get out of his way."

"Were you frightened?" Lana asked.

Syd thought about that, chewing for a moment on her lower lip. "More like alarmed," she said. "He was big. But I wasn't afraid of him because I thought he was dangerous. It was more like the flash of fear you get when a car swerves into your lane and there's nowhere to go to avoid hitting it."

"Picture the moment that you first heard him coming," Lana suggested, "and try to flip it into slow motion. You hear him, then you see him. What are you thinking? Right at that second when you first spot him coming down the stairs?"

Syd looked up from untying the laces of her boots. "Kevin Manse," she said.

She was still leaning over, and Lucky got a sudden brief look down the open front of her shirt. She was wearing a black bra, and he got a very clear look at black lace against smooth pale skin. As she moved to untie her other boot, Lucky tried to look away. Tried and failed. He found himself watching her, hoping for another enticing glimpse of her small but perfectly, delicately, deliciously shaped, lace-covered breasts.

Sydney Jameson was enormously attractive, he realized with a jolt as he examined her face. Sure he'd always preferred women with a long mane of hair, but hers was darkly sleek and especially lustrous, and the short cut suited the shape of her face. Her eyes were the color of black coffee, with lashes that didn't need any makeup to look thick and dark.

She wasn't traditionally pretty, but whenever she stopped scowling and smiled, she was breathtaking.

And as far as her clothes...

Lucky had never particularly liked the Annie Hall look before, but with a flash of awareness, he suddenly completely understood its appeal. Buried beneath Syd's baggy,

mannish clothing was a body as elegantly, gracefully feminine as the soft curves of her face. And the glimpse he'd
had was sexy as hell—sexy in a way he'd never imagined
possible, considering that the women he usually found
attractive were far more generously endowed.

She straightened up, kicking off her boots. She wasn't
wearing socks, and her feet were elegantly shaped with
very high arches. God, what was wrong with him that the
sight of a woman's bare foot was enough to push him over
the edge into complete arousal?

Lucky shifted in his seat, crossing his legs, praying
Lana wouldn't ask him to fetch anything from her desk
all the way across the room.

"Who's Kevin Manse?" the psychologist asked Sydney.

Syd sat back, crossing her legs tailor-style, tucking her
sexy feet beneath her on the couch. "He was a football
player I, um…" she flashed a look in Lucky's direction
and actually blushed "…knew in college. I guess the sheer
size of this guy reminded me of Kevin."

Wasn't that interesting? And completely unexpected.
Syd Jameson certainly didn't seem the type to have dated
a football player in college. "Boyfriend?" Lucky asked.

"Um," Syd said. "Not exactly."

Ah. Maybe she'd liked the football player, and he hadn't
even noticed her. Maybe, like Lucky, Kevin had been
too busy trying to catch the eyes of the more bodacious
cheerleaders.

Lana scribbled a comment on her notepad. "Okay," she
said. "Let's give this a shot, shall we?"

Syd laughed nervously. "So how do you do this? All
I can think of is Elmer Fudd trying to hypnotize Bugs
Bunny with his pocket watch on a chain. You know, 'You
ah getting vewwy sweepy.'"

Laughing, Lana crossed the room and turned off the light. "Actually, I use a mirror ball, a flashlight and voiced suggestions. Lieutenant, I have to recommend that you step out into the waiting room for a few minutes. I've found that SEALs are highly susceptible to this form of light-induced hypnotism. My theory is that it has to do with the way you've trained yourself to take combat naps." She sat down again across from Syd. "They fall, quickly, into deep REM sleep for short periods of time," she explained before looking back at Lucky. "There may be a form of self-hypnosis involved when you do that." She smiled wryly. "I'm not sure though. Quinn won't let me experiment on him. You can try staying in here, but..."

"I'll leave the room—temporarily," Lucky said.

"Good idea. I'm sure Dr. Quinn doesn't want both of us waddling around quacking like ducks," Syd said.

Hot damn, she'd made a joke. Lucky laughed, and Syd actually smiled back at him. But her smile was far too small and it faded far too quickly.

"Seriously," she added. "If I do something to really embarrass myself, don't rub it in, all right?"

"I won't," he told her. "As long as you promise to return the same favor some day."

"I guess that's fair."

"Step outside, Lieutenant."

"You'll wait to ask her any questions until I come back in?"

Lana Quinn nodded. "I will."

"Quack, quack," Syd said.

Lucky closed the door behind him.

As he paced, he punched a number into his cell phone. Frisco picked up the phone on his office desk after only half a ring.

"Francisco."

"Answering your own phone," Lucky said. "Very impressive."

"Understaffed," Frisco said shortly. "S'up?"

"I'm wondering if you've heard anything about yesterday's diving accident."

Frisco said some choice words, none of them polite. "God, what a stupid-fest. The SEAL candidate—*former* SEAL candidate—who nearly had nitrogen bubbles turn his brain into Swiss cheese, apparently snuck out of the barracks the night before the accident. It was his birthday, and some well-meaning but equally idiotic friends flew him to Vegas to visit his girlfriend. The flight back was delayed, and he didn't land in San Diego until oh-three-hundred. The stupid bastard made it back into the barracks without being found out, but he was still completely skunked when the training op started at oh-four-thirty."

Lucky cringed. It was dangerous to dive any less than twenty-four hours after flying. And if this guy was diving drunk, to boot...

"If he'd spoken up then, he would've been forced out of BUD/S, but this way they're throwing the book at him," Frisco continued. "He's facing a dishonorable discharge at the very least."

The fool was lucky he was alive, but indeed, that was where his luck ended. "How many of the candidates were covering for him?" Lucky asked. An incident like this could well eliminate half of an entire class.

"Only five of 'em," Frisco said. "All officers. All gone as of 0600 this morning."

Lucky shook his head. One guy couldn't handle having a birthday without getting some from his girlfriend, and six promising careers were flushed.

The door opened, and Lana Quinn poked her head out of her office. "We're ready for you, Lieutenant."

"Whoops," Lucky said to Frisco. "I've got to go. It's hypno-time. Later, man."

He hung up on his commanding officer and snapped his phone shut, slipping it into his pocket.

"Move slowly," Lana told him. "She's pretty securely under, but no quick motions or sudden noises, please."

The blinds were down in the office and, with the over-head lights off, Lucky had to blink for a moment to let his eyes adjust to the dimness.

He moved carefully into the room, standing off to the side, as Lana sat down near Syd.

She was stretched out on the couch, her eyes closed, as if she were asleep. She looked deceptively peaceful and possibly even angelic. Lucky, however, knew better.

"Sydney, I want to go back, just a short amount of time, to the night you were coming home from the movies. Do you remember that night?"

As Lucky sat down, Syd was silent.

"Do you remember that night?" Lana persisted. "You were nearly knocked over by the man coming down the stairs."

"Kevin Manse," Syd said. Her eyes were still tightly shut, but her voice was strong and clear.

"That's right," Lana said. "He reminded you of Kevin Manse. Can you see him, Syd?"

Sydney nodded. "He nearly knocks me over on the stairs. He's angry. And drunk. I know he's drunk. I'm drunk, too. It's my first frat-house party."

"What the—"

Lana silenced Lucky with one swift motion. "How old are you, Sydney?"

"I'm eighteen," she told them, her husky voice breath-less and young-sounding. "He apologizes—oh, God, he's *so* cute, and we start talking. He's an honors student as well as the star of the football team and I can't believe he's talking to *me*."

"Now it's more than ten years later," Lana interrupted gently, "and the man on the stairs only *reminds* you of Kevin."

"I'm so dizzy," Syd continued, as if she hadn't heard Lana. "And the stairs are so crowded. Kevin tells me his room's upstairs. I can lie down for a while on his bed. And he kisses me and…" She sighed and smiled. "And I know he doesn't mean alone."

"Oh, God," Lucky said. He didn't want to hear this.

"Sydney," Lana said firmly. "I need you to come back to the present day now."

"I pretend not to be nervous when he locks the door behind us," Syd continued. "His books are out on his desk. Calculus and physics. And he kisses me again and…"

She made a soft noise of pleasure, and Lucky rocketed out of his seat. "Why won't she listen to you?"

Lana shrugged. "Could be any number of reasons. She's clearly strong-willed. And this could well have been a pivotal moment in her life. Whatever her reasons, she doesn't want to leave it right now."

Syd moved slightly on the couch, her head back, her lips slightly parted as she made another of those intense little sounds. Dear God.

"Why don't we see if we can get to the end of this episode," Lana suggested. "Maybe she'll be more receptive to moving into the more recent past if we let her take her time."

"What," Lucky said, "we're just going to sit here while she relives having sex with this guy?"

"I've never done this before," Syd whispered. "Not really, and— *Oh!*"

Lucky couldn't look at her, couldn't not look at her. She

was breathing hard, with a slight sheen of perspiration on her face. "Okay," he said, unable to stand this another second. "Okay, Syd. You do the deed with Mr. Wonderful. It's over. Let's move on."

"He's so sweet," Syd sighed. "He says he's afraid people will talk if I stay there all night, so he asks a friend to drive me back to my dorm. He says he'll call me, and he kisses me good night and I'm...I'm so amazed at how good that felt, at how much I love him— I can't wait to do it again."

Okay. So now he knew that not only was Sydney hot, she was hot-blooded as well.

"Sydney," Lana's voice left no room for argument. "Now it's just a little less than a week ago. You're on the stairs, in your apartment building. You're coming home from the movies—"

"God." Sydney laughed aloud. "Did that movie *suck*. I can't believe I spent all that money on it. The highlight was that pop singer who used to be a model who now thinks he's an actor. And I'm not talking about his acting. I'm talking about the scene that featured his bare butt. It alone was truly worthy of the big screen. And," she laughed again, a rich, sexy sound, "if you want to know the truth, these days the movies is the closest I seem to be able to get to a naked man."

Lucky knew one easy way to change that, fast. But he kept his mouth shut and let Lana do her shrink thing.

"You're climbing the stairs to your apartment," she told Syd. "It's late, and you're heading home and you hear a noise."

"Footsteps," Syd responded. "Someone's coming down the stairs. Kevin Manse—no, he just looks for half a second like Kevin Manse, but he's not."

"Can you mentally push a pause button," Lana asked, "and hold him in a freeze-frame?"

Syd nodded. "He's not Kevin Manse."

"Can you describe his face? Is he wearing a mask? Panty hose over his head?"

"No, but he's in shadow," Syd told them. "The light's behind him. He's got a short crew cut, I can see the hair on his head sticking straight up, lit the way he is. But his face is dark. I can't really see him, but I know he's not Kevin. He moves differently. He's more muscle-bound— you know, top-heavy from lifting weights. Kevin was just big all over."

Lucky could well imagine. God, this was stupid. He was jealous of this Kevin Manse guy.

"Let him move toward you," Lana suggested, "but in slow motion, if you can. Does the light ever hit his face?"

Syd was frowning now, her eyes still closed, concentrating intensely. "No," she finally said. "He swerves around me, hits me with his shoulder. *Sorry, bud.* He turns his face toward me and I can see that he's white. His hair looks golden, but maybe it's just brown, just the reflected light."

"Are you sure he's not wearing a mask?" Lana asked.

"No. He's still moving down the stairs, but he's turning his head to look at me, and I turn away."

"*You* turn away," Lana repeated. "Why?"

Syd laughed, but there was no humor in it. "I'm embarrassed," she admitted. "He thought I was a man. It's happened to me before, and it's worse when they realize they've made a mistake. I hate the apologies. *That's* when it's humiliating."

"So why do you dress that way?" Lucky had to ask.

Lana shot him an appalled "what are you doing?" look. He didn't give a damn. He wanted to know.

"It's safe," Syd told him.

"Safe."

"Lieutenant," Lana said sternly.

"Back to the guy on the stairs," Lucky said. "What's *he* wearing?"

"Jeans," Syd said without hesitating. "And a plain dark sweatshirt."

"Tattoos?" Lucky asked.

"His sleeves are down."

"On his feet?"

She was silent for several long seconds. "I don't know."

"You turn away," Lana said. "But do you look back at him as he goes down the stairs?"

"No. I hear him, though. He slams the front door on his way out. I'm glad—it sometimes doesn't latch and then anyone can get in."

"Do you hear anything else?" Lucky asked. "Stop and listen carefully."

Syd was silent. "A car starts. And then pulls away. A fan belt must be loose or old or something because it squeals a little. I'm glad when it's gone. It's an annoying sound—it's not an expensive part, and it doesn't take much to learn how to—"

"When you're home, do you park in a garage," Lucky interrupted, "or on the street?"

"Street," she told him.

"When you pulled up," he asked, "after the movie, were there any cars near your apartment building that you didn't recognize?"

Syd chewed on her lip, frowning slightly. "I don't remember."

Lucky looked at Lana. "Can you take her back there?"

"I can try, but..."

"Gina's door is open," Syd said.

"Syd, let's try to backtrack a few minutes," Lana said. "Let's go back to your car, after you've left the movie theater. You're driving home."

"Why is her door open?" Syd asked, and Lana glanced at Lucky, shaking her head.

"Her boyfriend must've left it open," Syd continued. "Figures a guy can't replace a fan belt also can't manage to shut a door and..." She sat up suddenly, her eyes wide open. She was looking straight at Lucky, but through him, or in front of him, not at him. She didn't see him. Instead, she saw something else, something he couldn't see. "Oh, my *God!*"

Her hair was damp with perspiration, and she reached up with a shaking hand to push it away from her eyes.

Lana leaned forward. "Sydney, let's go back—"

"Oh, my God, *Gina!* She's in the corner of the living room, and her face is bleeding! Her eye's swollen shut and...oh, God, oh, God. She wasn't just beaten. Her clothes are torn and..." Her voice changed, calmer, more controlled. "Yes, I need the police to come here right away." She recited the address as if she were talking on the telephone. "We'll need an ambulance, too. And a police-woman, please. My neighbor's been...raped." Her voice broke, and she took a deep breath. "Gina, here's your robe. I think it would be okay if you put it around yourself. Let me help you, hon..."

"Sydney," Lana said gently. "I'm going to bring you back now. It's time to go."

"Go?" Syd's voice cracked. "I can't leave Gina. How could you even *think* that I could just leave Gina? God, it's bad enough I have to pretend everything's going to be okay. Look at her! *Look* at her!" She started to cry; deep, racking sobs that shook her entire body, a fountain of emotion brimming over and spilling down her cheeks. "What kind of monster could have done this to this girl? Look in her eyes—all of her hopes, her dreams, her *life,* they're *gone!* And you know with that mother of hers, she's going to live the rest of her life hiding from the world, too afraid ever to come back out again. And why? Because she left the window in the kitchen unlocked. She wasn't careful, because nobody had *bothered* to warn any of us that this son of a bitch was out there! They knew, the police *knew,* but nobody said a single word!"

Lucky couldn't stop himself. He sat next to Sydney, and pulled her into his arms. "Oh, Syd, I'm sorry," he said.

But she pushed him away, curling into herself, turning into a small ball in the corner of the couch, completely inconsolable.

Lucky looked at Lana helplessly.

"Syd," she said loudly. "I'm going to clap my hands twice, and you're going to fall asleep. You'll wake up in one minute, feeling completely refreshed. You won't remember any of this."

Lana clapped her hands, and just like that, Syd's body relaxed. The room was suddenly very silent.

Lucky sat back, resting his head against the back of the couch. He drew in a deep breath and let it out with a whoosh. "I had no idea," he said. Syd was always so strong, so in control.... He remembered that message he'd found on his answering machine last night when he'd gotten home. The way she hadn't quite managed to hide the fear in her voice when she'd called him for help, thinking she was being followed by a stranger. *You scared me to death,* she'd told him, but he hadn't really believed it until he'd heard that phone message.

What else was she hiding?

"She clearly considers her stake in this to be personal," Lana said quietly. She stood up. "I think it would be better if you were in the waiting room when she wakes up."

CHAPTER SIX

"WHERE ARE WE GOING?" Syd asked, following Luke down toward the beach.

"I want to show you something," he said.

He'd been quiet ever since they'd left Lana Quinn's office—not just quiet, but subdued. Introspective. Brooding.

It made her nervous. What exactly had she said and done while under the hypnotist's spell to make the ever-smiling Navy Ken *brood*?

Syd had come out of the session feeling a little disoriented. At first she'd thought the hypnosis hadn't worked, but then she'd realized that about half an hour had passed from the time she'd first sat down. A half hour of which she remembered nothing.

To Syd's disappointment, Lana told her she *hadn't* got a clear look at the rapist's unmasked face as he'd come down the stairs. They weren't any closer to identifying the man.

Luke O'Donlon hadn't said a word to her. Not in Lana's office, not in his truck as they'd headed back here to the base. He'd parked by the beach and gotten out, saying only, "Come on."

They stood now at the edge of the sand, watching the activity. And there was a great deal of activity on this beach, although there was nary a beach ball, a bikini-clad girl, a picnic basket or a colorful umbrella in sight.

There were men on the beach, lots of men, dressed in long pants and combat boots despite the heat. One group ran down by the water at a pounding pace. The other group was split into smaller teams of six or seven, each of which wrestled a huge, heavy-looking, ungainly rubber raft toward the water, carrying it high above their heads while men with bullhorns shouted at them.

"This is part of BUD/S," Luke told her. "SEAL training. These men are SEAL candidates. If they make it through all the phases of this training, they'll go on to join one of the teams."

Syd nodded. "I've read about this," she said. "There's a drop-out rate of something incredible, like fifty percent, right?"

"Sometimes more." He pointed down the beach toward the group of men that were running through the surf. "Those guys are in phase two, which is mostly diving instruction, along with additional PT. That particular class started with a hundred men and today they're down to twenty-two. Most guys ring out in the first few days of phase one, which consists mostly of intense PT—that's physical training."

"I'd kind of figured that out."

"Navyspeak contains a lot of shorthand," he told her. "Let me know if you need anything explained."

Why was he being so nice? He could have managed to sound patronizing, but he just sounded...nice. "Thanks," Syd managed.

"Anyway, this class," he pointed again to the beach, "is down to only twenty-two because they had a string of bad luck—some kind of stomach flu hit during the start of Hell Week, and a record number of men were evac-ed out." He smiled, as if in fond memory. "If it was just a matter of barf and keep going, most of 'em probably would've stayed in, but this flu came with a dangerously high fever. Medical wouldn't let them stay. Those guys were rolled back to the next class—most of them are going through the first weeks of phase one again right now. To top that off, this particular class also just lost six men in the fallout from that diving accident. So their number's low."

Syd watched the men who were running through the water—the candidates Luke had said were in the second phase of BUD/S training. "Somehow I was under the impression that the physical training ended after Hell Week."

Luke laughed. "Are you kidding? PT never ends. Being a SEAL is kind of like being a continuous work in progress. You always keep running—every day. You've got to be able to do consistent seven-and-a-half-minute miles tomorrow and next month—and next year. If you let it slip, your whole team suffers. See, a SEAL team can only move as fast as its slowest man when it's moving as a unit."

He gestured toward the men still carrying the black rubber boats above their heads. "That's what these guys are starting to learn. Teamwork. Identify an individual's strengths and weaknesses and use that information to keep your team operating at its highest potential."

A red-haired girl on a bicycle rode into the parking lot. She skidded to a stop in the soft sand a few yards away from Luke and Syd, and sat down, watching the men on the beach.

"Yo, Tash!" Luke called to her.

She barely even glanced up, barely waved, so intent was she on watching the men on the beach. It was the girl Syd had met yesterday, the one who'd been at the base with Lieutenant Commander Francisco's wife. She was looking for someone, searching the beach, shading her eyes with her hand.

"Frisco's not out here right now," Luke called to her.

"I know," she said and went right on looking.

Luke shrugged and turned back to Syd. "Check out this group here." He pointed at the men with the boats. "See this team with the short guy? He's not pulling his weight, right? He's not carrying much of the IBS—the inflatable boat—because he can hardly reach the damn thing. The taller men have to compensate for him. But you better believe that the vertically challenged dude will make up for it somewhere down the road. He's light, probably fast. Maybe he's good at climbing. Or he can fit into tight places—places the bigger men can't. Shorty may not help too much when it comes to carrying something like an IBS, but, guaranteed, he'll do more than his share in the long run."

He was quiet then, just watching the SEAL candidates. The group of runners—the candidates in the second phase of BUD/S training—collapsed on the sand.

"Five minutes," Syd heard distantly but distinctly through a bullhorn. "And then, ladies, we do it all over again."

The instructor with the bullhorn was Bobby Taylor, his long dark hair pulled back into a braid.

As Syd watched, one of the candidates approached Bobby, pointing up toward the edge of the beach, toward them. Bobby seemed to shrug, and the candidate took off, running toward them through the soft sand.

He was young and black, and the short, nearly shaved hairstyle that all the candidates sported served to emphasize the sharp angles of his face. He had a few scars, one disrupting the line of his right eyebrow, the other on his cheek, and they added to his aura of danger.

Syd thought he was coming to talk to Luke, but he headed straight for the little girl on the bike.

"Are you crazy?" His less-than-friendly greeting was accompanied by a scowl. "What did I tell you about riding your bike out here alone? And that was *before* this psycho-on-the-loose crap."

"No one wanted to ride all the way out here with me." Tasha lifted her chin. They were both speaking loudly enough for Syd to easily overhear. "Besides, I'm fast. If I see any weirdos, I can get away, no problem."

Sweat was literally pouring off the young man's face as he bent over to catch his breath, hands on his knees. "You're fast," he repeated skeptically. "Faster than a car?"

She was exasperated. "No."

"No." He glared at her. "Then it's *not* no problem, is it?"

"I don't see what the big deal—"

The black man exploded. "The *big deal* is that there's some son-of-a-bitch psycho running around town raping and beating the hell out of women. The *big* deal is that, as a female, you're a potential target. As a pretty, young female who's riding her bike alone, you're an attractive, easy target. You might as well wear a sign around your neck that says *victim*."

"I read this guy breaks into women's homes," Tasha countered. "I don't see what that has to do with me riding my bike."

Syd couldn't keep her mouth shut any longer. "Actually," she said, "serial rapists tend to do something called *troll* for victims. That means they drive around and look for a likely target—someone who's alone and potentially defenseless—and they follow her home. It's possible once they pick a victim, they follow her for several days or even weeks, searching for the time and place she's the most vulnerable. Just because all of the other attacks we know about occurred in the victims' homes doesn't mean he's not going to pull his next victim into the woods."

"Thank you, voice of reason," the young man said. He gave Tasha a hard look. "Hear that, wild thing? Uncle Lucky's girlfriend here sounds like she knows what she's talking about."

Uncle Lucky's girlfriend…? "Oh," Syd said. "No. I'm not his—"

"So, what am I supposed to do?" The girl was exasperated and indignant. "Stay home all day?"

Tasha and her friend were back to their fight, intently squaring off, neither of them paying any attention to Syd's protests.

Luke, however, cleared his throat. Syd didn't dare look at him.

"Yes," the young man answered Tasha's question just as fiercely and without hesitation. "Until this is over, *yes. Stay home.*"

She gave him an incredulous look. "But, Thomas—"

"How many times in the years that we've been friends have I ever asked you for a favor, princess?" Thomas asked, his voice suddenly quiet, but no less intense. "I'm asking for one now."

Tears welled suddenly in Tasha's eyes and she blinked rapidly. "I needed to see you. After hearing about that diving accident…"

The harsh lines of his face softened slightly. "I'm fine, baby."

"I see that," she said. "*Now.*"

Syd turned away, aware that she was watching them, afraid that her curiosity about their relationship was written all over her face. Thomas had to be in his twenties, and Tasha was only in her teens. He'd referred to them as friends, but it didn't take a genius-level IQ to see that the girl's attachment to this man was much stronger. But he was being careful not to touch her, careful to use words like *friends,* careful to keep his distance.

"How about I call you?" he suggested, kindly. "Three times a week, a few minutes before 2100—nine o'clock? Check in and let you know how I'm doing. Would that work?"

Tasha chewed on her lower lip. "Make it five times a week, and you've got a deal."

"I'll try for four," he countered. "But—"

She shook her head. "*Five.*"

He looked at her crossed arms, at the angle of her tough-kid chin and assumed the same pose. "*Four.* But I don't get every evening off, you know, so some weeks it might be only three. But if I get weekend liberty, I'll drop by, okay? In return, you've got to promise me you don't go anywhere alone until this bad guy is caught."

She gave in, nodding her acceptance, gazing up at him as if she were memorizing his face.

"Say it," he insisted.

"I promise."

"I promise, too," he said then glanced at his watch. "Damn, I gotta go."

He turned, focusing on Luke and Syd as if for the first time. "Hey, Uncle Lucky. Drive Tasha home."

It was, without a doubt, a direct order. Luke saluted. "Yes, sir, *Ensign* King, sir."

Thomas's harshly featured face relaxed into a smile that made him look his age. "Sorry, Lieutenant," he said. "I meant, *please* drive Tasha home, *sir.* It's not safe right now for a young woman to ride all that distance alone."

Luke nodded. "Consider it done."

"Thank you, sir." The young man pointed his finger

at Tasha. "I don't want to see you here again. At least not without Mia or Frisco."

And he was gone, lifting his hand in a farewell as he ran back to the rest of his class.

Luke cleared his throat. "Tash, you mind hanging for a minute? I've got—"

The girl had already moved down the beach, out of earshot. She sat in the sand, arms around her knees, watching the SEAL candidates. Watching Thomas.

"I've got to finish this really important discussion I was having with my *girlfriend*," Luke finished, purely for Syd's benefit.

She narrowed her eyes at him. "Not funny."

"Damn," he said with a smile. "I was hoping I could get you to squawk again. 'I'm not his girlfriend,'" he imitated her badly.

"Also not funny."

His smile widened. "Yes, it is."

"No, it's—"

"Let's call it a healthy difference of opinions and let it go at that."

Syd closed her mouth and nodded. Fair enough.

He looked out over the glistening ocean, squinting slightly against the glare. "The reason I wanted you to see this, you know, BUD/S, was to give you a look at the teamwork that takes place in the SEAL units."

"I know you think I'm going to get in your way over the next few days or weeks," Syd started. "But—"

Luke cut her off. "I *know* you'll get in my way," he countered. "When was the last time you ran a seven-and-a-half minute mile?"

"Never, but—"

"The way I see it, we can make this work by utilizing

your strengths and being completely honest about your weaknesses."

"But—" This time Syd cut her own self off. Did he say *make this work?*

"Here's what I think we should do," Luke said. He was completely serious. "I think we should put you to work doing what you do best. Investigative reporting. Research. I want you to be in charge of finding a pattern, finding *some*thing among the facts we know that will bring us closer to the rapist."

"But the police are already doing that."

"We need to do it, too." The breeze off the ocean stirred his already tousled hair. "There's got to be something they've missed, and I'm counting on you to find it. I know you will, because I know how badly you want to catch this guy." He gazed back at the ocean. "You, uh, kind of gave that away in Lana Quinn's office."

"Oh," Syd said. "God." What else had she said or done? She couldn't bring herself to ask.

"We're both on the same page, Syd," Luke said quietly, intensely. "I really want to catch this guy, too. And I'm willing to have you on my team, but only if you're willing to be a team player. That means you contribute by using your strengths—your brain and your ability to research. And you contribute equally by sitting back and letting the rest of us handle the physical stuff. You stay out of danger. We get a lead, you stay back at the base or in the equipment van. No arguments. You haven't trained for combat, you haven't done enough PT to keep up, and I won't have you endanger the rest of the team or yourself."

"I'm not *that* out of shape," she protested.

"You want to prove it?" he countered. "If you can run four miles in thirty minutes while wearing boots, and complete the BUD/S obstacle course in ten minutes—"

"Okay," she said. "Good point. Not in this lifetime. I'll stay in the van."

"Last but not least," he said, still earnestly, "I'm in command. If you're part of this team, you need to remember that I'm the CO. When I give an order you say 'yes, sir.'"

"Yes, sir."

He smiled. "So are we in agreement?"

"Yes, sir."

"You obviously need to learn the difference between a question and an order."

Syd shook her head. "No," she said, "I don't."

"OKAY," SYD ASKED, "it's ten against one. Do you fight or flee?"

"Fight. Definitely fight." Petty Officer Rio Rosetti's Brooklyn accent came and went depending on who he was talking to, and right now it was one hundred percent there. When he was with Syd, he was one hundred percent tough guy.

Lucky stood outside his temporary office, eavesdropping as Lieutenant Michael Lee added his quiet opinion.

"Depends on who the ten are," Lee mused. "And what they're carrying. Ten of Japan's elite commandos—I might choose the old 'live to fight another day' rule and run."

"What I want to know," Ensign Thomas King's rich voice chimed in, "is what I'm doing in a ten-to-one situation without the rest of my SEAL team."

Syd fit right in. For the past two days, she and Lucky and Bobby had been working around the clock, trying to find something that the police might've missed. Syd worked with the information they had on the victims, and Bobby and Lucky went through file after file of personnel records, looking for anything that connected any of the officers and enlisted men currently stationed in Coronado to any hint of a sex crime.

Admiral Stonegate's handpicked trio of SEAL candidates spent their off hours helping. They were a solid group—good, reliable men, despite their connection to Admiral Stonehead.

And after only two days, Syd was best friends with all three of them. And Bobby, too.

She laughed, she smiled, she joked, she fumed at the computers. It was only with Lucky that she was strictly business. All "yes, sir," and "no, sir," and that too-polite, slightly forced smile, even when they were alone and still working at oh-one-hundred....

Lucky had managed to negotiate a truce with her. They had a definite understanding, but he couldn't help but wish he could've gone with the girlfriend alliance scenario. Yes, it would've been messy further down the road, but it would have been much more fun.

Especially since he still hadn't been able to stop thinking about that kiss.

"Here's another 'what if' situation for you," Lucky heard Syd say. "You're a woman—"

"What?" Rio hooted. "I thought you wanted to know about being a SEAL?"

"This is related to this assignment," she explained. "Just hear me out. You're a woman, and you turn around to find a man wearing panty hose on his head in your apartment in the middle of the night."

"You tell him, 'no darling, that shade of taupe simply doesn't work with your clothing.'" Rio laughed at his joke.

"You want me to kill him or muzzle him?" Thomas King asked.

"Rosetti, I'm serious here," Syd said. "This has happened to eleven women. There's nothing funny about it. Maybe you don't understand because you're *not* a woman, but personally I find the thought terrifying. I saw this guy. He was big—about Thomas's size."

"Flee," Mike Lee said.

"But what if you can't?" Syd asked. "What if there's no place to run? If you're trapped in your own apartment by a known rapist? Do you fight? Or do you submit?"

Silence.

Submit. The word made Lucky squirm. He stepped into the room. "Fight," he said. "How could you do anything but fight?"

The three other men agreed, Rio pulling his boots down off the table and sitting up a little straighter.

Syd glanced up at him, her brown eyes subdued.

"But we're not women," Rio said with a burst of wisdom and insight. "We're not even men anymore."

"Hey, speak for yourself," Thomas said.

"I mean, we're *more* than men," Rio countered. "We're SEALs. Well, *almost* SEALs. And with the training I've had, I'm not really afraid of anyone—and I'm not exactly the biggest guy in the world. Most women haven't got either the training or the strength to kick ass in a fight with a guy who outweighs 'em by seventy pounds."

Lucky looked at Syd. She was wearing a plain T-shirt with her trademark baggy pants, sandals on her feet instead of her boots. Sometime between last night and this morning, she'd put red polish on her toenails.

"What would you do?" he asked her, taking a doughnut from the box that was open on the table. "Fight or…" He couldn't even say it.

She met his gaze steadily. "I've been going through the interviews with the victims, looking for a pattern of violence that correlates to their responses to his attack.

A majority of the women fought back, but some of them didn't. One of them pretended to faint—went limp. Several others say they froze—they were so frightened they couldn't move. A few others, like Gina, just cowered."

"And?" Lucky said, dragging a chair up to the table.

"And I wish I could say that there's a direct relationship between the amount of violence the rapist inflicted on the victim and the amount that she fought back. In the first half-dozen or so attacks, it seemed as if the more the woman fought, the more viciously he beat her. And there were actually two cases where our perp walked away from women who didn't fight back. As if he didn't want to waste his time."

"So then it makes sense to advise women to submit," Lucky figured.

"Maybe at first, but I'm not so sure about that anymore. His pattern's changed over the past few weeks." Syd scowled down at the papers in front of her. "We have eleven victims, spanning a seven-week period. During those seven weeks, the level of violence our guy is using to dominate his victims has begun to intensify."

Lucky nodded. He'd overheard Syd and Lucy discussing this several nights ago.

"Out of the six most recent victims, we've had four who fought back right from the start, one who pretended to faint, and Gina, the most recent, who cowered and didn't resist. Out of those six, Gina got the worst beating. Yet—go figure—the other woman who didn't resist was barely touched."

"So if you fight this guy, you can guarantee you'll be hurt," Lucky concluded. "But if you submit, you've got a fifty-fifty chance of his walking away from you."

"And a chance of being beaten within an inch of your life," Syd said grimly. "Keep in mind, too, that we're making projections and assumptions based on six instances. We'd really need a much higher number of cases to develop any kind of an accurate pattern."

"Let's hope we don't get that opportunity," Mike Lee said quietly.

"Amen to that," Thomas King seconded.

"I still think, knowing that, I would recommend zero resistance," Lucky said. "I mean, if you had a shot at this guy just walking away…"

"That's true." Syd chewed on her lower lip. "But actually, there's more to this—something that puts a weird spin on the situation. It has to do with, um…" She glanced almost apologetically at the other men. "Ejaculation."

Rio stood up. "Whoops, look at the time. Gotta go."

Syd made a face. "I know this is kind of creepy," she said, "but I think it's important you guys know all the details."

"Sit," Lucky ordered.

Rio sat, but only on the edge of his seat.

"Actually, Lieutenant," Mike said evenly, "we've got a required class in five minutes. If we leave now, we'll be on time." He looked at Syd. "I assume you'll be writing a memo about…this for the other members of the task force…?"

Syd nodded.

"There you go," Rio said with relief. "We'll read all about it in your memo."

All three men stood up, and Lucky felt a surge of panic. They were going to go, leaving him alone with Syd, who wanted to discuss… Yikes. Still, what was he supposed to say, "no, you can't go to class?"

"Go," he said, and they all nearly ran out the door.

Syd laughed. "Well," she said, "I sure know how to clear a room, don't I?" She raised an eyebrow. "Are you sure you don't want to follow them, Lieutenant? Read about this in my memo instead?"

Lucky stood up to pour himself a cup of coffee from the setup by the door. He had to search for a mug that was clean, and he was glad for the excuse to keep his back to her. "Nothing about this assignment has been pleasant. So if you think this is something I need to hear..."

"I do."

Lucky poured himself a cup of coffee, then, taking a deep breath, he turned to face her. He carried it back to the table and sat down across from her. "Okay," he said. "Shoot."

"According to the medical reports, our man didn't... shall we say, achieve sexual completion, unless the woman fought back," Syd told him.

Oh, God.

"We need to keep in mind," she continued, "the fact that rape isn't about sex. It's about violence and power. Domination. Truth is, many serial rapists never ejaculate at all. And in fact, out of these eleven cases of rape, we've got only four instances of sexual, um, completion. Like I said, all of them occurred when the victim fought back, or—and this is important—when the victim was *forced* to fight back."

"But wait. You said a majority of the victims fought back." Lucky leaned forward. "Couldn't he have been wearing a condom the other times?"

"Not according to the victims' statements." Syd stood up and started to pace. "There's more, Luke, listen to this. Gina said in her interview that she didn't resist. She cowered, and he hit her, and she cowered some more. And then, she says he spent about ten minutes trashing her apartment. I went in there. The place looked like there'd been one hell of a fight. But she *didn't fight back*.

"I'm wondering if this guy was trying to simulate the kind of environment in which the victim *has* fought back, in an attempt to achieve some kind of sexual release. When he went back to Gina after he tore the place up, he kicked the hell out of her, but she still didn't do more than curl into a ball—and, if my theory's right, she therefore didn't give him what he wanted. So what does he do? He's angry as hell and he tears at her clothes, but she still doesn't resist. So he grabs her by the throat and starts squeezing. Bingo. Instant response. She can't breathe—she starts struggling for air. She starts fighting. And that does the trick for him, maybe that plus the sheer terror he can see in her eyes, because now, you know, she thinks he's going to kill her. He achieves sexual completion, inflicts his final moment of pain upon her by burning her, then leaves. The victim's still alive—this time."

Oh, God.

"It's really just a matter of time before he squeezes someone's throat too hard, or for too long, and she dies," Syd continued grimly. "And if taking a life gives him the right kind of rush—and it's hard to believe that it won't—he'll have transitioned. Serial rapist to serial killer. We already know he's into fear. He likes terrorizing his victims. He likes the power that gives him. And letting someone know she's going to die can generate an awful lot of terror for her and pleasure for him."

Syd carried her half-empty mug to the sink and tossed the remnants of her coffee down the drain. "Fight or submit," she said. "Fighting gives him what he wants, but gets you a severe beating. Still, submitting pisses him off. And it could enrage him enough to kill."

Lucky threw his half-eaten doughnut into the trash can, feeling completely sick. "We've got to catch this guy."

"That," Syd agreed, "would be nice."

CHAPTER SEVEN

LUKE O'DONLON WAS WAITING when Syd pulled up.

"Is she alive?" she asked as she got out of her car.

The quiet residential area was lit up, the street filled with police cars and ambulances, even a fire truck. Every light was blazing in the upscale house.

Luke nodded. "Yes."

"Thank God. Have you been inside?"

He shook his head. "Not yet. I took a...walk around the neighborhood. If he's still here, he's well hidden. I've got the rest of the team going over the area more carefully."

It was remarkable, really. When Syd had received Luke's phone call telling her Lucy had just called, that there'd been another attack, she'd been fast asleep. She'd quickly pulled on clothes, splashed water on her face and hurried out to her car. She felt rumpled and mismatched, slightly off-balance and sick to her stomach from exhaustion and fear that this time the attacker had gone too far.

Luke, on the other hand, looked as if he'd been grimly alert for hours. He was wearing what he'd referred to before as his summer uniform—short-sleeved, light fabric—definitely part of the Navy Ken clothing action pack. His shoes were polished and his hair was neatly combed. He'd even managed to shave, probably while he was driving over. Or maybe he shaved every night before he went to bed on the off chance he'd need to show up somewhere and be presentable at a moment's notice.

"Is the victim…?"

"Badly beaten," he said tersely.

As if on cue, a team of paramedics carried a stretcher from the house, one of them holding an IV bag high. The victim was strapped down, her neck in a brace. She was carried right past them—the poor woman looked as if she'd been hit by a truck, both eyes swollen shut, her face savaged with bruises and cuts.

"God," Luke breathed.

It was one thing to read about the victims. Even the horror of photographs was one step removed from the violence. But seeing this poor woman, a mere hour after the attack…

Syd knew the sight of that battered face had brought the reality of this situation home to the SEAL in a way nothing else could have.

"Let's go inside,"she said.

Luke was still watching the victim as she was gently loaded into the ambulance. He turned his head toward Syd almost jerkily.

Uh-oh. "You okay?" she asked quietly.

"God," he said again.

"It's awful, isn't it? That's pretty much what Gina looked like," she told him. "Like she'd gone ten rounds with a heavyweight champ on speed. And what he did to her face is the least of it."

He shook his head. "You know, I've seen guys who were injured. I've helped patch up guys who've been in combat. I'm not squeamish, really, but knowing that some-one did that to her and got *pleasure* from it…." He took a deep breath and blew it out hard. "I'm feeling a little… sick."

He'd gone completely pale beneath his tan. Oh, boy,

unless she did something fast, the big tough warrior was going to keel over in a dead faint.

"I am, too," Syd said. "Mind if we take a minute and sit down?" She took his arm and gently pulled him down next to her on the stairs that led to the front door, all but pushing his head down between his knees.

They sat there in silence for many long minutes after the ambulance pulled away. Syd carefully kept her eyes on the activity in the street—the neighbors who'd come out in their yards, the policemen keeping the more curious at a safe distance—looking anywhere but at Luke. She was aware of his breathing, aware that he'd dropped his head slightly in an attempt to fight his dizziness. She took many steadying breaths herself—but her own dizziness was more from her amazement that he could be affected this completely, this powerfully.

After what seemed like forever, she sensed more than saw Luke straighten up, heard him draw in one last deep breath and blow it out in a burst.

"Thanks," he said.

Syd finally risked a glance at him. Most of the color had returned to his face. He reached for her hand, loosely lacing her fingers with his as he gave her a rueful smile. "That would've been really embarrassing if I'd fainted."

"Oh," she said innocently, "were you feeling faint, too? I know I'm not taking enough time to eat right these days, and that plus the lack of sleep...."

He gently squeezed her hand. "And thanks, also, for not rubbing in the fact that right now *I'm* the one slowing *you* down."

"Well, now that you mention it...."

Luke laughed. God, he was good-looking when he laughed. Syd felt her hands start to sweat. If she hadn't been light-headed before, she sure as hell was now.

"Let's go inside," Luke said. "Find out if this guy left a calling card this time."

Syd gently pulled her hand free as she stood up. "Wouldn't that be nice?"

"MARY BETH HOLLIS..." Detective Lucy McCoy told Syd over the phone "...is twenty-nine years old. She works in San Diego as an administrative assistant to a bank president."

Syd was sitting in the airless office at the naval base, entering the information about the latest victim into the computer. "Single?" she asked.

"Recently married."

Syd crossed her fingers. "Please tell me her husband works here at the base..." She had a theory about the victims, and she was hoping she was right.

But Lucy made the sound of the loser button. "Sorry," she said. "He works in legal services at the same bank."

"Her father?"

"Deceased. Her mother owns her own flower shop in Coronado."

Syd didn't give up. "Brothers?"

"She's an only child."

"How about her husband. Did he have any brothers or sisters in the Navy?"

Lucy knew where she was going. "I'm sorry, Syd, Mary Beth has no family ties to the base."

Syd swore. That made her theory a lot less viable.

"But..." Lucy said.

Syd sat up. "What? You've got something?"

"Don't get too excited. You know the official police and FInCOM position—"

"That the fact that eight out of twelve victims are connected to the base is mere coincidence?" Syd said a most indelicate word. "Where's the connection with Mary Beth?"

"It's a stretch," Lucy admitted.

"Tell me."

"Former boyfriend. And I mean former. As in nearly ancient history. Although Mary Beth just got married, she's been living with her lawyer for close to four years. Way before that, she was hot and heavy with a captain who still works as a doctor at the military hospital. Captain Steven Horowitz."

Syd sighed. Four years ago. That *was* a stretch.

"Still think there's a connection?" Lucy asked.

"Yes."

Lucky poked his head in the door. "Ready to go?"

Like Syd, he'd been working nonstop since last night's late-night phone call about the most recent attack. But unlike Syd, he still looked crisp and fresh, as if he'd spent the afternoon napping rather than sifting through the remaining personnel files of the men on the naval base.

"I gotta run," Syd told Lucy. "I'm going back to the hypnotist, see if I noticed any strange cars parked in front of my house on the night Gina was attacked. Wish me luck."

"Good luck," Lucy said. "If you could remember the license-plate number, I'd be most appreciative."

"Yeah, what are the odds of that? I don't even know my own plate number. Later, Lucy." Syd hung up the phone, saved her computer file and stood, trying to stretch the kinks out of her back.

"Anything new turn up?" Lucky asked as they started down the hall.

"Four years ago, Mary Beth Hollis—victim twelve—used to date a Captain Horowitz."

"Used to *date*," he repeated. He gave her a sidelong glance. "You're working hard to keep your theory alive, eh?"

"Don't even think of teasing me about this," Syd countered. "Considering all the women who lived in San Felipe and Coronado, it *couldn't* be coincidence that nine out of twelve victims were related to *someone* who worked at the base. There's a connection between these women and the base, I'm sure of it. However, what that connection is…" She shook her head in frustration. "It's there—I just can't see it. Yet," she added. "I know I'm close. I have this feeling in my…" She broke off, realizing how ridiculous she sounded. She had a *feeling*….

"In your gut?" he finished for her.

"Okay." She was resigned. "Go ahead. Laugh at me. I know. It's just a crazy hunch."

"Why should I laugh at you," Luke said, "when I believe that you're probably on to something?" He snorted. "Hell, I'd trust your hunches over FInCOM's any day."

He wasn't laughing. He actually believed her.

As Syd followed Lieutenant Lucky O'Donlon out into the brilliant afternoon, she realized that over the past few days, something most unlikely had occurred.

She and Navy Ken had actually started to become friends.

SYD OPENED HER EYES and found herself gazing up at an unfamiliar ceiling in a darkened room. She was lying on her back on a couch and…

She turned her head and saw Dr. Lana Quinn's gentle smile.

"How'd I do?" she asked.

Lana made a slight face and shook her head. "A 'dark, old-model sedan' was the best you could come up with. When I asked you what make or model, you said *ugly*.

You didn't see the plates—not that anyone expected you to—but I have to confess I'd hoped."

"Yeah, me, too." Syd tiredly pulled herself up into a sitting position. "I'm not a car person. I'm sorry—" She looked around. "Where's Luke?"

"Waiting room," Lana said as she pulled open the curtains, brightening up the room. "He fell asleep while he was out there—while I was putting you under. He looked so completely wiped out, I couldn't bring myself to wake him."

"It's been a tough couple of days," Syd told the doctor.

"I heard another woman was attacked last night."

"It's been frustrating," Syd admitted. "Particularly for Luke. We haven't had a whole lot of clues to go on. There's not much to do besides wait for this guy to screw up. I think if Luke had the manpower, he'd put every woman in both of these cities in protective custody. I keep expecting him to start driving around with a bullhorn warning women to leave town."

"Quinn's in DC this week," Lana said. "He's worried, too. He actually asked Wes Skelly to check up on me. I left for work earlier than usual this morning, and Wes was sitting in his truck in front of my house. It's crazy."

"Luke keeps trying to get me to stay overnight at the base," Syd told her, "and for the first time in his life, it's for platonic reasons."

Lana laughed as she opened the door to the waiting room. "I'm sorry to have to kick you out so soon, but I've got another patient."

"No problem. Dark, old-model sedan," Syd repeated. "Thanks again."

"Sorry I couldn't be of more help."

Syd went into the waiting room, where a painfully thin

woman sat as far away as possible from Luke, who lay sprawled on the couch, still fast asleep.

He was adorable when he slept—completely, utterly, disgustingly adorable.

The skinny woman went into Lana's office, closing the door tightly behind her as Syd approached Luke.

"Time to go," she announced briskly.

No response.

"O'Donlon."

He didn't even twitch. His eyes remained shut, his lashes about a mile long, thick and dark against his perfect, tanned cheeks.

No way was she going to touch him. She'd read far too many books where professional soldiers nearly killed the hapless fool who tried to shake them awake.

She clapped her hands, and still he slept on. "Damn it, Luke, wake up."

Nothing. Not that she blamed him. She was exhausted, too.

All right. She wasn't going to touch him, but she *was* going to poke him from a safe distance. She took the copy of *Psychology Today* that was on the end table, rolled it up and, trying to stay as far back from him as possible, jabbed him in the ribs.

It happened so fast, she wasn't completely sure she even saw him move. One moment, his eyes were closed, the next he had her pinned to the waiting-room floor, one hand holding both of her wrists above her head, his other forearm heavy against her throat.

The eyes that gazed into hers were those of an animal—soulless and fierce. The face those eyes belonged to was hard and severe and completely deadly, his mouth a taut line, his teeth slightly bared.

But then he blinked and turned back into Luke O'Donlon, aka Lucky, aka her own living Navy Ken.

"Jeez." He lifted his arm from her throat so that she could breathe again. "What the hell were you trying to do?"

"Not this," Syd said, clearing her throat, her head starting to throb from where it had made hard contact with the floor. "In fact, I was trying to do the exact opposite of this. But I couldn't wake you up."

"Oh, man, I must've…" He shook his head, still groggy. "Usually I can take a combat nap and wake up at the least little noise."

"Not this time."

"Sometimes, if I'm really tired, and if I know I'm in a safe place, my body takes over and I go into a deep sleep and—" his eyes narrowed slightly. "You're supposed to be hypnotized," he remembered. "How come you're not hypnotized?"

As Syd stared up into the perfect blueness of his eyes, she wasn't sure she *wasn't* hypnotized. Why else would she just lie here on the floor with the full weight of his body pressing down on top of her without protesting even a little?

Maybe she'd gotten a concussion.

Maybe that was what had rendered her so completely stupid.

But maybe not. Her head hurt, but not that much. Maybe her stupidity was from more natural causes.

"Dark, old-model sedan," she told him. "Lana didn't want to wake you, and it's just as well. I'm an idiot when it comes to cars. That and calling it ugly was the best I could do."

Was he never going to get off her ever again? She could

feel the muscular tautness of his thigh pressed between her legs. She could feel... Oh, God.

"Are you okay?" he asked, rolling away from her. "Last time you were hypnotized it was something of an emotional roller coaster. I'm sorry I fell asleep. I really wanted to be there, in case..." He laughed sheepishly, giving her what she thought of as his best Harrison Ford self-deprecating smile. It was as charming on Luke as it was on Harrison. "Well, this sounds really presumptuous, but I wanted to be there in case you needed me."

She would have found his words impossibly sweet—if she were the type to be swayed by sweet words. And she would've missed the warmth of his body if she were the type to long for strong arms to hold her. And if she were the type to wish he'd pull her close again and kiss her and kiss her and kiss her...

But she wasn't. She *wasn't*.

Having a man around was nice, but not a necessity.

Besides, she never took matters of the heart and all of their physical, sexual trappings lightly. Sex was a serious thing, and Luke, with his completely unplastic, extremely warm body, didn't do serious. He'd told her that himself.

"I *was* okay," she said, desperately trying to bring them back to a familiar place she could handle—that irreverent place of friendly insults and challenges, "until you hit me with a World Wrestling Federation-quality body slam, Earthquake McGoon."

"Ho," he said, almost as if he were relieved to be done with the dangerously sweet words and their accompanying illusion of intimacy himself, as if he were as eager to follow her back to the outlined safety of their completely platonic friendship. "You're a fine one to complain, genius, considering you woke me up by sticking a gun barrel into my ribs."

"A *gun* barrel!" She laughed her disbelief. "Get real!"

"What the hell was that, anyway?"

Syd picked up the magazine and tightly rolled it, showing him.

"It felt like a gun barrel." He pulled himself to his feet and held out his hand to help Syd up. "Next time you want to wake me, and calling my name won't do it," he said, "think Sleeping Beauty. A kiss'll do the trick every time."

Yeah, right. Like she'd ever try to kiss Luke O'Donlon awake. He'd probably grab her and throw her down and...

And kiss her until the room spun, until she surrendered her clothes, her pride, her identity, her very soul. And probably her heart, as well.

"Maybe we shouldn't leave," she said tartly, as she followed Luke out the door. "It seems to me that the safest place for a Navy SEAL who fantasizes that he's Sleeping Beauty is right here, in a psychologist's waiting room."

"Ha," Luke said, "ha."

"WHAT'S ON THE SCHEDULE for this afternoon?" Syd asked as Luke pulled his truck into the parking lot by the administration building.

"I'm going to start hanging out in bars," Luke told her. "The seedier the better."

She turned to look at him. "Well, *that's* productive. Drinking yourself into oblivion while the rest of us sweat away in the office?"

He turned off the engine but didn't move to get out of the truck. "You know as well as I do that I have no intention of partying."

"You think you'll single-handedly find this guy by going to bar after bar?" she asked. "You don't even know what he looks like."

He ran his hands through his hair in frustration. "Syd, I've got to do something before he hurts someone else."

"His pattern is four to seven days between attacks."

Luke snorted. "That's supposed to make me feel better?" He swore, hitting the steering wheel with the heel of his hand. "I feel like I'm sitting on a time bomb. What if this guy goes after Veronica Catalanotto next? She's home all alone, with only a toddler in her house. Melody Jones is out of town with her baby, thank God." He ticked them off on his fingers—the wives of his teammates in Alpha Squad. "Nell Hawken lives over in San Diego. She's safe—at least until this bastard decides to widen his target area. PJ Becker works for FInCOM. Both she and Lucy are best qualified to deal with this. They're both tough but, hell, no one's invincible. And there's you."

He turned to look at her again. "You live alone. Doesn't that scare you, even a little bit?"

Syd thought about last night. About that noise she thought she'd heard as she was brushing her teeth. She'd locked herself in the bathroom, and if she'd had the cell phone with her, she would have called Luke in a complete panic.

But she hadn't had her phone—in hindsight she could say thank God—and she'd sat, silently, fear coursing through her veins, for nearly thirty minutes, barely breathing as she waited, listening to hear that noise outside the bathroom door again.

Fight or submit.

She'd thought about little else for all thirty of those minutes.

And fight pretty much won.

There was nothing in the bathroom that could be used as a weapon except for the heavy ceramic lid to the back of the toilet. She'd brandished it high over her head as she'd finally emerged from the bathroom to find she was, indeed, alone in her apartment. But she'd turned on every lamp in the place, checked all the window locks twice, and slept—badly—with the lights blazing.

"Nah," she said now. "I'm just not the type that scares easily."

He smiled as if he knew she was lying. "What, did you get spooked and sleep with all the lights on last night?" he asked.

"Me?" She tried to sound affronted. "No way."

"That's funny," he said. "Because when I drove past your place at about 1:00 a.m. it sure looked as if you had about four million watts of electricity working."

She was taken aback. "You drove past my apartment…?"

He realized he'd given himself away. "Well, yeah…I was in the neighborhood…."

"How many nights have you been spending your time cruising the streets of San Felipe instead of sleeping?" she asked.

He looked away, and she realized she'd collided with the truth. "No wonder you nearly fainted last night," she said. No wonder he'd looked as if he had been pulled from bed.

"I wasn't going to faint," he protested.

"You were *so* going to faint."

"No way. I was just a little dizzy."

She glared at him. "How on earth do you expect to catch this guy if you don't take care of yourself—if you don't get a good night's sleep?"

"How on earth can I get a good night's sleep," he said through gritted teeth, "*until* I catch this guy?"

He was serious. He was completely serious. "My God," Syd said slowly. "It's the real you."

"The real me?" he repeated, obviously not understanding. Or at least pretending that he didn't understand.

"The insensitive macho thing's just an act," she accused him. She was certain of that now. "Mr. Aren't-I-Wonderful? in a gleaming uniform—a little bit dumb, but with too many other enticements to care. Most people can't see beyond that, can they?"

"Well," he said modestly, "I don't have *that* much to offer...."

The truth was, he was a superhero for the new millenium. "You're a great guy—a really intriguing mix of alpha male and sensitive beta. Why do you feel that you have to hide that?"

"I'm not sure," he said, "but I think you're insulting me."

"Cut the crap," she commanded. "Because I also know you've got a beta's IQ, smart boy."

"Smart boy," he mused. "Much better than Ken, huh, Midge?"

Syd tried not to blush. How many times had she slipped and actually addressed him as Ken? Too many, obviously. "What can I say? You had me fooled with the ultraplastic veneer."

"As long as we're doing the *Invasion of the Body-Snatchers* thing and pointing fingers at the non-pod people, I'd like to do the same to you." He extended his arm so that his index finger nearly touched her face, and let out an awful-sounding squawk.

Syd raised one eyebrow as she gazed silently at him.

"There," he said, triumphantly. "That look. That disdained dismay. You hide behind that all the time."

"Right," she said. "And what exactly is it that I'm bothering to hide from you?"

"I think you're hiding," he paused dramatically, "the fact that you cry at movies."

She gave him her best "you must be crazy" look. "I do not."

"Or maybe I should just say *you cry*. You pretend to be so tough. So…unmovable. Methodically going about trying to find a connection between the rape victims, as if it's all just a giant puzzle to be solved, another step in the road to success which starts with you writing an exclusive story about the capture of the San Felipe Rapist. As if the human part of the story—these poor, traumatized women—doesn't make you want to cry."

She couldn't meet his gaze. "Even if I were the type of person who cried, there's no time," she said as briskly as she possibly could. She didn't want him to know she'd cried buckets for Gina and all of the other victims in the safety and privacy of her shower.

"I think you're secretly a softy," he continued. "I think you can't resist giving to every charity that sends you a piece of junk mail. But I also think someone once told you that you'll be bulldozed over for being too nice, so you try to be tough, when in truth you're a pushover."

Syd rolled her eyes. "If you really need to think that about me, go right a—"

"So what are *you* doing this afternoon?"

Syd opened the door to the cab, ready to end this conversation. How had it gotten so out of hand? "Nothing. Working. Learning all there is to know about serial rapists. Trying to figure out what it is I'm missing that ties the victims together."

"Frisco told me you asked his permission to bring Gina Sokoloski onto the base."

Busted. Syd shrugged, trying to downplay it. "I need to talk to her, get more information. Find out if there's anyone connecting her to the Navy—anyone we might have missed."

"You could have done that over the phone."

Syd climbed out of the truck, slamming the door behind her. Luke followed. "Yeah, well, I thought it would be a good idea if Gina actually left her mother's house. It's nearly been two weeks, and she still won't open her bedroom curtains. I may not even be able to convince her to come with me."

"See?" he said. "You're nice. In fact, that's not just regular nice, that's *gooey* nice. It's prize-winning nice. It's—"

She turned toward him, ready to gag him if necessary. "All right! Enough! I'm nice. Thank you!"

"Sweet," he said. "You're sweet."

"Grrrr," said Syd.

But he just laughed, clearly unafraid.

LUCKY STOOD ON THE BEACH, about a dozen yards behind the blanket Syd had spread on the sand. She'd brought wide-brimmed hats—one for Gina and one for herself, no doubt to shade the younger woman's still-battered face from the hot afternoon sun. Syd had bought sunglasses, too. Big ones that helped hide Gina's bruised eyes. Together they looked like a pair of exotic movie stars who'd filtered through some time portal direct from the 1950s.

Syd had brought a cooler with cans of soda, one of which she was sipping delicately through a straw. No doubt Syd had thought of the straws on account of Gina's recently split lips.

Gina clutched her soda tightly, her legs pulled in to her chest, her arms wrapped around them, her head down. It was as close to a fetal position as she could get. She was a picture of tension and fear.

But Syd was undaunted. She sprawled on her stomach, elbows propping up her chin, keeping up a nearly continuous stream of chatter.

Down on the beach, the phase-one SEAL candidates were doing a teamwork exercise with telephone poles. And, just for kicks, during a so-called break, Wes and Aztec and the other instructors had them do a set of sugar-cookie drills—running into the surf to get soaked, and then rolling over and over so that the white powdery sand stuck to every available inch of them, faces included. Faces in particular. Then it was back to the telephone poles.

Syd gestured toward the hard-working, sand-covered men with her cola can, and Lucky knew she was telling Gina about BUD/S. About Hell Week. About the will-power the men needed to get through the relentless discomfort and physical pain day after day after day after day, with only four blessed hours of sleep the whole week long.

Perseverance. If you had enough of that mysterious quality that made you persevere, you'd survive. You'd make it through.

You'd be wet, you'd be cold, you'd be shaking with fatigue, muscles cramping and aching, blisters not just on your feet, but in places you didn't ever imagine you could get blisters, and you'd break it all down into the tiniest segments possible. Life became not a day or an hour or even a minute.

It became a footstep. Right foot. Then left. Then right again.

It became a heartbeat, a lungful of air, a nanosecond of existence to be endured and triumphed over.

Lucky knew what Syd was telling Gina, because she'd

asked him—and Bobby, and Rio, Thomas and Michael—countless questions about BUD/S, and about Hell Week in particular.

As he watched, whatever precisely Syd was saying caught Gina's attention. As he watched, the younger woman lifted her head and seemed to focus on the men on the beach. As he watched, Syd, with her gentle magic, helped Gina take the first shaky steps back to life.

Gina, like the SEAL candidates in BUD/S, needed to persevere. Yeah, being assaulted sucked. Life had given her a completely unfair, losing hand to play—a deal that was about as bad as it could get. But she needed to keep going, to move forward, to work through it one painful step at a time, instead of ringing out and quitting life.

And Syd, sweet, kind Syd, was trying to help her do just that.

Lucky leaned against Syd's ridiculous excuse for a car, knowing he should get back to work, but wanting nothing more than to spend a few more minutes here in the warm sun. Wishing he were on that blanket with Syd, wishing she had brought a soda for him, wishing he could lose himself in the fabulously textured richness of her eyes, wishing she would lean toward him and lift her mouth and...

Ooo-kay.

It was definitely time to go. Definitely time to...

Over on the blanket, Syd leapt to her feet. As Lucky watched, she danced in a circle around Gina, spinning and jumping. Miracle of miracles, Gina was actually laughing at her.

But then Syd turned and spotted him.

Yeesh. Caught spying.

But Syd seemed happy to see him. She ran a few steps

toward him, but then ran back to Gina, leaning over to say something to the young woman.

And then she was flying toward him, holding on to that silly floppy hat with one hand, her sunglasses falling into the sand. Her feet were bare and she hopped awkwardly and painfully over the gravel at the edge of the parking area to get closer to him.

"Luke, I think I've found it!"

He immediately knew which *it* she was talking about. The elusive connection among the rape victims.

"I've got to take Gina back home," she said, talking a mile a minute. "I need you to get some information for me. The two other women who had no obvious ties to the base? I need you to find out if they have or *had* a close relationship with someone who was stationed here four years ago."

She was so revved up, he hated to be a wet blanket, but he didn't get it. She looked at the expression on his face and laughed. "You think I'm nuts."

"I think it's a possibility."

"I'm not. Remember Mary Beth Hollis?"

"Yeah." He was never going to forget Mary Beth Hollis. The sight of her being carried to the ambulance was one he'd carry with him to his dying day.

"Remember she dated Captain Horowitz four years ago, before she was married?"

He remembered hearing about the woman's romantic connection to the navy doctor, but he hadn't committed the details to memory.

"Gina just told me that her mother's second husband was a master chief in the regular Navy," Syd continued. "Stationed where? Stationed *here*. He was transferred to the east coast when he and Gina's mom were divorced—when? Four years ago. Four. Years. Ago."

Understanding dawned. "You think all these women are connected in that they know someone who was stationed here—"

"Four years ago," she finished for him, her entire face glowing with excitement. "Or maybe it's not exactly four years ago, maybe it's more or less than that. What we need to do is talk to the two victims who've got no obvious connection to the base, see if they *had* a connection, past tense. Call Lucy McCoy," she ordered him. "What are you waiting for? Go. Hurry! I'll meet you in the office as soon as I drive Gina home."

She started hopping back over the rocks, and Lucky couldn't resist. He scooped her up and carried her the few feet to the soft sand. Problem was, once he had her in his arms, he didn't want to put her down. Especially when she looked up at him with such surprised laughter in her eyes.

"Thank you," she said. "Actually, my *feet* thank you."

She squirmed, and he released her, and then it was *his* turn to be surprised when she threw her arms around his neck and gave him an exuberant hug.

"Oh, baby, this is it," she said. "This is the connection! It's going to help us identify and protect the women this guy is targeting."

Lucky closed his eyes as he held her tightly, breathing in the sweet scent of her sunblock.

She pulled free far too soon. "Hurry," she said again, pushing him in the direction of the administration building.

Lucky went, breaking into an obedient trot, even though he was far from convinced they'd find anything new. He hoped with all of his heart that Syd wouldn't be too disappointed.

Of course, if she was, he could always comfort her. He

was good at providing comfort—particularly the kind that slid neatly into seduction.

God, what was he thinking? This was *Syd.*

Syd—who'd kissed him as if the world were coming to an end. Syd—whose body had felt so tempting beneath his just this morning. Syd—whose lit-up windows he'd stared at for nearly an hour last night, dying to ring her bell for more reasons than simply to make sure she was safe.

Okay. True confession time. Yes, it was Syd, and yes, he wanted to seduce her. But he liked her. A lot. Too much to trade in their solid friendship for his typical two-week, molten-lava, short-term fling.

He wasn't going to do it.

He was going to stay away from her, keep it platonic.

Yeah. Right.

CHAPTER EIGHT

"ANOTHER FORMER BOYFRIEND and a father who's since died," Luke said to Syd as she hurried into the office.

She stopped short. "Oh, my God, I'm *right?*"

"You're amazingly, perfectly, *brilliantly* right." He grabbed her and danced her around the room.

It was a lot like this morning in Lana Quinn's waiting room. One minute she was standing there and the next she was in motion. She clung to him for dear life as he spun her around and around.

"Finally," he said, "something that we might be able to go on."

She looked up at him breathlessly. "Only *might?*"

"I'm trying to be restrained." He narrowly avoided a head-on collision with a file cabinet.

She had to laugh at that. "This is you, *restrained?*"

Luke laughed, too, as he finally slowed to a stop, as he once more let her feet touch the ground. "This is me, *extremely* restrained."

He was still holding her as tightly as she was holding him, and suddenly, as he gazed into her eyes, he wasn't laughing anymore.

She was pressed against him from her shoulders to her thighs and the fit felt impossibly good. He was warm and solid and he smelled good, too.

He was looking down at her, her face tipped up to his, his mouth mere inches from hers, and for several long, heart-stopping moments, Syd was certain that he was going to kiss her.

Like the last time he'd kissed her, she saw it coming, but this go-round seemed so much more unrehearsed. The shift of emotions and the heightened awareness in his eyes couldn't possibly be an act, could it? Or the way his gaze dropped for just an instant to her lips, the way his own lips parted just a tiny bit, the tip of his tongue wetting them slightly in an unconscious move.

But then, instead of planting a big knee-weakening one on her, he released her. He let her go and even stepped back.

Whoa, what just happened here?

Luke grabbed her hand and pulled her over to the main computer. "Check *this* out. Show her the thing," he commanded the SEAL candidates.

Thomas was at the keyboard with Rio hovering over his shoulder, and they both moved slightly to the side so that Syd could see the screen. As if her eyes could focus on the screen.

She still felt completely disoriented. Luke hadn't kissed her. Of course, this was an office in a building on a U.S. naval base, she told herself, and he was the team's commanding officer. This was the U.S. Navy and there were probably rules about kissing.

Restrained, he'd said, indeed. Syd had to smile. Funny, she wouldn't have thought he'd have had it in him.

Thomas was talking to her, explaining what they'd done on the computer. "We pulled up the personnel files of all twelve of the servicemen and women—living and dead, active duty and retired—who're connected to the victims."

"All twelve," Rio chimed in, "were stationed here in Coronado during the same eight-week period in 1996."

Eight weeks, four years ago. That *couldn't* be a coincidence, could it? Syd leaned closer to look at the numbers on the screen for herself.

"According to the information we've been given directly from the women who were attacked, the servicemen and woman also all knew their corresponding victim during that time," Thomas pointed out.

"We've pulled a complete list of personnel who were here during that eight-week period," Luke said handing her a thick tome that was stapled together with what looked like a railroad spike. "Even if they were only here for a day during that time, their name's on this list. Mike's out delivering a copy to Lucy McCoy. She's going to run these names through the police computer, see if anyone left the service and ended up with a police record—particularly one that includes charges of sexual assault."

"We already have ten good candidates," Bobby added. "Ten of the men on that list were given dishonorable discharges either at that time or later in their careers."

"Basically, that means they were kicked out of the Navy," Luke explained.

Syd was overwhelmed. "I can't believe you did all this so quickly—that you actually managed to figure out the connection."

"*You* figured out the connection," Luke told her. "We just filled in the blanks."

She looked down at the enormous list of names she still held in her hands. "So now what do we do? Contact all these men and women and warn them that they or someone they love—or used to love—is in danger of being attacked?"

"Only a percentage of those men and women are still living in this area," Bobby said.

"A percentage of a billion is still a huge number," Syd countered.

"There's not a billion names on that list," Luke told her.

She hefted the list. "It feels as if there is."

"Most of Alpha Squad's in there," Bobby told her. "The squad came to Coronado for a training op, I remember, and ended up pulling extra duty as BUD/S instructors. There was this one class, where the dropout rate was close to zero. I think three guys rang out, total. It was the most amazing thing, but as they went into Hell Week, we were completely understaffed."

"I remember that," Luke said. "Most of us had done a rotation assisting the instructors, so we ended up shanghaied into helping take these guys through their paces."

"Most of Alpha Squad," Syd echoed, realizing just what that meant. Anyone female and connected to anyone on this list was a potential target for attack. She looked at Luke. "Have you called—"

"Already done," he said, anticipating her question. "I've talked to all the guys' wives except Ronnie Catalanotto, and I left a pretty detailed message on her machine and told her to call me on my cell phone ASAP."

"You know, Lieutenant Lucky, sir," Rio said, "one way to catch this guy might be to set Syd here up as bait, make it look like she's your girlfriend and—"

"Uh-uh," Luke said. "No way."

Well, wasn't he vehemently opposed to *that?*

"I'm not talking about sending her out into the bad part of San Felipe in the middle of the night," Rio persisted. "In fact, she'll be safer than she is right now, considering we'll be watching her whenever she's alone."

"She lives on the third floor of a house in a neighborhood that's more concrete and asphalt than landscaping,"

Luke argued. "How are you going to watch her? Unless you're hiding someplace in her apartment—"

"We can plant microphones," Thomas suggested. "Set up a surveillance system, have a van down on the street."

"We can bring the skel's attention to you, too." Rio was really excited about this. Syd could tell he'd watched too many episodes of *NYPD Blue*. Skel. Oh, brother. "You could go on TV, do an interview, insult him in some way. Claim that there's no way in hell he could be a SEAL. Obviously he's trying to make *some*body believe he's one— maybe he's trying to make himself believe it. Throw some reality into his face. Tick him off, then appear in public with Syd, do some kissy-face stuff and—"

"No. This is crazy."

Syd sat down at the conference table, trying to look unaffected and even slightly bored, as if she hadn't just realized that she'd completely misinterpreted that almost-kiss that she and Luke hadn't shared not quite five minutes ago. He'd spun her around, and she'd latched onto him. He hadn't looked at her as if he wanted to kiss her. No, she'd probably been looking at him that way. And he'd stopped laughing because he felt awkward. He wasn't being restrained because they were at his place of work. He simply wasn't interested.

How could she have thought he'd be even remotely interested in her?

Bobby cleared his throat. "You know, this *could* work."

"Yeah, but think of his reputation," Syd said dryly, "if he were seen in public with *me*."

Luke turned to look at her, the expression on his face unreadable. "You actually want to *do* this?" His voice cracked with disbelief. "Are you completely insane? Your job is research, remember? We had an agreement. You're supposed to be the one in the surveillance van, not the one used as bait. *Bait*. Dear Lord, save me from a conspiracy of fools!"

"Hey, what happened to brilliant?" Syd asked sharply.

He glared at her. "You tell me! You're the one who's lost your mind!"

"Maybe we could get Detective McCoy to pretend she's your girlfriend," Thomas volunteered.

"Oh, that would work," Syd rolled her eyes. "Clearly this guy pays attention to details. You don't think he'd notice that Luke sends out this 'come and get me and mine' message, and then starts getting chummy with the wife of one of his best friends? Oh, and she's a police detective, too. Anyone notice that not-too-fresh smell? Could that possibly be the stench of a *setup?*"

"Do you have *any* idea at all how much damage this dirtwad could do to you in the amount of time it would take the fastest SEAL team in the world to get from a van on the street to your third-floor apartment?" Luke asked hotly. "Do you know that this son of a bitch broke Mary Beth Hollis's cheekbone with his first punch? Do you really want to find out what that feels like? My God, Sydney! Think about *that,* will you *please?*"

"So maybe the setup should be at your house," she countered. "We can make like I move in with you, and set up a pattern where you come home extremely late—where there's a repeated block of time when I'm there alone. The team can hide in your backyard. Shoot, they can hide in your basement."

"No, they can't. I don't have a basement."

She nearly growled at him in exasperation. "Luke, think about this! If we can guarantee that the team will be close, then, yes, *yes,* I'm willing to do this to catch this guy. I really, *really* want to catch this guy. As far as I can see, the only real objection is that you and I will have to spend more time together, that we'll have to put on a show of a relationship in public. But, shoot, I can stomach that for the greater good of mankind, if *you* can."

Luke laughed in disbelief. If she didn't know better, she'd think his feelings were hurt. "Well, gee, that's big of you."

Syd stood there, staring at him, both wanting him to give in, and praying that he'd refuse. God, how on earth was she going to play boyfriend-girlfriend with this impossible, incredible man for any length of time? How was she going to share a house with him? If she were a gambler, she'd bet big money that she'd end up in his bed within a day or two. No, make that an hour or two. It was a sure thing—except for one little important detail. He didn't want her in his bed.

"I think this could really work," Bobby said, his calm voice breaking the charged silence.

"I do, too," Mike said, speaking up for the first time. "I think we should do it."

Luke said something completely, foully unrepeatable—something having to do with barnyard animals, something that implied that he was out of his mind, then stomped out of the room.

Bobby smiled at Syd's confused expression. "That was a green light," he interpreted. "A go-ahead. Why don't you use those media contacts you have and set up whatever kind of interview for the lieutenant that you can? TV's best, of course. Oh, and Syd—let's keep this to ourselves. The fewer people who know this relationship between you and Luke isn't real, the better."

Syd rolled her eyes. "Anyone who knows him will take one look at me and realize something's up."

"Anyone who knows him," Bobby said, "will take one look at you, and think he's finally found someone worthy of his time."

LUCKY COULDN'T REMEMBER THE last time he'd felt this nervous because of a woman.

He had to park his truck three houses down from the Catalanottos'. Veronica's "little" cookout had turned into a full-blown party, judging from all the cars and trucks parked on the street. Bobby's truck and Wes's bike were there. PJ Becker's lime-green Volkswagen bug. Frisco's Jeep. Lucy McCoy's unassuming little subcompact.

"We'll just stop in so I can talk Veronica into leaving town for a week or so," he told Syd as they walked down the driveway toward the little house. "We can use this party as a dress rehearsal for when we go into town later. If we can fool this group of people into thinking we're together, we can fool anyone."

Syd looked over at him, one perfect eyebrow slightly raised. "Do you really think we can fool them? We don't look like we're together."

She was right. In fact, they looked about as un-together as a man and woman could. "What do you think I...? Should I put my arm around your shoulders?"

Yeesh, he hadn't sounded this stupidly uncertain since that eighth-grade dance he'd been invited to as a sixth-grader.

"I don't know," she admitted. "Would you put your arm around my shoulders if we really were together?"

"I'd..." He put his arm around her waist, tucking her body perfectly alongside his. He didn't mean for it to happen, but his hand slipped up beneath the edge of her T-shirt and his fingers encountered satiny smooth skin.

Uh-oh.

He braced himself, waiting for her to hit him, or at least to pull away and assault him with a severe scolding. But she didn't. In fact, she slipped her arm around him, tucking her own hand neatly into the back pocket of his shorts, nearly sending him into outer space.

Lucky had to clear his throat before he could speak. "You think this is okay?" With his hand where it was against her bare skin, it was far more intimate and possessive than an arm thrown around her shoulders.

Syd cleared her throat, too. Hah, she wasn't as matter-of-fact as she was pretending to be.

"God, this is weird." She lifted her head to look up at him. "This *is* weird, isn't it?"

"Yes."

"Are you as nervous about this as I am?"

"Yes," Lucky said, glad to be able to admit it.

"If you have to kiss me," Syd told him, "try not to kiss me on the mouth, okay?"

Have to?

"Oh," he said, "well, sure. I mean, that's good. You tell me what you don't want me to do and I'll make sure I don't cross those boundaries—"

"No!" She sounded completely flustered. "It's not about boundaries. It's just…I had about a ton of garlic on my pizza for lunch yesterday, and I still have Dominic's Italian Café-breath. I just…I didn't want to gross you out."

Lucky laughed—it was such a lame excuse. "There's no way you could still have garlic-breath more than twenty-four hours later."

"You've obviously never had one of Dominic's deluxe garlic pizzas."

"Look, Syd." He stopped about ten feet from the Catalanottos' front steps, pulling her to face him. "It's okay. You don't need to make up reasons why I shouldn't kiss you."

"I'm not making up reasons," she insisted.

"So then, if I don't mind about the alleged garlic-breath, *you* don't mind if I kiss you?"

The early evening shadows played artfully across Syd's face as she laughed. "I can't believe we're having this conversation."

And standing there, looking down at her, with his arm still around her waist, Lucky wanted to kiss her about as badly as he'd ever wanted to kiss anyone.

And damn it, as long as they were playing this pretend girlfriend game, he might as well take advantage of the fact that it would only *help* their cover if he *did* kiss her.

But how the hell did one go about kissing a friend? He knew all there was to know about how to kiss a stranger, but this was different. This was far more dangerous.

And suddenly he knew exactly what to do, what to say.

"You've got me dying to find out if you really do taste like garlic," he said.

"Oh, believe me, I do."

"Do you mind...?" He tipped her chin up to his. "For the sake of scientific experimentation...?"

She laughed. That was when he knew he had her. That was when he knew he *could* kiss her without having her get all ticked off at him. She might pull away really fast, but she wasn't going to hit him.

So he lowered his head those extra inches and covered her mouth with his.

And, oh, my. Just like when he'd kissed her on that deck just off his kitchen, she turned to fire in his arms.

Just like when he'd kissed her on his deck, she wrapped her arms around him and pulled him closer, kissing him just as hungrily as he kissed her.

It was the kind of kiss that screamed of pure sex, the kind that lit him up pretty damn instantly, the kind that made him want to tear her clothes from her body so he could take her, right here and right now—on his captain's front lawn.

It was the kind of kiss that made him instantly aware that it had been forty-nine long days, seventeen agonizing hours and twelve very impatient minutes since he'd last had sex. It was the kind of kiss that made him instantly forget whomever it was he'd last had sex with. Hell, it made him forget every other woman he'd ever known in his entire women-filled life.

It was the kind of kiss he might normally have ended only to spend the rest of the evening actively plotting ways he could get away with kissing this woman again. But—ha! He laughed as well as he could, considering he was still kissing her. They were playing the pretend girlfriend game. He *could kiss her whenever he wanted!*

Oh, my, she tasted hot and sweet and delicious. And yes, he thought just maybe he could taste the slightest, subtlest spicy hint of garlic, too.

Syd pulled back, and he let her come up for air, ready to protest that he thought he needed to kiss her again just to make sure he wasn't imagining the garlic, ready to give her a mile-long list of reasons why he should probably kiss her again, ready to…

He realized belatedly that the light had gone on next to the Catalanottos' front door. He turned his head, and sure enough. Veronica was standing there, laughing at him.

"You," she said. "Figures it would be you."

Lucky saw that they'd drawn a crowd. PJ Becker was

behind Veronica. And Mia Francisco peeked through the front window, Frisco right behind her. Frisco gave him a smile and a thumbs-up.

Syd jettisoned herself from his arms, but he caught her hand and reeled her back in.

"It's okay," he murmured to her. "I knew someone would be bound to notice us. We're together, remember? You're my new girlfriend—I'm allowed to kiss you."

"Sorry," Veronica called through the screen in her crisp British accent. "Frankie came out onto the back deck, insisting that a man and a lady were making a baby in the front yard, and we just had to see for ourselves."

"Oh, my God," Syd said, her face turning bright pink.

"I obviously need to discuss the details of conception with him again," she said, laughter in her voice. "I'd thought we'd been over that 'kissing doesn't make a baby' stuff, but apparently it didn't stick. I suppose it's all right—he's only four."

"Do you want to come in?" PJ called out, "or should we just all go away? Give you some privacy—close the door and turn off the light?"

Lucky laughed as he pulled Syd to the door.

The introductions took no time, and then Veronica was pulling Syd through the house to the back deck. "You've got to see the view we've got of the ocean," she said, as if she'd known Syd for years, "and I've got to check the chicken that's on the grill."

"Bobby already checked the chicken," about four voices called out.

"Everyone here is convinced I can't cook," Veronica told Syd as she opened the slider. She made a face. "Unfortunately they're right."

"Hey, Syd," Bobby said serenely from his place at the grill.

He was wearing only a bathing suit, and with all his muscles gleaming, his long hair tied back in a braid, he looked as if he belonged on the cover of one of those historical romances. Syd did a major double take, and Lucky poked her in the side, leaning close to whisper, "Don't stare—you're with me, remember?"

"You know Lucy McCoy," Veronica said to Syd. "And Tasha Francisco, and Wes Skelly—"

"Actually, we've never met," Wes said. He didn't stand up from where he was sprawled in a lounge chair. "See, I'm not allowed to help with this op," he told Veronica, his voice tinged with sarcasm and coated with perhaps just a little too much beer. "I'm not a member of the team because I'm a potential suspect, right, Lieutenant?"

Lucky kept his voice cheerful. "Come on, Skelly, you know I didn't have anything to do with picking my team. Admiral Stonehead did it for me."

"Hi, everyone. Sorry, I'm late—I was held up at the office, and then it was such a nice evening I couldn't resist walking over."

Lucky turned to see Lana Quinn climbing the stairs that led from the beach.

Bobby greeted her with a hug. "Where's Wizard, the mighty Quinn? I thought he was coming home today."

She made a face. "Team Six has been sidetracked. What else is new? He's going to be away at least another few weeks. I know, I know—I should feel lucky he even got a chance to call."

Wes lurched to his feet, knocking over the little plastic table next to him, spilling pretzels across the deck. He swore sharply. "I'm sorry," he said. "Ron, I'm sorry, I forgot I… I have to go…do something. I'm sorry."

He vanished into the house, nearly knocking Syd over on his way. Lucky turned to Bobby, making the motion of keys turning in the ignition, silently asking if Wes was okay to drive.

Bobby shook his head no, then pulled his hand out of his bathing-suit pocket, opening it briefly—just long enough so that Lucky could see he'd already claimed possession of his friend's keys. Bobby made a walking motion with his fingers. Wes would walk back to the base.

On the other side of the deck, Syd helped Lana Quinn clean up the spilled pretzels.

"So. Does the new GF know you're a jerk?"

Lucky turned to see PJ Becker grinning at him, but he knew her words were only half in jest. Which, of course, made them half-serious, as well. This woman *still* hadn't forgotten the way he'd hit on her back when they'd first met. She'd forgiven, sure, but she'd probably never forget. It was one of the things he liked best about her. She'd never, ever let him get away with anything.

"Yeah," he said. "She knows. She likes me anyway." It wasn't entirely a lie. Syd *did* like him. Just not in the way PJ meant.

Senior Chief Harvard Becker's wife gazed at Syd with her gorgeous, liquid-brown eyes—eyes that never missed anything. "You know, O'Donlon, if you're smart enough to have hooked up with someone like Syd Jameson, maybe I seriously underestimated you. She's a good writer—she had a weekly column in the local paper about a year ago, you know. I tried never to miss it. There's a good brain—a thinking brain—in that girl's head." She gave him another brilliant smile and a kiss on the cheek. "Who knows? Maybe you're not such a jerk after all."

As Lucky laughed, PJ went to give her best evil eye to

the extremely pregnant Mia, who looked as if she were thinking about helping pick up pretzels.

Lucky sidled up to Bobby. "What's up with Wes?"

Bobby shrugged. "It hasn't been his year."

"Is he gonna be okay?"

"The walk will do him good. I'll throw his Harley into the back of my truck."

"Anything I can do to help?" Lucky asked.

"Nope."

"Let me know if that changes."

"Yep."

Lucky grabbed Veronica's arm as she went past carrying a broom. "Got a sec?"

She looked down at the broom. "Well…"

He took it from her and tossed it gracefully to PJ, who caught it with one hand. Show off.

"Yes, I suppose I do have a sec now," Veronica said cheerfully. "What's up?"

"I need you to go to New York," he said.

"How's a 10:00 a.m. flight tomorrow sound?"

He kissed her, relief flooding through him. "Thank you."

"Lucy was pretty persuasive. This monster you're trying to catch sounds awful. However, I've noticed that neither she nor PJ are planning to come with me."

"Lucy's SFPD and PJ's FInCOM."

"And you're convinced they can take care of themselves?" She searched his eyes, her concern written plainly on her face.

He tried to make it a joke. "Can you imagine the fallout if I even so much as *implied* PJ couldn't handle this on her own? And as for Lucy…" he glanced across the deck to where the detective was leaning against the railing, talking to Lana Quinn and Syd "…I'm going to strongly encourage her to bunk down at the police station until this is over."

Veronica followed his gaze. "You make sure Syd is careful, too."

"Oh, yeah," Lucky said. "Don't worry about that. She's, uh…she's moving in with me."

It was the weirdest thing. It was all part of the pretend girlfriend game, designed to catch the rapist, but as he said the words aloud—words he'd never before uttered, not ever in his entire life—it felt remarkably real. He felt a little embarrassed, a little proud, a little terrified, and a whole hell of a lot of anticipation.

Syd *was* moving in with him. She was going to go home with him tonight. It was true that she was going to sleep in the guest bedroom, but for the first time in God knows how long he wouldn't have to worry about her safety. Maybe, just maybe, he'd get some sleep tonight.

On the other hand, maybe not, considering she was going to be in the next room, and considering he was *still* half-aroused from that incredible kiss.

Veronica's eyes widened, and then filled with tears. She threw her arms around his neck and hugged him. "Oh, Luke, I'm so happy for you!" She pulled back to gaze into his eyes. "I was so certain you were just going to bounce from Heather to Heather for the rest of your life." She raised her voice. "Everyone, Lucky's finally living up to his nickname! He just told me Syd's moving in with him!"

There was a scramble for cans of beer—soda for Frisco and Mia and Tash—as Veronica made a toast. Lucky didn't dare look at Syd directly—he could feel her embarrassment from all the way across the room. And he could feel Frisco's eyes on him, too. His swim buddy and temporary CO was smiling, but there were questions in his eyes. Like, wow, didn't *this* happen incredibly fast? And, why didn't you mention this to me before now?

Tomorrow he'd sit down with Frisco and fill him in on the details—tell him the truth.

But right now...

He had to get Syd out of there before she died of embarrassment.

He put down the beer someone had thrust into his hand and rescued her from PJ, Mia, Lana and Veronica. "I hate to drop a bomb and run," he said.

"Speech!" someone said. It was Bobby, the bastard. He knew it was just a setup and he was probably having a good laugh behind that inscrutable calm.

"Speech," PJ echoed. "This is too good. No way are we going to let you get away without telling us at least *some* of the juicy details. Where'd you guys meet? How long have you been seeing each other?" She approached Lucky and gazed hard into his eyes from about four inches away. "Who are you really, and what have you done with our commitment-shy friend Lucky?"

"Very funny," Lucky said, tugging Syd past PJ and over to the door.

"Oh, come on," PJ said. "At least tell us how she managed to talk you into sharing a house. I mean, that's a major step. A grown-up decision." She smiled at Syd. "I'm proud of you. Good job! Way to make him follow *your* rules."

"Actually, *I* was the one who talked her into moving in with me," Lucky lied. "I'm finally in love." He shrugged. "What can I say?"

"WHO KNOWS?" SYD ASKED as they got into his truck.

"That this is just an act? Only Bobby. And Lucy McCoy," Luke admitted. "I had to tell Lucy, especially considering she's supposed to be informed of my team's every move. She called this afternoon, mad as hell about that TV interview. She was ready to wring my neck." He started the engine, switched on the headlights and pulled out into the street, turning around in a neighbor's driveway. "Officially, she's pissed, but unofficially, she hopes this works. She knows we'll keep you as safe—safer—than the police would."

He glanced at her in the dimness of the cab. "I'm going to tell Frisco tomorrow, but I'm going to ask him not to tell Mia. I think Bobby's right. The fewer people who know, the better."

Syd sat as far away from him as she possibly could on the bench seat, trying desperately not to think about the way he'd kissed her. About the way she'd kissed him. At the words he'd said so casually as they left the party: *I'm finally in love....*

Yeah, like that would ever happen. Syd had figured Luke O'Donlon out. He wasn't ever going to fall in love. At least not all the way. He thought he was safe as long as he kept himself surrounded by the beautiful, intelligent, exceptional and *already married* wives of his best friends. He could cruise through life, half in love with Lucy and Veronica and PJ and Mia, never having to worry about getting in too deep. He could have meaningless sexual relationships with self-absorbed, vacuous young women like Heather—again, without risking his heart.

But what if he was wrong? Not about Heather—Syd didn't think for one instant that Luke would ever lose his heart to her. But Lucy McCoy was an entirely different story. As was that outrageously beautiful African American woman she'd met just tonight—PJ Becker. It would be too tragic if Luke actually fell in love with a woman he couldn't have.

"So how long have you had a thing for PJ Becker?" she asked him.

He managed to pull off a completely astonished look. *"What?"*

"Don't play dumb," she told him. "And don't worry, I don't think everyone knows. It's just I've learned to read you pretty well, and you reacted differently to her than you did to Veronica or Lana."

He was embarrassed and rather vehement. "I don't have a thing for her."

"But you *did*," she guessed.

He gave it to her, but grudgingly. "Well, yeah, like a million years ago, before she even hooked up with the senior chief."

"And let me guess, *a million years ago,* you did something really dumb, like, oh, say, you hit on her?"

He was silent, and she just waited. He finally glanced at her out of the corner of his eyes, and then couldn't keep his lips from curling up into a rueful smile. "Don't you hate being right *all* the time?"

"It's not that I'm right all the time," she countered, "it's that you're so predictable. Why don't you surprise everyone next time you meet an attractive woman—and *not* hit on her first thing?"

"What," Luke said, "you mean, if this moving-in-to-gether thing doesn't work out and I don't end up married to you?"

She had to laugh. As if.

"Sorry about Veronica's announcement," he continued. "I honestly had no idea she was going to do that."

Syd shrugged. "It's okay. It was a little strange—all your friends looking at me sideways, wondering what type of alien mind control I was using to make you want to live with me."

"That's not what they were thinking," Luke scoffed.

Yes, it most certainly was. Syd kept her mouth closed.

"After seeing that kiss," he said with a laugh, "they think they *know* why I want to live with you."

That kiss.

For many, many pounding heartbeats, Syd had stood on the front walk of that cute little beach house with her arms wrapped around Luke O'Donlon, her lips locked on his. For many pounding heartbeats, she had dared to imagine that that kiss was real, that it had nothing to do with their game of pretend.

She'd thought she'd seen something warm, something special, deep in his eyes, right before he lowered his mouth to hers.

Okay, face it, she'd thought she'd seen his awareness of his genuine attraction, based on genuine liking and genuine respect.

She'd seen awareness, all right—awareness of the fact that they were being watched through the window. He'd known they were being watched. *That* was why he'd kissed her.

They drove in silence for several long minutes. And then he glanced at her again.

"Maybe you should scoot over here—sit closer to me. If this guy does start following us…"

Syd gave him a look. "Scoot?" she said, trying desperately to keep things light. If she moved next to him, and if he put his arm around her shoulders, she just might forget how to breathe. Unless she could somehow keep him laughing. "I'm sorry, but I never, ever *scoot* anywhere."

Luke laughed. Jackpot. "That's what I love most about you, Sydney, dear. You can pick a fight about *any*thing."

"Can not."

He laughed again and patted the seat next to him. "Come on. Move your skinny butt down here."

"Skinny?" she said, sidling a little bit closer, but nowhere near close enough to touch him. "Excuse me. Have you even *looked* at my butt? It's double wide."

"What, are you nuts?" He reached for her, pulling her so that she was sitting with her thigh pressed firmly against his, his arm draped across her shoulders. "You have a great butt. A classic butt."

"Thanks a million. You know, these days *classic* means old. Classic Coke, Classic Trek. *Old.*"

"It doesn't mean old, it means *incomparable*," he countered. "How old are you, anyway?"

"Old enough to know better than to sit this close to someone who's driving. Old enough to know I should have my seat belt on," she grumbled. "Older than you."

"No way."

"Yes way," she said, praying as he braked to a red light that he wouldn't look down at her. "I'm one year older than you."

If he looked down at her, his mouth—that incredible, amazing mouth—would be mere inches from hers. And if his mouth was mere inches from hers, she would be able to think of nothing but kissing him again.

She wanted to kiss him again.

He turned and looked down at her.

"Where are we going now?" she asked, not that she particularly cared. But she figured maybe if she used her mouth to talk, she wouldn't be tempted to use it for other things.

Like kissing Luke O'Donlon.

"There's a seafood shack down by the water here in

San Felipe," he told her. "It's usually packed this time of night. I figured we'd go get some steamed clams. And maybe after that, we could do a little barhopping."

"I've never been barhopping," she admitted, mostly to fill the pause in the conversation. "I always thought it sounded so exotic."

"Actually, it can be pretty depressing," Luke told her as the light turned green and he focused on the road again, thank God. "I've been barhopping with the other single guys from Alpha Squad. Mostly Bobby and Wes. Although occasionally their buddy Quinn would come along. The Wizard. He's married—you know, to Lana—which never sat quite right with me, because our goal was to cruise the clubs, looking to pick up college girls. But I didn't really know him, didn't really know Lana—I figured it was none of my business."

"God," Syd said. "Did she know?"

Luke shook her head. "No. Quinn used to say that they had an arrangement. He wouldn't tell her and she wouldn't find out. Wes used to get so mad at him. One night he actually broke Quinn's nose."

"Wes is Bobby's swim buddy, right?" Syd thought about the SEAL she'd met for the first time tonight. He was bigger than she'd imagined from the way Luke had described him. Something about him had been disturbingly familiar. When he'd slammed into her on his way out of the party...

"Bob and Wes are the best example of a two-man team I've ever seen," Luke told her, the muscles in his thigh flexing as he braked to make a right turn into a crowded restaurant parking lot. "They're good operators separately, but together—it's like instead of getting two regular guys, you're getting two super men. They know each other so well, they play off of each other perfectly—they anticipate each other's every move. They're remarkably efficient."

"Bobby knows Wes really well, then, I guess," Syd said.

"Probably better than Wes knows himself."

"And Bobby's certain Wes couldn't be—" She cut herself off, realizing how awful her words sounded. Just because he was broad-shouldered and wore his hair exactly like the man they were looking for....

Luke parked his truck, then pushed her slightly away from him, turning to face her, to look penetratingly into her eyes. "What aren't you telling me?"

"It was weird," she admitted. "When he bumped into me... It was like déjà vu."

"Wes isn't our guy." Luke was adamant.

She couldn't help herself. "Are you sure? Are you *absolutely* positive?"

"Yes. I know him."

"There was *some*thing about him...." And then she knew. "Luke, he smelled like the guy on the stairs."

"Smelled?"

"Yeah, like stale cigarettes. Wes is a smoker, right?"

"No. Last year Bobby made Wes quit. He *used* to be a smoker, but—"

"Sorry, he's smoking again. Maybe not in front of anybody, but he's definitely smoking, even if it's only on the sly. It was faint, but I could smell it. He smelled just like the man we're looking for."

Luke shook his head. "Wes isn't our guy," he said again. "No way. I can't—I *won't* accept that."

"What if you're wrong?" she asked. "What if you find out that all this time he's been right here, right under our noses?"

"I'm not wrong," Luke said tightly. "I know this man. You didn't see him at his best tonight, but I know him, all right?"

It wasn't all right, but Syd wisely kept her mouth shut.

CHAPTER NINE

"SO HERE'S THE SCENARIO," Syd said as Luke opened the door, letting her into the quiet coolness of his house. "You're the only man inside an enemy stronghold when a battle, what do you call it, a firefight starts. Your team is being pushed back. You're outnumbered and outgunned. Do you fight or flee?"

He locked the door behind them, the sound of the dead-bolt clicking into place seeming to echo around them.

They were here.

Together.

Alone.

For the night.

Syd's lips were still warm from the last time he'd kissed her—at a bar called Shaky Stan's. He'd kissed her at the Mousehole, too, and at Ginger's, and at the Shark's Run Grill as well. In fact, they'd kissed their way pretty much clear across San Felipe's waterfront district.

Syd had tried to keep the kisses short. She'd tried desperately to keep from melting in his arms. But far too often, she'd failed.

If they *were* truly moving in together, after that series of temperature-raising kisses, there was no way in hell either of them would still have their clothes on within five seconds of Luke's locking that door.

Aware of that fact, with her clothes firmly on, Syd kept talking, posing one of her military scenarios. She wasn't allowed to ask any of the SEALs specific questions about their operations, but she *could* pose hypotheticals. And she did, as often as possible.

"What's inside this hypothetical stronghold?" he asked, tossing his keys onto a small table near the front door. "Is this a rescue mission or an info-gathering op?"

"Rescue mission," she decided. "Hostages. There are hostages inside. Hostaged *children*."

He gave her a comically disbelieving look as he moved to the thermostat and adjusted the setting so that the air conditioning switched on. That was good. It was too still in here, too warm. The AC would get the air moving, make it a little less stuffy. A little less...sultry.

"Make it impossibly difficult, why don't you?" he said.

He went into the kitchen, and she followed. "I'm just trying to provide a challenge."

"Okay, great." He opened the refrigerator and scowled at the cluttered shelves. "If we've been sent in to rescue hostaged children, you better believe we've been given a direct order not to fail." He reached in behind a gallon of milk and pulled out a container that looked as if it held iced tea. "Want some?"

Syd nodded, leaning against the door frame. "Thanks."

She watched as he took two tall glasses from a cabinet and filled them with ice.

"So," she said, mostly to fill the silence. "What do you do in that situation?"

He turned to look at her. "We don't fail."

She had to laugh. "You want to be a *little* more specific?"

"I'm inside, right?" he said, pouring the tea over the ice in the glasses. "Alone. But I've got radio contact with my men outside. I guess what I do is, I use stealth and I find the enemy's points of vulnerability from inside. And then I let my team know when and where to attack. Then I find and protect the hostages, and wait for the rest of my team to come get us all out." He handed her the glass. "Lemon? Sugar?"

"Black is fine," she said. "Thanks."

God, this was weird. This man leaning against the counter in his kitchen had spent a good portion of the evening exploring the inside of her mouth with his tongue. And now they were having a refreshing glass of iced tea and a casual, impersonal chat about military strategies.

She wondered if he knew how badly she was dying for him to kiss her again. For real, this time. Inwardly she rolled her eyes. Like that would ever happen.

It was amazing really. It had only been a matter of days since Luke had first kissed her, just a few feet away from where they were standing, on the deck outside this very kitchen. They'd stood there as virtual strangers, and he'd made the wrong choice. Instead of trying to win her friendship, he'd tried to control her through his powerful sexual appeal. Little did he know that would almost entirely ruin his chances at ever becoming her friend.

Almost, but not entirely.

And somewhere, somehow, over the past few days, Luke had redeemed himself.

So now they stood here as friends. And now Syd actually *wanted* him to kiss her.

Except now that they were friends, he had no reason to kiss her.

"So," she said, trying desperately to fill the silence. "Tell me...why did you join the SEALs?"

Luke didn't answer right away. He finished stirring lemon and a small mountain of sugar into his iced tea, rinsed the spoon in the sink and put it neatly into the dishwasher. Then he picked up his glass, and went back into the living room, gesturing with his head for Syd to follow.

So she followed him. Right over to a wall that was filled with framed photographs. She'd noticed them the last time she was here. Pictures of Luke as a child, his sun-bleached hair even lighter than it was now. Pictures of young Luke with his arms around a chubby, dark-haired little girl. Pictures of Luke with a painfully thin blond woman who had to be his mother. And pictures of young Luke with a dark-haired, dark complexioned man.

He pointed now to the pictures of the man.

"This," he said, "is Isidro Ramos. He's why I joined the SEALs."

Syd looked more closely at the photograph. She could see the warmth in the man's eyes, one arm looped around young Luke's shoulder. She could see the answering adoration on the boy's smiling face. "Who is he?" she asked.

"Was," he told her, sitting down on the couch, taking a sip from his iced tea and stretching his legs out on the coffee table.

Syd knew him well enough by now to know his casualness was entirely feigned. In truth he was on edge. But was it the topic of conversation he was having trouble with—or her presence here?

"Isidro died when I was sixteen," he said. "He was my father."

His…? Syd did a double take. No way could a man that dark have had a son as fair as Luke.

"Not my biological father," he added. "Obviously. But he *was* my father far more than Shaun O'Donlon ever bothered to be."

Syd sat down on the other end of the couch. "And he's why you joined the SEALs?"

He turned and looked at her. "You want the long or the short story?"

"Long," she said, kicking off her sandals and tucking her feet up underneath her. "Start at the beginning. I want to hear it all. Why don't you start when you were born. How much did you weigh?"

As long as they kept talking, they wouldn't have to deal with such awkward topics as where she should sleep. Or rather, where she should *pretend* to sleep. She couldn't imagine being able to sleep at all, God help her, knowing Luke was in bed in the next room.

"You're kidding, right?" She shook her head and he laughed.

"Nine pounds, fourteen ounces. My mother was five feet two. She used to tell me I was nearly as big as she was at the time." He paused for a moment, looking up at the photographs. "My mother was pretty fragile," he said quietly. "You can't really tell from these pictures, because she was so happy with Isidro. The day he died, though, she pretty much gave up. She pretended to keep going, to try to fight her bad health for Ellen's—my sister's—sake. But it was a losing battle. Don't get me wrong," he added. "I loved her. She just…she wasn't very strong. She'd never been strong."

Syd took a sip of her tea, waiting for him to continue.

"Nineteen sixty-six wasn't a good year for her," he said, "considering her choices were to marry Shaun O'Donlon or have a baby out of wedlock. She was living in San Francisco, but she didn't quite have the 'flowers in her hair' thing down—at least not in '66. So she married Shaun in the shotgun wedding of the year, and I got the dubious honor of being legitimate. And—" he turned slightly so that he was facing her on the couch. "Are you really sure you want to hear *all* of this?"

"I'm interested," she told him. "A lot can be revealed about a person simply by listening to them talk about their childhood."

"If that's the case, then where did *you* grow up?" he asked.

"New Rochelle, New York. My father is a doctor, my mother was a nurse before she quit to have us. Four kids, I'm the youngest. My brothers and sister are all incredibly rich, incredibly successful, with perfect spouses, perfect wardrobes and perfect tans, cranking out perfect grand-kids for my parents right on schedule." She smiled at him. "Note that I don't seem to be on the family track. I'm generally spoken of in hushed tones. The black sheep. Serves them right for giving me a boy's name."

Luke laughed. She really liked making him laugh. The lines around his eyes crinkled in a way that was com-pletely adorable. And his mouth…

She looked down into her tea to avoid staring at his mouth.

"Actually," she confessed, "my family is lovely. They're very nice—if somewhat clueless. And they're quite okay and very supportive about my deviation from the norm. My mother keeps trying to buy me Laura Ashley dresses, though. Every Christmas, without fail. 'Gee, thanks, Mom. In *pink?* Wow, you shouldn't have. No, you *really* shouldn't have,' but next year, the exact same thing."

Syd risked another glance at Luke. He was still laughing.

"So come on, finish up your story. Your father was a jerk. I think I know how it probably goes—he left before you turned two—"

"I wish," Luke said. "But Shaun stayed until I was eight, sucking my mother dry, both emotionally and fi-nancially. But the year I turned eight, he inherited a small

fortune from old Great-Uncle Barnaby, and he split for
Tibet. My mother filed for divorce and actually won a
substantial amount in the settlement. She bought a house
in San Diego, and with the mortgage paid, she started
working full time for a refugee center. This was back
when people were leaving Central America in droves.
That's where she met Isidro—at the center.

"We had an extra apartment over our garage, back
behind our house, and he was one of about six men who
lived there, kind of as a temporary thing. I remember I
was a little afraid of them. They were like ghosts, just kind
of floating around, as if they were in shock. I realize now
that they probably were. They'd managed to escape, but
their families had all been killed—some right in front of
their eyes. Isidro later told me he'd been out trading for
gasoline on the black market, and when he came home, his
entire town had been burned and everyone—men, women
and children, even infants—had been massacred. He told
me he was one of the lucky ones, that he actually was able
to identify the bodies of his wife and children. So many
people never knew, and they were left wondering forever
if maybe their families were still back there, maybe their
kids were still alive."

His eyes were distant, unfocused. But then the condensation from his glass of iced tea dripped onto his leg, and
he looked down and then over at Syd and smiled. "You
know, it's been a long time since I've talked about Isidro.
Ellen used to like to hear about him, but I didn't tell her
too much of this darker stuff. I mean, the guy essentially
had an entire life back in Central America before he even
met my mother. He married her—my mother, I mean—so
that he wouldn't be deported. If he'd been sent back to his
own country, he would've been killed.

"My mother sat the two of us—me and Isidro—down

at the kitchen table and told us she was going to marry him." Luke laughed, remembering. "He was completely against it. He knew she'd had to get married before, when she was younger. He told her she'd gotten married for the wrong reasons the first time, and that he wasn't going to let her do that again. And she told him that marrying him so that he wouldn't die was the best reason she could imagine. I think she was in love with him, even back then. She convinced him that she was right, they got married, and he moved out of the apartment over the garage and into our house."

His mother had been pretty damn shrewd. She'd known what she wanted, and she'd gone about getting it. She'd known if she could get Isidro into her home, it wouldn't be long before their marriage was consummated. And she'd been right on the money.

It was funny the way life seemed to go in circles, Lucky mused as he gazed at Syd, who was way, *way* down on the other end of the couch, as far away from him as she could possibly sit. Because here he was, playing the same game his mother had played. Pretending that he was acting out of some big-picture necessity, rather than from his own personal need.

Pretending that, oh, yeah, jeez, if he really *had* to, he'd cope with the *inconvenience* of having Sydney around all day and all night.

Yeah, right. Like he didn't hope—the way his mother had hoped with Isidro—that the pressure from being with Syd constantly would trigger some kind of unavoidable and unstoppable sexual explosion. That sooner or later—if not tonight, then maybe tomorrow or the next day—Syd would push open his bedroom door with a crash and announce that she couldn't stand it another minute, that she had to have him right now.

He laughed. Yeah, like *that* was really going to happen.

"What's so funny?" she asked.

He almost told her. Somehow he managed to shrug instead. "Ellen was born just about a year after their wedding. Their marriage turned pretty real pretty fast."

She nodded, understanding, glancing up at the wall, at his mother's picture. "The proximity thing. She was beautiful, and if she was in love with him...he probably didn't stand a chance."

"He used to talk to me about his other family," Lucky remembered. "I think he probably didn't say much about them to my mother, but I asked, and he needed to talk about them. I used to go with him to meetings where he would tell about these horrible human rights violations he'd witnessed in his home country. The things he saw, Syd, the things he could bear witness to..." He shook his head. "He told me to value my freedom as an American above all else. Every day he reminded me that I lived in a land of freedom, every day we'd hang an American flag outside our house. He used to tell me that he could go to sleep at night and be certain that no one would break into our house and tear us from our beds. No one would drag us into the street and put bullets in our heads simply for something we believed in. Because of him, I learned to value the freedom that most Americans take for granted.

"Isidro taught me a lot of things, but that was something that really stuck. Because he'd lived with that fear. Because his other family *had* been murdered."

Syd was silent, just watching him.

"He became a naturalized citizen when I was thirteen years old," he told her, letting himself lose himself a little bit in the softness of her eyes. "That's one day of my life I'll never forget. He was so proud of becoming a real American. And God!" He laughed. "That November, on election day! He took me and Ellen to the polls with him, so we could watch him vote. And he made us both promise—even though El could barely talk—that we would vote every chance we got."

"So your stepfather is why you became a SEAL."

"Father," he corrected gently. "There was nothing step about him. And, yeah, the things he taught me stuck." Lucky shrugged, knowing that a cynical newspaper journalist probably wouldn't see it the same way he—and Isidro—had. Knowing that she would probably laugh, hoping she wouldn't, wanting to try to explain just the same. "I know there's a lot wrong with this country, but there's also a lot right. I *believe* in America. And I joined the Navy—the SEAL teams in particular—because I wanted to give something back. I wanted to be a part of making sure we remained the land of the free and the home of the brave. And I stayed in the Navy for longer than I'd ever dreamed of because I ended up getting as much as I gave."

She laughed.

He tried to hide his disappointment. "Yeah, I know. It sounds so hokey."

"Oh—" she sat up "—no! I wasn't laughing because of what you said. God, you've just impressed the hell out of me—please don't think I'm laughing at you."

"I have?" Lucky tried to sound casual. "Impressed you? Really?" Yeesh, he sounded like a dork, pathetically fishing for more compliments.

She didn't seem to notice, caught up in her own intensity. Man, when she got serious, she got *serious*. "I was laughing because back when I first met you, I thought I had you all figured out. I thought you were one of those testosterone-laden types who'd joined the SEALs purely because they liked the idea of blowing stuff up."

"Well, yeah." Lucky needed her to stop looking at him like that, with those blazing eyes that seemed able to look right through him and see his very soul. He needed her to lighten up so that he wouldn't do something really stupid like pull her into his arms and kiss her. "What do you think I mean when I talk about getting something back from being a SEAL? What I get is to blow stuff up."

Syd laughed. Thank God.

"Tell me," she said, "about your sister. Ellen. She's getting married, right?"

"In about a week," he told her. "You better put it on your calendar. It'll look really weird if we're supposedly living together but you don't attend my only sister's wedding."

"Oh, no." She made a face. "That really stinks. You can't possibly want to drag me along to your sister's wedding."

"I suppose we can make up some excuse for why you're not there," Lucky said. "I mean, if you really don't want to go."

"I'd love to go," she countered, "but I know what an important day this is for you. Bobby told me how you turned down a…what did he call it? A silver bullet assignment— something you really, really wanted—just so you could be in town."

"If I'm not there," he said, "who's going to walk her down the aisle? Look, just plan to go with me, okay? And if you could plan to wear a dress—something formal— while you're at it…"

"God." She gazed at him in mock horror. "You must think I'm a complete idiot. What did you think I'd wear to a formal wedding? A clean pair of jeans?"

"Well, yeah," he admitted. "Either jeans or your khakis. I've noticed a certain… repetitiveness to your attire."

"Great," she said. "First I'm an idiot, and then I'm *boring?*"

She was laughing, so he knew she wasn't completely serious, but he still felt the need to try to explain. "That's not what I meant—"

"Quit while you're ahead," she told him. "Just tell me about your sister."

It was nearly 0100 hours, but Lucky wasn't tired. Syd didn't look tired either.

So he told her about his sister, ready and willing to talk all night if she wanted him to.

He wished she wanted more than conversation from him. He wanted to touch her, to take her to his bedroom and make love to her. But he wasn't going to risk destroying this quiet intimacy they shared.

She liked him. He knew that. But this was too new and far too fragile to gamble with.

He wanted to touch her, but he knew he shouldn't. Tonight he was going to have to settle for touching her with his words.

"BLADE," RIO ROSETTI SAID. "Or Panther."

"How about Hawk?" Thomas suggested, tongue firmly in cheek.

"Yeah, Hawk's good, too."

Rio was unhappy with his current nickname and was trying to talk his friends into calling him something else.

"Personally, I think we should be developing a kinder, gentler group of SEALs, with kinder, gentler nicknames," Michael Lee said with a completely straight face. "How about Bunny?"

The look on Rio's face was comical.

Thomas cracked up. "I like it," he said. "Bunny."

"Whoa," Rio said. "Whoa, whoa, whoa—"

"Works for me," Lucky said.

They were sitting in the office, waiting for Lucy's electronic transmission of a list she'd got from the police computer.

Out of all the many men and women who had served at the Navy base during the same few-month period four years ago, nearly thirty of them—all men—had gotten into trouble with the law. Twenty-three had served time. Five were still incarcerated.

The police computer had spat out names, aliases and last-known addresses for all of them. They were going to cross-reference this list again with the information they had in the navy's personnel files.

"Lucky," Rio said. "Now *there's* a nickname I'd love."

"It's taken," Mike pointed out. "Whoops, here we go. List's in. I'll print out a couple of hard copies."

"It's not as if the luck comes with the name," Thomas told Rio. "According to legend, the lieutenant here has led a charmed existence, *hence* the name."

"Charmed indeed," Rio agreed. He glanced at Lucky, who'd gone to look over Mike's shoulder at the computer screen.

The list contained name, aliases, last-known address, and a short rap sheet of charges, convictions and jail time served—their criminal résumé, so to speak.

"I couldn't help but notice that Sydney came to work this morning wearing one of your Hawaiian shirts, sir," Rio continued. "I guess your little sleepover last night went…well."

Lucky looked up to find Thomas and Bobby waiting

for him to comment, too. Even Michael Lee had lifted his eyes from the computer screen. He laughed. "You guys are kidding, right? You know as well as I do that this is just a ruse to try to trap the rapist. Sure, Syd stayed over, but..." he shrugged, "...nothing happened. I mean, there's really nothing going on between us."

"She *is* wearing one of your shirts," Bobby said.

"Yeah, because last night, in a genius move, I insulted her wardrobe."

He'd fallen asleep on the couch last night and woken to the scent of coffee brewing. He'd thrown off the blanket Syd must've put over him and staggered into the kitchen to find her already showered and dressed—and wearing one of his shirts. It was weird—and a little scary. It was his full-blown morning-after nightmare, in which a woman he barely knew and didn't particularly like would move in and make herself completely at home, right down to stealing from his closet. Except in this case, there had been no night before. *And* in this case, it wasn't a nightmare.

The coffee smelled great, Syd looked amazing in his shirt, and, as she smiled at him, his stomach didn't twist with anxiety. It twisted, all right, but in anticipation.

He liked her, liked having her in his house, liked having her be a part of his morning.

And maybe, if he were really lucky, if he lived up to this nickname of his, he'd wake up tomorrow with her in his bed. Mike handed him three copies of the printed list, and he handed one to Bobby, the others to Thomas and Rio.

Rio was now looking at him as if he were mentally challenged. "Let me get this straight. You had Syd alone. Syd. One of the most incredibly fascinating and sexy women in the world. And she's alone with you, all night. And instead of taking advantage of that incredible opportunity, you spent your time insulting her clothes?"

"Hey, guys, I went to Starbuck's. Who wants coffee?"

Syd breezed in carrying a cardboard tray filled with paper coffee cups before Lucky could tell Rio to mind his own business. "Oh, good, the list finally came in?"

"Hot off the press," Lucky told her.

She smiled as she set a cup down in front of him. "Special delivery. Extra sugar. I figured you could use it after last night."

Rio cleared his throat pointedly. "Excuse me?"

Syd smacked him lightly on the shoulder. "Don't you dare think that—that's not what I mean, dirt brain. Luke and I are friends. I kept him up all night *talking*. He fell asleep on the living-room couch at about 3:30. He's running on way too little sleep and it's all my fault."

Rio shot Lucky a disbelieving look. "You fell asleep on the living-room couch...?"

"Hey," Thomas said, "Here's a guy who got out of prison in Kentucky four weeks before the first attack was reported."

"First known attack," Lucky reminded him, giving him a grateful look for changing the subject. He rolled his chair closer to the young ensign, to look over his shoulder at the list. "Kentucky's a stretch. He'd have to be motivated to reach San Diego with the amount of money he had on him."

"Yeah, but check this out. He's already wanted again," Thomas said, "in connection with a liquor store robbery in Dallas. That happened a week after his release."

Syd leaned over Lucky's shoulder. "Can a convict just leave the state like that? Doesn't he have to check in with a parole officer?"

He turned his head to look at her and found himself

eye to eye with her breasts. He looked away, his mind instantly blank. What was he just about to say?

Bobby answered for him. "As far as I understand it, parole is for when a prisoner is released early. If he serves out his full sentence, there's usually no parole."

"What's this guy's name?" Syd asked. "Where is he on the list?"

"Owen Finn." Lucky pointed to the list and she leaned even closer to read the small print. She was wearing his deodorant. It smelled different on her. Delicate and femininely fresh.

Damn, he *was* nuts. He should have at least said something to Syd last night. *So, hey, like, what do you say we get it on?* Well, maybe not that. But certainly something in between that and the great big nothing he'd uttered. Because what if this attraction was mutual? What if she'd spent all night wishing they could get physical, too? What could it hurt to be honest?

They were, after all, friends—by her own admission. As his friend, she would appreciate his honesty.

Wouldn't she?

"Finn was convicted of burglary," Syd said, straightening up. "I thought we were looking for someone with a record of sexual assault or some other violent crime."

"Finn," Bobby reported from the Navy Computer's personnel files. "Owen Franklin. Son of a medal of honor winner, entered the U.S. Naval Academy even though his grades weren't quite up to par. Rang out of BUD/S in '96, given a dishonorable discharge four months later, charged and convicted of theft. Yeah, this guy definitely has sticky fingers. No mention of violence, though."

"How about this one?" Thomas pointed to the list, and Syd leaned over Lucky again. "Martin Taus. Charged with four counts of sexual assault but never convicted. Got off on a technicality. Never served time but paid fines and did community service for damage done in a street fight back in '98. His last-known address is a post-office box in San Diego."

"How do we find these guys?" Syd asked. "Can't we just bring in everyone on this list?"

She sat down next to him, and he resisted the urge to put his arm around her. If they were out in public, he could've gotten away with it. But here in the office they didn't need to play the girlfriend game.

It was too bad.

"Most of them aren't local," Lucky told her. "And their last-known addresses are probably out of date. But FIn-COM's definitely looking to have them all brought in for questioning."

"Some of them aren't going to be easy to find," Thomas pointed out. "Like this Owen Finn who's wanted in Texas. He's clearly on the move."

"When are we going to start dangling me out there as bait?" Syd asked. "We need to establish a pattern of time that I'm home alone."

"We'll start tonight," Lucky told her. "I spoke to Frisco this morning. The phase-one SEAL candidates are going to be doing a series of night swims over the next week. I'm going to be visible at the base from the time the exercise starts at about twenty-three hundred, right up until the point I put on my gear. Then one of the other instructors will take over for me—masked and suited up, anyone who's watching won't know it's not me. I'll leave the base covertly and join Bobby and our junior frogmen, who will have concealed themselves strategically around the outside of our house. *My* house," he quickly corrected himself.

Alan Francisco had been disappointed—he'd said as much—when Lucky'd admitted his relationship with Syd was just an act. But he didn't say anything more, except that he was there to talk, if Lucky wanted someone to talk to. About what, Lucky'd asked. Yeah, he was a little worried about Syd putting herself in danger, but this way at least he could keep an eye on her. Everything was cool. There was nothing to talk about.

"I'll be going over to Luke's in about an hour to set up interior microphones," Bobby said.

"So, I'm going to be alone in the house starting at about seven until…two or three in the morning?" she guessed.

"No, we'll have time before the exercise starts," Lucky told her. "We can have dinner downtown. We'll leave here together at about 1800—six o'clock. After dinner, we'll go to my place, and around 2230, after Bobby and the guys have moved into position, I'll make a big show of kissing you goodbye, and I'll come here. You'll be alone from then until around 0200. About three and a half hours."

Syd nodded. "Maybe if we're lucky, FInCOM will round up most of the suspects on our list before tonight. And if we're *really* lucky, one of them will be our guy."

Lucky nodded, hoping the golden luck for which he'd been nicknamed would, indeed, shine through.

CHAPTER TEN

THE MELTINGLY PERFECT LOBSTER and the hundred-dollar bottle of wine had been completely wasted on Syd.

What with the blazing sunset, the incredible outdoor patio, the million-dollar view of the Pacific, and—last but certainly not least—the glowing golden good looks of the man sitting across the restaurant table from her, Syd had barely noticed the gourmet food or drink.

It might as well have been peanut butter sandwiches and grape juice for all the attention she gave to it.

She spent most of the meal wishing Luke would hold her hand. And when he finally did, reaching across the table to intertwine their fingers, she spent the rest of the meal wishing he'd kiss her again.

He'd kissed her outside the restaurant after giving the valet his keys. Slow, lingering kisses that rendered her speechless.

He'd kissed her in the bar, too, as they'd waited for a table. Delicate kisses. Elegant kisses. Five-star restaurant kisses.

She wasn't dressed for this place, but no one besides her seemed to care. The maitre d' was attentive, the waiters were respectful, and Luke...

Well, he'd nearly had *her* believing they were completely, totally, thrillingly in love.

"You're so quiet," he said now, his thumb tracing circles on the palm of her hand as they waited for the waiter to return with Luke's credit card, sitting beneath that perfect, color-streaked sky. The way he was looking at her, the quiet timbre of his voice—his behavior was completely that of an attentive lover. He was remarkably good at playing this part. "What are you thinking about?"

"Kissing you," she admitted.

For an eighth of a second, his guard dropped, his thumb stopped moving and she saw real surprise in his eyes. He opened his mouth to speak, but the waiter returned. And all Luke did was laugh as he gently reclaimed his fingers and signed the bill. He pocketed his receipt and stood, holding out his hand to her.

"Let's walk on the beach."

They went down the wooden steps hand in hand, and when they reached the bottom, he knelt in the sand and took off her sandals, then carried them for her, along with his own shoes. The sand was sensuously cool between her toes.

They walked in silence for about a minute, then Luke cleared his throat. "So, when you were thinking about kissing me, was it a good thought or…?"

"It was more of an amused thought," she admitted. "Like, here I am, with the best-looking man in the state of California, and oh, just in case that's not thrilling enough, he's going to kiss me a few dozen more times before the night is through. You kiss like a dream, you know? Of course you know."

"You're pretty good at it yourself."

"I'm an amateur compared to you. I can't seem to do that thing you do with your eyes. And that little 'I'm going to kiss you now' smile. Only someone with a face like yours can pull that off."

His laughter sounded embarrassed. "Oh, come on. I'm not—"

"Don't be coy," she reprimanded him. "You know what you look like. All you need to do is smile, and every woman within a hundred feet goes into heavy fantasy mode. Walk into any room and flash those teeth, and women start lining up for a chance to go home with you."

"Gee, if I'd only known that was all it would take..." He gave her his best smile.

She yawned. "Doesn't work on me. Not since I heard you snore last night."

"I do *not* snore."

Syd just smiled.

"I *don't*."

"Okay," she said, clearly just humoring him.

"You try to pick fights," he said, realization in his voice, "even these silly, teasing ones, because you're afraid to have a serious conversation with me."

That was *so* not true. "We had a very serious conversation last night," she argued.

"Yeah, but I did most of the talking. That was *my* serious conversation."

"I told you about my family," she protested.

"Barely."

"Well, they're boring. None of them have run off to Tibet. I mean, if anyone's Tibet-bound, it's probably *me*."

"There you go," he said. "Trying to get me to argue with you about whether you would or wouldn't actually go to Tibet if you had the cash."

Tibet no, but New York, *yes*. Or Boston or Philly. She wanted to return to the east coast, she reminded herself. That's what all this was about. It was about helping catch a serial rapist, and then writing the best, most detailed, most emotionally connected yet factual article about a city-wide task force ever written.

She wasn't here simply to kiss this man in the moonlight.

The last of the dusk was fading fast, and the moon was just a sliver in the sky. Syd could hear the party sounds from the Surf Club farther down the beach—the echo of laughter and distant rock and roll.

Luke's face was entirely in shadow. "I like you, Syd," he told her softly. "You make me laugh. But I want to *know* you. I want to know what you want, who you really are. I want to know where you see yourself in fifty years. I want to…" He laughed, and she could've sworn it was self-consciously, that is, if it was possible that Luke O'Donlon could be self-conscious. "I want to know about Kevin Manse. I want to know if you're still in love with him, if you still measure every man you bump into against him."

Syd was so completely surprised, it very nearly qualified as stunned. Kevin *Manse?* What the…? She wished she could see Luke's eyes in the darkness. "What do… *how* do you know about Kevin Manse?"

He cleared his throat. "He, um, came up in some detail when Lana Quinn first hypnotized you."

"*Some* detail…?"

"You, um, flashed back to the first time you, uh, met him."

Syd said a very impolite word. "*Flashed back?* What do you mean, *flashed back?*"

"Um, I guess *relived* is more accurate."

"*Relived?*" Her voice went up several octaves. "What is that supposed to mean?"

"You, um, partly told us what happened, partly talked to Kevin as if he were in the room. You told us you bumped into him on the stairs at some frat party, and that he took you up to his room. We kind of tried to rush through the 'oh, Kevin, yes, Kevin' part, but—"

Syd said another equally impolite word and sat down in the sand, covering her face with her hands. God, how mortifying. "I suppose you also heard how that pitiful story ended?"

"Actually, no, I don't know how it ended." She felt more than heard Luke sit down beside her. "Syd, I'm sorry. I wasn't trying to embarrass you. I was just... I've been thinking about it a lot lately, wondering..."

She peeked out at him through her fingers. He *didn't* know how the story ended. She was saved from complete and total mortification.

"Do you, um, still love him?"

Syd laughed. She laughed and laughed and laughed, lying back on the sand, staring up at the vastness of the sky and gasping for air.

She laughed, because if she didn't laugh, she'd cry. And there was no way she would *ever* cry in front of this man. Not if she could help it.

Luke laughed, too, mostly because laughter was contagious, partly because he was confused. "I didn't mean for that to be such a funny question."

"No," she said when she finally could talk, drawing in a deep breath and letting it out in a shudder of air. "No, I *definitely* don't still love him. In fact, I never loved him."

"You said you did. While you were hypnotized."

"I was eighteen," she said. "I lost my virginity to the bastard. I temporarily confused sex with love."

As she gazed at the sky, the stars slowly appeared.

He sighed. "It was only a one-nighter, huh?"

Syd turned her head to look at him, a darker lump of

a shadow against the darkness of the night. "A one-night stand. How many times have *you* done that?"

He answered honestly. "Too many."

"You're probably someone's Kevin Manse," she said. He was silent.

"I'm sorry," she said. "That was harsh."

"But probably true. I've tried to stay away from the eighteen-year-old virgins, though."

"Oh," Syd said. "Well. Then that makes it *all* better."

Luke laughed ruefully. "Man, you are unmerciful."

"I'll cut you down, but not yet—I like seeing you twisting in the wind, baby." Syd laughed. "You want serious? I'll give you the whole pathetic story—that'll really make you squirm. But if you repeat it to *any*one, our friendship is over, do you understand?"

"I'm going to hate this, aren't I?"

"It's pretty hateful." Syd sat up and looked out over the water. "I've never told this to anyone. Not my college roommate, not my sister, not my mother, not anyone. But I'm going to tell you, because we're friends, and maybe you'll learn something from it."

"I feel like I'm approaching a car wreck. I'm horrified at the thought of the carnage, but unable to turn away."

She laughed. "It's not *that* bad."

"No?"

"Well, maybe it was at the time." She hugged her knees close to her chest and sighed. Where to start…? "Kevin was a big football star."

"Yeah," Luke said. "You mentioned that. You said he was a scholar, too. Smart as hell. And probably handsome."

"On a scale from one to ten…" Syd squinted as she thought about it. "A twelve."

"Whoa!"

On that same scale, Luke was a fifty. But she wasn't going to tell *him* that.

"So I ran into him, the big, famous football hero, on the stairs of this frat-house party," she said, "and—"

"Yeah," he interrupted. "I know that part. You went upstairs with him, and I know *that* part, too. That's the part where you started going 'oh, Kevin, yes, Kevin—'"

"Wow, you are really the funniest man in the world. Oh, wait—no, you're not! You just *think* you are."

Luke laughed softly. "I'm sorry, I'm just…being a jerk. I'm really anxious about where this is going, and I was just trying to…" he exhaled noisily. "Truth is, when you were doing that in Lana's office, it was really incredibly sexy. It was kind of hard to sit through."

She closed her eyes. "God, I'm sorry. I hope I didn't offend you."

"Yeah, right. It's always offensive to find out that the woman I'm going to be working closely with for the next few weeks is completely *hot*."

She snorted. "Yeah, right. That's me. One hot chick."

"You steam," he told her.

"And I suppose the fact that you now know I had sex with some guy about an hour after I met him had nothing to do with your decision to hit on me?"

"I hit on you before you were hypnotized."

He was right. That *had* happened the day before—on the first day they'd met. And *after* she'd been hypnotized…

"After the session with Lana Quinn," he said, "was when I asked you to join the team, as a team player, remember?"

Syd was completely confused. "I'm not even going to *try* to make any sense out of that."

"Just finish the story," he told her. "You told me and

Lana that Kevin had one of his friends drive you back to your dorm, later that night."

"Yeah," she said. "He said he thought my staying all night would be bad for my reputation. Ha." She rested her chin on her knees, still holding on to herself tightly. "Okay. Next day. Act Two. It's Sunday. There's a big game. And me, I'm a genius. I'm thinking about the fact that thanks to the bottle of Jack Daniel's we put a solid dent in up in Kevin's room, I managed to leave without giving my new soul mate my telephone number. So I spend the morning writing him a note. I think I went through about a hundred drafts before I got it right. 'Dear Kevin, Last night was truly wonderful…'"

She had to swallow to clear away the sudden, aching lump that formed in her throat. God, she was such a sap. All these years later, and Kevin Manse could *still* make her want to cry, damn him.

She felt Luke touch her, his fingers gentle in her hair, light against her back.

"You really don't have to tell me any more of this," he said quietly. "I already feel really bad, and if you want, right now I'll swear to you that I'll never do a one-nighter again. I mean, it's been years since I have anyway, and—"

"I went to the football game," she told him. "With my pathetic little note. And I sat there in the stands and I watched my lover from the night before play a perfect game. After it was over, I tried to get into the stadium locker rooms, but there were security guards who laughed at me when I told them I was Kevin's girlfriend. I didn't get upset. I just smiled. I figured they'd have plenty of time to get to know me—the season was just starting. They told me that Kevin always came out the south entrance after a game to greet his fans. They told me I should wait there if I wanted to see him. So I waited."

"Oh, God," Luke said. "I know exactly where this is going."

"I waited by the south gate, with a crowd of about fifty people, for over an hour," Syd continued.

She remembered the smell of the spilled beer, the sweat, and the humid afternoon heat. She remembered that nervous feeling in her stomach, that anticipation at the thought of seeing Kevin again. She'd stood there, fantasizing, wondering what he'd do when he saw her. Would he laugh and hold out his arms to her? Would he get that soft look in his eyes, just as he had the night before, when they'd done those things that still made her blush? Would he pick her up and spin her around in a victory dance, and then kiss her? Syd remembered thinking that the crowd would cheer at that kiss, the way crowds always did at the end of romantic movies, when the hero and heroine were together at last.

"He finally came out," she told Luke, "and started signing autographs. It took me forever, but I made my way to the front of the crowd. And he turned to me and…"

The lump was back, damn it, and she had to clear it out of her throat.

"And he didn't remember me," she whispered. "He looked right into my eyes, and he didn't even recognize that I was the girl he'd had sex with the night before. He gave me his high-voltage, football-star smile, and took my note right out of my hand. He asked me what my name was, asked me how to spell it, and he signed his autograph on that piece of paper and gave it back to me. 'To Sydney— Stay happy, Kevin Manse.'"

Lucky sat in the sand and stared up at the now slightly

hazy sky. "Can I try to find him?" he asked. "Can I track him down and beat the hell out of him?"

Syd managed a shaky laugh.

He wanted to touch her again, to put his arms around her and hold her close, but it seemed like the wrong thing to do, given the circumstances.

"I'm so sorry," he said, and his words seemed so inadequate.

Especially since he'd spent nearly all of dinner planning exactly how he was going to talk Syd into his bed tonight. Late tonight. After 0200. In the small hours of the night, when she would be at her most vulnerable. He'd turn off the microphones, send the rest of his team home. And in the privacy of his living room...

He'd told himself that it would be good for him to be honest with her. To tell her he was attracted, admit that he was having trouble thinking about much else besides the fact that he wanted her. He was planning to move closer and closer as they sat on the couch, closing in on her until she was in his arms. He was planning to kiss her until she lost all sense of direction. He was planning to kiss her until she surrendered.

But in truth, he wasn't really being honest. He was merely calculating that this feigned honesty would get him some.

He hadn't given much thought at all to tomorrow. He hadn't considered Syd's feelings. Or her expectations.

Just like Kevin Manse, he'd thought only about his own immediate gratification. God, he was such a jerk.

Syd drew in a deep breath and let it out in a rush. "We should probably go. It's getting late. You have to head over to the base, and I've...I've got to go tattoo the word *victim* on my forehead, just to be sure our bad guy gets the right idea."

She stood up and stretched, then turned and offered Lucky a hand. He took it, and she helped him up. He'd known all along that she was strong, but she was much, much stronger than he'd ever imagined.

He held on to her hand, suddenly afraid that she didn't really like him, afraid that she was simply enduring his company, afraid of what she'd write about him in her article after this was all over. And, he was afraid that after it was over, he'd never see her again. "Syd, do you hate me?"

She turned toward him and touched his face, her fingers cool against his cheek. "Are you kidding?" Her husky voice was filled with amusement and something else. Something warm that wrapped around him and brought him more than mere relief. "I know it sounds crazy, but I think you're probably the best friend I've ever had."

CHAPTER ELEVEN

SYD WOKE TO THE SHRILL SOUND of the telephone ringing.

The clock on the bedside table in Luke's guest room read 3:52. It was nearly four in the morning. Who could possibly be calling now?

She knew instantly, sitting up, her heart pounding.

The rapist hadn't taken the bait. Instead, some other poor woman had been attacked.

She could hear the low murmur of Luke's voice from the other room.

His voice got louder, and, although she couldn't make out the words, she could pick up his anger loud and clear. No, this wasn't good news, that was for sure.

Luke had come home just after two. He'd been unnaturally quiet, almost pensive, and very, very tired. He'd made a quick circuit of the house, making sure all the doors and windows were securely locked, and then he'd gone into his bedroom and shut the door.

Syd had climbed into the narrow bed in this room that had probably once been Luke's sister's, and had tried to sleep.

Tried and failed. It seemed as if she'd just drifted off when the sound of the phone jerked her back to consciousness.

From the other side of the wall, she heard a crash from Luke's room as something was noisily knocked over. She

stood up, uncertain as to whether she should go make sure
he was all right, when her door opened with a bang.

Luke stood there, wearing only a pair of boxers, breathing hard, backlit by the light from the hallway. "Get your
clothes on. Fast. We're going to the hospital." His voice was
harsh, his face grim. "Lucy McCoy's been attacked."

SYD HAD TO RUN TO keep up with Luke as she followed
him down the hospital corridor.

Lucy McCoy. God, not Lucy....

Whoever had called Luke to give him the news hadn't
known any details. How badly had she been hurt? Was
she even alive?

Bobby appeared at the end of the hallway, and Luke
moved even faster.

"Sit-rep," he ordered the chief as soon as they were
close enough to talk without shouting.

Bobby's face was somber. "She's alive and she wasn't
raped," he told them as they continued down the hall.
"But that's where the good news ends. They've got her in
ICU—intensive care. I...persuaded a doctor to talk to me,
and he used words like *massive head injury* and *coma*.
She's got a broken collarbone, broken arm, and a broken
rib that punctured her lung, as well."

"Who's with her?" Luke's voice was tight.

"Wes and Mia," Bobby reported. "Frisco's taking care
of the paperwork."

"Has someone tried to reach Blue?"

"Yeah, I've tried, Frisco's tried, but we're both getting
a lot of static. Wherever Alpha Squad is, they're in deep. I
can't even get anyone to tell me which hemisphere they're
on."

"Call Admiral Robinson," Luke ordered as they stopped

outside the entrance to the intensive care unit. "If anyone can get word to Alpha Squad, he can."

Bobby moved briskly off as Mia Francisco pushed open the door and stepped out of ICU.

"I thought I heard your voice." She gave Luke a hug, her eyes red from crying.

"Should you be here?" Luke asked her, putting a hand on her enormous belly.

Mia hugged Syd, too. "How could I not be here?" she said. Her lip trembled. "The doctor says the next few hours are critical. If she makes it through the night—" Her voice broke.

"Oh, God," Syd said. "It's that bad?"

Mia nodded.

"Can I see her?" Luke asked.

Mia nodded again. "She's in room four. There's usually a family-members-only rule with patients in ICU, but with Blue out of the country, the doctors and nurses are letting us sit with her. I called Veronica and Melody. They're both flying in in the morning. And Nell and Becca should be here in about an hour. PJ's already over at the crime scene."

Luke pushed open the door to the intensive care wing, and Syd followed him in.

Nighttime didn't exist in ICU. It was as brightly lit and as filled with busy doctors and nurses as if it were high noon.

Luke stopped outside room four, just looking in. Syd took his hand.

Lucy looked impossibly small and fragile lying in that hospital bed. She was hooked up to all kinds of machines and monitors. Her head was swathed in bandages, her face pale—except for where it was savagely bruised. She had an angry-looking row of stitches above her left eyebrow, and her mouth looked scraped and raw, her lips swollen and split. Her left eye was purple and yellow and completely swollen shut.

Wes sat next to her bed, head bowed as he held her hand.

He looked up as Luke slowly went into the room, Syd following him to the foot of Lucy's bed.

Wes's eyes were as red as Mia's had been. He was crying.

Wes—whom Syd still thought of as a potential suspect. God, wasn't that an awful thought? Was it possible Wes could have done this to Lucy and then come here to sit by her bed—to make sure that she died? It was like something out of a bad movie.

"Hey, Luce," Luke said, trying his best to sound cheerful, but barely able to do more than whisper. "I don't suppose you want to wake up and tell me what happened, huh?"

Lucy didn't move. On the wall, the screen monitoring her heart continued its steady beeping.

Wes gave no guilty starts. His eyes didn't move shiftily. He didn't start to sweat or shake at the thought of Lucy opening her eyes and giving out information. He just sat there, crying, holding Lucy's hand, occasionally wiping his eyes with his T-shirt sleeve.

"Well, you know what?" Luke said to her. "I'm going to come back later and we can talk then, okay?"

Nothing.

Luke was holding Syd's hand so tightly, her fingers were starting to ache from lack of blood.

"Just…hang on, Lucy," he said, his voice thick with emotion. "Blue will be here soon, I promise. Just…hang on."

LUCKY STOOD IN BLUE AND Lucy McCoy's second-floor bedroom, grimly taking in the crushed and twisted lamps, the knocked-over rocking chair, the mattress half off its frame, the blood smeared on the sheets and the pale yellow wall, and the broken bay window that had looked out over the McCoys' flower-filled backyard.

Dawn was sending delicate, fairy-like light into the yard and, as he stepped closer to the window, the bits and pieces of broken glass glittered prettily on the grass below.

Syd stood quietly by the door. He'd heard her slip into the bathroom after they'd first arrived and seen the evidence of the violent and bloody fight that had taken place in this very room. He'd heard her get sick. But she'd come out almost right away. Pale and shaking but unwilling to leave.

PJ Becker came into the room, followed by one of the FInCOM agents who'd been assigned to the task force. PJ's recent promotion had pushed her way high up in FInCOM's chain of command, and the agent who was with her looked a little dazed at her presence.

"Dave, you already know Lieutenant O'Donlon and Sydney Jameson. Lieutenant, Dave Sudenberg's one of our top forensics experts," PJ said. "I thought you'd be interested in hearing his take on what happened here last night, since Detective McCoy's not yet able to give us a statement."

Lucky nodded and Dave Sudenberg cleared his throat. "As far as I can tell, the perpetrator entered the premises through a downstairs window," he told them. "He managed to bypass a portion of the security system without shutting the whole thing down, which was good, since the system's lights and alarms later played a large part in saving the detective's life."

He pointed to the door that Syd was still standing near. "He entered this room through that door, and from the pattern of blood on the sheets, we can assume that Lucy was in bed at the time, and probably asleep when he landed the first blow—probably the one that broke her nose. He struck her with his fists—there would have been far more blood had he used something other than his hands.

"Lucy came up swinging. She was probably trying to get to the weapon she kept just under the bed, but he wouldn't let her near it. She hit him with this lamp," he said, pointing to the twisted wreckage of what had once been a tall, freestanding halogen. "Preliminary tests already show that the blood on this thing isn't Lucy's.

"So she clobbers him, and he goes ballistic, throws her against this wall, battering the hell out of her, and delivering what I believe was the worst of Lucy's head injuries, and wrapping his hands around her neck. But somehow, she breaks free. Somehow she doesn't lose consciousness right away. And she does the one thing that I think saved her life. She dives out the window, right through the glass, setting off the alarm system, waking the neighbors. Perp runs, and the police come and find her, half dead in the backyard."

Lucky met Syd's eyes. Dear God, now *he* was going to be sick. Lucy had to have known that a fall like that could have killed her. Had she thought she'd have zero chance of survival by staying in the room with the attacker? Fight or submit. Had she believed either would have gotten her killed, and opted to flee, despite the health risks of jumping out a second-story window?

There was a real chance he'd never find out, that Lucy wouldn't live through the night, or that, even if she did, she'd never awaken from the coma she'd slipped into.

There was a real chance Blue would come home to bury his wife.

PJ moved to the window and looked all the way down at the yard below. "Dave thinks her broken collarbone and arm were from the dive she took out the window," she said grimly. "But the broken rib, broken nose, bruised throat and near-fatal head injuries were from your guy."

"We've got enough of his DNA to see if it matches the semen and skin samples he left behind with his other victims," Sudenberg told them. "I've already sent samples to the lab."

"What's it gonna take," Lucky asked, his chest and his throat both feeling so tight he had to push to squeeze his voice out, "to get the police or FInCOM to actually pick up the likely suspects on the list Lucy helped compile?"

"It's getting done, but these things take time," PJ told him as she headed for the door. She motioned for Sudenberg to follow her. "I'll see that you're given updated status reports as they come in."

Lucky nodded. "Thanks."

"See you back at the hospital," PJ said.

LUCKY STOOD IN HIS kitchen, his vision blurring as he stared out the window over the sink.

Lucy had made it through the night but still showed no signs of waking.

Blue could not be reached, not even with the help of Admiral Robinson. The admiral had known where Alpha Squad was though, and had been willing to break radio silence to contact them, but the mountains and rocky terrain were playing havoc with the signal. Lieutenant Mitch Shaw, one of the Admiral's Gray Group operatives, had volunteered to go in after them. To find Blue, to send him back out and to take his place on this critical mission.

Best-case scenario had Shaw taking a record four days to walk into the hostile and nearly impenetrable countryside and find Alpha Squad almost right away—another highly unlikely possibility. Another four days for Blue to get out. Best-case scenario didn't have him reaching his wife's side in fewer than nine or ten days.

Nine or ten *days*.

Damn it. *Damn* it.

He heard Syd in the doorway, but he didn't turn around. "Maybe I should go," she said quietly. "You probably want to be alone, and—"

He spun around, interrupting her with a very salty version of no. "Where would you go? To your apartment? I don't want you even to *think* of going back there alone, do you understand? Not unless I'm with you. From now on, you don't make a move on your own, is that absolutely clear?"

He was shouting at her, he realized. He was standing in his kitchen, blasting her for being considerate.

But she didn't shout back at him. She didn't recoil in horror. She didn't spin on her heel and walk away in a huff. Instead, she took a step toward him, reaching out her hand for him. "Luke, this isn't your fault. You know that, right?"

There was a solid lump in his throat, and no matter how hard he tried he couldn't swallow it. He couldn't push it down past the tightness in his chest. "I should have made her listen to me," he whispered. "I tried to talk her into staying at the police station, but she had such faith in her damned security system."

Syd was gazing at him with such compassion in her eyes. He knew that if she touched him, he'd be lost. If she touched him, everything he was fighting so hard to keep inside would break free, all the guilt and the anger and the fear—God, he was so afraid. It would escape, like water pouring over a dam.

He took a step back from her. "I don't want you doing this anymore. This bait thing. Not after this. No way. All bets are off. You're going to have to stay away from me from now on. I'll make sure Bobby's with you, 24-7."

She kept coming. "Luke. That doesn't make sense. This could well be the only way we'll catch this guy. I *know* you want to catch this guy."

He laughed, and it sounded sharp and brittle. "Understatement of the year."

"Maybe we should both get some sleep. We can talk about this later, after we've had time to think it through."

"There's nothing more to think about," he said. "There's too much that could go wrong. In the time it would take us to get inside the house, even from the backyard, you could be killed. You're smaller than Lucy, Syd. If he hit you the way he hit her—" His voice broke and he had to take a deep breath before he could go on. "I won't let you risk your life that way. The thought of you being alone with that guy even for one second..."

To Lucky's complete horror, the tears he was desperately fighting welled in his eyes, and this time he couldn't force them back. This time they escaped. He wiped at them savagely, but even that didn't stop them from coming.

Ah, God, he was crying. He was standing in front of Syd and crying like a two-year-old.

It was all over. He was completely unmanned.

Except she didn't laugh. She didn't give him one of those "wow, you are both lame *and* stupid" looks that she did so well.

Instead, she put her arms around him and held him

tightly. "It's okay if you cry," she told him softly. "I won't tell anyone."

He had to laugh at that. "Yeah, but you'll know."

She lifted her head to look up at him, gently pushing his hair back from his face, her eyes so soft. "I already knew."

The constriction in his chest got even tighter. God, it hurt. "I'd die if anything happened to you."

His voice broke as he thought about Blue, out there in some jungle somewhere, being told that the woman he loved more than life itself was lying in a hospital bed, maybe dying, maybe already dead.

And then Lucky wasn't just crying anymore. He was experiencing emotional meltdown. He was sobbing the way he hadn't done since Isidro had died, clinging tightly to Syd as if maybe she could save him.

His knees gave out and he crumpled, sliding down to sit on the kitchen floor.

And still Syd held on to him. She didn't say a word, didn't try to make him stop. She just sat next to him, rocking him gently.

Even if Lucy woke up, even if she opened her eyes tomorrow, she would have only *survived*. Blue could never go back and erase the trauma of what she'd been through. He could never take away the fear she must've known in what should have been the sanctuary of her bedroom, as she'd fought for her life, all alone with a man who wanted to violate her, to kill her. There would always, for the rest of their lives, be a permanent echo of that fear in her eyes.

And that was if she survived.

If she died...

How would Blue live, how would he even be able to breathe, with his heart ripped from his chest?

Would he spend the rest of his life haunted by the memory of Lucy's eyes? Would he be forever looking for her smile on a crowded street? Would the scent of her subtle perfume make him turn, searching for her, despite knowing full well that she was gone?

Lucky wasn't ever going to let himself be in that place where Blue was right now. He wasn't ever getting married. Never getting married. It had been his mantra for years as he'd struggled with the concept of commitment, yet now it held special meaning.

He didn't want to walk around feeling the fear that came with loving someone. He didn't want that, damn it!

Except look at him.

He was reduced to this quivering bowl of jelly not simply out of empathy for Blue. A solid part of the emotion that had reduced him to these stupid tears was this god-awful fear that tightened his chest and closed up his throat.

The thought of Syd spending even one single second with the man who had brutalized Lucy made him crazy. The thought of her being beaten into a coma was terrifying.

But the thought of Syd walking out of his life, after they'd caught and convicted the San Felipe Rapist, was nearly as frightening.

He loved her.

No! Dear God, where had *that* thought come from? An overdose of whatever bizarre hormones his emotional outburst had unleashed.

Lucky drew in a deep, shuddering breath and pulled free from Syd's arms. He didn't love her. That was insane. He was Lucky O'Donlon. He didn't *do* love.

He wiped his eyes, wiped his face, reached up for a

napkin from the holder on the kitchen table and blew his nose. He lived up to his nickname by tossing the napkin directly into the trash container all the way on the other side of the room with perfect aim, then sat leaning back, exhausted, against the kitchen cabinets.

No, he didn't love her. He was just a little confused, that's all. And, just to be safe, until he was able to sleep off this confusion, it would be smart for him to put a little distance between them.

Now was definitely not the time to act on his raging physical attraction for this woman. As much as he would have given for the comfort of losing himself in some highly charged sex before slipping into mind-numbing sleep, he wasn't going to do it.

Of course, there was also the not-so-small matter of his taking advantage of her.

Assuming that she'd even *let* him take advantage of her after he'd revealed just how completely pathetic a wimp he was.

Syd was silent as she sat beside him. He couldn't bring himself even to glance at her as he attempted an apologetic smile. "Sheesh. I'm sorry about that."

He sensed more than saw her turn so that she was sitting on her knees, facing him.

But then she touched him. Her fingers were cool against the heat of his face as she gently pushed his hair back from his forehead. He looked at her then—he couldn't really avoid it, she'd leaned forward and her face was about two inches from his.

Her eyes were so warm, he had to close his, for fear he'd start crying all over again.

And with his eyes closed, he didn't see her lean even farther forward. But she must have, because she kissed him.

She kissed him.

Here in his kitchen, where no one was watching, where no one could see.

It was such a sweet kiss, such a gentle kiss, her lips featherlight against his. It made his knees go even weaker, made him glad he was already sitting down.

She kissed him again, and this time he was ready for her. This time he kissed her, too, catching her mouth with his, careful to be as gentle, tasting the salt of his tears on her lips with the very tip of his tongue.

He heard her sigh and he kissed her again, longer this time, deeper. She opened her mouth to him, slowly, exquisitely meeting his tongue with hers, and Lucky threw it all away. Everything that he'd been trying to convince himself about putting distance between them went right out the window.

To hell with his confusion. He liked confusion. He *loved* confusion. If this was confusion, then damn it, give him more.

He reached for her, and she slid into his arms, her fingers in his hair, on his neck, on his back, her body so supple against him, her breasts so soft.

He'd kissed her before, but never like this. It had never been this real. It had never held this promise, this achingly pure glimpse of attainable paradise.

He kissed her again and again, slowly, lazily losing himself in the soft sweetness of her mouth, deliberately taking his time, purposely not pressuring her for anything more.

These kisses were enough. He wanted her, sure, but even if they only spent the next four hours just kissing, that would be good enough. Kissing her for four hours wouldn't be taking advantage, would it?

But Syd was the one who pushed them over the line.

She moved onto his lap, straddling him. She started unfastening the buttons on his shirt. She kissed him possessively—long, hard, deep, hungry kisses that lifted him up and made him tumble with her into a breathless, passionate, turbulent place. A place where the entire world disappeared, where nothing existed but the softness of her eyes, the warmth of her body.

She pushed his shirt off his shoulders, still kissing him.

He reached to unbutton her Hawaiian shirt—his shirt—and was completely sidetracked by the softness of her body beneath the silk, by the way her breasts fit perfectly in his hands, by the desire-tightened tips of her nipples.

She moved forward on his lap, pressing the heat between her legs against his arousal, nearly making him weep all over again.

She wanted him as badly as he wanted her.

And still she kissed him, fierce kisses now, kisses that stole his breath from his lungs, that made his heart pound in his chest.

He gave up trying to unfasten her shirt and yanked it up and over her head.

She unfastened the black lace of her bra, and then her bare breasts were in his hands, in his mouth. He kissed her, tasted her, pulling back to gaze at her. Small but perfect, she was quite possibly the most exquisitely feminine woman he'd ever seen. Her shoulders were so smooth, so slender. Her collarbone and the base of her throat were works of art. And her breasts… what on earth had she been thinking to keep all that covered up all the time?

He pulled her close and kissed her again, his arms wrapped around all that amazing satiny skin, her breasts cool against his chest.

She reached between them for the buckle on his belt.

It wasn't easy to get open, but she had it unfastened and his zipper undone in a matter of seconds.

Lucky's fingers fumbled at the button on her jeans, and she pulled out of his arms to kick off her sandals, to skim her pants down her legs. He did the same with his own pants, kicking off his shoes.

"Where do you keep your condoms?" she asked huskily.

"Bathroom. In the medicine cabinet."

For some reason that surprised her. "Really?" she said. "Not in the top drawer of your bedside table, next to your water bed?"

He had to laugh. "I hate to break it to you, but I don't have a water bed."

"No lava lamp?"

He shook his head, grinning at her like an idiot. "And nary a single black light, either. My apologies. As a bachelor pad, it's definitely lacking."

She took it in stride. "I suppose not having a water bed is better than not having any condoms." She was naked and so incredibly beautiful as she stood there, looking down at him. "As appealing an idea as it is to get it on right here on the kitchen floor, do you suppose if I went into your bedroom via a quick stop in the bathroom, I could convince you to follow me?"

The bedroom. The bedroom suddenly made this all so real. Lucky had to ask. "Syd, are you sure...?"

She gave him her 'I don't believe you' look. "I'm standing here naked, Luke, about to fetch a condom from your bathroom so that you and I can have raw, screaming sex. If that's not an unequivocal yes, I don't know what is."

"Raw, screaming sex," he repeated, his mouth suddenly dry.

"Wildly passionate, deliriously orgasmic, exquisitely

delicious, savage, pounding, rapture-inducing, sweaty, nasty, scorchingly ecstatic, heart-stopping, brain-meltingly raw, screaming sex." She gave him a very innocent smile. "You up for it?"

Lucky could only nod yes. His vocal cords had seized up. But his legs were working.

Somehow she managed to beat him into his bedroom. She tossed the condom on his bedside table and knelt on his bed, her gaze skimming his nearly naked body. She looked rather pointedly at his briefs. "Are you planning to keep those on?"

"I didn't want to scare you," he said modestly.

She laughed, just as he'd hoped she would.

"Come here," she said.

He did, and she kissed him as she pulled him back with her onto his bed.

The sensation of her naked body beneath his, of the silkiness of her legs intertwined with his was one he'd fantasized about often. Lucky had been with many, many women and found fantasy better than reality. But that wasn't so with Syd. In his fantasies about her, he hadn't even scratched the surface of how good it would feel to be with her this way, because it went so far beyond mere physical pleasure.

He loved the way her eyes lit up, the way she smiled at him as if making love to him was the most fun she'd ever had in her entire life.

He ran his hands down her back to the curve of her rear end. She was all his, and he laughed aloud as he touched her. He couldn't get enough of touching her.

He parted her legs with gentle pressure from his thighs, and as he kissed her, he ran his hand from her breasts to her stomach and lower, cupping her, touching her lightly at first. She was so slick and hot, it was dizzying. She opened herself to him, lifting her hips and pushing his exploring fingers more deeply inside her.

"I think now would be a very good time for you to lose the briefs," she breathed, tugging at his waistband.

He helped her peel them off, and she sighed her approval. He shut his eyes as her hand closed around him.

"I guess you don't scare easily," he murmured.

"I'm terrified," she told him, lowering her head and kissing him.

Her mouth was warm and wet and so soft, and sheer pleasure made fireworks of color explode behind his closed eyes.

And Lucky couldn't wait. He pulled her beneath him, cradling himself between her legs, his body so beyond ready for her that he was trembling.

Condom. Man, he'd nearly forgotten the condom. He reached for it on the bedside table, where she'd put it, tearing open the wrapper as he rolled off her and quickly covered himself.

But he didn't get a chance to roll back on top of her, because Syd straddled him. With one smooth move, she drove him deeply inside her.

If he'd been prone to heart attacks, he'd be a dead man.

Fortunately, his heart was healthy despite the fact it was going at about four hundred beats per minute.

Wild, she'd said. Passionate. Delirious...

Lucky couldn't tell where he ended and Syd began. They moved together, perfectly in sync, kissing, touching, breathing.

Delicious, savage, pounding...

He rolled them both over so that he was on top, so that he had control of their movement. He moved faster and harder and she liked it all, her body straining to meet him, to take him even more deeply inside her, her kisses feeding his fire.

He was slick with sweat, her body plastered exquisitely to him as they rolled once more, bringing Syd back on top. She pushed herself up so she sat astride him, her breasts glistening with perspiration, her damp hair clinging to her face as she threw her head back and laughed.

She looked down at him. "Is it just me, or is this amazingly, incredibly good?"

"Good," he managed to say. "Amazingly…"

She was moving slowly now, and each stroke took him closer and closer to the edge.

She was smiling at him, and he reached up and touched her, her face, her throat, her breasts, and he felt the start of her release. She held his gaze and breathed his name on a low, throaty sob of air that was without a doubt the sexiest sound he'd ever heard.

He pulled her close and kissed her as his own release rocketed through him.

It was heart-stopping. It *was* brain-melting. It was rapture and ecstasy.

But it wasn't sex.

It was making love, because, damn it, he was in love with her.

CHAPTER TWELVE

"NOTHING'S CHANGED," LUKE SAID, tracing circles around her belly button, head propped up on one elbow as he and Syd lay among his rumpled sheets.

They'd slept for about five hours, and the sun was high in the sky. Luke had put in a call to the hospital—nothing had changed with Lucy's condition, either.

"I really don't want to use you as bait," he continued. "I honestly don't think I can do it, Syd."

His hair was charmingly rumpled, and for the first time since they'd met, he was in need of a shave. It was amazing, really, but not entirely unexpected—even his stubble was golden.

She touched his chin, ran her thumb across his incredible lips. "So what do we do?"

"Pretend to break up."

"Pretend?" she asked, praying that he wouldn't be able to tell that her heart was in her throat. She couldn't bear to look at him.

"I don't want this to end," he told her. "But I need you to be safe."

It was an excuse. Had to be. Because, like he'd said, nothing really had changed. Breaking up with him wouldn't make her any safer.

"Look," she said, pulling away from him and covering herself with the sheet. She tried hard to keep her voice light. "I think it's pretty obvious that neither of us expected this to happen. We've had a tough couple of days and things just kind of got out of hand and—"

Luke laughed in disbelief. "Is that really what you think this was? Things getting out of hand?"

Syd staunchly forced herself to meet his gaze. "Wasn't it?"

"No," he said flatly. "And as far as neither of us expecting this, well, *I* sure as hell did. I planned for it. I counted on it. I *wanted* it." He kissed her hard, on the mouth. "I wanted you. I *still* want you. But more than that, I want you to be safe."

Syd was dizzy. "You *planned*…"

"I've been hot for you for weeks, baby cakes."

"We've only known each other a few weeks."

"Exactly."

Syd was looking into his eyes, and she believed him. My God, she really believed him. *I've been hot for you for weeks….* She had no idea. Except for all the times he'd kissed her. Playing the pretend girlfriend game, he'd called it. Those kisses had seemed so real.

"I thought you were making up some stupid excuse to break up because you didn't want me around," she admitted. "I thought…"

He knew what she'd thought. "That this was just a one-nighter?" He flopped back on the pillows, staring up at the ceiling. "You honestly thought I'd do that to you? After you told me about…the football player who shall remain nameless because the mere mention of his name enrages me?"

"Well…"

He lifted his head to look at her, his eyes suddenly sharp. "Did *you* mean for this to be a one-nighter?"

"I didn't think it would ever really happen," she told him honestly. "I mean, until it was happening, and then…"

She didn't know what to tell him. "We probably shouldn't have done this, because it's really going to screw up our friendship. You know, I really like you, Luke. I mean, as a friend..."

Oh, brother, could she sound any more stupid? And she was lying, too, by great big omission. Yeah, she really liked him as a friend, but she loved him as a lover, too.

Loved.

L-O-V-E-D.

As in, here, take my heart and crush it into a thousand tiny pieces. As in, here, take my heart and leave me here, emotionally bleeding to death as you move on to bigger and better things. As in, here, take my heart even though you don't really want it.

It was stupid, really. *She* was stupid. She'd realized it when she was having sex with the guy. The fact that she *was* having sex with the guy should have been a dead giveaway that she'd fallen for him in the first place. But, no, she had been too dumb to realize that those warm feelings she felt every time she looked at Luke O'Donlon were far more than feelings of friendship.

She'd gone and let herself fall in love with a Ken doll. Except, Luke wasn't really plastic. He was real, and he was perfect. Well, not *perfect* perfect, but perfect for *her.* Perfect except for the fact that he didn't do serious—he'd warned her about that himself—and that his usual girl-friends had had larger bra sizes back when they were twelve than Syd had now.

Perfect except for the fact that, if she let him, he *would* crush her heart into a thousand tiny pieces. Not intention-ally. But it didn't have to be intentional to hurt.

"I like you, too," he told her quietly. "But as more than a friend. *Way* more."

When he said things like that, lying back in his bed,

naked and gorgeous, all blue eyes and golden hair and
tan skin, it was like playing her older sister's Mystery
Date game and opening the door to the picture of the
perfect, blond, tuxedo-clad young Mr. Right. It was like
finding the "win a free year's supply" coupon in her bag of
M&M's. It was like living the perfect Hollywood movie,
the kind of romantic comedy that ended with two complete
opposites in each other's arms, locked in a kiss. The kind
of romantic comedy that ended way before the divorce two
years later.

Divorce. God, what was she thinking? It wasn't as if
Luke had asked her to marry him. There was a long, long
road between, "Honey, I like you as more than a friend,"
and "Will you marry me?"

Syd cleared her throat. "It won't make any difference
if we pretend to break up," she told him, "because our
guy has gone after ex-girlfriends, too, remember? He's
not picky. I wouldn't be any safer."

"You would be if you left town," he countered.

She was dumbstruck. "You want me to leave town?"

"Yeah." He was serious.

"No. No way. Absolutely not." Syd couldn't sit still, so
she leapt out of bed. "I'm part of this task force, part of
your team, remember?"

She was standing there naked, glaring at him, and she
grabbed the sheet from the bed and wrapped it around
herself.

Luke was trying not to smile. "I don't know," he said.
"The argumentative stance worked better for me without
the sheet."

"Don't change the subject, because I'm not leaving."

"Syd, baby, I've been trying to think of another way
this could work and—"

"Don't you dare *baby* me! Sheesh, sleep with a guy

once, and he thinks he's got the right to tell you what to do! Sleep with a guy once, and suddenly you're in Patronizing City! I'm *not* leaving town, *Luke, baby,* so just forget about it!"

"All right!" His temper snapped, too, and he sat forward, the muscles in his shoulders taut as he pushed himself up. "Great. I'll forget about it. I'll forget about the fact that the thought of you ending up in a hospital bed in a coma like Lucy is making me *freaking crazy!*"

He was serious. He really was scared to death for her. As Syd gazed into his eyes, her anger instantly deflated. She sat on the edge of the bed, wishing she could compromise, but knowing that this was one fight she had to win.

"I'm sorry," she said, reaching for him. "But I can't leave, Luke. This story is too important to me."

"Is it really worth risking your life?"

She touched his hair, his shoulder, traced the definition of the powerful muscles in his arm. "You're a fine one to talk about risking your life and whether a job is worth it."

"I'm trained for it," he said. "You're not. You're a writer."

She met his gaze. "And what if I never wrote anything that I thought was important? What if I always played it safe? I could be very safe, you know, and write copy for the back of cereal boxes. Do you really think that's what I should do for the rest of my life?"

It was hard for him, but he shook his head, no.

"I have a great opportunity here," she told him. "There's a job I really, really want as an editor and staff writer of a magazine I really, *really admire. Think* Magazine."

"I've never heard of it," Luke admitted.

"It's targeted to young women," Syd told him, "as kind

of an alternative to all those fashion magazines that tell you that you need to make yourself beautiful and thin if you want to win Mr. Right's heart—and also send you the message that you'll never be beautiful enough or thin enough."

"Is that your dream job?" he asked. "To write for this magazine?"

"My *dream* job is to write a book. I'd love to be able to afford to take a year or two and try writing fiction," she admitted. "But at the rate I'm saving, I'm going to be ninety before that happens. I either have to win the lottery or find a patron. And the odds of either of those things happening is like four billion to one. This job with *Think* is the next best thing." They'd somehow gotten off the topic. "This story," Syd said, steering them back onto track, "when I write it, is going to help me get that job. But that's just part of why I don't want to leave, Luke. You need to understand—the other part is intensely personal. The other part comes from knowing that I can help catch this guy. *I can help!*"

"You've already helped," he told her.

"If I leave, you're back to square one. You've got to start from scratch. Establish a new relationship—with whom, Luke? Some policewoman? You don't think that would look really suspicious? You don't think this guy pays attention to things like that? A guy who probably follows his victim around for days, searching for patterns, learning her schedule, watching for times when she's all alone...?"

She had him, and she knew it, as he flopped back onto the bed, put his arm over his eyes and swore.

"He's probably too smart, too suspicious to come near me anyway," she told him.

He lifted his arm to look at her. "You don't believe that

any more than I do." He reached for her, pulling her close, holding her tightly. "Promise me you won't go *any*where by yourself. Promise you'll always make sure someone from the team is watching you."

"I promise," Syd said.

"I'm talking about running down to the convenience store for some milk. It doesn't happen until we catch this guy, do you understand? I'm either right here, right next to you, or Bobby's breathing down your neck."

"I got it," Syd said. "Although, personally, I'd prefer *you* breathing down my neck."

"That can definitely be arranged." He kissed her, hard. "You *will* be safe. I'm going to make *damn* sure of it."

He kissed her again—her throat, her breasts, her stomach, moving even lower, his breath hot against her skin. That wasn't her neck he was breathing down, but Syd didn't bother to tell him. She figured he probably knew.

She closed her eyes, losing herself in the torrents of pleasure that rushed past her, over her, through her. Pleasure and emotion—thick, rich, *deep* emotion that surrounded her completely and made her feel as if she were drowning.

When it came to the things Luke O'Donlon could make her feel, she was in way over her head.

SOUNDS OF LAUGHTER RANG from Lucy McCoy's hospital room.

Hope expanded inside Lucky as he ran the last few steps and pushed open the door and...

He stopped short, and Syd, who was right behind him, bumped into him.

Lucy still lay motionless in her hospital bed, breathing with the help of a respirator.

But she was surrounded by her friends. The room was

filled with women. Veronica Catalanotto sat by Lucy's
bed and held her hand. Mia Francisco sat nearby, using
her enormously rounded belly as a table for a bowl of raw
vegetables, her legs propped up on another chair. Melody
Jones, Cowboy's wife, was perched on the windowsill, her
feet bare, next to Mitch Shaw's wife, Becca, who'd kept on
her cowboy boots. It figured they'd sit together, be close
friends. They both looked like something out of a very
wholesome country music video.

Melody waved at him. "Hey, Lucky. I was just tell-
ing Wes that my sister, Brittany, came out here with me.
She and Andy, my nephew, are watching the kids, so that
Ronnie and I can both be here. I was just suggesting that
as long as Brittany's in town, we try to set her up with
Wesley."

Lucky realized that Wes Skelly was in the room, too,
sitting on the floor by Lucy's bed, next to Nell Hawken,
Crash's wife. They both had their backs to the wall.

Wes rolled his eyes. "Why is it always me?" he com-
plained. "Why don't you women torment Bobby for a
change?"

"For a change?" Bobby deadpanned. He was there,
too, sitting cross-legged in front of young Tasha, who
was putting his long black hair into dozens of braids of
varying sizes.

There was more laughter, and Veronica leaned over
Lucy, as if she were hoping for something. A smile. A
movement. A twitch. She looked up, caught Lucky watching her and shook her head. Nothing. The strain that was
just below the surface on all of their faces showed through
at the tight edges of her mouth.

But she forced a smile. "Hey, Lucy, Lucky's here with
Syd." She looked around the room. "Who here hasn't
met Sydney Jameson? Brace yourself, ladies, no fainting

please, I know we all thought it would never happen, but our Luke has been smitten at last. Syd's moving in with him."

The noise of all those female voices talking at once as introductions were made and congratulations given—along with hugs and kisses—should have been enough to wake the dead, but Lucy still didn't move.

And Syd was embarrassed. Lucky met her eyes, and knew exactly what she was thinking. The moving in together thing wasn't real. It was part of the girlfriend game. Despite the fact that their relationship had become intimate, he *hadn't* asked her to move in with him.

And she hadn't accepted.

He tried to imagine asking such a thing. How did a man go about it? It wasn't a marriage proposal, so there wasn't any need to get down on your knees, was there? Would you do it casually? While you were making dinner? Or maybe over breakfast? "Hey, babe, by the way…it's occurred to me that as long as you're here all the time…"

It didn't seem very romantic, far more like a convenience than a commitment.

PJ Becker stuck her head in the door. "O'Donlon. About time you graced us with your appearance. Anyone in here given him a sit-rep yet?"

"Situation report," Tasha told Syd. "They talk in code, but don't worry. You'll learn it in no time."

"Well, I found out that Melody wants to set Wes up with her sister," Lucky said to PJ, "but I doubt that's what you meant."

"Mitch left last night," Mitch's wife Becca said quietly. "As soon as Admiral Robinson called. He's going to find Blue, and send him back here, but it's probably going to take some time."

"We've decided to take turns sitting with Lucy,"

Veronica reported. "One of us is going to be here around the clock until Blue gets back. We've worked out a schedule."

"Her doctor said it was good if we talked to her and held her hand—tried to establish some kind of contact," Nell Hawken, Crash's wife, blond and delicately pretty, added. "We thought we'd try getting together—all of us, like this—in the early evening, right before dinnertime. We figured we'd have sort of a party, tell stories and talk— see if maybe Lucy would want to wake up and join us."

"So far it hasn't worked," Mia said, "but we've just got to be patient. The doctor said the procedure they did to relieve the pressure from the subdural injury has made the swelling go down significantly. That's a good sign."

It was amazing. Lucky was standing in a room filled with beautiful women—the wives of some of his best friends in the world. He'd had crushes on most of them at one time or another, and he'd never dated anyone—even the illustrious Miss Georgia—that he didn't compare to them and find lacking.

Until now.

Until Syd, with her sleek dark hair, and her heart-shaped face. He'd made her wear another of his shirts today—one that was missing the top two buttons, and the collar gapped open, revealing her throat and her incredibly delicate collarbones.

But the truth was, it wasn't her body that put her into the same league as these incomparable women he adored. It was her sense of humor, her sharp wit, her brilliance— all of which shone clearly through in her incredible smile and her amazing brown eyes.

Across the room, Melody Jones slid down off the windowsill, slipping her feet into a pair of sneakers. "I better get back. Tyler's probably driving my sister nuts." She looked at Veronica. "Take your time coming over, Ron. Frankie will be fine. In fact, he can just spend the night in the baby's room, if you want."

"Thanks," Veronica said. "That would be great."

Melody turned to Becca. "You don't need a ride, right? You've got your own car...?"

On the other side of the room, Nell stood up and stretched. "I've got to go, too. I'll be back tomorrow, Lucy."

"Whoa," Lucky said, blocking the door. "Wait a minute. Where are you going?"

"Home," they said in unison.

"No, you're not," he said. "There's no way in *hell* I'm letting *any* of you just go home. You're all potential targets. You're not walking out of here without protection."

Melody looked at Veronica. Veronica looked at Nell and Becca. Mia stood up gracefully—no small feat—and they all turned to look at her.

"He's right," she said.

God, it was a logistical nightmare. All these women going in all these different directions....

Melody didn't look convinced. "It's not like I'm alone at home. My sister and the kids are there."

"And *I* certainly don't need protection," PJ added.

"My ranch is *way* out of town," Becca said. "I'm not really worried."

Mutiny. No way was he going to let them mutiny. Lucky bristled, ready to let them know in no uncertain terms that they were *all*, star FInCOM agent PJ Becker included, going to follow the law that he was about to lay down.

But Syd put her hand on his arm.

"*I'm* worried," she said to the other women. She looked down at Lucy, lying there so still and silent in that bed.

"And I'm betting that if Lucy really can hear everything we're saying, that *she's* worried, too."

She leaned over the bed. "This would be a really perfect time for you to wake up, detective," she continued, "because your friends need a crash course in exactly who this monster is we're all up against. Of course, if you don't mind, I can speak for you. I saw the way he came into your house through a locked living-room window—the way he bypassed your fancy alarm system."

Syd looked up, looked directly at Melody. "I saw the blood in your bed and on your bedroom wall—your blood."

She looked at Becca and her voice shook. "I saw the second-story window you dove through, risking a broken neck from the fall, because you knew that if he got his hands around your throat again, he *would* kill you."

She looked at PJ through the tears that brimmed in her eyes. Her voice was just a whisper now. "And I saw the gun you kept just under your bed, thinking that it—and your training as a police detective—made you safe. The gun you never even got a chance to use."

The room was dead silent.

Syd looked around at all of them. "If you're still not worried, think about your husbands. Think about the men who love you receiving the same awful message that Blue McCoy's going to get in just a few days, in just a few hours. Think about Blue, finding out that he may have lost Lucy forever."

"Oh, my God," Veronica breathed. "Lucy just squeezed my hand!"

CHAPTER THIRTEEN

SYD PACED.

And when she looked at the clock again, it was only six minutes past one—just two minutes later than it had been the *last* time she'd looked.

Luke's house was so silent.

Except, that is, for the booming sound of her pounding heart.

This must be the way it felt to be a worm, stuck on the end of a fishing hook. Or a mouse slipped into a snake trap.

Of course, Luke and Bobby and Thomas and Rio and Mike were hidden in the yard. They were watching all sides of the house, and listening in via strategically placed microphones.

"Damn," she said aloud. "I wish these mikes were two-way. I could use a little heated debate right about now, guys. Fight, flee or surrender. I realized there was an option we haven't discussed—hide. Anyone for *hide?* I'm telling you, those are some really tough choices. Right now it's all I can do to choose between Rocky Road or Fudge Ripple."

The phone rang.

Syd swore. "All right," she said as it rang again. "I know." She wasn't supposed to watch TV or listen to music. Or talk. They couldn't hear potential sounds of forced entry if she was talking. "Roger that, Lieutenant O'Donlon. I'll behave, I promise."

The phone stopped right in the middle of the third ring.

And Syd was alone once again with the silence.

The past few days had been crazy. Luke had worked around the clock to set up a safe house for the wives of the SEALs who were out of town. He and PJ Becker had organized teams of security guards and drivers who would take the women to and from the hospital and wherever else they needed to go. After Syd's little speech at the hospital, no one was complaining.

Luke also rode the police and FInCOM, trying to get them to work faster in picking up the men who were on the likely suspects list Lucy had helped compile. So far, they'd only picked up six of the men on the list—most of whom had had strong alibis for a good number of the attacks. The others had willingly volunteered to submit DNA samples, and so far, none had matched.

Luke also gave interviews to TV reporters, looking splendid in his gleaming white Navy Ken uniform, saying things guaranteed to enrage—or at least annoy—the man they were after. Come and get me, he all but said. Just *try* to come and get me or mine.

He sat by Lucy's bed and held her hand, hoping that Blue would be found soon, and praying with the rest of them that that single hand-squeeze hadn't been just a muscle spasm—the explanation the doctors had offered.

At night, he'd kiss Syd goodbye with real trepidation in his eyes and he'd leave her alone, pretending to help with BUD/S training, but in truth sneaking back to help guard her as she sat here in silence and alone—as serial rapist bait.

At 1:30 or 2:00 a.m., he'd return through the front door and fall into bed, completely exhausted.

But never too exhausted to make exquisite love to her.

The phone rang. Syd nearly jumped through the roof, then instantly berated herself. It wasn't as if the San Felipe Rapist were going to call her on the phone, was it?

She glanced again at the clock. It was quarter after one in the morning. It had to be Lucky. Or Bobby. Or maybe it was Veronica, calling from the hospital with news about Lucy.

Please, God, let it be good news.

It rang again, and she picked it up. "Hello?"

"Syd." The voice was low and male and unrecognizable.

"I'm sorry," she said briskly. "Who's—"

"Is Lucky there?"

The hair on the back of her neck went up. Dear God, what if it *were* the rapist, calling to make sure she was alone?

"No, sorry." She kept her voice steady. "He's teaching tonight. Who's calling?"

"It's Wes."

Chief Wes Skelly. That information didn't make her feel any better. In fact, it made her even more tense. Wes—who smelled just like the man who'd nearly run her down on the stairs after brutally attacking Gina. Wes—who had the same hair, same build, same accentless voice. Wes, who was—according to Bobby—having a rough year.

How rough, exactly?

Rough enough to completely lose it? Rough enough to turn into a homicidal maniac?

"Are you safe there, all by yourself?" Wes asked. He sounded odd, possibly drunk.

"I don't know," she said. "Maybe you should tell me."

"No," he said. "No, you're not safe. Why don't you go to this safe house thing and stay with Ronnie and Melody?"

"I think you probably know why I'm not there." Syd's heart was pounding again. She knew Luke didn't believe Wes could be the attacker, but she didn't have years of camaraderie to go on. Frankly, Wes Skelly spooked her, with his barbed-wire tattoo and his crew-cut hair. Whenever she saw him, he was grimly quiet, always watching, rarely smiling.

"What?" he said. "You *wanna* go one on one with this guy?" He laughed. "Figures a woman who thinks she's going to get any kind of commitment from Lucky O'Donlon's a little wacky in the head."

"Hey," she said indignantly. "I resent that—"

He hung up abruptly, and she swore. So much for keeping her cool, keeping him talking, for coaxing a confession out of him.

"Luke, that was Wes on the phone," she told the listening microphones as she dropped the receiver into the cradle on the wall. "He was looking for you, and he sounded really strange."

Silence.

The entire house was silent.

The phone didn't ring again, nothing moved, nothing made a sound.

If this were a movie, Syd thought, the camera would cut to the outside of the house, to the places where Luke and Bobby and the SEAL candidates were completely hidden. And the camera would reveal their unconscious faces and the ropes that bound them—that would keep them from coming to her rescue when she needed them.

And she *would* need them.

The camera would pull back to show the shadowy shape of a very muscular man with Wes's short hair, with Wes's wide shoulders, creeping across the yard, toward the house.

Bad image. *Bad* image. Syd shook her head, cleared her throat. "Um, Luke, I'm a little spooked, will you please call me?"

Silence.

The phone didn't ring. She stared at it, and it *still* didn't ring.

"Luke, I'm sorry about this, but I'm serious," Syd said. "I just need to know that you're out there and—"

She heard it. A scuffling noise out back.

Flee.

The urge to run was intense, and she scurried for the living room. But the front door was bolted shut—for her own protection—and she didn't have the key. Last night that bolt had made her feel safe. Now it didn't. Now she was trapped.

"I hear a noise outside, guys," she said, praying that she was wrong, that Luke was still listening in. "Out back. Please be listening."

The front windows were painted shut, and the glass looked impossibly thick. How had Lucy managed to break through her bedroom window?

She heard the noise again, closer to the back door this time. "Someone's definitely out there."

Fight.

She turned around in a full circle, looking for something, *any*thing with which to arm herself. Luke didn't have a fireplace, so there were no fireplace pokers. There was nothing, *nothing*. Only a newspaper she could roll up. Perfect—provided the attacker was a bad dog.

"Any time, Luke," she said. *"Please."*

Baseball bat. Luke had told her he'd played in high school, that he still sometimes went over to the batting cages on the west side of San Felipe.

He didn't have a garage, didn't have a basement. Where would a guy without those things keep a baseball bat?

Front closet.

Syd scrambled for the closet, threw open the door.

It was filled with U.S. Navy-issue overcoats of all weights and sizes. She pushed through to the back and found...

Fishing poles.

And lacrosse sticks.

A set of lawn darts.

And three different baseball bats.

She grabbed one as she heard the kitchen door creak open.

Hide.

Hiding suddenly seemed the most intelligent option, and she slipped into the closet, silently closing the door behind her.

Her palms were sweating, and her mouth was dry, and her heart was beating so loudly she couldn't hear anything else.

She gripped the baseball bat as tightly as she could and prayed. Please God, whatever happened to her, don't let Luke be badly hurt. Don't let them find him hidden in the backyard, with his throat slit, staring sightlessly up at the sky and...

Whoever was inside the house wasn't trying to be quiet anymore. Footsteps went down the hall toward the bedroom, and then faster, heading back. She heard the bathroom door slam open, heard, "Syd? *Syd!*"

It was Luke. That was Luke's voice. Relief made her

knees give out, and she sat down hard, right there in the closet, knocking over fishing poles and lacrosse sticks and God knows what else.

The closet door was yanked open and there was Luke. The panic in his eyes would have been sweet if her relief hadn't morphed instantly into anger.

"What the hell did you think you were doing?" She nearly came out of the closet swinging that bat. "You damn near scared me to *death!*"

"I scared *you?*" He was just as mad as she was. "God, Syd, I came in here and you were gone! I thought—"

"You should have called me, told me you would be here early," she said accusingly.

"It's not *that* early," he countered. "It's nearly 0130. What's early about that?"

It was. The clock on the VCR said 1:27.

"But…" Syd regrouped, thinking fast. Why had she been so frightened? She pointed toward the kitchen. "You came in through the back door. You always come in through the front—which was locked with a deadbolt, you genius! If you *had* been the San Felipe Rapist, I would have been trapped!"

She had him with that one. It stopped him cold and doused his anger. He looked at the lock on the door and then at her. She could see him absorbing the baseball bat that still dangled from her hand. She watched him notice the fact that she was still shaking, notice the tears that were threatening to spill from her eyes.

Damn it, she *wasn't* going to cry in front of him.

"My God," he said. "You don't have a key? Why the hell don't you have a key?"

Syd shook her head, unable to say anything, using all her energy to keep from crying.

Luke *wasn't* lying dead in the backyard. Thank God.

Frowning, he looked down at his belt, and pulled his cell phone free. It was shaking silently. He flipped it open, switched it on. "O'Donlon." He listened then said, "Yeah. We're both okay. She got…" He looked at her.

"Scared," Syd said, shakily lowering herself onto the couch. "I was scared. You can say it. I admit it."

"She didn't know it was me coming in," Luke said into his phone, "and she opted for the *hide* solution to the nightmare scenario." He looked at the baseball bat. "With maybe a little *fight* thrown in." He took a deep breath, running his other hand back through his hair, making it stand on end. "I came in, couldn't find her and—" He froze. He stood absolutely, completely still. "It's not?"

Syd's pulse was just starting to drop below one hundred, but something in his voice made it kick into higher gear again. "What's not?" she asked.

Luke turned to look at her. "Thomas says he heard your requests for a phone call, but that he couldn't get through. He said he called twice before he realized he couldn't hear the phone ringing over the microphones. Something's wrong with the phone."

Syd stared at him. "I got a phone call just a few minutes ago. Wes called, looking for you."

"Wes called *here?*"

"Yeah," Syd said. "Didn't you hear at least my side of the conversation?"

"I must've been already circling back," he said, "driving home—pretending I was coming from the base." He held out his hand to her. "Come here. I want you near me until we check this out."

Syd took his hand and he pulled her up from the couch as he spoke to Thomas once again. "Stay in position. Full alert. I want eyes open and brains working."

"This is probably nothing," he said to Syd, but she knew he didn't believe that.

The lights were still on in the kitchen. Everything looked completely normal. There were a few dirty dishes in the sink, a newspaper open to the sports page on the kitchen table.

As Syd watched, Luke picked up the telephone and put the receiver to his ear.

He looked at Syd as he hung it up, as he spoke once more to Thomas over his cell phone. "Phone's dead. Stay in position. I'm calling for backup."

A CLEAN CUT.

Probably with a knife, possibly with a scissors.

Lucky sat on his living-room sofa, trying to rub away his massive headache by massaging his forehead.

It wasn't working.

Somehow, someone had gotten close enough to the house tonight to cut the phone wire. Somehow, the son of a bitch had gotten past two experienced Navy SEALs and three bright, young SEAL candidates who had been looking for him.

He hadn't gone inside, but his message had been clear.

He could have.

He'd been right there, just on the other side of a wall from Sydney. If he'd wanted to, he could've gone in, used that knife to kill her as dead as the phone and been gone before Lucky had ever reached the back door.

The thought made him sick to his stomach.

As the FInCOM and police members of the task force filtered through his house, Lucky sat with Syd on the couch, his arm securely around her shoulder—he didn't give a damn who saw.

"I'm sorry," he told her for the fourteenth time. "I've been trying to figure out how he got past us."

"It's all right," she said.

"No, it's not." He shook his head. "We were distracted pretty much all night. It started around 0050 when Bobby got a page from Lana Quinn. She sent him an urgent code, so he called her back. The rest of us were watching the house—it should have been no big deal. So Bob calls Lana, who tells him that Wes just came by her place, completely skunked. Wes told her he needed to talk, but then left without saying anything. She managed to get his keys away from him, but he walked to a nearby bar—a place called Dandelion's. She followed because she was worried, and sure enough, as soon as he got there, he tried to start a bar fight. She stepped in and he backed down, but he wouldn't leave with her. So she called Bobby."

Lucky sighed. "Bobby called Frisco, but he's got Mia and Tasha to worry about, he can't just leave them home alone. Meanwhile, it's getting later and later. Lana's paging Bobby again, telling him she lost Wes in the crowd at Dandelion's, and now she's not sure *where* he's gone and—"

"Wait a minute," Syd said. "Lana *lost* Wes?"

"Well, no, not really," Lucky told her. "She thought she'd lost him for about twenty minutes, but he was only in the men's."

"He was in the men's room for twenty minutes?"

Lucky bristled. "No," he said. "I know what you're implying and *no*."

She held his gaze. "Dandelion's is only about a four-minute drive from here."

"Wes is not a suspect."

"I'm sorry, Luke, but he's still on *my* list."

"Lana took the keys to his bike."

"A clever move," she countered. "Particularly if he

wanted to establish an alibi and convince everyone that he'd actually been in the men's room for all that time—instead of here at your house, at the exact time your phone wire was cut during a distraction that he knew about."

Lucky shook his head. "No," he said. "Syd, you've got to go with me on this one. It's *not* Wes. It can't be. You've got to trust me."

She gazed at him, looking into his eyes. She'd been scared tonight, badly. When she'd come out of that closet, that was the closest Lucky had ever seen her come to losing it. She was tough, she was strong, she was smart and she was as afraid of all this as he was. And that made her desire to catch this bastard that much crazier. Crazier and completely admirable.

She nodded. "Okay," she said. "If you're that certain... he's off my list. It's not Wes."

She wasn't humoring him, wasn't being patronizing. She was accepting—on faith—something that he believed in absolutely. She trusted him that much. It was a remarkably good feeling. *Remarkably* good.

Lucky kissed her. Right in front of the task force, in front of Chief Zale.

"Tomorrow," he said, "I'll talk to Wes. See if he wouldn't mind voluntarily giving us a DNA sample, just so we can run it by the lab and then officially take him off the suspect list."

"I don't need you to do that," she said.

"I know." He kissed her again, trying to make light of it despite the tight feeling that was filling his chest from the inside out. "Pissing off Wes Skelly while he's got a killer hangover isn't my idea of fun. But hey, I don't have anything else to do tomorrow."

"Tomorrow," Syd reminded him, "your sister's getting married."

CHAPTER FOURTEEN

LUKE O'DONLON CRIED AT his little sister's wedding.

It wasn't a surprise to Syd. In fact, she would have been surprised if he *hadn't* cried.

He looked incredible in his dress uniform—nearly as good, in fact, as he looked naked.

Ellen, his sister, was as dramatically gorgeous as he was, except while he was golden, she was dark-haired and mocha-skinned. Her new husband, Gregory Price, however, was completely average looking, completely normal—right down to his slightly thinning hair and the glasses.

Syd stood at the edge of the restaurant dance floor, one of a very small number of relatives and intimate friends of the bride and groom, and watched as the newlyweds danced.

Greg made Syd feel slightly better about herself. If he could dare to *marry* Ellen, then Syd—also extremely average looking—could certainly have a fling with Luke.

"Have I told you how incredibly beautiful you look tonight?"

Syd turned around to give Luke an arched eyebrow. "That's slinging it a little thick, don't you think?"

She knew what she looked like. Her dress was black and basic, and yes, maybe it did hide her imperfections and accentuate the better parts of her figure, but it was a simple illusion. And yes, she *had* taken time with her hair and had even put on a little makeup this evening, but she was, at best, interestingly pretty. Passable. Accept-able. But not even remotely close to *incredibly* anything, particularly not beautiful.

Luke actually looked surprised. "You think I'm—" He caught himself, and laughed. "Uh-uh," he said. "Nope. No way. I'm not going to let you pick a fight with me over the fact that I think you look great."

He pulled her close and kissed her, surprising her by giving her a private kiss instead of a public one. It was one of those kisses that melted her bones, turned her to jelly, and left her dizzy, dazed and clinging to him. It was one of those kisses he gave her before he scooped her into his arms and carried her into his bedroom. It was one of those kisses he gave her when he wanted them to stop talking and start communicating in an entirely different manner. It was one of those kisses she could never, ever resist.

"I think you look incredibly beautiful tonight," he mur-mured into her ear. "Now what *you* do, is *you* say, thank you, Luke."

"Thank you, Luke," she managed.

"Was that so hard?"

He was smiling down at her, with his heavenly blue eyes and his gorgeous face and his sunstreaked hair. *He* was the one who was incredibly beautiful. It seemed im-possible that the heated look in his eyes could be real, but it was. He'd somehow pulled her onto the dance floor, and as they moved slowly in time to the music, he was holding her close enough for her to know that that kiss had done the exact opposite of turning *him* to jelly.

He wanted her.

At least for now.

"You two are so perfect together." Gregory's mother, platinum-haired, rail-thin, with a smile as warm as her son's, winked as she danced past them. "We'll be dancing at *your* wedding next, won't we, Luke?"

Oh, God. How embarrassing. Syd kept her own smile pasted on as she quickly answered for Luke, saving him— and saving herself from having to listen to him stammer and choke on his hasty negative response.

"I'm afraid it's a little too soon for that kind of prediction, Mrs. Price," she called to the other woman. "Luke and I haven't really known each other for *that* long."

"Well, it's my son's wedding, and I'm predicting wonderful things for everyone," Mrs. Price enthused. "And my predictions usually do come true."

"In that case," Syd murmured to Luke as the older woman moved out of earshot, trying to turn this into a total joke, "maybe she could predict a lottery win for me. I could really use the cash. My car's in serious need of a complete overhaul."

As she'd hoped, Luke laughed.

Crisis averted, thank God. There was nothing that created tension quite like bringing up the subject of marriage with a man who, like Luke, was commitment-shy.

Syd didn't want him looking at her and feeling the walls closing in. She didn't want him to assume that just because she was female, she wouldn't be able to resist thinking about fairy-tale endings with wedding bells and happily-ever-afters. She didn't want him thinking that *she* was even *remotely* thinking about such an impossibility as marriage.

Marriage. Syd and Luke, *married?*

It was absurd.

It was insane.

It was…

Something she couldn't keep herself from thinking about. Especially not today.

There'd been a message this afternoon on her answering machine. *Think* magazine had called from New York. The series of pieces she'd written on women's safety, along with her proposal for an in-depth article on catching serial criminals, had given buoyancy to the résumé she'd sent them months ago. In fact, it had floated right to the top of their pile of editorial candidates' résumés. They wanted her to come for an interview with their publisher and managing editor, Eileen Hess. Ms. Hess was going to be in Phoenix for a few days at a conference. Perhaps it would be more convenient for Syd to meet with her there, rather than flying all the way to New York? It would be more affordable for Syd, too. They were a small magazine, and unfortunately they couldn't afford to pay Syd's airfare.

Syd had called back to let them know that she wouldn't be able to leave California until the San Felipe Rapist was apprehended. She didn't know how long that would be, and if that meant she'd be out of the running for the job, she hoped they'd consider her in the future.

She'd found out they were willing to wait. She could fly to New York next week or even next month. This job was virtually in her pocket, if she wanted it.

If she wanted it.

Of *course* she wanted it.

Didn't she?

Luke kissed her neck, and she knew what she *really* wanted.

She wanted Luke, ready and willing to spend the rest of his life with her.

Talk about pipe dreams.

Her problem was that she had too vivid an imagination. It was far too easy for her to take this make-believe relationship and pretend it was something real.

Syd closed her eyes as he kissed her again, lightly this time, on the lips, and she knew what the real problem was.

Her problem was simply that she loved him. And when she was with him—which was damn near all the time—the lines between make-believe and reality began to blur.

Yes, they were lovers, but no, she hadn't really moved in with him. That was just pretend. Yes, he'd told his friends that he loved her, but he'd never said those words to her, and even if he did, she wasn't sure she'd believe him, Lothario that he was.

Yes, she was here with him at his sister's wedding, and yes, they looked like a real couple. But in truth, they were merely co-workers who had become friends—friends who had a good time together in bed.

To think anything else would be a mistake.

But, as Syd swayed to the music, held close in Luke's arms, she knew the mistake had already been made. She was in love with him. There was nothing left to do now except endure the coming pain. And, like the removal of a Band-Aid, doing it fast and getting it over with always hurt far less in the long run.

After they caught the rapist, she'd go to New York. As fast as she possibly could.

THE CALL CAME AS LUCKY and Syd were leaving the reception.

Ellen and Gregory had left for their honeymoon and, at nearly 2300 hours, the party was winding down.

Lucky's pager and cell phone went off simultaneously.

His first thought was a bad one—that another woman had been attacked. His second thought was that it was good news. That Lucy McCoy had come out of her coma, or that they'd found Blue and he was on his way home.

The number on the pager was Frisco's—and so was the voice on the other end of the phone.

"Hey," Frisco said. "You're there. Good news. We caught him."

It was a possibility Lucky hadn't even considered, and he nearly dropped the phone. "Repeat that."

"Martin Taus," Frisco said. "Ex-regular Navy, enlisted, served here at Coronado during the spring and summer of 1996. Discharged in late '96 with lots of little dings against him—nothing big enough to warrant a dishonorable. He served time in Nevada in early '98 for indecent exposure. He's been picked up for sexual assault at least twice before, both times he got off on a technicality. He was brought in early this evening for questioning by the San Felipe PD. He just finished making a videotaped confession about twenty minutes ago."

Syd was watching him, concern in her eyes.

"They caught the rapist," Luke told her, hardly believing it himself.

"Are they sure?" She asked the question exactly as Luke asked Frisco.

"Apparently, he's been pretty specific in describing the attacks," Frisco said. "Chief Zale's getting ready to give a press conference—just in time for the eleven o'clock news. I'm heading over to the police station. Can you meet me there?"

"I'm on my way," Lucky said, and hung up.

Syd wasn't smiling. In fact, she looked extremely skeptical. "Do they actually have evidence, tying this guy to—"

"He confessed," he told her. "Apparently in detail."

"Can we talk to him?" she asked.

"Let's go find out."

SYD TURNED OFF THE videotape and went back to her laptop computer, unable to listen for another second as the man named Martin Taus described the way he'd slammed Lucy McCoy into the wall. He knew the names of all the victims, knew the extent of their injuries. He was the right height, the right size, had the right hair—a short crew cut.

After Zale's press conference, Syd and Luke had waited for hours to see Taus, only to be told that the police were limiting the people in the interview room to the three FInCOM agents from the task force. When the police had tried to take a blood sample in order to match his DNA to that left behind during the attacks, Taus had thrown a nutty. He'd threatened a lawsuit if they so much as touched one hair on his head.

Normally, the police would get a warrant to search his home and take a hair sample from his hairbrush for the DNA test. But Taus was homeless. He lived under a bridge down by the water. He didn't even own a hairbrush.

Huang, Sudenberg and Novak were in there with him now, trying to talk him into consenting to the test. Once they succeeded, there would be a wait of a number of days before the results came in. But those results, along with Martin Taus's confession, would prove his guilt beyond a shadow of a doubt. With that confession and a guilty plea, they'd skip the trial and go straight to sentencing.

Martin Taus was going to go to jail for a long, long time.

Luke looked over Syd's shoulder at her laptop's screen. She was glad she'd made him stop at home to pick it up—at *his house,* she corrected herself—before coming to the police station last night. During all this waiting, she'd written a variety of different articles, from features to hard news, on various aspects of the case.

"Don't even *think* about reading over my shoulder," she warned him, her fingers flying over the keyboard, working on her story for *Think* magazine. She'd already sent the hard news story out electronically to the *San Felipe Journal,* and they'd called to tell her it was being picked up by *USA Today.*

"So you buy it, huh?" Luke asked. "You believe this is really our guy and, just like that, it's all over?"

"It *does* seem a little anticlimactic," she had to admit. "But real life isn't always as exciting as the movies. Personally, I prefer it *this* way." She looked up at him. "Are you finally ready to go?"

He sat down wearily next to her at the interview-room table. It had been a long night, and they were both still dressed in their formal clothes despite the fact that it was well after 8:00 a.m. "Yeah, I just wanted to see him," he said. "I just wanted to be in the same room with him for a minute. I knew if I stood there long enough, they'd eventually let me in."

"And?"

"And they did. He was…" Luke shook his head. "I don't think he's our guy."

"Luke, he *confessed.*"

"*I* could confess. That wouldn't make *me* the rapist."

"Did you even *watch* the videotape? It's chilling the way he—"

"Maybe I'm wrong," he countered. "I just…there was something that wasn't right. I was standing there, right next to him, but I couldn't put my finger on it."

"Maybe it's just lack of sleep."

"I know what lack of sleep feels like and no, it's not

helping that I'm tired, but there's something else wrong," he told her. "All I'm saying is that I'm not just going to go along with Zale and stamp the case file 'solved' until the DNA tests come back with a match."

Syd looked at him with dismay. "Luke, that could be days."

He gave her a very tired version of his best smile. "Guess you'll just have to stay at my place for a few more days. Too bad, huh?"

She saved her file and shut down her computer, closing it up. "Actually," she said, choosing her words carefully, "I was just thinking how convenient it was that Martin Taus picked last night to get himself caught, because now I can take advantage of a really excellent opportunity and drive out to Phoenix for a job interview."

He sat back in his chair, his mouth dropping open. "Since when have you been thinking about moving to Phoenix? To *Arizona?*"

"The interview's in Phoenix," she told him. "The job's in New York. Remember? *Think* magazine. I told you I'd sent them my résumé for a position as an editor and staff writer."

"New York?" He swore. "Syd, that's worse than Phoenix! You didn't say a thing about New York!"

"Well, where did you think a job like that would be?"

"Here," he said. "I thought it would be here. San Diego, maybe. God, Syd, *New York?* Do you really want to live in New York?"

"Yeah," she said. "I do."

It wasn't really lying. Because she didn't really care where she lived. Her options had been split into only two possibilities. *With Luke* was her real first choice, but completely unrealistic. And everywhere else in the world fell under the heading *without Luke*. Everywhere else was exactly the same. New York, San Diego, Chicago. They would all *feel* exactly the same—lonely as hell, at least for a while.

"Wow," Luke said, rubbing his eyes. "I'm stunned. I'm…" He shook his head. "Here I was thinking, I don't know, maybe that we had something here that was worth spending some time on."

Syd couldn't keep from laughing. "Luke. Get real. We both know exactly what we've got going. It's fun, it's great, but it's not serious. You told me yourself—you don't do serious."

"Well…what if I've changed my mind?"

"What if you only *think* you've changed your mind?" she countered gently. "And what if I give up a great career move—something I've worked for and wanted for *years*—and your 'what if' turns out to be wrong?"

He cleared his throat. "I was thinking, um, maybe you really could move in with me."

Syd couldn't believe it. Luke wanted her to move in with him? Mr. I'm-never-serious? For a nanosecond, she let herself believe it was possible.

But then he winced, giving himself away. He didn't really want her to move in with him. He just wasn't used to being the one in a relationship who got dumped. It was a competitive thing. He was grabbing on to anything—no matter how stupid an idea it was in reality—in order to keep her around temporarily, in order to win.

But once he had her, he'd soon tire of her. And she'd move out. Maybe not right away, but eventually. And then she'd be in Coronado without Luke.

The job in New York wouldn't keep her warm at night, but neither would Luke after they'd split up.

"I think," Syd said slowly, "that a decision of that

magnitude deserves a massive amount of thought. On both our parts."

"I've thought about it some," Luke said, "and I know it's not...perfect, but—"

"Think again," Syd said, her heart aching. She couldn't believe she was the one who was turning him down, but what he was saying wasn't real, she told herself. It wasn't honest. "Think about it while I'm in Phoenix."

"NEW YORK," LUCKY TOLD Lucy McCoy as he sat beside her hospital bed. "The job's in New York. Syd's having the interview right now, this morning in Phoenix, and of course she's going to get this job. I mean, who wouldn't hire her? She's brilliant, she's funny, she's a great writer, she's...she's perfect."

Lucy was silent, her brain still securely locked shut by the coma.

Lucky lifted her hand to his lips and kissed it. "Come on, Luce," he said. "Wake up. I could really use some advice."

Nothing.

He sighed. "I feel like a complete ass—both for letting her drive to Phoenix by herself in that crappy car of hers, and for—" He laughed. "God, Lucy, you're not going to believe what I did. I asked her to move in with me for real. What a jerk. I couldn't believe the words were actually coming out of my mouth. I mean, I felt so cheap, like why am I only doing this halfway?" He lowered his voice. "I love her. I do. I never really understood this thing you've got going with Blue. Or Joe with Ronnie. I mean, I could *appreciate* it, sure, but I didn't *get* it. Until I met Syd. And now it all makes sense. My entire *life* makes sense—except for the fact that Syd is going to move to New York."

"So why don't you ask her to marry you?"

Lucky jumped, turning to see Veronica standing in the door. He swore. "Ron, are you taking lessons in stealth from the Captain? Jeez, way to give a guy a heart attack."

She came into the room, sat down on the other side of the bed, taking Lucy's other hand. "Hi, Lucy, I'm back." She looked up at Lucky and smiled. "Sorry for eavesdropping."

"Like hell you are."

"So why *don't* you ask Syd to marry you?"

He couldn't answer.

Veronica answered for him. "You're afraid."

Lucky gritted his teeth and answered honestly. "I'm scared she'll turn me down, *and* I'm scared that she won't."

"Well," Veronica said in her crisp British accent. "She'll do neither—and go to New York—unless you do something drastic."

There was a commotion out in the hall, and the door was pushed open. One of the younger nurses blocked the doorway with her body. "I'm sorry, sir, but it might be best if you wait for the doctor to—"

"I talked to the doctor on the phone on my way over here from the airport." The voice from the hallway was soft but pure business, honeyed by a thick south-of-the-Mason-Dixon-Line drawl. "It's *not* best if I wait for the doctor. It's best if I go into that room and see my wife."

Blue McCoy.

Lucky stood up to see Lieutenant Commander Blue McCoy literally pick up the nurse and move her out of his way. And then he was in the room.

"Lucy." He didn't have eyes for anyone but the woman lying in the middle of that hospital bed.

Blue looked exhausted. He hadn't shaved in weeks, but

his hair was wet as if he'd taken a short shower—no doubt for sanitary purposes—moments before he'd arrived. The look on his face was terrible as he gazed down at Lucy, as he took in her bruises and cuts and the stark white bandage around her head. He sat down on the edge of her bed and took her hand.

"I'm here, Yankee," he said, his voice breaking slightly. "I'm sorry it took me so long, but I'm here now." His eyes filled with tears at her complete lack of response. "Come on, Lucy, the doctor said you're going to be just fine—all you have to do is open your eyes."

Nothing.

"I know it's going to be hard. I know you must've gone through some kind of hell, and it's probably easier to stay asleep and just not have to face it, but I'm here, and I'll help you. Whatever you need," Blue told his wife. "It's going to be okay, I promise. Together we can make anything okay."

Blue's tears escaped, and Lucky took Veronica's arm and dragged her to the door.

Captain Catalanotto was in the hallway. Veronica launched herself at her husband. "Joe!"

Joe Cat was an enormous man, and he enfolded her easily in his arms and kissed her.

No, he inhaled her. What Joe gave to Veronica was beyond a kiss. Lucky turned away, feeling as if he'd already gotten a glimpse of something far too private.

But he couldn't help but overhear Joe's rough whisper. "Are you all right?"

"I am now," Veronica told him.

"Is Lucy...?"

"Still nothing," she told him. "No response."

"What does the doctor really say?" Joe asked. "Is there really a chance she'll just wake up?"

"I hope so," she told him.

Lucky had spoken to the doctor just a few hours earlier. He turned to tell Joe that but did a quick about-face. Big, bad Joe Cat was crying as he held on tightly to his wife.

"Everything's going to be okay," he heard Veronica tell Joe through her own tears. "Now that Blue's here, now that you're here...everything's going to be okay. I know it."

And Lucky knew then exactly what he wanted. He wanted what Lucy shared with Blue. He wanted what Joe and Veronica had found.

And for the first time in his life, he thought that maybe, just *maybe* he'd found it, too.

Because when Syd was around him, everything *was* okay.

He was definitely going to do it. He was going to ask Syd to marry him.

The door at the end of the corridor opened, and the rest of Alpha Squad came in. Harvard, Cowboy and Crash. And Mitch Shaw was back, too. Lucky walked down to greet them, shooting Mitch a quizzical look.

"By the time I found them," he explained, "they'd completed their mission and were on their way out of the mountains."

"How's Lucy?" Harvard asked. "We don't want to get too close—Blue and Joe were the only ones who had time to shower."

"Lucy's still in a coma," Lucky told them. "It's kind of now-or-never time, as far as coming out of it goes. Her doctors were hoping Blue's voice would help pull her back to our side." He took a step back from them. "Jeez, you guys are ripe." They smelled like a combination of unwashed dog and stale campfire smoke.

Stale smoke...

Lucky swore. And grabbed for his phone, punching in Syd's cell phone number. Please, God, don't let her be conserving her batteries....

She picked up after only one ring. "Hello?"

"Stale cigarette smoke," Lucky said. "*That's* what's wrong with this Martin Taus guy."

"I'm sorry," Syd said. "Who's calling? Could it possibly be my insane friend Luke O'Donlon? The man who starts conversations in the middle instead of at the beginning?"

"Syd," he said. "Yes, you're funny. Thank you. Listen to me—Martin Taus isn't our guy. He's not a smoker. I stood right next to him, remember? I knew something was wrong, but I couldn't put my finger on it until two seconds ago. You said the man who nearly knocked you down the stairs smelled like Wes Skelly—like stale cigarette smoke, remember?"

There was a long silence. Then Syd laughed. "I could've been wrong. *You* could've been wrong."

"I could be," he agreed, "but I'm not. And you're not either. You need to be careful, Syd. You need to come right home." He corrected himself. "No, don't come home, come to the hospital. But don't get out of your car if the parking lot's deserted. Stay in your car, keep moving, call me on your cell phone and I'll come out to meet you, okay? God, I can't believe you talked me into letting you drive to Phoenix!"

Another long pause. "Well," she said. "I'm sure you're dying to know—my interview went really, really well."

"To hell with your interview," Lucky said in complete exasperation. "You're driving me crazy. I need you back here, I need you *safe*. Get your butt home and, and...marry me, damn it."

He looked up and found Harvard, Cowboy, Mitch and Crash all staring at him.

On the other end of the phone, Syd was equally silent.

"Wow," Lucky said. "That didn't come out quite the way I'd hoped it would."

Cowboy started to laugh, but when Harvard elbowed him hard in the chest, he fell instantly silent.

Lucky closed his eyes and turned away. "Syd, will you please come back here so we can talk?"

"Talk." Her voice sounded weak. She cleared her throat. "Yeah, that sounds smart. You're in luck. I'm nearly halfway home."

CHAPTER FIFTEEN

FIGHT, FLEE, HIDE, SUBMIT.

Hide was definitely not a working option in this scenario.

Please be there, please be there, please be there, Syd silently chanted as she dialed Lucky's number on her cell phone.

She held the steering wheel with one hand, her phone with the other as she drove. Her map was spread out on the seat beside her.

"O'Donlon."

"Luke, thank God!"

"I'm sorry, who's this?" Luke shouted. "I'm having a little trouble hearing—there's a lot of noise over here. Hang on, let me move into…" There was a pause, and then he was back, normal-voiced. "Sorry about that. Let's start over. O'Donlon."

"Luke, it's Syd. I have a little problem."

He didn't hear her. He spoke over her words as soon as he heard her voice. "Hey, excellent timing! I was just about to call you. I have some *great* news. Lucy's back! She opened her eyes about an hour after Blue arrived, and—get this! She looks at him and she goes, 'I'm bald. They had to shave my head.' Her first words after being in a coma for all that time. Typical woman—she nearly died and she's worrying about her hair. And it kills me that she knew. She must've been able to hear everything that was going on last week, because how else would she have known?"

"Luke."

"And Blue goes, 'I've always thought you'd look damn good in a crew cut, Yankee,' and it was all over. There were seven of us here—all SEALs, all crying like babies and—"

"*Luke.*"

"I'm sorry. I'm nervous. I'm talking because I'm nervous, because I'm scared to death that you called me back to tell me to go to hell."

Syd waited for a few seconds to make sure he was finally done. "I called you," she said, glancing into her rearview mirror, "because I've got a little problem. I'm out here, in the middle of nowhere, and I'm...I'm pretty sure that I'm being followed."

LUCKY'S HEART STOPPED. "This is real, right?" he said. "Not just some make-believe scenario game you're playing?"

"It's real. I noticed the car behind me about fifteen miles ago." Over the telephone, Syd's voice sounded very small. "When I slow down, he slows down. When I speed up, he speeds up. And now that I'm thinking about it, I saw this car back at the gas station, last time I stopped."

"Where are you?" he asked. His heart had started up again, but now it was lodged securely in his throat. He stuck his head out of the men's room, braving the noise out in the hospital cafeteria, waving until he caught Frisco's attention. He gestured for his swim buddy to follow him into the men's as Syd answered him.

"Route 78," she was telling him. "Just inside the California state line. I'm about forty miles south of Route 10, heading for Route 8. There's nothing out here, Luke. Not even another car, not for miles. As far as I can tell from the map, the next town isn't for another thirty miles. I tried calling the local police, but I couldn't get through. I'm not even sure what I'd say— Hi, I'm out here on the state road and there's a car behind me...? Maybe it's just a coincidence. Maybe..."

"Whatever you do," Lucky said, "don't stop. Don't pull over. Keep your car moving, Syd."

Frisco came into the men's room, curiosity on his face.

"I need the captain and the senior chief and a state map," Lucky told him. "I think Syd's being followed by the guy who put Lucy into this hospital."

Frisco had been at Chief Zale's press conference—the one in which the SFPD and FInCOM had announced that the San Felipe Rapist had been apprehended. But Frisco didn't ask any questions. He didn't waste any time. He nodded and went to get the other two men.

"SYD, I'M GOING TO figure out a way to get to you," Luke told her. "Just keep heading south and west, okay? Stay on Route 78, okay?"

Syd took a deep breath. "Okay."

"Tell me about the car behind you." He sounded so calm, so solid.

She looked in the rearview mirror. "It's dark blue. Ugly. One of those big old sedans from the late seventies and..." She realized what she was saying. Dark-colored, old-model sedan. Ugly. That was how she'd described that unfamiliar car that had been parked on her street on the night Gina was attacked.

Behind her, the car started to speed up. The driver pulled into the oncoming lane.

"He's going to pass me," Syd told Luke, filled with a flash of relief.

The dark sedan was moving faster now, moving up alongside of her.

"God, this was just my imagination," she said. "I'm so sorry, I feel so stupid and—"

The sedan was keeping pace with her. She could see the driver through the window. He was big, broad, built like a football player. His hair was short and brownish blond, worn in a crew cut.

And he had a pair of feature-distorting panty hose over his face.

Syd screamed and hit the gas, dropping the phone as her car surged forward.

"SIT-REP," LUCKY SHOUTED into his cell phone. Damn, she probably didn't remember what sit-rep was. "Syd! What's happening, damn it?"

Joe Cat and Harvard pushed their way into the men's room, their faces grim. Harvard had a map, bless him.

Lucky's voice shook as he briefly outlined the situation, as he took the map from Harvard's hands and opened it. "She's heading south on 78." He swore as he found it on the map. "What the hell is she doing on route 78? Why not 95? Why didn't she cut over to Route 8 closer to Phoenix? Why—" He took a deep breath. "Okay. I want to intercept. Fast. What are my options?" He was praying that he wasn't already too late.

The phone line was still open, and he thought he heard the sound of Syd's car's noisy engine. Please, God…

Joe Cat looked at Harvard. "The Black Hawk that brought us here is probably still on the roof. It had more than enough fuel…"

Harvard kicked into action. "I'll round up the team."

"Come on, Syd," Lucky said into his phone as he started for the roof. "Get back on the phone and tell me you're all right."

THE CAR WAS STARTING to shudder and shake. It wasn't made to travel at seventy miles per hour for more than short bursts.

Syd had managed to pull out in front of the other car, but she needed both hands on the steering wheel to control the shaking. She could see her phone bumping around on the passenger's-side floor, next to her Club steering wheel lock. The phone wasn't *that* far away. If she could just take one hand off the wheel for a few seconds and...

She grabbed for it.

And missed.

LUCKY TOOK A QUICK HEAD count as the Black Hawk helicopter rocketed east. Joe Cat, Harvard, Cowboy, Crash, Mitch. Also Thomas King, Rio Rosetti and Mike Lee—they'd been coming into the hospital, bringing flowers to Lucy when Harvard had grabbed them and dragged them to the roof. Nine men and...one *woman?* FInCOM agent PJ Becker, who hated to fly in anything smaller than a 737, was here, too. God bless her.

Her voice came through loud and clear over the radio headset Lucky had slipped on. "As Navy SEALs, you have no authority here," she told them. "So if anyone asks, this is a FInCOM operation, you got it? I'm the Officer in Charge, and you're—just think of yourselves as my posse. But that's just if anyone asks. This is your op, O'Donlon."

Lucky looked at the captain. "What weapons do we have on board, sir?"

"Considering that we pretty much came straight from a

mission that called for full battle dress, we've got enough to outfit a small army."

"If this guy so much as touches Syd…" Lucky couldn't go on.

But Joe Cat knew what he was saying. And he nodded. "It finally happened to you, huh, O'Donlon? This woman got under your skin."

"She's irreplaceable," Lucky admitted.

SYD RODE THE CLUTCH, trying to push a little extra power into her car's top speed. It was working, but for how long?

The temperature gauge was rising. It wasn't going to be long until she was out of time.

She had to get her phone off the floor. It had been at least ten minutes since she'd dropped it—Luke had to be going nuts. She had to talk to him. She had to tell him… what?

That she loved him, that she was sorry, that she wished it might've all turned out differently.

With a herculean effort, she reached for the phone and…

This time her hand connected with it. This time, her fingers scraped along the gritty floor mat. This time, she got it!

But the effort made her swerve, and she fought to control the car with only one hand.

Maybe it would be better if she died in a crash….

The thought was a wild one, and Syd rejected it instantly. That would be surrender of a permanent kind. And she'd never been fond of the surrender or submit solution to any "what if" scenario. If she were going to die, she would die fighting, damn it.

She tucked the phone under her chin and took a deep

breath. The line was still open. She didn't have to redial, thank God.

"Luke?"

"Syd, this is Alan Francisco. Lucky's in a chopper, heading toward you, fast. He gave me the phone because he was afraid he'd lose your signal moving at that kind of speed. I'm in radio contact with him, though. Are you all right? I'm sure he's going crazy...."

Syd's heart sank. She wasn't going to get to talk to Luke. At least not directly. God, she'd wanted to hear his voice just one more time.

"It's him," she told Frisco. "The San Felipe Rapist. In the car behind me. He pulled alongside me—he's wearing panty hose over his face. He tried to run me off the road."

"Okay," Frisco said calmly. "Keep moving, Syd. Straddle the center line, don't let him get in front of you. Hang on—let me relay this information to Lucky."

"Alan," she said. "My temperature gauge is about to go into the red zone. My car's about to overheat."

OVERHEATING. SYD'S CAR WAS OVERHEATING.

"Can we make this thing go any faster?" Lucky asked Harvard.

"We're pushing it as it is," the senior chief told him. "But we're close."

"Close isn't good enough," Lucky growled. "Frisco. Tell Syd..." Everyone was listening. Everyone but the one person he wanted to talk to more than anything. "Tell Syd to hang on. Tell her to try to keep moving. Tell her if this bastard gets out of his car, if she's got any power left at all, tell her to run the son of a bitch over. But if her car overheats and the engine dies, tell her to stay inside. Lock the doors. Make him break the windows to get to her. Tell her she should cover her head with something, a jacket or something, so she doesn't get cut by the glass. Tell her..." He had to say it. To hell with the fact that everyone was listening in. "Tell Syd I love her."

"HE SAID THAT?" Syd couldn't believe it. "He actually said those words?"

"He said, tell Syd I love her," Frisco repeated.

"Oh, God," Syd said, unsure whether to laugh or cry. "If he actually said that, he thinks I'm going to die, doesn't he?"

Steam started escaping from under the front hood of her car. This was it. "My radiator's going," she told Frisco. "It's funny, all those debates about whether to fight or submit. Who knew I'd actually have to make that choice?"

Luke wanted her to submit. He wanted her to stay in her car, wait for this behemoth to come in after her. But once he did, she wouldn't stand a chance.

But maybe, if she were outside the car, she could use her steering wheel lock as a very literal club. Maybe, if she opened the door and came out swinging...

"Tell Luke I'm sorry," Syd told Frisco. "But I choose *fight*."

Her radiator was sending out clouds of steam, and her car was starting to slow. This was it. The beginning of the end.

"Tell him...I love him, too."

Syd cut the connection and let the phone drop into her lap as the car behind hit her squarely. She had to hold on to the steering wheel with both hands to keep her car in the middle of the road. She had to keep him from moving alongside her and running her off onto the soft shoulder.

Except what would that do, really, but delay the inevitable?

Still, she couldn't quit. She couldn't just give up.

He rammed her again, pushing her up and over one last rise in the long, otherwise flat road stretching out in front of her, and…

And then Syd saw it.

A black speck, moving toward her, growing bigger by the second. It was some kind of jet plane or…no, it was a helicopter, moving faster than she'd ever seen a helicopter move in her entire life.

The sedan slammed into her again, this time pushing her off the road. She plowed into the soft dirt and braced herself for another impact. But the helicopter was on top of them then, swooping down like a giant, terrible, noisy hawk bent on revenge. It slowed only slightly as it turned, circling back, and Syd saw that the doors were open. There was a sharp noise—a gunshot—and the sedan swerved to a stop just in front of her. They'd shot out his front tire!

The helicopter was hovering, and at least a dozen men, armed to the teeth with enormous guns, swarmed down ropes.

Out her front window, Syd watched as the man who'd been terrorizing her was pulled from his car. He was big, but they were bigger, and even though he resisted, they had him down on his stomach on the pavement in a matter of seconds.

Her cell phone rang.

Syd picked it up. "Frisco?"

"No." The voice was Luke's. "I borrowed the captain's phone."

She looked up to find him walking toward her car, phone in one hand, gun in the other.

"How's that for timing?" he asked.

Syd dropped the phone and unlocked the door, and he pulled her up and out and into his arms.

CHAPTER SIXTEEN

"HIS NAME IS OWEN FINN," Lucky reported to Frisco from his kitchen phone. "He was at the Academy, got into BUD/S, but didn't make it through the program. He rang out—it was during the summer of '96. Apparently he was a nutcase. One of those guys who had a million opportunities handed to him on a platter, but he just kept on screwing up. And whenever he did, it was never his fault."

"Yeah," Frisco said. "I know the type. 'I didn't mean to beat my wife until she ended up in the hospital. It wasn't my fault—she got me so mad.'"

"Yeah, right. Four months after he quit BUD/S," Lucky told his friend, "he was charged and convicted of theft. That got him a dishonorable discharge as well as time served. When he got out, as a civilian, he got caught in a burglary attempt, did time in Kentucky as well. I guess he sat there for a few years, stewing on the fact that—in his mind at least—his abysmal record of failure started when he rang out of BUD/S. As soon as he got out of jail, he headed back to Coronado, via a short stop in Texas where he robbed a liquor store. God forbid he should actually *work* to earn money.

"The police psychologist thinks he probably came back here with some kind of vague idea of revenge—an idea that didn't gel until he got here. This psychologist told me and Syd that he thinks Finn got mileage out of being mistaken for a SEAL in the local bars—he was built up from all those years of pumping iron in prison. He thinks Finn's first act of violence was a date rape—a woman who willingly left the bar with him. According to the shrink, Finn enjoyed the power and the fear, and realized how he could get his pound of flesh, so to speak. He started going down his list, hitting women who were connected to the people he wanted to hurt. Some of them were women he remembered from '96, some he did research to find. He was always careful only to go after the women who had definite patterns of time in which they were alone in their homes. Syd was an exception. And even then, he told the shrink he'd been planning to hit her in her motel room in Phoenix. She foiled his plan by heading back to California a day early. Thank God."

Lucky closed his eyes, unable to deal with the thought of what might've happened had she stayed in Arizona as she'd first intended.

"We're still waiting for Finn's DNA tests to come back, but this time I think we've got him," Lucky said. "He definitely smelled like cigarette smoke. As for Martin Taus, we're not sure yet how he was able to describe Lucy's attack so accurately. I think he must've met Finn in a bar."

"How's Syd doing?" Frisco asked.

Lucky laughed "She's writing," he said. "She locked herself in the guest room, and she's been writing from the minute we walked in the door. She's working on a short piece for *USA Today* about Finn—a kind of follow-up to those other articles she wrote.

"Did she, uh…" Frisco was trying to be tactful. "Did she give you an answer yet?"

"No." Lucky knew exactly what his friend was talking about. His marriage proposal. His incredibly stupid and all-too-public marriage proposal. It figured that Frisco would've heard about it. In fact, Mia was probably standing next to him, tugging on his sleeve, waiting for the word so that she could call Veronica with an update. And Veronica would talk to PJ, and PJ would tell Harvard, who would send out a memo to the rest of Alpha Squad.

The fact that Lucky had actually proposed marriage wasn't being taken lightly by his friends. In fact, it was serious business.

Serious business.

Serious...

"Hang on a sec, can you?" Lucky said into the phone. He set the receiver down on the kitchen table, then went down the hall, and knocked on the closed guest-room door.

"Yeah." Syd sounded impatient. She was writing.

Lucky opened the door and made it quick. "Do you have an estimate for when you'll be done?"

"Two hours," she said. "Go away. Please."

Lucky closed the door, went back into the kitchen and picked up the phone. "Frisco, man, I need your help."

SYD SENT THE ARTICLE electronically, and shut down her laptop computer. She stood up, stretching out her back, knowing that she'd put it off as long as she possibly could.

Luke was out there in his living room, waiting so that they could talk.

To hell with your interview.... Get your butt home and marry me, damn it.

He couldn't have been serious. She *knew* he wasn't serious.

He'd been upset for a variety of reasons. He didn't like the idea of losing her, of losing, period. This marriage proposal was just a knee-jerk attempt to make her stick around.

Tell Syd I love her.

Yeah, sure, he loved her. He'd probably said the same three words to the four billion women who'd come before Syd. She just couldn't take it seriously.

And she was going to have to tell him that. She couldn't—and wouldn't—take *him* seriously. She cared for him deeply, but she couldn't make such a big gamble. This was her life, after all. She was sorry, but she was going to take the job in New York.

She'd leave quickly. They wanted her to start as soon as possible. So she'd pack her things and go. One sharp pain, and it would be over. Like pulling off a Band-Aid, she reminded herself.

He probably wouldn't miss her for more than a week.

She, on the other hand, was going to miss him for the rest of her life.

She braced herself, squared her shoulders and opened the door.

Luke was in the living room, standing at the front window, looking out. He turned when he heard her, and she realized with a jolt of shock that he was wearing his dress uniform. His hair was combed neatly back from his face, every strand carefully in place. He wasn't wearing just his rows of ribbons on his chest, but rather the full medals. It was a wonder he could stand up with so much extra poundage weighing him down.

"Are you going somewhere?" she asked him.

"I think," he said, "that that should be my question for you." He looked so serious, standing there like that, all spit and polish, without a smile on his handsome face.

Syd sat down on the couch. "Yes," she said. "I'm going

to New York. There was a message on my machine. They made me an offer. They want me."

"What about my offer?" Luke asked. "I want you, too."

She searched his eyes, but he still wasn't smiling. There was no sign that he was kidding, no sign that he acknowledged how completely out of character this was. "You seriously expect me to believe that you want to marry me?" She could barely say the words aloud.

"Yes. I need to apologize for the subpar delivery, but—"

"Luke. Marriage is forever. I take that *very* seriously. This isn't some game that we can play until you get bored."

"Do I look like I'm playing a game?" he countered.

She didn't get a chance to answer because the doorbell rang.

"Good," Luke said. "Just in time. Excuse me."

As Syd watched, he opened his door. Thomas King stood there, Rio Rosetti and Michael Lee right behind him. They, like Luke, were wearing their dress uniforms. Their arms were full of...*flowers?*

"Great," Luke said. "Come on in. Just put those down on the table, gentlemen. Perfect."

"Hey, Syd," Thomas said.

"If you don't mind waiting out on the back deck...?" Luke efficiently pushed them toward the kitchen door. "I've got a cooler out there with beer, wine and soda. Help yourselves."

Syd stared at Luke, stared at the flowers. They were gorgeous—all different kinds and colors. The bouquets completely covered the coffee table. "Luke, what is this for?"

"It's for you," he said. "And me."

The doorbell rang again.

This time it was Bobby Taylor and Wes Skelly. They both carried heavy boxes into the living room. Luke opened one and took out a bottle of champagne. He read the label. "Terrific," he said. "Thanks, guys."

"There're a couple bottles of non-alcoholic stuff, too," Wes told him. "For Frisco and Mia. We got it at the health food store."

"Hi, Syd," Bobby said. He pointed to the back of the house. "Deck?" he asked Luke, who nodded. He vanished, pulling Wes with him.

Flowers and champagne...? "Luke, what—"

Luke interrupted her. "Today you said that you love me. Were you serious?"

Oh, God. She was trying so hard to be realistic about this. "I thought I was going to die."

"So...you said something that wasn't really true?" he asked, sitting down next to her on the couch. "Something that you didn't really mean?"

Syd closed her eyes. She'd meant it, all right. She just probably wouldn't have *said* it if she'd known she was going to live.

"Do you love me?" he asked.

She couldn't lie to him. "Yes," she said. "But I don't—"

He kissed her. "The short answer's all I want."

Syd let herself look into his eyes. "It's just not that simple."

"It can be." He leaned forward to kiss her again, but the doorbell rang.

It was Harvard. What a surprise. He had PJ with him. And Crash and Nell Hawken. And Cowboy and Melody Jones. And Mitch and Becca Shaw. They were all dressed up, as if they were going to the opera or...

"Limos R Us," Cowboy announced with a grin. "Three of 'em. White, as ordered."

"Ready to roll, Lieutenant, sir," Harvard added. "Vegas, here we come."

Vegas? As in Las Vegas? Wedding capital of the world?

Syd stood up and looked out the window. Sure enough, three stretch limos, big enough to hold a small army, were idling at the curb. Her heart began to pound, triple time, in her chest. Was it possible Luke truly was serious...?

"Hi, Syd." PJ gave her a hug and a kiss. "You okay after this afternoon?"

Syd didn't have time to answer. PJ disappeared with the others, pushed into the kitchen and out the back door.

"So," Luke said when they were alone once again. "You love me. And I love you. I know this job in New York is good for your career, but you also told me that if you had a chance, if you could find a patron to support you for a year or two, you'd rather quit your day job and write a book." He spread his arms. "Well, here I—"

The doorbell rang.

"Excuse me."

This time it was Frisco and Mia. They came into the living room, followed by an elderly man in a dark suit who was carrying a large briefcase.

"This is George Majors," Frisco told Luke. "He owns that jewelry store over on Ventura."

Luke shook the old man's hand. "This is wonderful," he said. "I really appreciate your coming out here like this. Here, you can set up over here." He pushed aside some of the flowers on the table, pulled Syd down onto the couch.

Mr. Majors opened his briefcase, and inside was a display case of rings. Diamond rings and wedding rings. Syd couldn't breathe.

Luke got down on one knee beside her and took her hand. "Marry me, Syd." His eyes were so blue. She could drown in those eyes. She could lose herself forever.

Frisco cleared his throat and started inching toward the kitchen door. "Maybe we should—"

"Don't go anywhere. You guys are my best friends. If I can't grovel in front of you, who *can* I grovel in front of?" He pointed to the jeweler. "Him I don't really know, but I figure he's got to be a pretty cool guy to come all the way out here like this."

He looked back at Syd. "Marry me," he said. "Live here with me, write your book, have my babies, make my life complete."

Syd couldn't speak. He was serious. He was completely, totally serious. It was everything she had ever wanted. But she couldn't manage to utter even one short syllable to tell him yes.

And he took her silence for hesitation.

"Maybe I should put it like this," he said. "Here's the scenario, Syd. There's a guy who's never taken any romantic relationship seriously before in his life. But then he meets you, and his world turns upside-down. He loves you more than life itself, and he wants to marry you. Tonight. At the Igloo of Love Wedding Chapel in Vegas. Do you fight, flee, hide or surrender?"

Syd stared to laugh. "Igloo of Love?"

Luke was trying his damnedest to stay serious, but he couldn't keep a smile and then a laugh from escaping. "I knew you'd like that. With me, your life's going to be high class all the way, baby."

With Luke, her life was going to be laughter and sunshine all the way.

"I surrender," she whispered, and started to kiss him, but then she pulled back. She was wearing jeans and a T-shirt, and everyone else was dressed for...a *wedding*. "Tonight?" she said. "God, Luke, I don't have a dress!"

The doorbell rang.

It was Joe Cat and Veronica. Mia let them in.

"I have found," Veronica announced, "exactly what Luke asked me to find—the most *exquisite* wedding dress in all of Southern California."

"My God," Syd whispered to Luke. "You thought of everything."

"Damn right," he told her. "I wanted to make sure you knew I was serious. I figured if you saw that all my friends were taking me seriously, then you would, too."

He kissed her—and it was an extremely serious kiss.

"Marry me tonight," he said.

Syd laughed. "At the Igloo of Love? Definitely."

Smiling into his eyes, she knew her life would never be the same. She'd got Lucky. Permanently.

* * * * *

TAYLOR'S TEMPTATION

In loving memory of Melinda Helfer,
Romantic Times reviewer—a friend of mine,
and a friend of all romance. The first time I met
Melinda was at an RWA book signing years ago—
right after *Prince Joe* and *Forever Blue* had come
out. She rushed up to me, dropped to the floor
in front of my table and proceeded to kowtow!
She told me she loved those two books, and
couldn't wait for the next installment in the
TALL, DARK & DANGEROUS series to be released.
She was funny, enthusiastic and amazingly
intelligent—a fierce and passionate fan of
all romance, and a good friend. Melinda,
this one's for you. (But then again,
I think you probably knew that
all my TDD books were written for you!)
You will be missed.

PROLOGUE

"IT WAS AMAZING." Rio Rosetti shook his head, still unable to wrap his mind around last night's explosive events. "It was absolutely amazing."

Mike and Thomas sat across from him at the mess hall, their ham and eggs forgotten as they waited for him to continue.

Although neither of them let it show, Rio knew they were both envious as hell that he'd been smack in the middle of all the action, pulling his weight alongside the two legendary chiefs of Alpha Squad, Bobby Taylor and Wes Skelly.

"Hey, Little E., get your gear and strap on your blue-suede swim fins," Chief Skelly had said to Rio just six hours ago. Had it really only been six hours? "Me and Uncle Bobby are gonna show you how it's done."

Twin sons of different mothers. That's what Bobby and Wes were often called. Of *very* different mothers. The two men looked nothing alike. Chief Taylor was huge. In fact, the man was a total animal. Rio wasn't sure, because the air got kind of hazy way up by the top of Bobby Taylor's head, but he thought the chief stood at least six and a half feet tall, maybe even more. And he was nearly as wide. He had shoulders like a football player's protective padding, and, also like a football player, the man was remarkably fast. It was pretty freaky, actually, that a guy that big could achieve the kind of speed he did.

His size wasn't the only thing that set him apart from

Wes Skelly, who was normal-size—about Rio's height at five-eleven with a similar wiry build.

Bobby was at least part Native American. His heritage showed in his handsome face and in the rich color of his skin. He tanned a real nice shade of brown when he was out in the sun—a far nicer shade than Rio's own slightly olive-tinged complexion. The chief also had long, black, straight hair that he wore pulled severely from his face in a single braid down his back, giving him a faintly mystical, mysterious air.

Wes, on the other hand, was of Irish-American descent, with a slightly reddish tint to his light brown hair and leprechaun-like mischief gleaming in his blue eyes.

No doubt about it, Wes Skelly came into a room and bounced off the walls. He was always moving—like a human pinball. And if he wasn't moving, he was talking. He was funny and rude and loud and not entirely tactful in his impatience.

Bobby, however, was the king of laid-back cool. He was the kind of guy who could sit perfectly still, without fidgeting, just watching and listening, sometimes for hours, before he gave voice to any opinions or comments.

But as different as they seemed in looks and demeanor, Bobby and Wes shared a single brain. They knew each other so well they were completely in tune with the other's thoughts.

Which was probably why Bobby didn't do too much talking. He didn't need to. Wes read his mind and spoke—incessantly—for him.

Although when the giant chief actually *did* speak, men listened. Even the officers listened.

Rio listened, too. He'd learned early on in SEAL training, long before he got tapped to join SEAL Team Ten's legendary Alpha Squad, to pay particular attention to Chief Bobby Taylor's opinions and comments.

Bobby had been doing a stint as a BUD/S instructor in Coronado, and he'd taken Rio, along with Mike Lee and Thomas King, under his extremely large wing. Which wasn't to say he coddled them. No way. In fact, by marking them as the head of a class filled with smart, confident, determined men, he'd demanded more from them. He'd driven them harder than the others, accepted no excuses, asked nothing less than their personal best—each and every time.

They'd done all they could to deliver, and—no doubt due to Bobby's quiet influence with Captain Joe Catalanotto—won themselves coveted spots in the best SEAL team in the Navy.

Rewind to six hours ago, to last night's operation. SEAL Team Ten's Alpha Squad had been called in to assist a FInCOM/DEA task force.

A particularly nasty South American drug lord had parked his luxury yacht a very short, very cocky distance outside of U.S. waters. The Finks and the DEA agents couldn't or maybe just didn't want to for some reason—Rio wasn't sure which and it didn't really matter to him—snatch the bad dude up until he crossed that invisible line into U.S. territory.

And that was where the SEALs were to come in.

Lieutenant Lucky O'Donlon was in charge of the op—mostly because he'd come up with a particularly devious plan that had tickled Captain Joe Cat's dark sense of humor. The lieutenant had decided that a small team of SEALs would swim out to the yacht—named *Swiss Chocolate,* a stupid-ass name for a boat—board it covertly, gain access to the bridge and do a little creative work on their computerized navigational system.

As in making the yacht's captain think they were heading south when they were really heading northwest.

Bad dude would give the order to head back toward

South America, and instead they'd zoom toward Miami—
into the open arms of the Federal task force.

It was just too good.

Bobby and Wes had been selected by Lieutenant
O'Donlon to gain covert access to the bridge of the yacht.
And Rio was going along for the ride.

"I knew damn well they didn't need me there," he told
Thomas and Mike now. "In fact, I was aware I was slowing
them down." Bobby and Wes didn't need to talk, didn't
need to make hand signals. They barely even looked at
each other—they just read each other's minds. It was so
freaky. Rio had seen them do similar stuff on a training
op, but somehow out in the real world it seemed even more
weird.

"So what happened, Rosetti?" Thomas King asked.
The tall African-American ensign was impatient—not that
he'd ever let it show on his face. Thomas was an excellent
poker player. Rio knew that firsthand, having left the table
with empty pockets on more than one occasion.

Most of the time Thomas's face was unreadable, his
expression completely neutral, eyelids half-closed. The
combination of that almost-bland expression and his
scars—one bisecting his eyebrow and the other branding one of his high cheekbones—gave him a dangerous
edge that Rio wished his own far-too-average face had.

But it was Thomas's eyes that made most people cross
the street when they saw him coming. So dark-brown
as to seem black, his eyes glittered with a deep intelli-
gence—the man was Phi Beta Kappa *and* a member of
the Mensa club. His eyes also betrayed the fact that despite
his slouched demeanor, Thomas King was permanently
at Defcon Five—ready to launch a deadly attack without
hesitation if the need arose.

He was Thomas. Not Tommy. Not even Tom. *Thomas.* Not one member of Team Ten ever called him anything else.

Thomas had won the team's respect. Unlike Rio, who somehow, despite his hope for a nickname like Panther or Hawk, had been given the handle Elvis. Or even worse, Little Elvis or Little E.

Holy Chrysler. As if Elvis wasn't embarrassing enough.

"We took a rubber duck out toward the *Swiss Chocolate,*" Rio told Thomas and Mike. "Swam the rest of the way in." The swift ride in the little inflatable boat through the darkness of the ocean had made his heart pound. Knowing they were going to board a heavily guarded yacht and gain access to her bridge without anyone seeing them had a lot to do with it. But he was also worried.

What if he blew it?

Bobby apparently could read Rio's mind almost as easily as he read Wes Skelly's, because he'd touched Rio's shoulder—just a brief squeeze of reassurance—before they'd crept out of the water and onto the yacht.

"The damn thing was lit up like a Christmas tree and crawling with guards," Rio continued. "They all dressed alike and carried these cute little Uzi's. It was almost like their boss got off on pretending he had his own little army. But they weren't any kind of army. Not even close. They were really just street kids in expensive uniforms. They didn't know how to stand watch, didn't know what to look for. I swear to God, you guys, we moved right past them. They didn't have a clue we were there—not with all the noise they were making and the lights shining in their eyes. It was so easy it was a joke."

"If it were a joke," Mike Lee asked, "then what's Chief Taylor doing in the hospital?"

Rio shook his head. "No, that part wasn't a joke." Someone on board the yacht had decided to move the party up from down below and go for a midnight swim. Spotlights had switched on, shining down into the ocean, and all hell had broken loose. "But up until the time we were heading back into the water, it was a piece of cake. You know that thing Bobby and Wes can do? The telepathic communication thing?"

Thomas smiled. "Oh, yeah. I've seen them look at each other and—"

"This time they didn't," Rio interrupted his friend. "Look at each other, I mean. You guys, I'm telling you, this was beyond cool—watching them in action like this. There was one guard on the bridge, okay? Other than that, it was deserted and pretty dark. The captain and crew are all below deck, right? Probably getting stoned with the party girls and the guests. So anyway, the chiefs see this guard and they don't break stride. They just take him temporarily out of the picture before he even sees us, before he can even make a sound. Both of them did it—together, like it's some kind of choreographed move they've been practicing for years. I'm telling you, it was a thing of beauty."

"They've been working with each other for a long time," Mike pointed out.

"They went through BUD/S together," Thomas reminded them. "They've been swim buddies from day one."

"It was perfection." Rio shook his head in admiration. "Sheer perfection. I stood in the guard's place, in case anyone looked up through the window, then there'd be someone standing there, you know? Meanwhile Skelly disabled the conventional compass. And Bobby broke into the navigational computers in about four seconds."

That was another freaky thing about Bobby Taylor. He had fingers the size of ballpark franks, but he could manipulate a computer keyboard faster than Rio would have thought humanly possible. He could scan the images that scrolled past on the screen at remarkable speeds, too.

"It took him less than three minutes to do whatever it was he had to do," he continued, "and then we were out of there—off the bridge. Lucky and Spaceman were in the water, giving us the all-clear." He shook his head, remembering how close they'd been to slipping silently away into the night. "And then all these babes in bikinis came running up on deck, heading straight for us. It was the absolute worst luck—if we'd been anywhere else on the vessel, the diversion would've been perfect. We would've been completely invisible. I mean, if you're an inexperienced guard are you going to be watching to see who's crawling around in the shadows or are you going to pay attention to the beach bunnies in the thong bikinis? But someone decided to go for a swim off the starboard side—right where we were hiding. These heavy-duty searchlights came on, probably just so the guys on board could watch the women in the water, but wham, there we were. Lit up. There was no place to hide—and nowhere to go but over the side."

"Bobby picked me up and threw me overboard," Rio admitted. He must not have been moving fast enough— he was still kicking himself for that. "I didn't see what happened next, but according to Wes, Bobby stepped in front of him and blocked him from the bullets that started flying while they both went into the water. That was when Bobby caught a few—one in his shoulder, another in the top of his thigh. He was the one who was hurt, but he pulled both me and Wes down, under the water—out of sight and out of range."

Sirens went on. Rio had been able to hear them along with the tearing sound of the guards' assault weapons and the screams from the women, even as he was pulled underwater.

"That was when the *Swiss Chocolate* took off," Rio said. He had to smile. "Right for Miami."

They'd surfaced to watch, and Bobby had laughed along with Wes Skelly. Rio and Wes hadn't even realized he'd been hit. Not until he spoke, in his normal, matter-of-fact manner.

"We better get moving, get back to the boat, ASAP," Bobby had said evenly. "I'm shark bait."

"The chief was bleeding badly," Rio told his friends. "He was hurt worse even than he realized." And the water hadn't been cold enough to staunch the flow of his blood. "We did the best we could to tie off his leg, right there in the water. Lucky and Spaceman went on ahead—as fast as they could—to connect with the rubber duck and bring it back toward us."

Bobby Taylor had been in serious pain, but he'd kept moving, slowly and steadily through the darkness. Apparently he'd been afraid if he didn't keep moving, if he let Wes tow him back to the little rubber boat, he'd black out. And he didn't want to do that. The sharks in these waters *did* pose a serious threat, and if he were unconscious, that could have put Rio and Wes into even more significant danger.

"Wes and I swam alongside Bobby. Wes was talking the entire time—I don't know how he did it without swallowing a gallon of seawater—bitching at Bobby for playing the hero like that, making fun of him for getting shot in the ass—basically, just ragging on him to keep him alert.

"It wasn't until Bobby finally slowed to a crawl, until he told us he wasn't going to make it—that he needed help—that Wes stopped talking. He took Bobby in a lifeguard hold and hauled ass, focusing all his energy on getting back to the rubber duck in record time."

Rio sat back in his seat. "When we finally connected with the boat, Lucky had already radioed for help. It wasn't much longer before a helo came to evac Bobby to the hospital.

"He's going to be okay," he told both Thomas and Mike again. That was the first thing he'd said about their beloved chief's injuries, before they'd even sat down to breakfast. "The leg wound wasn't all that bad, and the bullet that went into his shoulder somehow managed to miss the bone. He'll be off the active-duty list for a few weeks, maybe a month, but after that..." Rio grinned. "Chief Bobby Taylor will be back. You can count on that."

CHAPTER ONE

NAVY SEAL CHIEF Bobby Taylor was in trouble.

Big trouble.

"You gotta help me, man," Wes said. "She's determined to go, she flippin' hung up on me and wouldn't pick up the phone when I called back, and I'm going wheels-up in less than twenty minutes. All I could do was send her email—though fat lotta good that'll do."

"She" was Colleen Mary Skelly, his best friend's little sister. No, not *little* sister. *Younger* sister. Colleen wasn't little, not anymore. She hadn't been little for a long, long time.

A fact that Wes didn't seem quite able to grasp.

"If *I* call her," Bobby pointed out reasonably, "she'll just hang up on me, too."

"I don't want you to call her." Wes shouldered his seabag and dropped his bomb. "I want you to go there."

Bobby laughed. Not aloud. He would never laugh in his best friend's face when he went into overprotective brother mode. But inside of his own head, he was rolling on the floor in hysterics.

Outside of his head, he only lifted a quizzical eyebrow. "To Boston." It wasn't really a question.

Wesley Skelly knew that this time he was asking an awful lot, but he squared his shoulders and looked Bobby straight in the eyes. "Yes."

Problem was, Wes didn't know just how much he was asking.

"You want me to take leave and go to Boston," Bobby didn't really enjoy making Wes squirm, but he needed his best friend to see just how absurd this sounded, "because you and Colleen got into another argument." He still didn't turn it into a question. He just let it quietly hang there.

"No, Bobby," Wes said, the urgency in his voice turned up to high. "You don't get it. She's signed on with some kind of bleeding-heart, touchy-feely volunteer organization, and next she and her touchy-feely friends are flying out to flippin' Tulgeria." He said it again, louder, as if it were unprintable, then followed it up by a string of words that truly were.

Bobby could see that Wes was beyond upset. This wasn't just another ridiculous argument. This was serious.

"She's going to provide earthquake relief," Wes continued. "That's lovely. That's wonderful, I told her. Be Mother Teresa. Be Florence Nightingale. Have your goody two-shoes permanently glued to your feet. But stay *way* the hell away from Tulgeria! Tulgeria—the flippin' terrorist capital of the world!"

"Wes—"

"I tried to get leave," Wes told him. "I was just in the captain's office, but with you still down and H. out with food poisoning, I'm mission essential."

"I'm there," Bobby said. "I'm on the next flight to Boston."

Wes was willing to give up Alpha Squad's current assignment—something he was really looking forward to, something involving plenty of C-4 explosives—to go to Boston. That meant that Colleen wasn't just pushing her brother's buttons. That meant she was serious about this. That she really was planning to travel to a part of the world where Bobby himself didn't feel safe. And he wasn't a freshly pretty, generously endowed, long-legged—*very* long-legged—redheaded and extremely female second-year law student.

With a big mouth, a fiery temper and a stubborn streak. No, Colleen's last name wasn't Skelly for nothing.

Bobby swore softly. If she'd made up her mind to go, talking her out of it wasn't going to be easy.

"Thank you for doing this," Wes said, as if Bobby had already succeeded in keeping Colleen off that international flight. "Look, I gotta run. Literally."

Wes owed Bobby for this one. But he already knew it. Bobby didn't bother to say the words aloud.

Wes was almost out the door before he turned back. "Hey, as long as you're going to Boston…"

Ah. Here it came. Colleen was probably dating some new guy and… Bobby was already shaking his head.

"Check out this lawyer I think Colleen's dating, would you?" Wes asked.

"No," Bobby said.

But Wes was already gone.

COLLEEN SKELLY WAS IN TROUBLE.

Big trouble.

It wasn't fair. The sky was far too blue today for this kind of trouble. The June air held a crisp sweetness that only a New England summer could provide.

But the men standing in front of her provided nothing sweet to the day. And nothing unique to New England, either.

Their kind of hatred, unfortunately, was universal.

She didn't smile at them. She'd tried smiling in the past, and it hadn't helped at all.

"Look," she said, trying to sound as reasonable and calm as she possibly could, given that she was facing down six very big men. Ten pairs of young eyes were watching her, so she kept her temper, kept it cool and clean. "I'm well aware that you don't like—"

"'Don't like' doesn't have anything to do with it," the man at the front of the gang—John Morrison—cut her off. "We don't want your center here, we don't want *you* here." He looked at the kids, who'd stopped washing Mrs. O'Brien's car and stood watching the exchange, wide-eyed and dripping with water and suds. "You, Sean Sullivan. Does your father know you're down here with *her?* With the hippie chick?"

"Keep going, guys," Colleen told the kids, giving them what she hoped was a reassuring smile. *Hippie chick.* Sheesh. "Mrs. O'Brien doesn't have all day. And there's a line, remember. This car wash team has a rep for doing a good job—swiftly and efficiently. Let's not lose any customers over a little distraction."

She turned back to John Morrison and his gang. And they *were* a gang, despite the fact that they were all in their late thirties and early forties and led by a respectable local businessman. Well, on second thought, calling Morrison *respectable* was probably a little too generous.

"Yes, Mr. Sullivan does know where his son is," she told them levelly. "The St. Margaret's Junior High Youth Group is helping raise money for the Tulgeria Earthquake Relief Fund. All of the money from this car wash is going to help people who've lost their homes and nearly all of their possessions. I don't see how even *you* could have a problem with that."

Morrison bristled.

And Colleen silently berated herself. Despite her efforts, her antagonism and anger toward these Neanderthals had leaked out.

"Why don't you go back to wherever it was you came from?" he told her harshly. "Get the hell out of our neighborhood and take your damn bleeding-heart liberal ideas and stick them up your—"

No one was going to use that language around her kids. Not while she was in charge. "Out," she said. "Get out. Shame on you! Get off this property before I wash your mouth out with soap. And charge you for it."

Oh, that was a big mistake. Her threat hinted at violence—something she had to be careful to avoid with this group.

Yes, she was nearly six feet tall and somewhat solidly built, but she wasn't a Navy SEAL like her brother and his best friend, Bobby Taylor. Unlike them, she couldn't take on all six of these guys at once, if it came down to that.

The scary thing was that this was a neighborhood in which some men didn't particularly have a problem with hitting a woman, no matter her size. And she suspected that John Morrison was one of those men.

She imagined she saw it in his eyes—a barely tempered urge to backhand her—hard—across the face.

Usually she resented her brother's interference. But right now she found herself wishing he and Bobby were standing right here, beside her.

God knows she'd been yelling for years about her independence, but this wasn't exactly an independent kind of situation.

She stood her ground all alone, wishing she was holding something more effective against attack than a giant-size sponge, and then glad that she wasn't. She was just mad enough to turn the hose on them like a pack of wild dogs, and that would only make this worse.

There were children here, and all she needed was Sean or Harry or Melissa to come leaping to her aid. And they would. These kids could be fierce.

But then again, so could she. And she would not let

these children get hurt. She would do whatever she had to do, including trying again to make friends with these dirt wads.

"I apologize for losing my temper, Shantel," she called to one of the girls, her eyes still on Morrison and his goons. "Run inside and see if Father Timothy's coming out with more of that lemonade soon. Tell him to bring six extra paper cups for Mr. Morrison and his friends. I think we could probably all use some cooling off."

Maybe that would work. Kill them with kindness. Drown them with lemonade.

The twelve-year-old ran swiftly for the church door.

"How about it, guys?" Colleen forced herself to smile at the men, praying that this time it would work. "Some lemonade?"

Morrison's expression didn't change, and she knew that this was where he was going to step forward, inform her he didn't want any of their lemonade—expletive deleted—and challenge her to just try washing out his mouth. He'd then imply—ridiculously, and solely because of her pro bono legal work for the HIV Testing and AIDS Education Center that was struggling to establish a foothold in this narrow-minded but desperately needy corner of the city—that she was a lesbian and offer to "cure her" in fifteen unforgettable minutes in the closest back alley.

It would almost be funny. Except for the fact that Morrison was dead serious. He'd made similar disgusting threats to her before.

But now, to her surprise, John Morrison didn't say another word. He just looked long and hard at the group of eleven- and twelve-year-olds standing behind her, then did an about face, muttering something unprintable.

It was amazing. Just like that, he and his boys were walking away.

Colleen stared after them, laughing—softly—in disbelief.

She'd done it. She'd stood her ground, and Morrison had backed down without any interference from the police or the parish priest. Although at 260 pounds, Father Timothy was a heart attack waiting to happen. His usefulness in a fist fight would be extremely limited.

Was it possible Morrison and his clowns were finally hearing what she was saying? Were they finally starting to believe that she wasn't going to let herself be intimidated by their bogus threats and ugly comments?

Behind her the hoses were still silent, and she turned around. "Okay, you guys, let's get back to—"

Colleen dropped her sponge.

Bobby Taylor. It was Bobby Taylor. Standing right there, behind her, in the St. Margaret's parking lot. Somehow, some way, her brother's best friend had materialized there, as if Colleen's most fervent wishes had been granted.

He stood in a Hawaiian shirt and cargo shorts, planted in a superhero pose—legs spread and massive arms crossed in front of his equally massive chest. His eyes were hard, and his face stony as he still glared in the direction John Morrison and his gang had departed. He was wearing a version of his "war face."

He and Wes had completely cracked Colleen up on more than one occasion by practicing their "war faces" in the bathroom mirror during their far-too-infrequent visits home. She'd always thought it was silly—what did the expression on their faces matter when they went into a fight?—until now. Now she saw that that grim look on Bobby's usually so-agreeably handsome face was startlingly effective. He looked hard and tough and even mean—as if he'd get quite a bit of enjoyment and satisfaction in tearing John Morrison and his friends limb from limb.

But then he looked at her and smiled, and warmth seeped back into his dark-brown eyes.

He had the world's most beautiful eyes.

"Hey, Colleen," he said in his matter-of-fact, no worries, easygoing voice. "How's it going?"

He held out his arms to her, and in a flash she was running across the asphalt and hugging him. He smelled faintly of cigarette smoke—no doubt thanks to her brother, Mr. Just-One-More-Cigarette-Before-I-Quit—and coffee. He was warm and huge and solid and one of very few men in the world who could actually make her feel if not quite petite then pretty darn close.

As long as she'd wished him here, she should have wished for more. Like for him to have shown up with a million-dollar lottery win in his pocket. Or—better yet—a diamond ring and a promise of his undying love.

Yes, she'd had a wild crush on this man for close to ten years now. And just once she wanted him to take her into his arms like this and kiss her senseless, instead of giving her a brotherly noogie on the top of her head as he released her.

Over the past few years she'd imagined she'd seen appreciation in his eyes as he'd looked at her. And once or twice she could've sworn she'd actually seen heat—but only when he thought both she and Wes weren't looking. Bobby was attracted to her. Or at the very least she wished he were. But even if he were, there was no way in hell he'd ever act on that attraction—not with Wes watching his every move and breathing down his neck.

Colleen hugged him tightly. She had only two chances each visit to get this close to him—once during hello and once during goodbye—and she always made sure to take full advantage.

But this time he winced. "Easy."

Oh, God, he'd been hurt. She pulled back to look up

at him, and she actually had to tilt her head. He was
that tall.

"I'm a little sore," he told her, releasing her completely
and stepping back, away from her. "Shoulder and leg.
Nothing serious. You got me in the dead perfect spot,
that's all."

"I'm sorry."

He shrugged. "It's no big deal. I'm taking some down
time to get back to speed."

"What happened—or can you not tell me?"

He shook his head, smiling apologetically. He was such
a good-looking man. And that little smile... What would
he look like with his thick hair loose from the single braid
he wore down his back? Although, she realized, he wasn't
wearing a braid today. Instead, he wore his hair pulled
back into a simple ponytail.

Every time she saw him, she expected him to have his
hair cut short again. But each time it was even longer.

The first time they'd met, back when he and Wes were
training to become SEALs, he'd had a crew cut.

Colleen gestured to the kids, aware they were all still
watching. "Come on, gang, let's keep going here."

"Are you all right?" Bobby stepped closer to her, to
avoid the spray from the hose. "What's the deal with those
guys?"

"You're why they left," she realized suddenly. And even
though mere minutes ago she'd wished desperately for
Bobby's and her brother's presence, she felt a flare of anger
and frustration. Darn it! She'd wanted Morrison's retreat
to be because of her. As nice as it would be, she couldn't
walk around with a Navy SEAL by her side every minute
of every day.

"What was that about, Colleen?" Bobby pressed.

"Nothing," she said tersely.

He nodded, regarding her steadily. "It didn't feel like 'nothing.'"

"Nothing *you* have to worry about," she countered. "I'm doing some pro bono legal work for the AIDS Education Center, and not everyone is happy about it. That's what litigation's all about. Where's Wes? Parking the car?"

"Actually, he's—"

"I know why you're here. You came to try to talk me out of going to Tulgeria. Wes probably came to forbid me from going. Hah. As if he could." She picked up her sponge and rinsed it in a bucket. "I'm not going to listen to either of you, so you might as well just save your breath, turn around and go back to California. I'm not fifteen anymore, in case you haven't noticed."

"Hey, I've noticed," Bobby said. He smiled. "But Wes needs a little work in that area."

"You know, my living room is completely filled with boxes," Colleen told him. "Donations of supplies and clothing. I don't have any room for you guys. I mean, I guess you can throw sleeping bags on the floor of my bedroom, but I swear to God, if Wes snores, I'm kicking him out into the street."

"No," Bobby said. "That's okay. I made hotel reservations. This week is kind of my vacation, and—"

"Where *is* Wes?" Colleen asked, shading her eyes and looking down the busy city street. "Parking the car in Kuwait?"

"Actually." Bobby cleared his throat. "Yeah."

She looked at him.

"Wes is out on an op," he told her. "It's not quite Kuwait, but…"

"He asked *you* to come to Boston," Colleen realized. "For him. He asked you to play big brother and talk me out of going to Tulgeria, didn't he? I don't believe it. And you *agreed?* You jerk!"

"Colleen, come on. He's my best friend. He's worried about you."

"And you don't think I worry about him? Or you?" she countered hotly. "Do *I* come out to California to try to talk you out of risking *your* lives? Do *I* ever say, don't be a SEAL? No! Because I respect you. I respect the choices and decisions you make."

Father Timothy and Shantel emerged from the church kitchen with a huge thermos of lemonade and a stack of cups.

"Everything all right?" Father T. asked, eyeing Bobby apprehensively.

Bobby held out his hand. "I'm Bobby Taylor, a friend of Colleen's," he introduced himself.

"A friend of my brother, Wes's," she corrected him as the two men shook hands. "He's here as a surrogate brother. Father, plug your ears. I'm about to be extremely rude to him."

Timothy laughed. "I'll see if the other children want lemonade."

"Go away," Colleen told Bobby. "Go home. I don't want another big brother. I don't *need* one. I've got plenty already."

Bobby shook his head. "Wes asked me to—"

Damn Wes. "He probably also asked you to sift through my dresser drawers, too," she countered, lowering her voice. "Although I'm not sure what you're going to tell him when you find my collection of whips and chains, my black leather bustier and matching crotchless panties."

Bobby looked at her, something unrecognizable on his face.

And as Colleen looked back at him, for a moment she spun out, losing herself in the outer-space darkness of his eyes. She'd never imagined outer space could be so very *warm*.

He looked away, clearly embarrassed, and she realized suddenly that her brother wasn't here.

Wes wasn't here.

Bobby was in town *without Wes.* And without Wes, if she played it right, the rules of this game they'd been playing for the past decade could change.

Radically.

Oh, my goodness.

"Look." She cleared her throat. "You're here, so…let's make the best of this. When's your return flight?"

He smiled ruefully. "I figured I'd need the full week to talk you out of going."

He was here for a whole week. Thank you, Lord. "You're not going to talk me out of anything, but you cling to that thought if it helps you," she told him.

"I will." He laughed. "It's good to see you, Colleen."

"It's good to see you, too. Look, as long as there's only one of you, I can probably make room in my apartment—"

He laughed again. "Thanks, but I don't think that would be a very good idea."

"Why waste good money on a hotel room?" she asked. "After all, you're practically my brother."

"No," Bobby said emphatically. "I'm not."

There was something in his tone that made her bold. Colleen looked at him then in a way she'd never dared let herself look at him before. She let her gaze move down his broad chest, taking in the outline of his muscles, admiring the trim line of his waist and hips. She looked all the way down his long legs and then all the way back up again. She lingered a moment on his beautiful mouth, on his full, gracefully shaped lips, before gazing back into his eyes.

She'd shocked him with that obvious once-over. Well,

good. It was the Skelly family motto: everyone needs a good shocking every now and then.

She gave him a decidedly nonsisterly smile. "Glad we got that established. About time, huh?"

He laughed, clearly nervous. "Um…"

"Grab a sponge," she told him. "We've got some cars to wash."

CHAPTER TWO

WES WOULD KILL HIM if he found out.

No doubt about it.

If Wes knew even *half* the thoughts that were steam-rolling through Bobby's head about his sister, Colleen, Bobby would be a dead man.

Lord have mercy on his soul, the woman was hot. She was also funny and smart. Smart enough to have figured out the ultimate way to get back at him for showing up here as her brother's mouthpiece.

If she were planning to go anywhere besides Tulgeria, Bobby would have turned around. He would have headed for the airport and caught the next flight out of Boston.

Because Colleen was right. He and Wes had absolutely no business telling her what she should and shouldn't do. She was twenty-three years old—old enough to make her own decisions.

Except both Bobby and Wes had been to Tulgeria, and Colleen hadn't. No doubt she'd heard stories about the warring factions of terrorists that roamed the dirt-poor countryside. But she hadn't heard Bobby and Wes's stories. She didn't know what they'd seen, with their own eyes.

At least not yet.

But she would before the week was out.

And he'd take the opportunity to find out what that run-in with the local chapter of the KKK had been about, too.

Apparently, like her brother, Wes, trouble followed

Colleen Skelly around. And no doubt, also like Wes, when it didn't follow her, she went out and flagged it down.

But as for right now, Bobby desperately needed to re-group. He had to go to his hotel and take an icy-cold shower. He had to lock himself in his room and away—far away—from Colleen.

Lord save him, somehow he'd given himself away. Somehow she'd figured out that the last thing that came to mind when he looked at her was brotherly love.

He could hear her laughter, rich and thick, from the far end of the parking lot, where she stood talking to a woman in a beat-up station wagon, who'd come to pick up the last of the junior-size car washers.

The late-afternoon sunlight made Colleen's hair gleam. With the work done, she'd changed into a summer dress and taken down her ponytail, and her hair hung in shimmering red-gold waves around her face.

She was almost unbearably beautiful.

Some people might not agree. And taken individually, most of the features of her face were far from perfect. Her mouth was too wide, her cheeks too full, her nose too small, her face too round, her skin too freckled and prone to sunburn.

Put it all together, though, and the effect was amazing.

And add those heartstoppingly gorgeous eyes…

Colleen's eyes were sometimes blue, sometimes green, and always dancing with light and life. When she smiled—which was most of the time—her eyes actually twinkled. It was corny but true. Being around Colleen Skelly was like being in the middle of a continuous, joyful, always-in-full-swing party.

And as for her body…

Ouch.

The woman was beyond hot. She wasn't one of those anemic little bony anorexic girls who were plastered all over TV and magazines, looking more like malnourished 12-year-old boys. No, Colleen Skelly was a woman—with a capital *W*. She was the kind of woman that a real man could wrap his arms around and really get a grip on. She actually had hips and breasts—and not only was that the understatement of the century, but it was the thought that would send him to hell, directly to hell. 'Do not pass Go, do not collect two hundred dollars,' do not live another minute longer.

If Wes ever found out that Bobby spent any amount of time at all thinking about Colleen's breasts, well, that would be it. The end. Game over.

But right now Wes—being more than three thousand miles away—wasn't Bobby's problem.

No, Bobby's problem was that somehow *Colleen* had realized that he was spending far too much time thinking about her breasts.

She'd figured out that he was completely and mindlessly in lust with her.

And Wesley wasn't around to save him. Or beat him senseless.

Of course, it was possible that she was just toying with him, just messing with his mind. *Look at what you can't have, you big loser.*

After all, she was dating some lawyer. Wasn't that what Wes had said? And these days, wasn't *dating* just a euphemism for *in a relationship with?* And that was really just a polite way of saying that they were sleeping together, lucky son of a bitch.

Colleen glanced up from her conversation with the station-wagon mom and caught him looking at her butt.

Help.

He'd known that this was going to be a mistake back in California—the second the plea for help had left Wes's lips. Bobby should have admitted it, right there and then.

*Don't send me to Boston, man. I've got a crippling jones
for your sister. The temptation may be too much for me
to handle, and then you'll kill me.*

"I've gotta go," Bobby heard Colleen say as she straight-
ened up. "I've got a million things to do before I leave."
She waved to the kids in the back. "Thanks again, guys.
You did a terrific job today. I probably won't see you until
I get back, so..."

There was an outcry from the back seat, something
Bobby couldn't make out, but Colleen laughed.

"Absolutely," she said. "I'll deliver your letters to
Analena and the other kids. And I'll bring my camera
and take pictures. I promise."

She waved as the station wagon drove away, and then
she was walking toward him. As she approached, as she
gazed at him, there was a funny little smile on her face.

Bobby was familiar with the full arsenal of devious
Skelly smiles, and it was all he could do not to back away
from this one.

"I have an errand to run, but after, we could get dinner.
Are you hungry?" she asked.

No, he was terrified. He sidled back a bit, but she came
right up to him, close enough for him to put his arms
around. Close enough to pull her in for a kiss.

He couldn't kiss her. *Don't you dare,* he ordered
himself.

He'd wanted to kiss her for years.

"I know this great Chinese place," she continued, twin-
kling her eyes at him. "Great food, great atmosphere, too.
Very dark and cool and mysterious."

Oh, no. No, no. Atmosphere was the dead-last thing he
wanted or needed. Standing here on the blazing-hot asphalt in broad daylight was bad enough. He had to clench
his fists to keep from reaching for her. No way was he

trusting himself around Colleen Skelly someplace dark and cool and mysterious.

She touched him, reaching up to brush something off his sleeve, and he jumped about a mile straight up.

Colleen laughed. "Whoa. What's with you?"

I want to sink back with you on your brightly colored bedspread, undress you with my teeth and lose myself in your laughter, your eyes and the sweet heat of your body.

Not necessarily in that order.

Bobby shrugged, forced a smile. "Sorry."

"So how 'bout it? You want to get Chinese?"

"Oh," he said, stepping back a bit and shifting around to pick up his seabag and swing it over his shoulder, glad he had something with which to occupy his hands. "I don't know. I should probably go try to find my hotel. It's the Sheraton, just outside of Harvard Square?"

"You're sure I can't talk you into spending the night with me?"

It was possible that she had no idea how suggestive it was when she asked a question like that, combined with a smile like that.

On the other hand, she probably knew damn well what she was doing to him. She was, after all, a Skelly.

He laughed. It was either that or cry. *Evasive maneuvers, Mr. Sulu.* "Why don't we just plan to have lunch tomorrow?"

Lunch was good. Lunch was safe. It was businesslike and well lit.

"Hmm. I'm working straight through lunch tomorrow," she told him. "I'm going to be driving the truck all day, picking up donations to take to Tulgeria. But I'd love to have breakfast with you."

This time it wasn't so much the words but the way she said it, lowering her voice and smiling slightly.

Bobby could picture her at breakfast—still in bed, her hair sexily mussed, her gorgeous eyes heavy-lidded. Her mouth curving up into a sleepy smile, her breasts soft and full against the almost-transparent cotton of that innocent little nightgown he'd once seen hanging in her bathroom....

Everything about her body language was screaming for him to kiss her. Unless he was seriously mistaken, everything she was saying and doing was one great big, giant green light.

God help him, why did she have to be Wes Skelly's little sister?

TRAFFIC WAS HEAVY THROUGH the Back Bay and out toward Cambridge.

For once, Colleen didn't mind. This was probably the last time for a while that she'd make this drive up Comm. Ave. and over the BU bridge. It was certainly the last time she'd do it in this car.

She refused to feel remorse, refused even to acknowledge the twinge of regret that tightened her throat every time she thought about signing over the title. She'd done too much pro bono work this past year. It was her fault entirely, and the only way to make ends meet now was to sell her car. It was a shame, but she had to do it.

At least this final ride was a memorable one.

She glanced at Bobby Taylor, sitting there beside her, looking like the perfect accessory for a lipstick-red 1969 Ford Mustang, with his long hair and exotic cheekbones and those melted-chocolate eyes.

Yeah, he was another very solid reason why she didn't mind at all about the traffic.

For the first time she could remember, she had Bobby Taylor alone in her car, and the longer it took to reach Harvard Square, the better. She needed all the time she could to figure out a way to keep him from getting out when they arrived at his hotel.

She'd been pretty obvious so far, and she wondered just how blatant she was going to have to be. She laughed aloud as she imagined herself laying it all on the table, bringing it down to the barest bottom line, asking him if he wanted to get with her, using the rudest, least-elegant language she knew.

"So…what are you going to do tonight?" she asked him instead.

He glanced at her warily, as if he were somehow able to read her mind and knew what she really wanted to ask him.

"Your hair's getting really long," she interrupted him before he could even start to answer. "Do you ever wear it down?"

"Not too often," he told her.

Say it. Just say it. "Not even in bed?"

He hesitated only briefly. "No, I usually sleep with it braided or at least pulled back. Otherwise it takes forever to untangle in the morning."

She hadn't meant while he slept. She knew from the way he wasn't looking at her that he was well aware of what she had meant.

"I guess from your hair that you're still doing the covert stuff, huh?" she asked. "Oops, sorry. Don't answer that." She rolled her eyes. "Not that you would."

Bobby laughed. He had a great laugh, a low-pitched rumble that was always accompanied by the most gorgeous smile and extremely attractive laughter lines around his eyes. "I think it's fine if I say yes," he told her. "And you're right—the long hair makes it kind of obvious, anyway."

"So is Wes out on a training op or is it the real thing this time?" she asked.

"I don't know that myself," he admitted. "Really," he added as she shot him a skeptical glance.

The traffic light was red, and she chewed her lip as she braked to a stop and stared at the taillights of the cars in front of them. "It worries me that he's out there without you."

When she looked at him again, he was watching her. And he actually held her gaze for the first time since they'd gotten into her car. "He's good at what he does, Colleen," he told her gently. She loved the way he said her name.

"I know. It's just… Well, I don't worry so much when he's with you." She forced a smile. "And I don't worry so much about you when you're with him."

Bobby didn't smile. He didn't do much of anything but look into her eyes. No, when he looked at her like that, he wasn't just looking into her eyes. He was looking into her mind, into her soul. Colleen found herself holding her breath, hypnotized, praying that he would like what he saw. Wishing that he would kiss her.

How could he look at her like that—and the way he'd looked at her in the church parking lot, too—and then *not* kiss her?

The car behind her honked, and she realized that the light had changed. The line of traffic had already moved. She fumbled with the stick shift, suddenly afraid she was making a huge fool of herself.

One of Wes's recent emails had mentioned that Bobby had finally ended his on-again, off-again relationship with a woman he'd met in Arizona or New Mexico or some-place else equally unlikely, considering the man spent most of his waking hours in the ocean.

Of course, that so-called *recent* email from her brother had arrived nearly two months ago. A lot might've hap-pened in the past two months. Bobby could well have hooked up with someone new. Or gotten back together with what's-her-name. Kyra Something.

"Wes told me you and Kyra called it quits." There was absolutely no point in sitting here wondering. So what if she came across as obvious? She was tired of guessing. Did she have a chance here, or didn't she? Inquiring minds wanted to know.

"Um," Bobby said. "Yeah, well... She, uh, found someone who wasn't gone all the time. She's actually getting married in October."

"Oh, yikes." Colleen made a face at him. "The *M* word." Wes always sounded as if he were on the verge of a panic attack when that word came up.

But Bobby just smiled. "Yeah, I think she called to tell me about it because she was looking for a counteroffer, but I just couldn't do it. We had a lot of fun, but..." He shook his head. "I wasn't about to leave the teams for her, you know, and that's what she wanted." He was quiet for a moment. "She deserved way more than I could give her, anyway."

"And you deserve more than someone who'll ask you to change your whole life for them," Colleen countered.

He looked startled at that, as if he'd never considered such a thing, as if he'd viewed himself as the bad guy in the relationship—the primary reason for its failure.

Kyra Whomever was an idiot.

"How about you?" he asked. "Wes said you were dating some lawyer."

Oh, my God. Was it possible that Bobby was doing a little fishing of his own?

"No," she said, trying to sound casual. "Nope. That's funny, but... Oh, I know what he was thinking. I told him I went to Connecticut with Charlie Johannsen. Wes must've thought..." She had to laugh. "Charlie's longtime companion is an actor. He just got cast in a new musical at Goodspeed-at-Chester."

"Ah," Bobby said. "Wes will be relieved."

"Wes never wants me to have any fun," she countered. "How about you?" She used Bobby's own words. "Are you seeing someone new?"

"Nope. And Wes isn't, either."

Okay. She would talk about Wes. She'd gotten the info she'd wanted.

"Is he still carrying the torch for—" What was her name? "Laura?"

Bobby shook his head. "You'll have to ask him about that."

Yeah, like Wes would talk to her about this. "Lana," she remembered. "He once wrote me this really long email all about her. I think he was drunk when he wrote it."

"I'm sure he was." Bobby shook his head. "When you talk to him, Colleen, it's probably better not to mention her."

"Oh, my God, is she dead?"

"No. Do you mind if we talk about something else?"

He was the one who'd brought up Wes in the first place. "Not at all."

Silence.

Colleen waited for him to start a new topic of conversation—anything that wasn't about Wes—but he just sat there, distracted by the sight of the river out the window.

"Do you want to go see a movie later?" she finally asked. "Or we could rent a video. I've got an appointment at six-thirty with a guy who wants to buy my car. If everything goes right, I'll be done by seven-thirty, easy."

That got his attention, just the way she knew it would. "You're selling your car? *This* car?"

When she was fifteen, sixteen, seventeen, this Mustang

was all she could talk about. But people's priorities changed. It wasn't going to be easy to sell it, but she refused to let it be the end of her world—a world that was so much wider now, extending all the way to Tulgeria and beyond.

She made herself smile at him. "I am. Law school's expensive."

"Colleen, if you need a loan—"

"I've got a loan. Believe me I've got *many* loans. I've got loans to pay off loans. I've got—"

"It took you five years to rebuild this car. To find authentic parts and—"

"And now someone's going to pay top dollar for a very shiny, very well-maintained vintage Mustang that handles remarkably badly in the snow. I live in Cambridge, Massachusetts. I don't need a car—especially not one that skids if you so much as whisper the word *ice*. My apartment's two minutes from the T, and frankly, I have better things to spend my money on than parking tickets and gasoline."

"Okay," he said. "Okay. I have an idea. I've got some money saved. I'll lend you what you need—interest free— and we can take the next week and drive this car back to your parents' house in Oklahoma, garage it there. Then in a few years when you graduate—"

"Nice try," Colleen told him. "But my travel itinerary has me going to Tulgeria next Thursday. Oklahoma's not exactly in the flight path."

"Think about it this way—if you don't go to Tulgeria, you get to keep your car and have an interest-free loan."

She took advantage of another red light to turn and look at him. "Are you attempting to bribe me?"

He didn't hesitate. "Absolutely."

She had to laugh. "You really want me to stay home?

It's gonna cost you. A million dollars, babe. I'll accept nothing less."

He rolled his eyes. "Colleen—"

"Put up or shut up."

"Seriously, Colleen, I've been to Tulgeria and—"

"I'm *dead* serious, Robert. *And* if you want to lecture me about the dangers of Tulgeria, you've got to buy me dinner. But first you've got to come with me while I sell my car—make sure the buyer's really a buyer and not some psycho killer who answers vintage car ads in the *Boston Globe*."

He didn't hesitate. "Of course I'll come with you."

Jackpot. "Great," Colleen said. "We'll go take care of business, then drop your stuff at your hotel before we grab some dinner. Is that a plan?"

He looked at her. "I never really stood a chance here, did I?"

She smiled at him happily. "Nope."

Bobby nodded, then turned to look out the window. He murmured something that Colleen wasn't quite sure she caught, but it sounded an awful lot like, "I'm a dead man."

CHAPTER THREE

Dark, cool and mysterious.

Somehow, despite his best intentions, Bobby had ended up sitting across from Colleen in a restaurant that was decidedly dark, cool and mysterious.

The food *was* great. Colleen had been right about that, too.

Although she didn't seem to be eating too much.

The meeting with the buyer had gone well. The man had accepted her price for the car—no haggling.

It turned out that that meeting had been held in the well-lit office of a reputable escrow agent, complete with security guard. Colleen had known damn well there was absolutely no danger from psycho killers or anyone else.

Still, Bobby had been glad that he was there while the buyer handed over a certified check and she handed over the title and keys to the Mustang.

She'd smiled and even laughed, but it was brittle, and he'd wanted to touch her. But he hadn't. He knew that he couldn't. Even just a hand on her shoulder would have been too intimate. And if she'd leaned back into him, he would have put his arms around her. And if he'd done that there in the office, he would have done it again, later, when they were alone, and there was no telling where that might lead.

No, strike that. Bobby knew damn well it would lead to him kissing her. And that could and would lead to a full meltdown, a complete and utter dissolving of his defenses and resolve.

It made him feel like a total skeeve. What kind of friend could he be to Colleen if he couldn't even offer her the most basic form of comfort as a hand on her shoulder? Was he really so weak that he couldn't control himself around her?

Yes.

The answer was a resounding, unchallenged *yes*.

No doubt about it—he was scum.

After leaving the escrow office, they'd taken the T into Harvard Square. Colleen had kept up a fairly steady stream of conversation. About law school. About her roommate—a woman named Ashley who'd gone back to Scarsdale for the summer to work in her father's law office, but who still sent monthly checks for her share of the rent, who didn't have the nerve to tell her father that, like Colleen, she'd far rather be a public defender and a pro bono civil litigant than a highly paid corporate tax attorney.

Bobby had checked into his hotel and given his bag and a tip to the bellhop. He didn't dare take it up to his room himself—not with Colleen trailing behind, no way. That transaction only took a few minutes, and then they were back out in the warm summer night.

The restaurant was only a short walk into Harvard Square. As he sat down across from Colleen, as he gazed at her pretty face in the dim candlelight, he'd ordered a cola. He was dying for a beer, but there was no way he'd trust himself to have even one. If he was going to survive this, he needed all of his wits about him.

They talked about the menu, about food—a nice safe topic—for a while. And then their order came, and Bobby ate while Colleen pushed the food around on her plate.

She was quiet by then, too. It was unusual to be around a Skelly who wasn't constantly talking.

"Are you okay?" he asked.

She looked up at him, and he realized that there were tears in her eyes. She shook her head. But then she forced a smile. "I'm just being stupid," she said before the smile wavered and disappeared. "I'm sorry."

She pushed herself out of the booth and would have rushed past him, toward the rest rooms at the back of the restaurant, if he hadn't reached out and grabbed her hand. He slid out of the bench seat, too, still holding on to her. It took him only a second to pull more than enough dollars to cover the bill out of his pocket and toss it onto the table.

This place had a rear exit. He'd automatically noted it when they'd first came in—years of practice in preparing an escape route—and he led her to it now, pushing open the door.

They had to go up a few steps, but then they were outside, on a side street. It was just a stone's throw to Brattle Street, but they were still far enough from the circus-like atmosphere of Harvard Square on a summer night to have a sense of distance and seclusion from the crowds.

"I'm sorry," Colleen said again, trying to wipe away her tears before they even fell. "I'm stupid—it's just a stupid car."

Bobby had something very close to an out-of-body experience. He saw himself standing there, in the shadows, next to her. Helplessly, with a sense of total doom, he watched himself reach for her, pull her close and enfold her in his arms.

Oh, dear Lord, she was so soft. And she held him tightly, her arms around his waist, her face buried in his shoulder as she quietly tried not to cry.

Don't do this. Get away from her. You're asking for trouble.

He must've made some kind of awful strangled sound because Colleen lifted her head and looked up at him. "Oh, no, am I hurting you?"

"No," he said. No, she was *killing* him. And count on Colleen to worry about someone else during a moment when most people wouldn't have been thinking of anyone but themselves.

Tears glistened on her cheeks and sparkled in her eyelashes, and the tip of her nose was red. Bozo the Clown, he and Wes had teased her whenever she'd cried back when she was thirteen.

She wasn't thirteen anymore.

Don't kiss her. Don't do it.

Bobby clenched his teeth and thought about Wes. He pictured the look on his best friend's face as he tried to explain. *See, she was right there, man, in my arms, and her mouth looked so soft and beautiful, and her body was so warm and lush and...*

She put her head back against his shoulder with a sigh, and Bobby realized he was running his fingers through the silk of her hair. She had hair like a baby's, soft and fine.

He knew he should make himself stop, but he couldn't. He'd wanted to touch her hair for more than four years now.

Besides, she really seemed to like it.

"You must think I'm a loser," she murmured.

"No."

She laughed softly. "Yeah, well, I am. Crying over a car. How dumb can I be?" She sighed. "It's just... When I was seventeen, I'd imagined I'd have that car forever—you know, hand it down to my grandchildren? I say it now, and it sounds stupid, but it didn't feel stupid back then."

The deal she'd just made gave her twenty-four hours to change her mind.

"It's not too late," he reminded her. He reminded himself, too. He could gently release her, take one step back, then two. He could—without touching her again—lead her back to the lights and crowd in Harvard Square. And then he'd never even have to mention anything to Wes. Because nothing would have happened.

But he didn't move. He told himself he would be okay, that he could handle this—as long as he didn't look into her eyes.

"No, I'm selling it," she told him, pulling back slightly to look up at him, wiping her nose on a tissue she'd taken from her shoulder pack. "I've made up my mind. I need this money. I loved that car, but I love going to law school, too. I love the work I do, I love being able to make a difference."

She was looking at him so earnestly he forgot about not looking into her eyes until it was too late. Until the earnest look morphed into something else, something loaded with longing and spiked with desire.

Her gaze dropped to his mouth, and her lips parted slightly, and when she looked once again into his eyes, he knew. She wanted to kiss him nearly as much as he wanted to kiss her.

Don't do this. Don't...

He could feel his heart pounding, hear the roar of his blood surging through his body, drowning out the sounds of the city night, blocking out all reason and harsh reality.

He couldn't not kiss her. How could he keep from kissing her when he needed to kiss her as much as he needed to fill his lungs with air?

But she didn't give him a chance to lean down toward her. She stood on her tiptoes and brushed her mouth across his in a kiss that was so achingly sweet that he thought for one paralyzingly weak-kneed moment he just might faint.

But she stepped back just a little to look at him again, to smile hesitantly into his eyes before reaching up, her hand cool against the too-hot back of his neck as she pulled his head down to kiss him again.

Her lips were so soft, so cool, so sweetly uncertain, such a contrast to the way his heart was hammering and to the tight, hot sensation in his rib cage—as if his entire chest were about to burst.

He was afraid to move. He was afraid to kiss her back, for fear he'd scare her to death with his hunger for her. He didn't even know how to kiss like this—with such delicate tenderness.

But he liked it. Lord, he liked it an awful lot. He'd had his share of women who'd given him deep, wet, soul kisses, sucking his tongue into their mouths in a decidedly unsubtle imitation of what they wanted to do with him later, in private.

But those kisses hadn't been even a fraction as sexy as what Colleen was doing to him right now.

She kissed his mouth, his chin and then his mouth again, her own lips slightly parted. She barely touched him. In fact, she touched him more with her breath—soft, unsteady puffs of air that caressed him enticingly.

He tried to kiss her the same way, tried to touch her without really touching her, skimming his hands down her back, his palms tingling from the almost-contact. It made him dizzy with anticipation.

Incredible anticipation.

She touched his lips with her tongue—just the very tiniest tip of her tongue—and pleasure crashed through him. It was so intense that for one blindingly unsteady moment he was afraid he might actually have embarrassed himself beyond recovery.

From just a kiss.

But he hadn't. Not yet, anyway. Still, he couldn't take it anymore, not another second longer, and he crushed her to him, filling his hands with the softness of her body, sweeping his tongue into her mouth.

She didn't seem to mind. In fact, her pack fell to the ground, and she kissed him back enthusiastically, welcoming the ferocity of his kisses, winding her arms around his neck, pressing herself even more tightly against him.

It was the heaven he'd dreamed of all these years.

Bobby kissed her, again and again—deep, explosively hungry kisses that she fired right back at him. She opened herself to him, wrapping one of her legs around his, moaning her pleasure as he filled his hand with her breast.

He caught himself glancing up, scanning a nearby narrow alleyway between two buildings, estimating whether it was dark enough for them to slip inside, dark enough for him to unzip his shorts and pull up her skirt, dark enough for him to take her, right there, beneath someone's kitchen window, with her legs around his waist and her back against the roughness of the brick wall.

He'd pulled her halfway into the alley before reality came screaming through.

Wes's sister. This was Wes's *sister.*

He had his tongue in Wes's sister's mouth. One hand was filled with the softness of Wes's sister's derriere as he pressed her hips hard against his arousal. His other hand was up Wes's sister's shirt.

Had he completely lost his mind?

Yes.

Bobby pulled back, breathing hard.

That was almost worse, because now he had to look at her. She was breathing hard, too, her breasts rising and falling rapidly, her nipples taut and clearly outlined beneath her shirt, her face flushed, her lips swollen and moist from his kisses.

But it was her eyes that almost killed him. They were smoky with desire, brimming with fire and unresolved passion.

"Let's go to my apartment," she whispered, her voice even huskier than usual.

Oh, God.

"I can't." His voice cracked, making him sound even more pathetic.

"Oh," she said. "Oh, I'm—" she shook her head "—I'm sorry, I thought… You said you weren't seeing anyone."

"No." He shook his head, tried to catch his breath. "It's not that."

"Then why stop?"

He couldn't respond. What could he possibly say? But shaking his head again wasn't a good enough response for Colleen.

"You really don't want to come back to my place and—"

"I can't. I just can't." He cut her off, unable to bear finding out just which words she would use to describe what they'd do if he did go home with her tonight. Whether she called it making love or something more crudely to the point, however she couched it, it would be a total turn-on.

And he was already *way* too turned on.

She took a step toward him, and he took a step back.

"You're serious," she said. "You really don't want to?"

He couldn't let her think that. "I want to," he told her. "God, I want to. More than you could possibly know. I just… I *can't*."

"What, have you taken some kind of vow of abstinence?"

Somehow he managed to smile at her. "Sort of."

Just like that she understood. He saw the realization dawn in her eyes and flare rapidly into anger. "Wesley," she said. "This is about my brother, isn't it?"

Bobby knew enough not to lie to her. "He's my best friend."

She was furious. "What did he do? Warn you to stay away from me? Did he tell you not to touch me? Did he tell you not to—"

"No. He warned me not even to *think* about it." Wes had said it jokingly, one night on liberty when they'd each had five or six too many beers. Wes hadn't really believed it was a warning he'd needed to give his best friend.

Colleen bristled. "Well, you know what? Wes can't tell *me* what to think, and *I've* been thinking about it. For a long time."

Bobby gazed at her. Suddenly it was hard to breathe again. A long time. "Really?"

She nodded, her anger subdued, as if she were suddenly shy. She looked everywhere but in his eyes. "Yeah. Wasn't that kind of obvious from the way I jumped you?"

"I thought I jumped you."

Colleen looked at him then, hope in her eyes. "Please come home with me. I really want you to—I want to make love to you, Bobby. You're only here for a week—let's not waste a minute."

Oh, God, she'd said it. Bobby couldn't bear to look at her, so he closed his eyes. "Colleen, I promised Wes I'd look out for you. That I'd take care of you."

"Perfect." She bent down to pick up her bag. "Take care of me. Please."

Oh, man. He laughed because, despite his agony, he

found her funny as hell. "I'm positive he didn't mean it like that."

"You know, he doesn't need to find out."

Bobby braced himself and met her gaze. "I can't be that kind of friend to him."

She sighed. "Terrific. Now I feel like a total worm." She started toward Brattle Street. "I think, considering all things, we should skip the movie. I'm going home. If you change your mind…"

"I won't."

"…you know where to find me." Bobby followed her about a dozen more steps, and she turned around. "Are you coming with me after all?"

"It's getting late. I'll see you home."

"No," Colleen said. "Thank you, but no."

Bobby knew not to press it. That look in her eyes was one he'd seen far too many times on a completely different Skelly.

"I'm sorry," he said again.

"Me, too," she told him before she walked away.

The sidewalk wasn't as crowded as it had been just a few hours ago, so Bobby let her get a good head start before he started after her.

He followed her all the way home, making certain she was safe without letting her see him again.

And then he stood there, outside her apartment building, watching the lights go on in her apartment, angry and frustrated and dying to be up there with her, and wondering what on earth he was going to do now.

CHAPTER FOUR

COLLEEN HAD PRINTED OUT the email late last night, and she now held it tightly in her hand as she approached Bobby.

He was exactly where he'd said he would be when he'd called—sitting on the grassy slope along the Charles River, looking out at the water, sipping coffee through a hot cup with a plastic lid.

He saw her coming and got to his feet. "Thanks for meeting me," he called.

He was so serious—no easygoing smile on his face. Or maybe he was nervous. It was hard to be sure. Unlike Wes, who twitched and bounced off the walls at twice his normal frenetic speed when he was nervous, Bobby showed no outward sign.

He didn't fiddle with his coffee cup. He just held it serenely. He'd gotten them both large cups, but in his hand, large looked small.

Colleen was going to have to hold hers with both hands.

He didn't tap his foot. He didn't nervously clench his teeth. He didn't chew his lip.

He just stood there and breathed as he solemnly watched her approach.

He'd called at 6:30 this morning. She'd just barely fallen asleep after a night spent mostly tossing and turning—and analyzing everything she'd done and said last night, trying to figure out what she'd done wrong.

She'd come to the conclusion that she'd done *every-*thing wrong. Starting with crying over a motor vehicle and ending with darn near throwing herself at the man.

This morning Bobby had apologized for calling so early and had told her he hadn't been sure what time she was leaving for work today. He'd remembered that she was driving the truck, remembered their tentative plan to meet for breakfast.

Last night she'd wanted him to *stay* for breakfast.

But he hadn't—because of some stupid idea that by having a relationship with her, he'd be betraying Wes.

Wes, whose life he'd most likely saved, probably count-less times. Including, so it seemed, one definite time just a few short weeks ago.

"I can't believe you didn't tell me you'd been *shot*." Colleen didn't bother saying good morning. She just thrust the copy of Wes's email at him.

He took it and read it quickly. It wasn't very long. Just a short, fast, grammatically creative hello from Wes, who didn't report where he was, who really just wanted to make sure Bobby had arrived in Boston. He mentioned almost in passing that Bobby had recently been shot while out in the real world—the SEALs' nickname for a real mission or operation.

They had been somewhere they weren't supposed to be, Wes reported vaguely, and due to circumstances out of their control, they'd been discovered. Men with as-sault weapons started shooting, and Bobby had stepped in front of Wes, taking some bullets and saving his scrawny hide.

"Be nice to him," Wes had written to Colleen. "He nearly died. He almost got his butt shot off, and his shoul-der's still giving him pain. Treat him kindly. I'll call as soon as I'm back in the States."

"If he can say all that in an email," Colleen told Bobby

sternly, "you could have told me at least a *little* about what happened. You could have told me you were shot instead of letting me think you'd hurt yourself in some normal way—like pulling a muscle playing basketball."

He handed her the piece of paper. "I didn't think it was useful information," he admitted. "I mean, what good is telling you that a bunch of bad guys with guns tried to kill your brother a few weeks ago? Does knowing that really help you in any way?"

"Yes, because *not* knowing hurts. You don't need to protect me from the truth," Colleen told him fiercely. "I'm not a little girl anymore." She rolled her eyes. "I thought we cleared *that* up last night."

Last night. When some extremely passionate kisses had nearly led to getting it on right out in the open, in an alley not far from Harvard Square.

"I got coffee and muffins," Bobby said, deftly changing the subject. "Do you have time to sit and talk?"

Colleen watched as he lowered himself back onto the grass. Gingerly. Why hadn't she noticed that last night? She was *so* self-absorbed. "Yes. Great. Let's talk. You can start by telling me how many times you were shot and exactly where."

He glanced at her as she sat down beside him, amusement in his dark eyes. "Trust Wes to be melodramatic. I took a round in the upper leg that bled kind of heavily. It's fine now—no problem." He pulled up the baggy leg of his shorts to reveal a deeply tanned, enormously muscular thigh. There was a fresh pink scar up high on his leg. Where it would really hurt a whole lot to be shot. Where there were major veins—or were they arteries?—which, if opened, could easily cause a man to bleed to death very quickly.

Wes hadn't been melodramatic at all. Colleen couldn't

breathe. She couldn't stop staring at that scar. Bobby could have died.

"It's my shoulder that's giving me the trouble," Bobby continued, pulling his shorts leg back down. "I was lucky I didn't break a bone, but it's still pretty sore. I've got limited mobility right now—which is frustrating. I can't lift my arm much higher than this."

He demonstrated, and Colleen realized that his ponytail wasn't a fashion statement after all. He was wearing his hair like that because he wasn't physically able to put it back in his usual neat braid.

"I'm supposed to take it easy," he told her. "You know, not push it for another week."

He handed her a cup of coffee and held open a bag that contained about a half a dozen enormous muffins. She shook her head. Her appetite was gone.

"Can you do me a favor?" she asked. "Next time you or Wes get hurt, even if it's just something really little, will you call me and let me know? Please? Otherwise I'm just going to worry about you all the time."

Bobby shook his head. "Colleen…"

"Don't *Colleen* me," she countered. "Just promise."

He looked at her. Sighed. "I promise. But—"

"No buts."

He started to say something, then stopped, shaking his head instead. No doubt he'd spent enough time around Skellys to know arguing was useless. Instead he took a sip of his coffee and gazed out at the river.

"How many times have you saved Wes's life?" she asked him, suddenly needing to know.

"I don't know. I think I lost count somewhere between two and three million." The laughter lines around his eyes crinkled as he smiled.

"Very funny."

"It's just not that big a deal," he said.

"It is to me," she returned. "And I'm betting it's a pretty big deal to my brother, too."

"It's really only a big deal to him because I'm winning," Bobby admitted.

At first his words didn't make sense. And then they made too much sense. "You guys keep score?" she asked in disbelief. "You have some kind of contest going…?"

Amusement danced in his eyes. "Twelve to five and a half. My favor."

"Five and a *half?*" she echoed.

"He got a half point for getting me back to the boat in one piece this last time," he explained. "He couldn't get a full point because it was partially his fault I needed his help in the first place."

He was laughing at her. Oh, he wasn't actually laughing aloud, but Colleen knew that, inside, he was silently chortling away.

"You know," she said with a completely straight face, "it seems only fair that if you save someone's life that many times, you ought to be able to have wild sex with that person's sister, guilt free."

Bobby choked on his coffee. Served him right.

"So what are you doing tonight?" Colleen asked, still in that same innocent voice.

He coughed even harder, trying to get the liquid out of his lungs.

"'Be nice to him,'" she read aloud from Wes's email. She held it out for him to see. "See, it says it right there."

"That's *not* what Wes meant," Bobby managed to gasp.

"How do you know?"

"I *know.*"

"Are you okay?" she asked.

His eyes were tearing, and he still seemed to have trouble breathing. "You're killing me."

"Good. I've got to go, so—" She started to stand up.

"Wait." He coughed again, tugging her back down beside him. "Please." He drew in a breath, and although he managed not to cough, he had to clear his throat several times. "I really need to talk to you about what happened last night."

"Don't you mean what *didn't* happen?" She pretended to be fascinated with her coffee cup, with folding up the little flap on the plastic lid so that she could take a sip without it bumping into her nose.

What had happened last night was that she had found out—the hard way—that Bobby Taylor didn't want her. At least not enough to take what she'd offered. At least not as much as she wanted him. It was possible he'd only used his fear of Wes's disapproval as an excuse to keep from going home with her. After all, it had worked, hadn't it? It had worked very well.

This morning she could only pretend not to care. She could be flip and say outrageous things, but the truth was, she was both embarrassed and afraid of what he might want to say to her.

Of course, if ever there were a perfect time for him to confess his undying love, it would be now. She supposed it *was* possible that he would haltingly tell her he'd fallen in love with her years ago, that he'd worshiped her from afar for all this time and now that they'd finally kissed, he couldn't bear to be apart from her any longer.

Bobby cleared his throat again. "Colleen, I, um…I don't want to lose you as a friend."

Or he could say that. He could give her the "let's stay friends" speech. She'd heard it before. It would contain the word *friend* at least seven more times. He would say *mistake* and *sorry* both at least twice and *honest* at least once. And he'd tell her that he hoped what happened last night wouldn't change things between them. Her friendship was very important to him.

"I really care about you," he told her. "But I have to be honest. What happened last night was, well, it was a mistake."

Yup. She'd definitely heard it before. She could have written it out for him on a three-by-five-card. Saved him some time.

"I know that I said last night that I couldn't...that we couldn't...because of *Wes* and, well, I need you to know that there's more to it than that."

Yeah, she'd suspected that.

"I can't possibly be what you really want," he said quietly.

Now *that* was different. She'd never heard that before.

"I'm not..." He started to continue, but then he shook his head and got back on track. "You mean too much to me. I can't take advantage of you, I *can't*. I'm ten years older than you, and—Colleen, I knew you when you were thirteen—that's just too weird. It would be crazy, it wouldn't go anywhere. It couldn't. *I* couldn't. We're too different and..." He swore softly, vehemently. "I really am sorry."

He looked about as miserable as she was feeling. Except he probably wasn't embarrassed to death. What had she been thinking, to throw herself at him like that last night?

She closed her eyes, feeling very young and very foolish—as well as ancient beyond her years. How could this be happening again? What was it about her that made men only want to be her friend?

She supposed she should be thankful. This time she got the "let's stay friends" speech *before* she'd gone to bed with the guy. That had been the lowest of a number of low-relationship moments. Or it should have been. Despite the fact that Bobby obviously cared enough not to let it get that far, he didn't care about her the way she wanted him to. And that hurt remarkably badly.

She stood up, brushing off the seat of her shorts. "I know you're probably not done. You still have one more *mistake* and another *sorry* to go, but I'll say 'em for you, okay? I'm sorry, too. The mistake was mine. Thanks for the coffee."

Colleen held her head up as she quickly walked away. And she didn't look back. She'd learned the hard way never to look back after the "let's stay friends" speech. And never to cry, either. After all, smart friends didn't cry when stupid, idiotic, completely clueless friends rejected them.

Tears welled in her eyes, but she forced them back.

God, she was such a fool.

BOBBY LAY BACK ON the grass and stared up at the sky.

In theory, telling Colleen that they should stay friends instead of rip each other's clothes off had seemed to be the least painful way of neatly dealing with something that was on the verge of turning into an emotional and physical bloodbath.

Physical—because if Wes found out that Bobby had messed with his little sister, he would have been mad enough to reach down Bobby's throat and rip his lungs out.

Bobby had been direct with Colleen. He'd been swift and, if not quite honest, he'd certainly been sincere.

Yet somehow he'd managed to hurt her. He'd seen it in her eyes as she'd turned and walked away.

Damn. Hurting her was the dead last thing he'd wanted to do.

That entire conversation had been impossibly difficult.

He'd been on the verge of telling her the truth—that he hadn't slept at all last night, that he'd spent the night alternately congratulating himself for doing the right thing and cursing himself for being an idiot.

Last night she made it clear that she wanted him. And Lord knows that the last thing he honestly wanted was to stay mere friends with her. In truth, he wanted to get naked with her—and stay naked for the entire rest of this week.

But he knew he wasn't the kind of man Colleen Skelly needed. She needed someone who would be there for her. Someone who came home every night without fail. Someone who could take care of her the way she deserved to be taken care of.

Someone who wanted more than a week of hot sex.

He didn't want another long-distance relationship. He couldn't take it. He'd just gotten out of one of those, and it wasn't much fun.

And would be even less fun with Colleen Skelly— because after Wes found out that Bobby was playing around with his sister, Wes would come after him with his diving knife.

Well, maybe not, but certainly he and Wes would argue. And *Colleen* and Wes would argue. And that was an awful lot of pain, considering Bobby would spend most of his time three thousand miles away from her, him missing her with every breath he took, her missing him, too.

No, hurting Colleen was bad, but telling her the truth would hurt them both even more in the long run.

CHAPTER FIVE

COLLEEN HAD JUST FINISHED picking up a load of blankets collected by a women's church group and was on her way to a half dozen senior centers to pick up their donations when a taxi pulled up. It stopped directly in front of her, blocking her exit from the parking lot with a TV-cop-drama squealing of brakes.

Her first thought was that someone was late to their own wedding. But other than the representative from the ladies' auxiliary who had handed over the bundles of blankets, the building had been silent and empty.

Her second thought was that someone was in a major hurry to repent their sins, probably before they sinned again. She had to laugh at that image, but her laughter faded as the absolute last person she'd expected to see here at the St. Augustus Church climbed out of the cab.

Bobby Taylor.

His hair had partially fallen out of his ponytail, and his face was covered with a sheen of perspiration, as if he'd been running. He ignored both his sweat and his hair as he came around to the passenger side of the truck's cab. She leaned across the bench seat, unlocked the door, and he opened it.

"Thank God," he said as if he really meant it. "I've been following you for an hour now."

More than just his face was sweaty. His shirt was as soaked as if he'd been running a marathon in this heat.

Wes. Her brother was the only reason she could come

up with for Bobby to search her out so desperately. Wes had to have been injured. Or—please, God, no—dead.

Colleen flashed hot and then cold. "Oh, no," she said. "What happened? How bad is it?"

Bobby stared at her. "Then you haven't heard? I was ready to yell at you because I thought you knew. I thought you went out to make these pickups, anyway."

"Just tell me he's not dead," she begged him. She'd lived through one dead brother—it was an experience she never wanted to repeat. "I can take anything as long as he's not dead."

His expression became one of even more perplexity as he climbed into the air-conditioned cab and closed the door. "He?" he asked. "It was a woman who was attacked. She's in ICU, in a coma, at Mass General."

A woman? At Mass General Hospital...? Now it was Colleen's turn to stare at him stupidly. "You didn't track me down because Wes is hurt?"

"Wes?" Bobby shook his head as he leaned forward to turn the air conditioner fan to high. "No, I'm sure he's fine. The mission was probably only a training op. He wouldn't have been able to send email if it were the real thing."

"Then what's going on?" Colleen's relief was mixed with irritation. He had a lot of nerve, coming after her like this and scaring her to death.

"Andrea Barker," he explained. "One of the chief administrators of the AIDS Education Center. She was found badly beaten—barely breathing—outside of her home in Newton. I saw it in the paper."

Colleen nodded. "Yeah," she said. "Yeah, I heard about that this morning. That's really awful. I don't know her that well—we talked on the phone only once. I've mostly met with her assistant when dealing with the center."

"So you *did* know she's in the hospital." Something

very much like anger flashed in his eyes, and his usually pleasantly relaxed mouth was back to a hard, grim line.

Bobby Taylor was mad at her. It was something Colleen had never experienced before. She hadn't thought he was capable of getting mad—he was so laid-back. Even more mind-blowing was the fact that she truly had no clue what she'd done to get him so upset.

"The article went into some depth about the problem they've—*you've*— You're part of them, providing legal services at no cost, right? The problem *you've* been having establishing a center in this one particular neighborhood in Boston. The same neighborhood where you just happened to be threatened yesterday while having a car wash…?"

And Colleen understood. She laughed in disbelief. "You really think the attack on Andrea Barker had something to do with her work for the education center?"

Bobby didn't shout at her the way Wesley did when he got mad. He spoke quietly, evenly, his voice dangerously soft. Combined with the spark of anger in his eyes, it was far more effective than any temper tantrum Wes had ever thrown. "And you don't?"

"No. Come on, Bobby. Don't be so paranoid. Look, I heard that the police theory is she startled a burglar coming out of her house."

"I heard a partial list of her injuries," Bobby countered, still in that same quietly intense voice. She had to wonder, what would ever set him off, make him raise his voice? What—if anything—would make this man lose his cool and detonate? If it ever happened, boy, look out. It would probably be quite an impressive show.

"They weren't the kind of injuries a woman would get from a burglar," he continued, "whose primary goal would have been to knock her down so he could run away as quickly as possible. No, I'm sorry, Colleen. I know you want to believe otherwise, but this woman was beaten deliberately, and if I know it, then the police know it, too. The burglar story is probably just something they threw out to the press, to make the real perpetrator think he's home-free."

"You don't know that for sure."

"Yes," he said. "You're right. I don't know it absolutely. But I'm 99 percent sure. Sure enough to be afraid that, as the legal representative to the AIDS Education Center, you could be the next target. Sure enough to know that the last thing you should be doing today is driving a truck around all by yourself."

He clenched his teeth, the muscles jumping in his jaw as he glared at her. That spark of anger made his eyes cold, as if she were talking to a stranger.

Well, maybe she was.

"Oh. Right." Colleen let her voice get louder with her growing anger. What did he care what happened to her? She was just an idiot who'd embarrassed both of them last night. She was just his *friend*. No, not even. The real truth was that she was just some pain-in-the-butt sister of a friend. "I'm supposed to lock myself in my apartment because there *might* be people who don't like what I do? Sorry, that's not going to happen."

"I spoke to some people," Bobby told her. "They seem to think this John Morrison who threatened you yesterday could be a real danger."

"Some people?" she asked. "Which people? If you talked to Mindy in the center's main office—well, she's afraid of her own shadow. And Charlie Johannsen is no—"

"I dare you," Bobby said, "to look me in the eye and tell me that you're not just a little bit afraid of this man."

She looked at him. Looked away. "Okay. So maybe I am a *little*—"

"And yet you came out here, anyway. By yourself."

She laughed in his face. "Yeah, and like *you* never do anything that you're a little afraid of. Like jumping out of airplanes. Or swimming in shark-infested waters. That's a particularly tough one for you, isn't it, Bobby? Wes told me you have a thing about sharks. Yet you do it. You jump into the water without hesitation. You face down your fear and get on with your life. Don't be a hypocrite, Taylor, and expect me to do anything less."

He was trying hard to be patient. "I'm trained to do those things."

"Yeah, well, I'm a woman," she countered. "I've been trained, too. I've had more than ten years of experience dealing with everything from subtle, male innuendo to overt threats. By virtue of being female, I'm a little bit afraid almost every single time I walk down a city street—and I'm twice as afraid at night."

He shook his head. "There's a big difference between that and a specific threat from a man like John Morrison."

"Is there?" Colleen asked. "Is there really? Because I don't see it that way. You know, there have been times when I walk past a group of men sitting out on the front steps of their apartment building, and one of them says, 'Hey, baby. Want to…'" She said it. It was impossibly crude, and Bobby actually flinched. "'Get over here now,' they say. 'Don't make me chase you to get what I *know* you want to give me.'"

She paused for emphasis. Bobby looked appropriately subdued. "After someone," she said more quietly now, "some *stranger* says something like that to you—and if you want a real dare, then I dare you to find a woman my age who *hasn't* had a similar experience—you get a little—just a little—nervous just going out of your apartment. And when you approach a man heading toward you on the sidewalk, you feel a little flicker of apprehension or maybe even fear. Is he going to say something rude? Is he going take it a step further and follow you? Or is he just going to look at you and maybe whistle, and let you see from his eyes that he's thinking about you in ways that you don't want him to be thinking about you?

"And each time that happens," Colleen told him, "it's no less specific—or potentially unreal—than John Morrison's threats."

Bobby was silent, just sitting there, looking out the window.

"I'm so sorry," he finally said. "What kind of world do we live in?" He laughed, but it wasn't laughter that had anything to do with humor. It was a burst of frustrated air. "The really embarrassing part is that I've been that guy. Not the one who actually says those things, I'd never do that. But I'm the one who looks and even whistles. I never really thought something like that might frighten a woman. I mean, that was *never* my intention."

"Think next time," she told him.

"Someone really said that to you?" He gave her a side-long glance. "In those words?"

She nodded, meeting his gaze. "Pretty rude, huh?"

"I wish I'd been there," he told her. "I would've put him in the hospital."

He said it so matter-of-factly, but she knew it wasn't just an idle threat. "If you had been there," she pointed out, "he wouldn't have said it."

"Maybe Wes is right." Bobby smiled at her ruefully. "Maybe you *should* have a twenty-four-hour armed escort, watching your every move."

"Oh, no," Colleen groaned. "Don't *you* start with that, too. Look, I've got a can of pepper spray in my purse and a whistle on my key ring. I know you don't think so, but I'm about as safe as I can be. I've been keeping the truck doors locked, I've called ahead to set up appointment times, I've—"

"You forgot me," Bobby interrupted. "You should have called me, Colleen. I would have gladly come along with you right from the start."

Oh, perfect. She knew without even asking that he was not going to leave, that he was here in the cab of this truck until she made the last of her pickups, dropped off both the donations and the truck, and took the T back to Cambridge.

"Has it occurred to you that I might not be overly eager to spend the day with you?" she asked him.

She could see his surprise. He'd never dreamed she would be so blunt and to the point. Still, he recovered nicely. And he surprised her back by being equally straightforward.

"It's already too late for our friendship, isn't it?" he said. "I really blew it last night."

No way was she going to let him take the blame. "I was the one who kissed you first."

"Yeah, but I was the one who didn't stop you right then and there," Bobby countered.

She jammed the truck into gear, silently cursing herself for being stupid enough to have even just a little hope left to be crushed. Yet there it was, flapping about like a deflated balloon on the gritty floor of the truck, right next to her shredded pride and pulverized heart.

"I'm sorry," he said. "I should have been able to control myself, but I couldn't. I'm…"

Colleen looked at him. She didn't mean to. She didn't want to. God forbid he see the total misery that his words brought her reflected in her eyes. But there was something in his voice that made her unable to keep from turning her head.

He was looking at her. He was just sitting there, *looking*

at her, and it was the exact same way he'd looked at her last night, right before he'd pulled her close and kissed the hell out of her. There was hunger in his eyes. Heat and need and *desire*.

He looked away quickly, as if he didn't want her to see those things. Colleen looked away, too, her mind and heart both racing.

He was lying. He'd lied this morning, too. He didn't want them to stay just friends any more than *she* did.

He hadn't given her the "let's stay friends" speech because he had an aversion to women like her, women who actually had hips and thighs and weighed more than ninety pounds, wet. He hadn't made that speech because he found her unattractive, because she didn't turn him on.

On the contrary...

With a sudden clarity that should have been accompanied by angelic voices and a brilliant light, Colleen knew.

She *knew*. Bobby had said there was more to it, but there wasn't. This was about Wes.

It was Wesley who had gotten in the way of her and Bobby Taylor, as surely as if he were sitting right there between them, stinking of stale cigarette smoke, in the cab of this truck.

But she wasn't going to call Bobby on that—no way. She was going to play—and win—this game, secure that she knew the cards he was holding in his hand.

Bobby wasn't going to know what hit him.

She glanced at him again as she pulled out of the parking lot. "So you really think Andrea's attack had something to do with her being an AIDS activist?" she asked.

He glanced at her, too, and this time he managed to keep his eyes mostly expressionless. But it was back there—a little flame of desire. Now that she knew what to look for, she couldn't help but see it. "I think until she comes out of that coma and tells the police what happened, we should err on the side of caution."

Colleen made herself shiver. "It's just so creepy—the thought of her being attacked right outside of her own home."

"You don't have to worry about that. I'll go home with you after we're done here."

Jackpot. She had to bite the insides of her cheeks to keep from smiling. She somehow managed to twist her mouth around into a face of displeasure. "Oh," she said. "I don't know if that's necessary—"

"I'll check your place out, see what we can do to heighten the security," he told her. "Worst-case scenario, I'll camp out in the living room tonight. I know you probably don't want me to, but…"

No, indeed, she did *not* want him camped out in her living room tonight.

She wanted him in her bedroom.

"Wait," Colleen said, when Bobby would've opened the truck door and climbed down, after she parked outside the next senior center on her list. She was fishing around in her backpack, and she came up brandishing a hairbrush. "The wild-Indian hairstyle needs a little work."

He had to laugh. "That's so completely un-PC."

"What, telling you that your hair is a mess?"

"Very funny," he said.

"That's me," she said. "Six laughs a minute, guaranteed. Turn around, I'll braid it for you."

How had that happened? Ten minutes ago they'd been fighting. Bobby had been convinced that their friendship was badly strained if not completely over, yet now things were back to where they'd been when he'd first arrived yesterday.

Colleen was no longer completely tense, no longer

looking wounded. She was relaxed and cheerful. He would even dare to call her happy.

Bobby didn't know how that had happened, but he wasn't about to complain.

"You don't have to braid it," he said. "A ponytail's good enough. And all I really need help with is tying it back. I can brush it myself."

He reached for the brush, but she pulled it back, away from him.

"I'll braid it," she said.

"If you really want to." He let her win. What harm could it do? Ever since he'd gotten injured, he'd had to ask for help with his hair. This morning he'd gone into a beauty salon not far from his hotel, tempted to cut it all off.

Back in California, he'd gotten help with his hair each day. Wes stopped by and braided it for him. Or Mia Francisco—the lieutenant commander's wife. Even the captain—Joe Cat—had helped him out once or twice.

He shifted slightly in the seat so Colleen had access to the back of his head, reaching up with his good arm to take out the elastic.

She ran both the brush and her fingers gently through his hair. And Bobby knew immediately that there was a major difference between Colleen braiding his hair and Wes braiding his hair. They were both Skellys, sure, but that was where all similarities ended.

"You have such beautiful hair," Colleen murmured, and he felt himself start to sweat.

This was a bad idea. A very, very bad idea. What could he possibly have been thinking? He closed his eyes as she brushed his hair back, gathering it at his neck with her other hand. And then she was done brushing, and she just used her hands. Her fingers felt cool against his forehead as she made sure she got the last stray locks off his face.

She was going to braid his hair, and he was going to sit here, acutely aware of each little, last, barely-touching-him movement of her fingers. He was going to sit here, wanting her, thinking of how soft she'd felt in his arms just last night, how ready and willing and eager she'd been. She wouldn't have stopped him from pushing up her skirt and burying himself inside of her and—

Sweat trickled down his back.

What harm was there in letting her braid his hair?

None—provided no one at the Parkvale Senior Center had enough of their eyesight left to notice the uncomfortably tight fit of his pants.

Provided Colleen didn't notice it, either. If she did, she would realize that he'd lied to her. It wouldn't take her long to figure out the truth. And then he'd be a dead man.

Bobby tried thinking about death, about rats, about plague, about pestilence. He tried thinking about sharks— all those teeth, those mean little eyes coming right at him. He thought about the day—and that day *was* coming, since he was no longer in his twenties—when he'd have to leave the SEAL teams, when he'd be too old to keep up with the newer recruits.

None of it worked to distract him.

Colleen's gentle touch cut through it all. It was far more real than any of his worst-imagined nightmares.

Yet it was remarkably easy to picture her touching him like that all over—not just on his head and his hair and the back of his neck, but *all* over. Oh, man...

"If I were a guy," Colleen murmured, "and I had hair like this, I'd wear it down. All the time. And I would have women falling at my feet. Lining up outside my bedroom door. All the time."

Bobby choked. "What?"

"Most women can't keep their hands off guys with long hair," she explained. "Particularly good-looking guys like you who are completely ripped. Hey, did you pack your uniform?"

She thought he was good-looking and *ripped*. Bobby had to smile. He liked that she thought of him that way, even though he wasn't sure it was completely true. He was a little too big, too solid to get the kind of muscle definition that someone like Lucky O'Donlon had.

Now, there was a man who was truly ripped. Of course, Lucky wasn't here right now as a comparison, which was just as well. Even though he was married, women were still drawn to him like flies to honey.

"Hello," Colleen said. "Did you fall asleep?"

"No," Bobby said. "Sorry." She'd asked him something. "Um…"

"Your uniform?"

"Oh," he said. "No. No, I'm not supposed to wear a uniform while my hair's long—unless there's some kind of formal affair that I can't get out of attending."

"No this one's not formal," she told him. "It's casual—a bon voyage party at the local VFW the night before we leave. But there will be VIPs there—senators and the mayor and… I just thought it would be cool for them to meet a real Navy SEAL."

"Ah," he said. She was almost done braiding his hair, and he was simultaneously relieved and disappointed. "You want me to be a circus attraction."

She laughed. "Absolutely. I want you to stand around and look mysterious and dangerous. You'd be the hit of the party." She reached over his shoulder, her arm warm against his slightly damp, air-conditioner-chilled T-shirt. "I need the elastic."

He tried to hand it to her, and they both fumbled. It dropped into his lap. He grabbed it quickly—God forbid she reach for it there—and held it out on his open palm for her to take.

Somehow she managed to touch nearly every inch of his palm as she took the elastic.

"You know what you're asking, don't you?" he said. "I'll spend the evening fending off all kinds of personal questions. Is it true SEALs know how to rip out an opponent's throat with their bare hands? How many men have you killed? Have you ever killed anyone in hand-to-hand combat? Did you like it? Is it true SEALs are rough in bed?" He let out a burst of exasperated air. "As soon as people find out I'm a SEAL, they change, Colleen. They look at me differently. The men size me up, and the women..." He shook his head.

She laughed as she sat back, finally done. "Yeah, right, Taylor. You tell me that you and my brother haven't taken advantage of the way women react when they find out you're a SEAL."

"No," he said. "You're right. I *have* taken advantage—too many times. It's just...these days I don't get much enjoyment out of it. It's not real. You know, I didn't tell Kyra I was a SEAL until we were together for two months."

"Did she treat you differently when she found out?" Colleen asked. Her eyes were more green than blue today, so luminous and beautiful.

"Yeah, she did," he had to admit. "It was subtle, but it was there." And she'd slept with him that very same night. Coincidence? Maybe. But unlikely.

"I'm sorry," she said. "Forget I asked. You don't even have to come to this thing. It's just...I have to go, and since you're doing this twenty-four-hour bodyguard thing, I thought—"

"I'll call Harvard, have him send my uniform."

"No," she said. "You can go incognito. With your hair down. Wearing leather pants. I'll tell everyone you're a supermodel from Paris. See what kind of questions you get asked then."

Bobby laughed as Colleen climbed down from the cab of the truck. "Hey," he said, sliding across the seat and keeping her from closing the door by sticking out his foot. "I'm glad we're still friends."

"You know, I've been thinking about this friend thing," she said, standing there, hands on her hips, looking up at him. "I think we should be the kind of friends who have wild sex three or four times a day."

She shot him a smile and turned toward the seniors center.

Bobby sat there, staring after her, watching the sunlight on her hair and the gentle swaying of her hips as she walked away.

She was kidding.

Wasn't she?

God, maybe she wasn't.

"Help," he said to no one in particular as he followed her inside.

CHAPTER SIX

BOBBY CAUGHT COLLEEN by the arm and pulled her back, almost on top of him, almost down the stairs that led to her third-floor apartment.

At first she thought she'd won. At first she thought that all the little glances and smiles, and all the thinly veiled—and some not so thinly veiled at all—comments she'd made all afternoon were finally paying off, that she'd succeeded in driving him crazy. She thought he was pulling her toward him to kiss her, the way he'd kissed her in Harvard Square last night.

Yeah, right, Colleen. Dream on.

Kissing her was the last thing on his mind. "Stay behind me," he ordered, pushing her so that her nose was practically pressed into the broad expanse of his back.

She realized then that her apartment door was ajar.

Someone was in her apartment.

Andrea Barker had come home, too, to find someone breaking into her house.

And had been beaten so badly she was still in a coma.

Colleen grabbed Bobby—it was about as effective as grabbing an aircraft carrier. "Don't go in there!"

"I won't," he said. "At least not before I get you out of here." He was holding on to her then, too, turning toward her and practically lifting her up, about to carry her down the stairs.

For the first time in her life Colleen actually felt fragile and petite and in need of rescue.

She wasn't quite sure she liked it.

She was scared, yes. She didn't want Bobby charging in, a one-man assault team, to find John Morrison and his gang in her living room. At the same time, if John Morrison and his gang *were* in her apartment, she didn't want to run away and lose the opportunity to have them all arrested.

"Put me down," she ordered him. They could go downstairs, call the police from Mr. Gheary's apartment.

To her surprise he did put her down, none too gently pushing her away from him. As she struggled to regain her balance, she realized he was charging up the last few stairs toward her apartment door. Toward a man who was coming out.

Wearing an unbelievably loud plaid shirt.

"Bobby, don't!"

She wasn't the only one shouting.

The owner of that shirt was shouting, too, shrieking, really, in pure terror.

It was Kenneth. Bobby had him against the entryway wall, his face pressed against the faded wallpaper, his armed twisted up behind his back.

"Bobby, *stop!* He's a friend of mine," Colleen shouted, taking the stairs two at a time, just as the door to her apartment opened wide, revealing the equally wide eyes of Ashley and her brother, Clark. She did a double take. Ashley's blue-haired brother, Clark.

"What are you doing here?" she asked Ashley, who was supposed to be spending the entire summer working at her father's law firm in New York.

"I escaped from Scarsdale," Ashley said faintly, staring at Bobby, who still had Kenneth pinned, his feet completely off the ground. "Clark and Kenneth came and broke me out."

That explained the blue hair. Nineteen-year-old Clark

knew he'd be seeing his extremely conservative father. Say no more.

"Bobby, meet my roommate, Ashley DeWitt," Colleen said. "Her brother, Clark, and his friend, Kenneth. Guys, this is my brother's friend, Chief Bobby Taylor."

"I'M YOUR FRIEND, TOO," Bobby reminded her as he gently lowered the kid back to the floor. "Sorry."

The kid was shaken, but he pulled himself together quickly. "That was...somewhat uncomfortable, but the adrenaline rush is quite nice, thanks."

"Kenneth's from England," Colleen told him.

"Yeah," Bobby said, following them all into her apartment. "I caught that from the accent."

Man, Colleen hadn't been kidding. It was worse in here than he'd imagined. The small living room was filled, in some cases from floor to ceiling, with boxes. Colleen was in the process of writing, in big, block letters, what seemed to be a Tulgerian address on each of them. As far as he could tell, she was only about a third of the way done.

"So you're a chief, huh?" Clark said as Bobby closed the door behind him. "What tribe?"

"Oh, God! Clark, he's not *that* kind of chief." Ashley gave Bobby an apologetic smile. She was what he thought of as a New York blonde. Average height and slender, with a figure that was just barely curvy enough to be considered feminine, but certainly not curvy enough to be lush. Everything about her was neat and perfectly in place, nothing too extreme. She was cool and beautiful—kind of the way a stone statue was cool and beautiful. You didn't mind looking, but you wouldn't want to touch.

Compared to Ashley, Colleen was a mess. Her hair was everywhere. Her smile was crooked. Her breasts looked as if they were about to explode out from under her T-shirt every time she moved. She was too much of everything—too tall, too stacked, too blunt, too funny, too into having a good time wherever she went. Laughter spilled out of her constantly. Her eyes were never the same color from one minute to the next, but they were always, *always* welcoming and warm.

Desire knifed through him so sharply he had to clench his fists.

"Forgive my brother," Ashley continued. "He's terminally stupid."

He yanked his gaze away from Colleen, aware he'd been staring at her with his tongue nearly hanging out. God, he couldn't let her catch him looking at her that way. If she knew the truth…

Who was he kidding? She'd probably already guessed the truth. And now she was trying to drive him slowly insane with all those deep looks and the seemingly innocently casual way she touched him damn near constantly in passing. A hand on his arm, on his knee. Fingers cool against his face as she fixed a stray lock of his hair. Brushing against him with her shoulder. Sitting so close that their thighs touched.

And the things she said to him! She thought they should be the kind of friends who had sex three or four times a day. She'd only been teasing. She liked being outrageous— saying things like that and trying to shake him up.

That one had worked.

"I'm a chief petty officer," Bobby explained to the kid with blue hair, working to keep up with the conversation. That kid's name was Clark. He was Ashley's brother— no doubt about that. He had the same perfectly sculpted nose and chin, slightly differently shaped eyes that were a warmer shade of gray. "I'm in the Navy."

"Whoa, dude," Clark said. "With long hair like that?" He laughed. "Hey, maybe they'll take me, huh?"

"Bobby's a—" Colleen cut herself off, and Bobby knew

she was remembering all that he'd told her about the way most people's attitudes changed when they found out he was a SEAL. She looked at him and as their eyes met he felt the small room shrink. It was as if he'd been caught in the beam of a searchlight—he and Colleen. Ashley, Clark and Kenneth vanished in the darkness outside his peripheral vision. All he could see was Colleen and her beautiful, laughing eyes.

They were very blue right now.

"Bobby's a very good friend of mine," she said softly, instead of telling them he was a SEAL.

"I should join the Navy," Clark's voice cut through. "Wouldn't *that* tick the old man off?"

"I had big plans for tonight," Colleen said, still looking into Bobby's eyes. "I was going to cook dinner for Bobby and then seduce him by dancing naked in the kitchen."

There she went again. More teasing. She was laughing at him—probably at the look of shock on his face. But as she turned away, as the world opened up again to include the other three people in the room, Bobby got the feeling that she wasn't completely kidding. She'd had plans for tonight, and those plans *had* included him.

"I should go," he said, wanting to stay at least as much as he wanted to keep breathing. But he couldn't stay. No way.

"No," Ashley said swiftly. "We were just going out."

"No, we weren't," Clark said with disdain. "You are such a liar. You have a headache—so bad that Kenneth was going to the drugstore to get you some painkillers." He turned to Colleen. "Unless you've got some hidden here. Ash wouldn't let me search your bedroom."

"Gee, I don't know why," Colleen said. "Could it maybe have something to do with the fact that the last time you searched my room I got home and called the police because I thought I'd been vandalized? Besides, you wouldn't have found any. I don't get headaches. Did you look in the bathroom?"

"I'm feeling much better," Ashley interrupted. Bobby had just met her, but even he could tell that she was lying. "We're going out."

"But what about that letter you were going to write to Dad?"

"It can wait." Ashley motioned toward the door with her head, making big eyes at her brother. "This is Bobby Taylor. Wes's friend?" Clark stared at her blankly, as only a younger brother can stare at an older sister. "The Navy SEAL…?"

"Oh," Clark said. "*Oh*. Right." He looked at Bobby. "You're a SEAL, huh? Cool."

Colleen's smile was rueful and apologetic. "Sorry," she told Bobby. "I tried."

Clark grinned at Kenneth. "Dude! You were almost killed by a Navy SEAL! You should definitely tell the girls at that party tonight. I bet one of 'em will go home with you."

"Ashley, you really don't have to go anywhere," Colleen said to her friend. "You look wiped. What happened? What'd your father do now?"

Ashley just shook her head.

"What's a Navy SEAL?" Kenneth asked. "And do you suppose if he actually *had* killed me then Jennifer Reilly might want to marry me? I mean, if you think she might go home with me if he *almost* killed me…."

"Oh, no way!" Clark countered. "I wasn't thinking Jenn Reilly, dude! Set your sights lower, man. Think B or C tier. Think Stacy Thurmond or Candy Fremont."

"You rank the women you know into *tiers?*" Colleen was outraged. "Get out of my house, scumball!"

"Whoa," Clark said, backing up and tripping over one

of the boxes. "We don't *tell* 'em we rank 'em. We'd never say it to their faces. They don't know. Honest."

"Yes, they do," Colleen countered. "Believe me, they know."

"Who is this *we* to whom you keep referring, scumball?" Kenneth asked Clark.

"What tier am *I* in?" Colleen's voice was dangerously quiet.

"A," Clark told her quickly. "Absolutely. You are so completely, gorgeously, perfectly A."

Colleen cut him down with a single word—a pungent profanity that Bobby realized he'd never heard her use before. Unlike Wes, she didn't pepper her everyday speech with four-letter words. As a matter of fact, he couldn't remember the last time he'd heard her say damn or even hell. It was pretty remarkable actually, considering how prone she was to blurting out whatever was on her mind.

I think we should be the kind of friends who have wild sex three or four times a day. Help.

"Once when I was running down by the river," Colleen told Clark tightly, "I went past these two guys who were grading all the women who ran by. The wind carried their voices to me right at the exact moment they were checking me out. They gave me a C minus—probably about the equivalent of your lower C tier."

Bobby couldn't stay silent another second. "They were fools."

"They were…several words I will not lower myself to use," she said, chin held high, pretending that a C-minus ranking by a pair of strangers didn't bother her one bit. Pretending she was above that. Pretending that she hadn't been hurt.

"You're on my A list," Bobby said. The moment the words left his lips, he realized he'd just made a fatal mistake. Although he'd meant it as the highest compliment, he'd just admitted that he had an A list. And that would make him little better than…what had she called Clark? A scumball.

"That came out really wrong," he told her quickly as her eyes started to narrow.

Clark, the genius, stepped up to the plate. "See? All guys have lists. It's a guy thing," he protested, not old enough to know that all either of them could do now was grovel, apologize and pray for forgiveness. "It doesn't mean anything."

"Bobby, strangle him, strangle his strange, plaid-clothed little friend," Colleen ordered him, "and then strangle yourself."

"What I *meant* to say," Bobby told her, moving close enough to catch her chin with his hand, so she now had to look up into his eyes, "was that I find you as beautiful on the outside as you are on the inside."

The searchlight clicked back on, and the rest of the world faded. Colleen was looking at him, her eyes wide, her lips slightly parted. She was the only other person in the entire universe. No one and nothing else existed. He couldn't even seem to move his hand away from the soft smoothness of her face.

"Strangle me?" Bobby heard Kenneth protest, his voice faint, as if coming from a great distance. "Why strangle *me?* I don't put anyone into tiers, thank you very much."

"Yeah, because you can't see past Jenn Reilly," Clark countered, also from somewhere way back there, beyond Colleen's eyes and Colleen's lips. "For you, Jenn's got her own gigantic tier—and everyone else is invisible. You and Jenn are *so* not going to happen, man. Even if hell froze over, she would walk right past you and date Frosty the Snowman. And then she would call you later to tell you how it went because you guys are *friends*. Sheesh. Don't you know friendship is the kiss of death between a man and a woman?"

"That was very sweet," Colleen told Bobby softly. "I forgive you."

She took his hand and kissed him, right on the palm, and Bobby felt something major snap in his chest.

Oh, God, he had to get out of here before it was too late. Before he reached for her and...

He turned away, forcing himself to focus on blue hair and a loud plaid. Anything but Colleen and her bone-melting smile.

"Yes, I'm thwarted by the curse of being the *friend*." Kenneth sighed. "I'm double damned because Jennifer thinks I'm gay. I'm her *gay* friend. I've told her that I'm quite not, thanks, but..."

"*Every*one thinks you're gay," Clark countered. "Tell me honestly, bro," he asked Bobby. "When you first saw Kenneth—I mean, Kenneth, come on, man. Only a gay dude would call himself Kenneth instead of Ken or Kenny—when you first saw him, Bobby, didn't you think—" he held out his hands to frame Kenneth, like a movie director "—*gay?*"

Bobby didn't bother to answer. He'd spent far too much time around Wes, who was the same kind of hyped-up, whirlwind talker as this kid, to know that his answer wasn't really needed. Which was just as well, because he wasn't completely convinced that he'd be able to speak.

Every time he looked into Colleen's eyes, his hands started to sweat, his chest felt squeezed and his throat tightened up. He was in desperate trouble.

"You know, my father thinks you're gay, too," Clark told Kenneth. "I enjoy that about you. You frighten him, dude."

"Well, I'm not gay," Kenneth said through clenched teeth.

Bobby cleared his throat experimentally. A few more times and he'd have his voice back. Provided he didn't look at Colleen again.

"Not that there's anything wrong with being gay," Kenneth added hastily, glancing at Bobby. "We should probably make sure we're not offending a gay Navy SEAL here—an extremely big, extremely tall gay Navy SEAL. Although I still am not quite certain as to exactly what a Navy SEAL might be."

Clark looked at Bobby with new interest. "Whoa. It never even occurred to me. *Are* you gay?"

For the first time in a good long number of minutes, there was complete and total silence. They were all looking at him. *Colleen* was looking at him, frowning slightly, speculation in her eyes.

Oh, great. Now she thought he'd told her he only wanted to be friends because he was—

He looked at her, wavering, unable to decide what to say. Should he just shut up and let her think whatever she thought, hoping that it would make her keep her distance?

Colleen found her voice. "Congratulations, Clark, you've managed to reach new heights of rudeness. Bobby, don't answer him—your sexual orientation is no one's business but your own."

"I'm straight," he admitted.

"I'm sure you are," Colleen said a little too heartily, implying that she suspected otherwise.

He laughed again. "Why would I lie?"

"I believe you," she said. "Absolutely." She winked at him. "Don't ask, don't tell. We'll just pretend Clark didn't ask."

Suddenly this wasn't funny anymore, and he laughed in disbelief. "What do you want me to do...?" Prove it? He stopped himself from saying those words. Oh, God.

She was giving him another of those killer smiles, complete with that two-thousand-degree incinerating heat in her eyes. Yes, she did want him to prove it. She didn't say it in words, but it was right there, written all over her face. She hadn't believed he was gay for one minute. She'd been baiting him. And he'd walked right into her trap. She waggled her eyebrows at him suggestively, implying that she was only teasing, but he knew better.

Help.

Please, God, let there be voice mail waiting for him, back in his hotel room. Please, God, let Wesley have called, announcing that he was back in the States and on his way to Boston. Please, God…

"Now that we've got *that* mystery solved, the two burning questions of the night that remain are why did you come back to Boston," Colleen said to her roommate, "and why blue?" She turned and looked at Clark's hair critically. "I'm not sure it's you…dude."

"What is a Navy SEAL?" Kenneth reminded her. "Burning question number three. I keep picturing beach balls and Seaworld, and I'm confident that's not quite right."

"SEALs are part of the U.S. military's special forces," Colleen said. "They're part of the Navy, so they spend a lot of time in and around the water—swimming, scuba diving, underwater demolition even. But SEAL stands for sea, air and land. They also jump out of airplanes and crawl across the desert and through the jungle, too. Most of the time no one knows that they're there. They carry great big guns—assault weapons, like commandos—but nearly all of their operations are covert." She looked at Clark. "Which means secret. Clandestine—99.9 percent of the time they insert and extract from their mission location without firing a single bullet."

She turned back to Bobby. "Did I miss anything vital?

Besides the fact that you SEALs frequently kill people—usually with your bare hands—and that you're known for being exceedingly rough in bed?"

Bobby started to laugh. He couldn't help it. And then Colleen was laughing, too, with the others just staring at them as if they were crazy.

She was so alive, so full of light and joy. And in less than a week she was going to get on an airplane and fly to a dangerous place where she could well be killed. And, Lord, what a loss to the world that would be. The thought was sobering.

"Please don't go," he said to her.

Somehow she knew he was talking about the trip to Tulgeria. She stopped laughing, too. "I have to."

"No, you don't. Colleen, you have no idea what it's like there."

"Yes, I do."

Ashley pulled her brother and Kenneth toward the door. "Coll, we're going to go out for a—"

"No, you're not." Colleen didn't look away from Bobby. "Kick Thing A and Thing B out onto the street, but if you're getting one of your headaches, you're not going anywhere but to bed."

"Well then, I'll be in my room," Ashley said quietly. "Come on, children. Let's leave Aunt Colleen alone."

"*Hasta la vista,* baby." Clark nodded to Bobby. "Dude."

"Thanks again for not killing me," Kenneth said cheerfully.

They went out the door, and Ashley faded quietly down the hallway.

Leaving him alone in the living room with Colleen.

"I should go, too." That would definitely be the smart thing. As opposed to kissing her. Which would definitely be the opposite of the smart thing. But he couldn't seem to get his feet to move toward the door.

"You should come into the kitchen," she countered. "Where there are chairs that aren't covered with boxes. We can actually sit down."

She took his hand and tugged him into the kitchen. Somehow his feet had no problem moving in that direction.

"Okay," she said, sitting at the kitchen table. "Spill. What happened in Tulgeria?"

Bobby rubbed his forehead. "I wish it was that easy," he said. "I wish it was one thing. I wish I was wrong, but I've been there a half dozen times, at least, and each time was more awful than the last. It's bad and getting worse, Colleen. Parts of the country are a war zone. The government's lost control everywhere but in the major cities, and even there they're on shaky ground. Terrorist groups are everywhere. There are Christian groups, Muslim groups. They work hard to kill each other, and if that wasn't enough, there's in-fighting among each of the groups. Nobody's safe. I went into a village and—"

Lord, he couldn't tell her—not the details. He didn't want to tell her *any* of it, but he made himself. He looked her straight in the eye and said it. "Everyone was dead. A rival group had come in and… Even the children, Colleen. They'd been methodically slaughtered."

She drew in a breath. "Oh, no!"

"We went in because there were rumors that one of the terrorist groups had gotten hold of some kind of chemical weapon. We were there to meet a team of Army Rangers, escort 'em out to a waiting submarine with samples of whatever they'd found. But they came up empty. These people had nothing. They had hardly any regular ammunition, let alone any kind of chemical threat. They killed each other with swords—these big machete-style things, with these curved, razor-sharp blades.

"No one is safe there." He said it again, hoping she was listening. "No one is safe."

She looked pale, but her gaze didn't waver. "I have to go. You tell me these things, and I have to go more than ever."

"More than half of these terrorists are zealots." He leaned across the table, willing her to hear him, to *really* hear him. "The other half are in it for the black market—for buying and selling anything. Including Americans. *Especially* Americans. Collecting ransom is probably the most lucrative business in Tulgeria today. How much would *your* parents pay to get you back?"

"Bobby, I know you think—"

He cut her off. "Our government has a rule—no negotiating with terrorists. But civilians in the private sector... Well, they can give it a go—pay the ransom and gamble that they'll actually get their loved one back. Truth is, they usually don't. Colleen, please listen to me. *They usually don't get the hostages back.*"

Colleen gazed at him searchingly. "I've heard rumors of mass slaughters of Tulgerian civilians in retaliation by the local government."

Bobby hesitated, then told her the truth. "I've heard those rumors, too."

"Is it true?"

He sighed. "Look, I know you don't want to hear this, but if you go there you might die. *That's* what you should be worrying about right now. Not—"

"*Is* it true?"

God, she was magnificent. Leaning across the table toward him, palms down on the faded formica top, shoulders set for a fight, her eyes blazing, her hair on fire.

"I can guarantee you that the U.S. has special forces

teams investigating that right this very moment," he told her. "NATO warned Tulgeria about such acts of genocide in the past. If they're up to their old tricks and if we find out about it—and if they are, we will, I guarantee it—then the U.S. ambassador and his staff will be pulled out of Tulibek immediately. The U.S. will cut all relations with the Tulgerian government. The embassy will be gone—potentially overnight. If that happens while you're there…"

Bobby took a steadying breath. "Colleen, if you go, you'll be in danger every minute of that entire week."

"I want to show you something," she said. "Don't go anywhere. I'll be right back."

CHAPTER SEVEN

THE PHOTOGRAPHS WERE IN her bedroom. Colleen grabbed the envelope from her dresser, stopping to knock softly on Ashley's door on her way back to the kitchen.

"Come in."

The room was barely lit, with the shades all pulled down. Ash was at her computer, and despite the dim lighting, Colleen could see that her eyes were red and swollen. She'd been crying.

"How's the headache?" Colleen asked.

"Pretty bad."

"Try to sleep."

Ashley shook her head. "I can't. I have to write this."

"Write what?"

"A brief. To my father. That's the only way he'll ever pay attention to me—if I write him a legal brief. Isn't that pathetic?"

Colleen sighed. It *was* pathetic. Everything about Ashley's relationship with her father was pathetic. She'd actually gotten caller-ID boxes for all of their telephones, so they'd know not to answer when Mr. DeWitt called. Colleen loved it when her own father called.

"Why don't you do it later?" she said to her friend. "After the headache's gone."

Ashley's headaches were notoriously awful. She'd been to the doctor, and although they weren't migraines, they were similar in many ways. Brought on by tension and stress, the doctor had said.

Great ailment for a future lawyer to have.

"I'll help you with it," Colleen continued. "You need to tell me what happened—why you haven't called or emailed me since mid-May. I assume it's all connected?" It was. She could see that from the look on Ashley's face. "Just let me get rid of Bobby, okay?"

"Don't you dare!" Indignation gave Ashley a burst of energy. "Colleen, my God! You've had a thing for this guy for *years!* He's gorgeous, by the way. And huge. I mean, you told me he was big, but I had no idea. How tall is he?"

"I don't know exactly. Six-six? Maybe taller."

"His hands are like baseball mitts."

"Yeah," Colleen said. "And you know what they say about guys with big hands."

"They have big gloves," they said in unison. Colleen grinned, and Ashley even managed a weak smile. But it was fleeting.

"I can't believe my rotten timing. Of all the times to come running back to Cambridge and get in the way…" Ashley rested her forehead in her hands, elbows on her desk. "I saw him looking at you, Coll. All you have to do is say the word and he'll spend the night."

"He gave me the friends speech," Colleen told her.

"You're kidding!"

"Let's see—would that be something that I, designated best friend to the entire world's male population, would kid about? No, I don't think so."

"I'm sorry."

"Yeah, well…" Colleen forced a smile. "Personally I think he's lying—that he's got some kind of code-of-honor thing going, you know, because I'm his best friend's sister. I have to convince him that it's okay, that he doesn't have to fall in love and marry me—that I just want us to have some fun."

Although if he *did* happen to fall in love with her... No, she couldn't let herself think that way. That path was fraught with the perils of disappointment and frustration. All she wanted was to have fun, she reminded herself again, wishing the words hadn't sounded so hollow when she'd said them aloud.

"He's probably wondering what happened to you," Ashley pointed out.

Colleen went out the door, stopping to look at her friend, her hand on the knob. "I'll be back in about thirty minutes to get your full report on Scarsdale and your dear old dad."

"That's really not necessary—"

"I know you," Colleen said. "You're not going to sleep until we talk, so we're going to talk."

BOBBY HEARD THE DOOR SHUT, heard Colleen coming back down the hall to the kitchen.

He'd heard the soft murmur of voices as she'd stopped to speak to her roommate.

The soundproofing in this old place was virtually nonexistent.

That meant that grabbing her when she came back into the room, and having hot, noisy sex right there, on top of the kitchen table was definitely not an option.

Oh, man, he had to get out of here.

He stood up, but Colleen came into the room, blocking his escape route.

"Sit," she ordered. "Just for a few more minutes. I want to show you something."

She took a photograph out of an envelope and slid it across the table toward him. It was a picture of a small girl, staring solemnly into the camera. She had enormous eyes—probably because she was so skinny. She was all narrow shoulders, with a pointy chin, dressed in ill-fitting clothes, with a ragged cap of dark-brown hair. She looked to be about six or seven years old, with the kind of desperate and almost feral air about her that would have made Bobby watch her from the corner of his eye had he happened upon her in the street. Yeah, he'd watch her, all right, *and* secure his wallet in an inside pocket.

"This was Analena," Colleen told him, "two years ago—before my student Children's Aid group adopted her."

She put another picture on the table. "This was taken just last month."

It was the same girl, only now her hair was longer—thick and glossy. She was smiling—laughing—as she ran across a field, kicking a soccer ball. Her cheeks were pink and healthy looking, and although she was still rail thin, it was because she was growing. She was gangly, gawky. She no longer looked as if she would snap in two. And the feral look was gone. She was a child again.

Colleen laid a letter in front of him—written in a large, loopy child's hand. "Dearest Colleen," he read silently:

I dream last night that I visit you in U.S. of A. It such wonderful dream—I want to no wake up. I hope you okay that I gifted Ivan with futball you gifted me. He try to steal many times, I think, why not he keep?

My English, she is getting better, no? It is gift from you—from America books and tape player and batteries you send. Blessed gift. More better than futball. Ivan make bad noise, don't think this. Still, I teach Ivan English words. Some day he thank me, thank you, also.

Send more letter soon. Love, Analena.

Colleen pulled other photos from the envelope. They were pictures of other kids.

"Analena and about twenty-five other children live in an

orphanage, St. Christof's, deep inside Tulgeria's so-called war zone," she told him, "which also happens to be the part of the country that sustained the most damage from the earthquake. My Children's Aid group has been corresponding—for over two years—with the nuns who run St. Christof's. We've been trying to find a legal loophole so we can get those children out of Tulgeria. These are unwanted children, Bobby. Most are of mixed heritage—and nobody wants them. The terrible irony is that we have lists of families here in the U.S. who want them desperately—who are dying to adopt. But the government won't let them go. They won't pay to feed them, yet they won't give them up."

The pictures showed the bleakness of the orphanage. Boarded-up windows, peeling paint, bombed-out walls. These children were living in a shell of a former house. In all of the pictures, the nuns—some clad in old-fashioned habits, some dressed in American jeans and sneakers— were always smiling, but Bobby could see the lines of strain and pain around their eyes and mouths.

"When this earthquake happened," Colleen continued, still in that same soft, even voice, "we jumped at the chance to actually go in there." She looked Bobby squarely in the eyes. "Bringing relief aid and supplies to the quake victims is just our cover. We're really going in to try to get those children moved out of the war zone, to a safer location. Best-case scenario would be to bring them back to the States with us, but we know the chances of that happening are slim to none."

Bobby looked at her. "I can go," he said. "Colleen, I'll do this for you. I'll go instead of you."

Yes, that would work. He could get some of the other men in Alpha Squad to come along. Rio Rosetti, Thomas King and Mike Lee were all young and foolish. They'd jump at the chance to spend a week's vacation in the number-one most dangerous hot spot in the world. And

Spaceman—Lieutenant Jim Slade. He was unmarried, too. He'd help if Bobby asked.

But no way would Bobby ask any of his married friends to spend any of their too-infrequent leave time away from their families, risking their lives.

"This could work," he told her, but she was already shaking her head.

"Bobby, I'm going." She said it firmly, absolutely, calmly. As if this was a fact that wasn't going to change no matter what he said or did. "I'm the liaison with the Tulgerian minister of Public Health. I believe he's our one hope of getting those children moved out of immediate danger. He knows me, he trusts me—I'm going."

"If you're going, I'm going, too," he told her just as absolutely.

She shook her head. "No, you're not."

He sighed. "Look, I know you probably think I'm just interfering, but—"

Colleen smiled. "No, you don't understand. I'd love it if you could come along. Honest. It would be great. But be practical, Bobby. We're leaving in less than a week. It's taken us nearly three weeks to get permission to enter the country and bring aid—despite the fact that people there are wandering around hungry, their homes destroyed by this earthquake. You'll have to go through the same diplomatic channels and—"

"No, I won't."

She made a face at him. "Yeah, right. What, are you going to call some admiral and snap your fingers and...?"

"I won't snap my fingers at Admiral Robinson," Bobby told her. "That would be rude."

She stared at him. "You're serious. You're really going to call an *admiral?*"

He nodded as he glanced at his watch. It was a little too

late to call tonight. The admiral and his wife, Zoe, had twins. Max and Sam.

The twins were pure energy in human form—as Bobby well knew. He baby-sat them once when the admiral and his wife were out in California, when their regular sitter had canceled at the last minute. Max and Sam were miniature versions of their father. They both had his striking-blue eyes and world-famous smile.

Jake would've just finished reading them a story and putting them to bed. Bobby knew he would then go in search of his wife, maybe make them both a cup of herbal tea and rub her shoulders or feet….

"I'll call him tomorrow morning," Bobby said.

Colleen smiled. She didn't believe he was tight enough with an admiral to be able to give the man a call. "Well, it would be nice if you could go, but I'm not going to hold my breath." She gathered up the pictures and put them back in the envelope.

"How many people are going?" he asked. "You know, in your group?"

"About twelve."

Twelve unprepared, untrained civilians running around loose…. Bobby didn't swear—at least not aloud.

"Most of them will actually be distributing supplies to the quake victims. They'll be hooking up with the Red Cross volunteers who are already in place in the country," she continued. "Of the twelve, there are five of us who'll be concentrating on getting those children moved."

Five was a much better, much more compact number. Five people could be whisked out of sight and removed from danger far more easily than twelve.

"Who's meeting you at the airport?" he asked.

"We've rented a bus and made arrangements to be picked up by the driver," she told him.

A bus. Oh, *man.* "How many guards?"

Colleen shook her head. "One. The driver insisted. We're still arguing over that. We don't want any guns. Our connection to the Red Cross—"

"Colleen, you'll need armed guards," he told her. "Way more than just one man hired by the driver. Three or four at the least. Even just for the short trip between the airport and your hotel. And you'll need twice as many if you're going up north."

"But—"

"The Red Cross means nothing in Tulgeria. In fact, it's often used as a bull's-eye for terrorists. Don't put the emblem on the bus, don't wear it on your clothes."

She was looking at him as if he were speaking Greek. "Are you serious?"

"Dead serious. And instead of a single bus, we should get you three or four Humvees. Something smaller and faster, that'll be less of a target."

"The bus is so that we can move the children if we get the opportunity," she told him.

Oh, damn. Yeah, they would definitely need a bus for that. "Okay," he said. "I'm going to do what I can to get Admiral Robinson involved—to make this an official operation for one of his Gray Group teams. But if it's official, there's a chance I won't be able to go. I'm still not 100 percent—"

"I'm not sure that's such a good idea," Colleen said. "If we go in there looking like some kind of commando team…"

"Whoever goes in with you, they'll be covert. There'll be three or four guys hanging around with assault weapons for show as if they were hired guards. But everyone else on the team will blend in with your group. I promise."

She looked at him. "You promise. Except you're not going to be there."

"I may not be there," he said. "But I'm sure as hell going to try."

Colleen smiled. "You know, every time someone says that they'll *try,* I think of that scene in *The Empire Strikes Back* with Luke Skywalker and Yoda. You know, the one where Yoda says, 'Try not. Do or do not.'"

"Yeah, I know that scene," Bobby told her. "And I'm sorry, but—"

She reached across the table and touched his hand. "No, don't apologize. I didn't mean to sound as if I were accusing you of anything. See, the truth is I've fought so many losing battles for so many years that I really appreciate someone who tries. In fact, a try is all I ever ask for anymore. It may not work out, but at least you know you gave it a shot, right?"

She wasn't talking about him coming to Tulgeria. She was talking about the way he'd kissed her. And the way he'd pushed her away, refusing to see where that kiss might lead. Refusing even to try.

Bobby wasn't sure what to say. He felt like the worst kind of coward. Too scared even to try.

Even when her hand was on top of his, her fingers so cool against the heat of his skin. Even when he wished with all of his heart that she would leave her hand right there for a decade or two.

But Colleen took her hand away as she stood. He watched as she placed the envelope with the pictures on the cluttered surface of a built-in desk in the corner of the room.

"You know, I've met most of the people who want to adopt these kids," she told him. "They're really wonderful. You look into their eyes, and you can see that they already love these children just from seeing their pictures, from reading their letters." Her voice wavered. "It just breaks my heart that those kids are in danger, that we can only *try* to help them. It kills me that there are no guarantees."

Bobby stood up. He didn't mean to. And as soon as he found himself on his feet, he forced himself to stop. To not move toward her, not take her into his arms. The last time he did that, he'd completely lost control.

But Colleen turned to face him. *She* came toward him. She reached for him, taking hold of both of his hands. "It's important to me that you know I'm not doing this purely to drive Wes crazy."

Her fingers were cool and strong and, again, he didn't want to let her go. *Help.* "I know."

But she didn't come any closer. She just smiled and squeezed his hands. "Good," she said as she released him. "So go. You're free. Escape. Lucky you—I need to hang with Ashley tonight. Guess I'll have to dance naked for you another night."

Her eyes sparkled as she laughed at him, at the pained look he couldn't keep off his face.

The door was right there. She'd given him permission to leave. He could have walked through it, walked out of her apartment, walked to a place where he—and she—were safe. Instead he didn't move. "Why do you keep doing that?"

She opted not to play dumb. She knew he was talking about her suggestive comments. "You're such an easy target and I want…"

"What?" He really wanted to know. Badly enough that he almost touched her again. Almost. "You want what, Colleen?"

"You."

He'd known she was gutsy. And when she teased, she could be pretty outrageous. But he'd never expected her to say that.

She lowered her eyes as if she were suddenly shy. "I always have, you know."

She spoke barely loud enough for him to hear her, but he did. He heard. His ears were working perfectly. It was his lungs that were having trouble functioning.

"So now you know," she said quietly. When she looked up at him, her smile was rueful. "How's that for a powerful rebuttal to the 'I just want to be friends' speech?"

He couldn't respond. He didn't have any idea at all of what to say. She wanted him. She always had. He felt like laughing and crying. He felt like grabbing her, right there in the kitchen. He felt like running—as hard and as fast and as far as he possibly could.

"I figure either I'm right, and you didn't mean what you said this morning," she told him. "Or I'm wrong, and I'm a complete idiot who deserves humiliation and rejection twice in two days."

Bobby kept his mouth shut, wishing he *were* the kind of man who could just run for the door—and keep running when he hit the street. But he knew that he wasn't going to get out of there without saying *some*thing.

He just wasn't sure what that something should be. Tell the truth and admit he hadn't meant what he'd said? That was one hell of a bad idea. If he did that, she'd smile and move closer and closer and...

And he'd wake up in her bed.

And then Wes would kill him.

Bobby was starting to think he could maybe handle death. It would be worth it for a chance at a night with Colleen.

What he would never be able to live with was the look of betrayal in his best friend's eyes. He clamped his mouth shut.

"I know I act as if it's otherwise," Colleen continued, turning away from him and fiddling with half a dozen organic apples that were on the kitchen counter. As she spoke, she arranged them into a pattern. Big, then little, then big. "But I haven't had too much experience. You know. With men, I mean. In fact, all I've had are a couple of really crummy short-term relationships. I've never been with someone who really wants me—I mean other than for the fact that I'm female and convenient." With the apples neatly arranged in two perfect rows, she turned to face him, to look him in the eye. "I know you say you don't— want me, that is. But I see something really different when I look into your eyes. And…Bobby, I just want to know what that's like—to be made love to the way you kissed me last night. It felt so right and…"

She took a deep breath. Smiled shakily. "So. You've been warned. Now you know. You also know that I'm not going to be talked out of going to Tulgeria. So if your admiral guy doesn't come through for you, you can tell my brother you did everything you could to keep me off that plane. And you can go back to California with a clear conscience. And I think you probably should go—if you really did mean what you said about just wanting to be friends. If you stay, though, you better put on your fireproof suit. Because starting tomorrow I'm turning up the heat."

"YOU REALLY SAID THAT?" Ashley laughed. "What did he do?"

After her little speech, Bobby hadn't grabbed her and kissed her. But then again, Colleen hadn't really thought he would.

"What did he *say*?" Ash persisted.

"Nothing," Colleen told her friend. "He looked a little pale—kind of like he was going to faint. So I told him we'd talk more tomorrow and I pushed him out the door."

Truth was, she hadn't wanted to hear what he might have to say in response to her painfully honest confession.

She'd pretty much been flashing hot and cold by then herself—alternately clapping herself on the back for her bravery and deriding herself for pure stupidity.

What if she *were* completely wrong? What if she were completely misinterpreting everything she'd seen in his eyes? What if he hadn't really been looking at her with barely concealed longing and desire? What if it had just been a bad case of indigestion?

"I had to try," Colleen told Ashley—and herself as well.

Ash was sitting cross-legged on her bed, hugging her beat-up, raggedy stuffed bear—the one she'd been given when she was three and had chicken pox. The one she still slept with despite the fact that she'd just turned twenty-four.

It was ironic. Colleen's friend had everything. Money. A beautiful face. A slim, perfect body. Weight that didn't fluctuate wildly given her moods. A 4.0 grade point average. Impeccable taste.

Of course, Colleen had something Ashley didn't have. And Colleen wouldn't have traded that one thing for Ashley's looks and body, even if her friend had thrown in all the gold in Ft. Knox, too.

Not a chance.

Because Colleen had parents who supported her, 100 percent. She knew, without a doubt, that no matter what she did, her mom and dad were behind her.

Unlike Mr. DeWitt, who criticized Ashley nonstop.

Colleen couldn't imagine what it had been like growing up in that house. She could picture Ash as a little girl, desperately trying to please her father and never quite succeeding.

"Ashley, what's this? A Father's Day gift? A ceramic bowl? You made it yourself on the wheel in pottery class? Oh, well, next time you'll do much better, won't you?"

It was true, Colleen's own parents weren't perfect. No one's parents were. But hers loved her unconditionally. She'd never doubted that.

"You ready to talk about what happened?" she asked Ashley now.

Her friend sighed. "I'm so stupid."

Colleen just waited.

"There was a new associate in my father's firm," Ash finally said. "Brad Hennesey." Tears filled her eyes, and she tried to laugh. "God, I'm such an idiot. I can't even say his name without..." She gestured to her face.

Colleen handed her a box of tissues and waited while Ashley blew her nose.

"He was so nice," Ash told her. "I mean, I didn't expect him *not* to be nice to me, because I'm the boss's daughter, but he seemed so genuine, and..."

"Oh, no," Colleen said. She was pretty sure she knew where this was going, and she prayed she was wrong.

"I did something really dumb," Ash admitted. "We started dating, and he was so..." She laughed but it was loaded with pain. "Yeah, he was completely perfect—smart and gorgeous with all those white teeth and that Land's End model body, and we loved the same books and movies, and... And I fell in love with him. God! How could I be so stupid?"

Colleen waited, praying that she was wrong.

"But then I found out that my father had hired him purposely. Brad was part of his plan to guarantee that I'd come home after law school and join the firm. He was going to be made partner instantly upon our engagement. I hear myself telling you this, and it sounds so ludicrous. Can you believe any of this?"

She could. She'd met Ashley's father. "Ah, Ash," Colleen said. "How did you find out?"

"Brad *told* me," Ashley said. "He confessed everything.

He called me in the middle of the night and told me he had to see me. Right then. So he came over to the house and we went into the garden and... He was really upset and he told me he was in love with me. He said he'd fallen for me, and he told me that he had to come clean before it went any further, that he couldn't live with himself any longer."

"But that's good," Colleen countered. "Isn't it? He was honest when it mattered the most."

"Colleen, he accepted a position where the job description included tricking the boss's daughter into marrying him." Ashley was still aghast at the idea. "What kind of person would do that?"

"One who maybe saw your picture?" Colleen suggested.

Ashley stared at her as if she were in league with Satan.

"I'm not saying it's a good thing," she added quickly. "But how bad could the guy be if he really did fall in love with you?"

"Did he?" Ashley asked darkly. "Or is he just saying that he did? Is this confession just another lie?"

Oh, ick. Colleen hadn't thought of it that way. But Ash was right. If *she* were trying to con someone into marrying her, she'd pretend to be in love with them, confess everything and beg for forgiveness. That would save her butt in the event that the truth ever did surface after the wedding.

"He slept with me, Colleen," Ashley said miserably. "And my father was *paying* him."

"Yeah," Colleen said, "I don't think your father was paying him to do that, though."

"It feels that way." Ashley was one of those women who still looked beautiful when she cried. "You know the really stupid thing?"

Colleen shook her head. "No."

"I didn't have the nerve to confront my father." Ashley's lip trembled. "I just ran away. I hid."

"But you're writing him a letter," Colleen pointed out. "That's a start."

"Clark keeps telling me I should take one of those assertiveness training courses. You know, the kind where you go out into the mountains with only a canteen of water and a hunting knife and come back after having killed a bear?"

Colleen laughed at the absurdity of that. "You'd take advice from a man with blue hair?"

Ash laughed, too. It was shaky, but it was laughter.

"You know what I think you should do?" Colleen said. "I think you should go back and have this raging, passionate affair with Brad. Flaunt it in your father's face. Make it really public. And then, next May, when you graduate from law school, you dump the creep and flip your father the bird. You pass the California bar exam, and take a job as a public defender in East L.A. and you do pro bono work for the community on the side just to *really* tick him off. That's what *I* would do."

"You could do that?" Ashley asked. "Really? Have that kind of a relationship with a man without falling even further in love? Without getting in too deep?"

Colleen thought about Bobby Taylor, about what would happen if she did succeed in talking her way into his bed. She thought about waking up beside him, smiling into his beautiful eyes as he bent to kiss her. She thought about driving him to the airport and watching his broad back and his long, easygoing stride as he headed into the terminal, as he walked away. From her. Without looking back.

She thought about the way that would make her heart die inside of her. Just a little bit.

Just enough to change her forever.

"No," she said quietly. "I guess I couldn't, either."

CHAPTER EIGHT

"WAIT," BOBBY SAID. "Zoe, no, if he's taking a day off, don't…" Bother him. But Zoe Robinson had already put him on hold.

"Hey, Chief!" Admiral Jake Robinson sounded cheerful and relaxed. "What's up? Zo tells me you're calling from Boston?"

"Uh, yes, sir," Bobby said. "But, sir, this can wait until tomorrow, because—"

"How's the shoulder?" the admiral interrupted. Admirals were allowed to interrupt whenever they wanted.

"Much better, sir," Bobby lied. It was exactly like Admiral Robinson to have made certain he'd be informed about the injuries of anyone on the SEAL teams—and to remember what he'd been told.

"These things take time." It was also like Robinson to see through Bobby's lie. "Slow and steady, Taylor. Don't push it too hard."

"Aye, sir. Admiral, I had no idea that your secretary would patch me through here, to your home."

"Well, you called to talk to me, didn't you?"

"Yes, sir, but you're an *admiral,* sir, and—"

"Ah." Robinson laughed. "You wanted it to be harder to reach me, huh? Well, if you need me to, I'll call Dottie in my office and tell her to put you on hold for a half an hour."

Bobby had to laugh, too. "No, thank you. I'm just… surprised."

"I don't take everyone's call," Jake Robinson's voice was serious now. "In fact, Dottie's probably kissed off half a dozen captains, commanders and lieutenant commanders already this morning. But when I set up the Gray Group, Chief, I made a point to make myself available 24/7 to the men I call to go out on my missions. You work for me—you need me? You got me. You probably don't know it, but you were on a Gray Group mission when you were injured. That cycled your name to the top of the list."

"I wasn't told, but…I knew."

"So talk to me, Chief. What's going on?"

Bobby told him. "Sir, I've become aware of a situation in which a dozen U.S. citizens—mostly students from here in Boston—are about to walk into Tulgeria with a single, locally hired armed guard."

Robinson swore, loudly and pungently.

Bobby told the admiral about the earthquake relief organization. About the bus and the children in the orphanage. About the fact that these American Good Samaritans were not going to be talked out of making this trip.

"What's your connection to this group, Chief?" Robinson asked. "Girlfriend?"

"Negative, sir," Bobby said hastily. "No, it's Wes Skelly's sister. She's one of the volunteers who's going."

"What, did Skelly send you to Boston to talk her out of it?" Robinson laughed. "God, you're a good friend to him, Bobby."

"He's out of the country, Admiral, and I had the time. Besides, he'd do the same for me."

"Yeah, and I suspect *your* sister is a little easier to handle than this sister of Skelly's—what's her name?"

"Colleen, sir."

"Is Colleen Skelly as much like her brother as I'm imagining her to be, God help us all?"

Bobby laughed again. "Yes and no, sir. She's…"

Wonderful. Beautiful. Amazingly sexy. Intelligent. *Perfect.* "She's special, sir. Actually, she reminds me of Zoe in a lot of ways. She's tough, but not really—it's just a screen she hides behind, if you know what I mean."

"Oh, yes. I do." The admiral laughed softly. "Oh, boy. So, I know it's none of my business, but does Wes know that you've got a thing for his sister?"

Bobby closed his eyes. Damn, he'd given himself away. There was no point in denying it. Not to Jake. The man may have been an admiral, but he was also Bobby's friend. "No, he doesn't."

"Hmm. Does *she* know?"

Good question. "Not really."

"Damn."

"I mean, she's incredible, Jake, and I think—no, I *know* she's looking for a fling. She's made that more than clear but I can't do it, and I'm…"

"Dying," Jake supplied the word. "Been there, done that. If she really is anything like Zoe, you don't stand a chance." He laughed. "Colleen Skelly, huh? With a name like that, I'm picturing a tiny red head, kind of built like her brother—compact. Skinny. With a smart mouth and a temper."

"She's a redhead," Bobby said. "And you're right about the mouth and the temper, but she's tall. She might even be taller than Wes. And she's not skinny. She's…" Stacked. Built like a brick house. Lush. Voluptuous. All those descriptions felt either disrespectful or as if he were exchanging locker-room confidences. "Statuesque," he finally came up with.

"Taller than Wes, huh? That must tick him off."

"She takes after their father, and he's built more like their mother's side of the family. It ticks Colleen off, too. She's gorgeous, but she doesn't think so."

"Genetics. It's proof that Mother Nature exists," Jake

said with a laugh. "She's got a strong sense of irony, doesn't she?"

"I need you to help me, sir." Bobby brought their conversation back to the point. "Colleen's determined to go to Tulgeria. This whole trip is an international incident waiting to happen. If this isn't something you want to get Alpha Squad or the Gray Group involved in, then I'm hoping you can give me—"

"It is," the admiral said. "Protection of U.S. citizens. In a case like this I like to think of it as preventative counter-terrorism. The Tulgerian government will bitch and moan about it, but we'll get you in. We'll tell the local officials that we need two teams," he decided. "One'll accompany Colleen Skelly and her friends, the other'll go in covert. The timing is really good on this, Taylor. You're actually the one doing *me* the favor here."

Admiral Robinson didn't say it. He couldn't say it, but Bobby knew he was going to use this seemingly standard protection op as a chance to send in an additional highly covert and top-secret team on an entirely different mission. It was probably related to the ongoing investigation of those rumors that the Tulgerian government was mass slaughtering its own citizens.

God, what a world.

"Alpha Squad will be back from their current training op in three days, tops," Robinson continued. "I'll have them rerouted here to the East Coast—to Little Creek. We'll both meet them there, Chief, you'll fill them in and work out a plan, then bring them back up to Boston to hash out the details with Colleen Skelly and her idealistic friends."

The admiral wanted Bobby to be part of the op. "I'm sorry, sir," he said. "I may have misled you about the status of my shoulder. I still have limited movement and—"

"I'm thinking you're valuable because you've already

established rapport with the civilians," Jake cut him off. "But I'll let it be your choice, Bobby. If you don't want to go—"

"Oh, no sir, I *want* to go." It was a no-brainer. He wanted to be there, himself, to make sure Colleen stayed safe.

Yes, it would have been easier to toss the entire problem into Admiral Robinson's capable hands and retreat, swiftly and immediately, to California. But Wes would be back in three days. Bobby could handle keeping his distance from Colleen for three days.

Couldn't he?

"Good," Jake said. "I'll get the ball rolling."

"Thank you, sir."

"Before you go, Chief, want some unsolicited advice?"

Bobby hesitated. "I'm not sure, sir."

The admiral laughed—a rich burst of genuine amusement. "Wrong answer, Taylor. This is one of those times that you're supposed to 'Aye, aye, sir' me, simply because I'm an admiral and you're not."

"Aye, aye, sir."

"Trust your heart, Chief. You've got a good one, and when the time comes, well, I'm confident you'll know what to do."

"Thank you, sir."

"See you in a few days. Thanks again for the call."

Bobby hung up the phone and lay back on his hotel room bed, staring up the ceiling.

When the time comes, you'll know what to do.

He already knew what he had to do.

He had to stay away from Colleen Skelly, who thought— God help them both—that she wanted him.

What did she know? She was ridiculously young. She had no clue how hard it was to sustain a relationship over long distances. She had no idea how difficult it was for *any*one to be involved with a SEAL, let alone someone ridiculously young. She was mistaking her desire for a physical relationship with a man she had a crush on, with her very real need for something more powerful and more permanent.

She said she wanted passion—well, he could give her that. He had no doubt. And maybe, if he were really lucky, she'd be so completely dazzled that she'd fall in love with him.

Yeah, right, *then* where would she be? In love with a man who spent most of his time out of the country with her brother—provided her brother would ever forgive him enough to speak to him again. But the key words there were *out of the country.* Colleen would get tired of *that* fast enough.

Eventually she'd be so tired of being second place in his life that she'd walk away.

And he wouldn't stop her.

But she'd want him to. And even though she was the one who left him, she'd end up hurt.

The last thing he wanted in the world was to leave her hurt.

Follow your heart. He would. Even though it meant killing this relationship before it even started. Even though it was the hardest thing he'd ever done.

COLLEEN SLID THE BACK door of the truck closed with a resounding bang.

"Okay," she said, as she attached a combination lock that was more to keep the door from bouncing open as they drove into Boston than to deter thieves. "Did someone lock my apartment?"

Kenneth looked blankly at Clark, and Clark looked blankly at Kenneth.

Colleen gave up on them and looked at Bobby, who nodded. "I took care of it," he said.

It was no surprise. He was dependable. Smart. Sexier than a man had the right to be at ten in the morning.

Their eyes met only briefly before he looked away—still it was enough to send a wave of heat through her. Shame. Embarrassment. Mortification. What exactly had she said to him last night? *I want you.* In broad daylight, she couldn't believe her audacity. What had she been thinking?

Still, he was here. He'd shown up bright and early this morning, hot cup of coffee in hand, to help lug all of the boxes of emergency supplies out of her living room and into the Relief Aid truck.

He'd said hardly anything to her. In fact, he'd only said, "Hi," and then got to work with Clark and Kenneth, hauling boxes down the entryway stairs and out to the truck. Bad shoulder or not, he could carry two at once without even breaking a sweat.

Colleen had spent the past ninety minutes analyzing that "Hi," as she'd built wall upon wall of boxes in the back of the truck. He'd sounded happy, hadn't he? Glad to see her? Well, if not glad to see her, he'd sounded neutral. Which was to say that at least he hadn't sounded *un*happy to see her. And that was a good thing.

Wasn't it?

Everything she'd said to him last night echoed in her head and made her stomach churn.

Any minute now they were going to be alone in the truck. Any minute now he was going to give her the friends speech, part two. Not that she'd ever been persistent and/or stupid enough before to have heard a part-two speech. But she had a good imagination. She knew what was coming. He would use the word *flattered* in reference to last night's no-holds-barred, bottom-line statement. He would focus on their differences in age, in background, in everything.

One major difference between them that she already knew was that she was an idiot.

Colleen climbed in behind the wheel and turned the key. Bobby got in beside her, picking her backpack up off the floor and placing it between them on the wide bench seat, like some kind of protective shield or definitive border.

She and her brother Ethan and her sister Peg, both who'd been closest to her in age among the seven Skelly children, had made similar boundaries in the far back seat of their father's Pontiac station wagon. Don't cross this line or else.

"Hey," Clark shouted over the roar of the diesel engine. "Can we bum a ride into Kenmore Square? You're going that way, right?"

"Sure," she said. "Squeeze in."

She felt Bobby tense. And then he moved. Quickly. He opened the passenger-side door, and would have leaped out to let the younger men sit in the middle—no doubt to keep from sitting pressed up against her—but Kenneth was already there, about to climb in.

As Colleen watched, Bobby braced himself and slid down the seat toward her.

She took her pack and set it on the floor, tucked between the seat and her door.

He moved as close as he possibly could without touching her. It was amazing, really, that he could be that close yet have absolutely no physical contact.

He smelled like baby shampoo and fresh laundry with a hint of the coffee that he seemed to drink each morning by the gallon. His hair was back in a ponytail again. She couldn't imagine him letting her braid it later today. She couldn't do it now, not the way they were sitting. And she knew that after Clark and Kenneth got out of the truck, Bobby wasn't going to let her get close enough to braid his hair ever again—not after what she'd said to him last night.

"Sorry," she said, her voice low. "I guess I must have embarrassed you to death last night."

"You scared me to death," he admitted, his voice pitched for her ears only. "Don't get me wrong, Colleen, I'm flattered. I really am. But this is one of those situations where what I want to do is completely different from what I should do. And should's got to win."

She looked up at him and found her face inches from his. A very small number of inches. Possibly two. Possibly fewer. The realization almost knocked what he'd just said out of her mind. Almost.

What he wanted *to do,* he'd said. True, he'd used the word *flattered* as she'd expected, but the rest of what he was saying was…

Colleen stared at that mouth, at those eyes, at the perfect chin and nose that were close enough for her to lean forward, if she wanted to, and kiss.

Oh, she wanted to.

And he'd just all but told her, beneath all those ridiculous *shoulds,* that he wanted her, too. She'd won. She'd *won!*

Look at me, she willed him, but he seemed intent upon reading the truck's odometer. *Kiss me.*

"I spoke to Admiral Robinson, who greenlighted U.S. military protection for your trip," he continued. "He wants me to remain in place as liaison with your group, and, well—" his gaze flicked in her direction "—I agreed. I'm here. I know what's going on. I have to stick around, even though I know you'd rather I go away."

"Whoa, Bobby." She put her hand on his knee. "I don't *want* you to go anywhere."

He glanced at her briefly again as he gently took her hand and deposited it back into her own lap. "The thing is..." He fixed his gaze on a point outside the truck. "I can't stay in the, uh—" he closed his eyes briefly "—the *capacity* in which you want me to stay."

She laughed in disbelief. "But that's crazy!"

He leaned forward to look out the passenger-side door, checking to see why Clark was taking so long to get in. Her roommate's brother was holding on to the door, blue head down, intent upon scraping something off the bottom of his shoe. "The admiral told me that Wes'll be back in about three days," Bobby told her.

Three days. That meant they didn't have a lot of time to—

"Once he's back, it'll be easier for me to, you know, do the right thing. Until then..."

"Do the right thing?" she repeated, loudly enough that Kenneth looked uncomfortable. "How could this," she gestured between them, "not be the *right thing* when everything about it feels so perfect?"

Bobby glanced back toward Kenneth and Clark before finally meeting and holding her gaze. "Please, Colleen, I'm begging you—don't make this more difficult for me than it has to be," he said, still softly, and she knew, just like that, that she hadn't won. She'd lost. He wanted her, too, but he was begging her—*begging* her—not to push this attraction that hung between them too far.

He wanted her, but he didn't want her. Not really. Not enough to let what he was feeling take priority over all their differences and all his asinine personal rules.

Colleen felt like crying. Instead she forced a smile. "Too bad, Taylor, it would have been amazingly great," she told him.

His smile was forced, too. He closed his eyes, as if he

couldn't bear looking at her, and shook his head slightly. "I know," he said. "Believe me, I know."

When he opened his eyes, he looked at her, briefly meeting her gaze again. He was sitting close—close enough for her to see that his eyes truly were completely, remarkably brown. There were no other flecks of color, no imperfections, no inconsistencies.

But far more hypnotizing than the pure, bottomless color was the brief glimpse of frustration and longing he let her see. Either on purpose or accidentally, it didn't matter which.

It took her breath away.

"I need about three more inches of seat before I can close this door," Clark announced. He shifted left in a move reminiscent of a football player's offensive drive, making Kenneth yelp and ramming Bobby tightly against Colleen.

Completely against Colleen. His muscular thigh was wedged against her softer one. He had nowhere to put his shoulder or his arm, and even though he tried to angle himself, that only made it worse. Suddenly she was practically sitting in the man's lap.

"There," Clark added with satisfaction as he closed the truck door. "I'm ready, dudes. Let's go."

Just drive. Colleen knew the smartest thing to do was to just drive. If traffic was light, it would take about fifteen minutes to reach Kenmore Square. Then Clark and Kenneth would get out, and she and Bobby wouldn't have to touch each other ever again.

She could feel him steaming, radiating heat from the summer day, from the work he'd just done, and he shifted, trying to move away, but he only succeeded in making her aware that they both wore shorts, and that his bare skin was pressed against hers.

She was okay, she told herself. She'd be okay as long as she kept breathing.

Colleen reached forward to put the truck into drive. Raising her arm to hold the steering wheel gave Bobby a little more space—except now his arm was pressed against the side of her breast.

He tried desperately to move away, but there was nowhere for him to go.

"I can't lift my arm enough to put it on the back of the seat," he said in a choked-sounding voice. "I'm sorry."

Colleen couldn't help it. She started to laugh.

And then she did the only thing she could do, given the situation. She threw the truck into Park and turned and kissed him.

It was obviously the last thing he'd expected. She could taste his disbelief. For the briefest moment he tried to pull away, but then she felt him surrender.

And then he kissed her back as desperately and as hungrily as she kissed him.

It was a kiss at least as potent as the one they'd shared in the alley. Did he always kiss like this, with his mouth a strange mix of hard and soft, with a voracious thirst and a feverish intensity, as if she were in danger of having her very life force sucked from her? His hands were in her hair, around her back, holding her in place so that he could claim her more completely. And claim her he did.

Colleen had never been kissed quite so possessively in all her life.

But, oh, she liked it. Very much.

Quiet, easygoing Bobby Taylor kissed with a delirious abandon that was on the verge of out of control.

He pulled her toward him, closer, tugging as if he wanted her on his lap, straddling him. As if he wanted...

"You know, on second thought, Kenneth, we might get to Kenmore faster on the T."

Oh, my *God*.

Colleen pulled back the same instant that Bobby released her.

He was breathing hard and staring at her, with a wild look in his eyes she'd never seen before. Not on him, anyway, the King of Cool.

"This is how you help?" he asked incredulously.

"Yes," she said. She couldn't breathe, either, and having him look at her that way wasn't helping. "I mean, no. I mean—"

"Gee, I'm sorry," Kenneth said brightly. "We've got to be going. Clark, *move* it."

"Clark, don't go anywhere," Colleen ordered, opening the door. "Bobby's going to drive. I'm coming around to sit on the other side."

She got out of the truck's cab, holding onto the door for a second while she waited for the jelly in her legs to turn back to bone.

She could feel Bobby watching her as she crossed around the front of the truck. She saw Clark lean forward, across Kenneth, and say something to him.

"Are you sure, man?" Clark was saying to Bobby as she opened the door.

"Yes," Bobby said with a definiteness that made her want to cry. Clark had no doubt asked if Bobby wanted the two of them to make themselves scarce. But Bobby didn't want them to leave. He didn't want to be alone with Colleen until he absolutely had to.

Well, she'd really messed *that* up.

As Bobby put the truck in gear, she leaned forward and said, across Clark and Kenneth, "I wasn't trying to make it worse for you. That was supposed to be like, I don't know, I guess a...a kind of a kiss goodbye."

He looked at her and it was a look of such total incomprehension, she tried to explain.

"It seemed to me as if we'd just decided that our relationship wasn't going to move beyond the…the, I don't know, platonic, I guess, and I just wanted—" She swore silently—words she'd never say aloud, words she usually didn't even *think*. This wasn't coming out right at all. *Just say it.* What was he going to do? Laugh at her for being so pathetic? "I just wanted to kiss you one last time. Is that so awful?"

"Excuse me," Clark said. "But that was a *platonic* kiss?"

Bobby's hair had come out of his ponytail. She must've done that when she'd wrapped her arms around his neck and kissed him as if there were no tomorrow. As she watched, he tried to gather it up with his right hand—his good arm. He settled for hooking it behind his ears.

"Dude. If *that* was a *platonic* kiss," Clark started, "then I want to see one that's—" Kenneth clapped his hand over his mouth, muffling the rest of his words.

"I'm sorry," Colleen said.

Bobby glanced up from the road and over at her. The mixture of remorse, anger, and whatever those other mysterious emotions were that seemed to glisten in his dark eyes, was going to haunt her dreams. Probably for the rest of her life. "I am, too."

CHAPTER NINE

THERE WERE PROTESTORS. On the sidewalk. In front of the AIDS Education Center. With signs saying NIMBY. Not In My Back Yard.

Bobby, following Colleen's directions, had taken a detour after letting Clark and Kenneth out near Kenmore Square. Colleen had something to drop at the center—some papers or a file having to do with the ongoing court battle with the neighborhood zoning board.

She'd been filling up the silence in the truck in typical Skelly fashion, by telling Bobby about how she'd gotten involved doing legal work for the center, through a student program at her law school.

Although she'd yet to pass the bar exam, there was such a shortage of lawyers willing to do pro bono work like this—to virtually work for free for desperately cash-poor nonprofit organizations—student volunteers were allowed to do a great deal of the work.

And Colleen had always been ready to step forward and volunteer.

Bobby could remember when she was thirteen—the year he'd first met her. She was just a little kid. A tomboy—with skinned knees and ragged cutoff jeans and badly cut red hair. She was a volunteer even back then, a member of some kind of local environmental club, always going out on neighborhood improvement hikes, which was just a fancy name for cleaning up roadside trash.

Once, he and Wes had had to drive her to the hospital

to get stitches and a tetanus shot. During one of her tromps through a particularly nasty area, a rusty nail went right through the cheap soles of her sneakers and into her foot.

It had hurt like hell, and she'd cried—a lot like the way she'd cried the other night. Wiping her tears away fast, so that, with luck, he and Wes wouldn't see.

It had been a bad year for her. And for Wes, too. Bobby had come home with Wes earlier that year—for a funeral. Wes and Colleen's brother, Ethan, had been killed in a head-on with a tree, in a car driven by a classmate with a blood-alcohol level high enough to poison him.

God, that had hurt. Wes had been numb for months after. Colleen had written to Bobby, telling him she'd joined a grief counseling group connected to Mothers Against Drunk Drivers. She'd written to ask Bobby to find a similar support group for Wes, who had loved Ethan best out of all his brothers and sisters, and was hurt the worst by the loss.

Bobby had tried, but Wes didn't want any of it. He ferociously threw himself into training and eventually learned how to laugh again.

"Pull over," Colleen said now.

"There's no place to stop."

"Double park," she ordered him. "I'll get out—you can stay with the truck."

"No way," he said, harshly throwing one of Wes's favorite—although unimaginative and fairly offensive—adjectives between the two words.

She looked at him in wide-eyed surprise. He'd never used that word in front of her before. Ever.

Her look wasn't reproachful, just startled. Still, he felt like a dirtball.

"I beg your pardon," he said stiffly, still angry at her for kissing him after he'd begged her—*begged* her—not to, angry at himself, as well, for kissing her back, "but if you think I'm going to sit here and watch while you face down an angry mob—"

"It's not an angry mob," she countered. "I don't see John Morrison, although you better believe he's behind this."

He had to stop for the light, and she opened the door and slipped down from the cab.

"Colleen!" Disbelief and something else, something darker that lurched in his stomach and spread fingers of ice through his blood, made his voice crack. Several of those signs were made with two-by-fours. Swung as a weapon, they could break a person's skull.

She heard his yelp, he knew she had, but she only waved at him as she moved gracefully across the street.

Fear. That cold dark feeling sliding through his veins was fear.

He'd learned to master his own personal fear. Sky diving, swimming in shark-infested waters, working with explosives that, with one stupid mistake, could tear a man into hamburger. He'd taken hold of that fear and controlled it with the knowledge that he was as highly skilled as a human being could be. He could deal with anything that came along—anything, that is, that was in his control. As for those things outside of his control, he'd developed a zen-like deal with the powers that be. He'd live life to its fullest, and when it was his turn to go, when he no longer had any other options, well then, he'd go—no regrets, no remorse, no panic.

He wasn't, however, without panic when it came to watching Colleen head into danger.

There was a lull in the traffic, so he ran the light, pulling as close to the line of parked cars in front of the building as possible. Putting on his flashers, he left the truck sitting in the street as he ran as fast as he could to intercept Colleen before she reached the protestors.

He stopped directly in front of her and made himself as big as possible—a wall that she couldn't get past.

"This," he said tightly, "is *the* last time you will *ever* disobey me."

"Excuse me," she said, her mouth open in outraged disbelief. "Did you just say...*disobey?*"

He'd pushed one of her buttons. He recognized that, but he was too angry, too upset to care. He was losing it, his voice getting louder. "In Tulgeria, you will not *move*, you will not lift a *finger* without my or Wes's permission. Do you understand?"

She laughed at him, right in his face. "Yeah, in your dreams."

"If you're going to act like a *child*—unable to control yourself—"

"What are you going to do?" she countered hotly. "Tie me up?"

"Yes, dammit, if I have to!" Bobby heard himself shouting. He was shouting at her. Bellowing. As loudly as he shouted in mock fury at the SEAL candidates going through BUD/S training back in Coronado. Except there was nothing mock about his fury now.

She wasn't in danger. Not now. He could see the protestors, and up close they were a far-less-dangerous-looking bunch than he'd imagined them to be. There were only eight of them, and six were women—two quite elderly.

But that was moot. She'd completely ignored his warning, and if she did that in Tulgeria, she could end up very dead very fast.

"Go on," she shouted back at him, standing like a boxer on the balls of her feet, as if she were ready to go a few rounds. "Tie me up. I dare you to try!" As if she honestly thought she could actually beat him in a physical fight.

As if she truly believed he would ever actually raise a hand against her or any other woman.

No, he'd never fight her. But there were other ways to win.

Bobby picked her up. He tossed her over his good shoulder, her stomach pressed against him, her head and arms dangling down his back. It was laughably easy to do, but once he got her there, she didn't stay still. She wriggled and kicked and howled and punched ineffectively at his butt and the backs of his legs. She was a big woman, and he wrenched his bad shoulder holding her in place, but it wasn't that that slowed him.

No, what made him falter was the fact that her T-shirt had gapped and he was holding her in place on his shoulder with his hand against the smooth bare skin of her back. He was holding her legs in place—keeping her from kicking him—with a hand against the silkiness of her upper thighs.

He was touching her in places he shouldn't be touching her. Places he'd been dying to touch her for years. But he didn't put her down. He just kept carrying her down the sidewalk, back toward the truck that was double parked in front of the center.

His hair was completely down, loose around his face, and she caught some of it with one of her flailing hands. Caught and yanked, hard enough to make his eyes tear.

"Ouch! God!" That was it. As soon as he got back to his room, he was shaving his head.

"Let! Me! Go!"

"You dared me," he reminded her, swearing again as she gave his hair another pull.

"I didn't think you were man enough to actually do it!"

Oh, ouch. That stung far worse than getting his hair pulled.

"Help!" she shrieked. "Someone *help!* Mrs. O'Hallaran!"

Mrs. who...?

"Excuse me, young man..."

Just like that, Bobby's path to the truck was blocked by the protestors.

One of the elderly women stood directly in front of him now, brandishing her sign as if it were a cross and he were a vampire. "What do you think you're doing?" she asked, narrowing her eyes at him from behind her thick glasses.

Take Back the Night, the sign said. Neighborhood Safety Council.

"He's being a jerk, Mrs. O'Hallaran," Colleen answered for him. "A complete idiotic, stupid, male-chauvinist *jerk*. Put me down, *jerk!*"

"I know this young lady from church," the elderly woman—Mrs. O'Hallaran—told him, her lips pursed in disapproval, "and I'm certain she doesn't deserve the indignity of your roughhousing, sir."

Colleen punched him in the back as she kneed him as hard as she could. She caught him in the stomach, but he knew she'd been aiming much lower. She'd wanted to bring him to his knees. "Put me *down!*"

"Colleen, do you want us to call the police?" one of the two men asked.

She knew these people. And they knew her—by name. From church, the old lady had said. Colleen had never even remotely been in danger.

Somehow that only served to make him even more mad. She could have told him she knew them, instead of letting him think...

He put her down. She straightened her shirt, hastily pulling it back down over her exposed stomach, giving him a glimpse of her belly button, God help him.

She ran her fingers quickly through her hair, and as she did, she gave him a look and a smile that was just a little too smug, as if she'd won and he'd lost.

He forced himself to stop thinking about her belly button and glared at her. "This is just some kind of game to you, isn't it?"

"No," she said, glaring back, "this is my life. I'm a woman, not a child, and I don't need to ask *any*one's permission before I 'so much as lift my finger,' thank you very much."

"So you just do whatever you want. You just walk around, doing whatever you want, *kissing* whoever you want, whenever you want—" Bobby shut himself up. What the hell did that have to do with this?

Everything.

She'd scared him, yes, by not telling him why she was so confident the protestors didn't pose a threat, and that fear had morphed into anger. And he'd also been angry, sure, that she'd completely ignored his warning.

But, really, most of his anger came from that kiss she'd given him, less than an hour ago, in front of her apartment building.

That incredible kiss that had completely turned him upside down and inside out and...

And made him want far more than he could take.

Worse and worse, now that he'd blurted it out, she knew where his anger had come from, too.

"I'm sorry," she said quietly, reaching up to push his hair back from his face.

He stepped away from her, unable to bear the softness of her touch, praying for a miracle, praying for Wes suddenly to appear. His personal guardian angel, walking down the sidewalk, toward them, with that unmistakable Skelly swagger.

Colleen had mercy on him, and didn't stand there,

staring at him with chagrin and pity in her luminous blue-green eyes. God, she was beautiful.

And, God, he was so pathetic.

He'd actually shouted at her. When was the last time he'd raised his voice in genuine anger?

He couldn't remember.

She'd turned back to the protestors and was talking to them now. "Did John Morrison tell you to come down here with these signs?"

They looked at each other.

As Bobby watched, Colleen spoke to them, telling them about the center, reassuring them that it would be an improvement to the neighborhood. This wasn't an abortion clinic. They wouldn't be handing out copious handfuls of free needles or condoms. They would provide HIV testing and counseling. They would provide AIDS education classes and workshops.

She invited them inside, to introduce them to the staff and give them a tour of the facility, while Bobby stayed outside with the truck.

A parking spot opened up down the street, and as he was parallel parking the beast, the truck's phone rang. It was Rene, the coordinator from the Relief Aid office, wondering where they were. She had ten volunteers ready to unpack the truck. Should they wait or should she let them take an early lunch?

Bobby promised that Colleen would call her right back. He was a half a block away from the center when he saw the protestors take their signs and go home. Knowing Colleen, she'd talked half of them into volunteering at the center. The other half had probably donated money to the cause.

She came out and met him halfway. "I don't know why John Morrison is so determined to cause trouble. I guess I should be glad he only sent protestors this time, instead of throwing cinder blocks through the front windows again."

"Again?" Bobby walked her more swiftly toward the truck, wanting her safely inside the cab and out of this wretched neighborhood. "He did that before?"

"Twice," she told him. "Of course, he got neighborhood kids to do the dirty work, so we can't prove he was behind it. You know, I find it a little ironic that the man owns a bar. And his place is not some upscale hangout…it's a dive. People go there to get seriously tanked or to connect with one of the girls from the local 'escort service,' which is really just a euphemism for Hookers R Us. I'm sure Morrison gets a cut of whatever money exchanges hands in his back room, the sleaze, and *we're* a threat to the neighborhood…? What's he afraid of?"

"Where's his bar?" Bobby asked.

She gave him an address that meant nothing to him. But with a map he'd find it easily enough.

He handed her the keys. "Call Rene on the cell phone and tell her you're on your way."

She tried to swallow her surprise. "You're not coming?"

He shook his head, unable to meet her eyes for more than the briefest fraction of a second.

"Oh," she said.

It was the way she said it, as if trying to hide her disappointment that made him try to explain. "I need to take some time to…" What? Hide from her? Yes. Run away? Absolutely. Pray that he'd last another two and a half days until Wes arrived?

"Look, it's all right," she said. "You don't need to—"

"You're driving me crazy," he told her. "Every time I turn around, I find myself kissing you. I can't seem to be able to stop."

"You're the only one of us who sees that as a bad thing."

"I'm scared to death to be alone with you," he admitted. "I don't trust myself to be able to keep the distance I need to keep."

She didn't step toward him. She didn't move. She didn't say anything. She just looked at him and let him see her wanting him. He had to take a step back to keep himself from taking a step forward, and then another step and another, and pulling her into his arms and...

"I've got to..." he said. "Go..."

He turned away. Turned back.

She still didn't say anything. She just waited. Standing there, wanting him.

It was the middle of the day, on the sidewalk of a busy city street. Did she really think he'd do something as crazy as kiss her?

Ah, God, he wanted to kiss her.

A goodbye kiss. Just one last time. He wanted to do it, to kiss her again, knowing this time that it would, indeed, be the last time.

He wanted—desperately—for her to kiss him the way she'd kissed him in the darkness of the backstreet off Harvard Square. So lightly. So sweetly. So perfectly.

Just one more time like that.

Yeah, like hell he could kiss her just one more time. If he so much as touched her again, they were both going to go up in flames.

"Get in the truck," he somehow managed to tell her. "Please."

For one awful moment he was certain she was going to reach for him. But then she turned and unlocked the door to the truck. "You know, we're going to have to talk about that 'obey' thing," she said. "Because if you don't lighten up, I'm going to recommend that we don't accept your admiral's protection. We don't have to, you know."

Oh, yes, they did. But Bobby kept his mouth shut. He

didn't say another word as she climbed into the truck from the passenger's side, as she slid behind the wheel and started the big engine.

As he watched, she maneuvered the truck onto the street and, with a cloud of exhaust, drove away.

Two and a half more days.

How the hell was he going to survive?

CHAPTER TEN

COLLEEN CLEANED OUT HER REFRIGERATOR.

She washed the bathroom floor and checked her email.

She called the center's main office to find out the status of Andrea Barker, who'd been attacked just outside her home. There was no change, she was told. The woman was still in a coma.

By 9:00, Bobby still hadn't called.

By 9:15, Colleen had picked up the phone once or twice, but each time talked herself out of calling his hotel.

Finally, at 9:45, the apartment building front door buzzer rang.

Colleen leaned on the intercom. "Bobby?"

"Uh, no." The male voice that came back was one she didn't know. "Actually, I'm looking for Ashley DeWitt?"

"I'm sorry," Colleen said. "She's not here."

"Look, I drove up from New York. I know she was coming here and... Hold on a sec," the voice said.

There was a long silence, and then a knock directly on her apartment door.

Colleen looked out through the peephole. Brad. Had to be. He was tall and slender, with dark-blond hair and a yacht-club face. She opened the door with the chain still on and gave him a very pointedly raised eyebrow.

"Hi," he said, trying to smile. He looked awful. Like he

hadn't slept in about a week. "Sorry, someone was coming out, so I came in."

"You mean, you sneaked in."

He gave up on the smile. "You must be Colleen, Ash's roommate. I'm Brad—the idiot who should be taken out and shot."

Colleen looked into his Paul-Newman-blue eyes and saw his pain. This was a man who was used to getting everything he wanted through his good looks and charisma. He was used to being Mr. Special, to winning, to being envied by half of the world and wanted by the other half.

But he'd blown it, big-time, with Ashley, and right now he hated himself.

She shut the door to remove the chain. When she opened it again, she stepped back to let him inside. He was wearing a dark business suit that was rumpled to the point of ruin—as if he'd had it on during that entire week he hadn't been sleeping.

He needed a shave, too.

"She's really not here," Colleen told him as he followed her into the living room. "She went to visit her aunt on Martha's Vineyard. Don't bother asking, because I don't know the details. Her aunt rents a different house each summer. I think it's in Edgartown this year, but I'm not sure."

"But she *was* here. God, I can smell her perfume." He sat down, heavily, on the sofa, and for one awful moment Colleen was certain that he was going to start to cry.

Somehow he managed not to. If this was an act, he deserved an Oscar.

"Do you know when she'll be back?" he asked.

Colleen shook her head. "No."

"Is this your place or hers?" He was looking around the living room, taking in the watercolors on the walls, the art prints, the batik-patterned curtains, the comfortable, secondhand furniture.

"Most of this stuff is mine," Colleen told him. "Although the curtains are Ashley's. She's a secret flower child, you know. Beneath those designer suits is a woman who's longing to wear tie-dyed T-shirts."

"Did she, uh, tell you what I did?" Brad asked.

"Yup."

He cleared his throat. "Do you think…" He had to start again. "Do you think she'll ever forgive me?"

"No," Colleen said.

Brad nodded. "Yeah," he said. "I don't think she will, either." He stood up. "The ferry to the Vineyard is out of Woods Hole, right?"

"Brad, she went there because she doesn't want to see you. What you did was unconscionable."

"So what do *you* recommend I do?" he asked her. "Give up?" His hands were shaking as if he'd had too much coffee on the drive up from New York. Or as if he were going into withdrawal without Ashley around.

Colleen shook her head. "No," she said. "Don't give up. Don't ever give up." She looked at the telephone—it still wasn't ringing. Bobby wasn't calling. That left only one alternative. She had to call him. Because *she* wasn't going to give up, either.

She followed Brad to the door.

"I quit my job," he told her. "You know, working for her father. If Ashley calls, will you tell her that?"

"If she calls," Colleen said, "I'll tell her you were here. And then, if she asks, I'll tell her what you said. But only if she asks."

"Fair enough."

"What should I tell her if she asks where you are?"

He started down the stairs. "Edgartown. Tell her I'm in Edgartown, too."

BOBBY STARED AT THE phone as it rang, knowing it was Colleen on the other end. Had to be. Who else would call him here? Maybe Wes, who had called earlier and left a message.

It rang again.

Bobby quickly did the math, figuring out the time difference.... No, it definitely wasn't Wes. Had to be Colleen.

A third time. Once more and the voice mail system would click on.

He reached for it as it began to ring that final time, silently cursing himself. "Taylor."

"Hi, it's me."

"Yeah," he said. "I figured."

"And yet you picked it up, anyway. How brave of you."

"What's happening?" he asked, trying to pretend that everything was fine, that he hadn't kissed her—again— and then spent the entire afternoon and evening wishing he was kissing her again.

"Nothing," Colleen said. "I was just wondering what you were up to all day."

"This and that." Mostly things he didn't want to tell her. That when he wasn't busy lusting after her, he'd been checking out John Morrison, for one. From what Bobby could tell from the locals, Morrison was mostly pathetic. Although, in his experience, pathetic men could be dangerous, too. Mostly to people they perceived to be weaker than they were. Like women. "Is your door locked?"

Colleen lowered her voice seductively. "Is yours?"

Oh, God. "This isn't a joke, Colleen," he said, working hard to keep his voice even. Calm. It wasn't easy. Inside he was ready to fly off the handle, to shout at her again. "A woman you work with was attacked—"

"Yes, my door is locked," she said. "But if someone

really wants in, they can get in, since my windows are all open wide. And don't ask me to close and lock them, because it's hot tonight."

It was. Very hot. Even here in his air-conditioned hotel room.

Funny, but it had seemed nice and cool right up until a few minutes ago. When the phone rang.

He'd showered earlier in an attempt to chill out, but his hair, still down around his shoulders, was starting to stick to his neck again. As soon as he got off the phone with Colleen, he'd put it into a ponytail.

Shoot, maybe he'd take another shower. A nice, freezing-cold one this time.

"Colleen," he said. Despite his attempts to sound calm, there was a tightness to his voice. "Please don't tell me you sleep with your windows unlocked."

She laughed. "All right," she said. "I won't tell you."

Bobby heard himself make a strangled sound.

"You know, if you want me to be really, absolutely safe, you could come over," she told him. "Although, you've got air-conditioning over there, don't you? So you should really ask *me* to come to the hotel. I could take a cab and be there in five minutes."

He managed a word this time. "Colleen..."

"Okay," she said. "Right. Never mind. It's a terrible idea. Forget it. Just forget about the fact that I'm here, sitting on my bed, all alone, and that you're just a short mile away, sitting on yours, presumably also all alone. Forget about the fact that kissing you is on my list of the five most wonderful things I've ever done in my life and—"

Oh, man.

"I can't do it," he said, giving up on not trying to sound as desperate as he felt. "Dammit, even if you *weren't* Wes's sister, I'm only here for a few more days. That's all I could give you. I can't handle another long-distance relationship right now. I can't do that to myself."

"I'll take the days," she said. "Day. Make it singular if you want. Just once. Bobby—"

"I can't do that to you." But oh, sweet heaven, he wanted to. He *could* be at her place in five minutes. Less. One kiss, and he'd have her clothes off. Two, and... Oh, *man.*

"I want to know what it's like." Her voice was husky, intimate across the phone line, as if she were whispering in his ear, her breath hot against him. "Just once. No strings, Bobby. Come on..."

Yeah, no strings—except for the noose Wes would tie around his neck when he found out.

Wes, who'd left a message for Bobby on his hotel voice mail...

"Hey, Bobby! Word is Alpha Squad's heading back to Little Creek in a few days to assist Admiral Robinson's Gray Group in Tulgeria as part of some kind of civilian protection gig. Did you set that up, man? Let me guess. Leenie dug in her heels, so you called the Jakester. Brilliant move, my friend. It would be perfect—if Spaceman wasn't being such a total jerk out here on my end.

"He's making all this noise about finally getting to meet Colleen. Remember that picture you had of her? It was a few months ago. I don't know where you got it, but Spaceman saw it and wouldn't stop asking about her. Where does she go to school? How old is she? Yada-yada-yada, on and on about her hair, her eyes, her smile. Give me a break! As if I'd ever let a SEAL within twenty-five feet of her—not even an officer and alleged gentleman like Spaceman, no way. Look, I'll call you when we get into Little Creek. In the meantime, stick close to her, all right? Put the fear of God or the U.S. Navy into any of those college jerks sniffing around her, trying to get too close. Thanks again for everything, Bobby. I hope your week hasn't been too miserable."

Miserable wasn't even close. Bobby had left misery behind a long time ago.

"Maybe we should have phone sex," Colleen suggested.

"What?" Bobby dropped the receiver. He moved fast and caught it before it bounced twice. "No!"

She was laughing at him again. "Ah, come on. Where's your sense of adventure, Taylor? What are you wearing? Isn't that the way you're supposed to start?"

"Colleen—"

She lowered her voice. "Don't you want to know what I've got on?"

"No. I have to go now." Bobby closed his eyes and didn't hang up the phone. *Yes.* Oh, man.

"My nightgown," she told him, her voice even softer. Slightly breathy now. Deep and husky, her voice was unbelievable even when she wasn't trying to give him a heart attack. Right now, she was trying, and it was pure sex. "It's white. Cotton." She left long pauses between her words, as if giving him plenty of time to picture her. "Sleeveless. It's got buttons down the front, and the top one fell off a long time ago, leaving it a little…daring, shall we say? It's old—nice and soft and a little worn-out."

He knew that nightgown. He'd seen it hanging on the back of her bathroom door the last time he and Wes had visited. He'd touched it by mistake when he'd come out of the shower, thinking it was his towel. It wasn't. It *was* very soft to the touch.

Her body, beneath it, would be even softer.

"Want me to guess what you're wearing?" she asked.

Bobby couldn't speak.

"A towel," she said. "Just a towel. Because I bet you just showered. You like to shower at night to cool down before you go to bed, right? If I touched you," her voice dropped another notch, "your skin would be clean and cool and smooth.

"And your hair's down—it's probably still a little damp, too. If I were there, I'd brush it out for you. I'd kneel behind you on the bed and—"

"If you were here," Bobby said, interrupting her, his voice rough to his own ears, "you wouldn't be brushing my hair."

"What would I be doing?" she shot back at him.

Images bombarded him. Colleen, flashing him her killer smile just before she lowered her head and took him into her mouth. Colleen, lying back on his bed, hair spread on his pillows, breasts peaked with desire, waiting for him, welcoming him as he came to her. Colleen, head back as she straddled him, as he filled her, hard and fast and deep and—

Reality intervened. Phone sex. Dear sweet heaven. What was she doing to him? Beneath the towel—yes, she was right about the towel he wore around his waist—he was completely aroused.

"What would you be doing? You'd be calling a cab to take you home," he told her.

"No, I wouldn't. I'd kiss you," she countered, "and you'd pick me up and carry me to your bed."

"No, I wouldn't," he lied. "Colleen, I have...I really have to go now. Really."

"Your towel would drop to the floor," she said, and he couldn't make himself hang up the phone, both dreading and dying to hear what she would say next. "And after you put me down, you'd let me look at you." She drew in a breath, and it caught—a soft little gasp that made him ache from wanting her. "I think you're the most beautiful man I've ever seen."

He wasn't sure if he wanted to laugh or cry. "I think you're crazy." His voice cracked.

"No. Oh, your shoulders are so wide, and your chest and arms...mmmmm." She made a sound deep in her throat that was so sexy he was sure he was going to die.

Stop this. Now. Somehow he couldn't make his lips form the words.

"And the muscles in your stomach, leading down to..." She made another sound, a sigh, this time. "Do you know how incredibly good you look naked? There's...so *much* of you. I'm a little nervous, but you smile at me, and your eyes are so soft and beautiful, I know you'd never hurt me."

Bobby stood up. His sudden, jerky movement was reflected in the mirror above the dresser, on the other side of the dimly lit room. He looked ridiculous standing there, his towel tenting out in front of him.

He must've made some anguished noise, because she quieted him. "Shhh. It's okay."

But it wasn't. Nothing about this was okay. Still, he couldn't hang up. He couldn't make her stop.

He couldn't stand the sight of himself like that, standing there like some absurd, pathetic clown, and he took the towel off, flinging it across the room. Only now he stood there naked. Naked and aching for someone he couldn't have. Not really.

"After I look at you for a long time..." Her voice was musical. Seductive. He could have listened to her read a phone book and gotten turned on. This was driving him mad. "I unbutton my nightgown. I've got nothing on underneath, nothing at all, and you know it. But you don't rush me. You just sit back and watch. One button at a time.

"Finally, I'm done, but...I'm shy." She was silent for a moment, and when she spoke again, her voice was very small. "I'm afraid you won't…like me." She was serious. She honestly thought—

"Are you kidding? I love your body," Bobby told her. "I dream about you wearing that nightgown. I dream about—"

Oh, my God. What was he doing?

"Oh, tell me," she breathed. "Please, Bobby, tell me what you dream."

"What do you think I dream?" he asked harshly, angry at her, angry at himself, knowing he still wasn't man enough to hang up the phone and end this, even though he knew damn well that he should. "I dream exactly what you're describing right now. You in my bed." His voice caught on his words. "Ready for me."

"I am," she told him. "Ready for you. Completely. You're still watching, so I…I touch myself—where I'm dying for you to touch me."

She made a noise that outdid all of the other noises she'd been making, and Bobby nearly started to cry. Oh, man, he couldn't do this. This was Wes's sister on the other end of this phone. This was wrong.

He turned his back to the mirror, unable to look at his reflection.

"Please," she gasped, "oh, please, tell me what you dream when you dream about me."

Oh, *man*. "Where did you learn to do this?" He had to know.

"I didn't," she said breathlessly. "I'm making it up as I go along. You want to know what I dream about you?"

No. Yes. It didn't matter. She didn't wait for him to answer.

"My fantasy is that the doorbell rings, and you're there when I answer it. You don't say anything. You just come inside and lock the door behind you. You just look at me and I know. This is it. You want me.

"And then you kiss me, and it starts out so slowly, so delicately, but it builds and it grows and it takes over everything—the whole world gets lost in the shadow of this one amazing kiss. You touch me and I touch you, and I love touching you, but I can't get close enough, and somehow you know that, and you make my clothes disappear. And you still kiss me and kiss me, and you don't stop kissing me until I'm on my back on my bed, and you're—" her voice dropped to a whisper "—inside of me."

"That's what I dream," Bobby whispered, too, struggling to breathe. "I dream about being inside you." Hell. He was going to burn in hell for saying that aloud.

Her breath was coming in gasps, too. "I love those dreams," she told him. "It feels *so* good…"

"Yes…"

"Oh, please," she begged. "Tell me more…."

Tell her… When he closed his eyes, he could see Colleen beneath him, beside him, her body straining to meet his, her breasts filling his hands and his mouth, her hair a fragrant curtain around his face, her skin smooth as silk, her mouth soft and wet and delicious, her hips moving in rhythm with his….

But he could tell her none of that. He couldn't even begin to put it into words.

"I dream of touching you," he admitted hoarsely. "Kissing you. Everywhere." It was woefully inadequate, compared to what she'd just described.

But she sighed as if he'd given her the verbal equivalent of the Hope Diamond.

So he tried again, even though he knew he shouldn't. He stood there, listening to himself open his mouth and say things he shouldn't say to his best friend's sister.

"I dream of you on top of me." His voice sounded distant and husky, thick with desire and need. Sexy. Who would have thought he'd be any good at this? "So I can watch your face, Colleen." He dragged out her name, taking his time with it, loving the way it felt in his mouth, on his tongue. *Colleen.* "So I can look into your eyes, your beautiful eyes. Oh, I love looking into your eyes, Colleen, while you…"

"Oh, yes," she gasped. "Oh, Bobby, oh—"

Oh, *man.*

CHAPTER ELEVEN

JUST AFTER MIDNIGHT THE PHONE RANG.

Colleen picked it up on the first ring, knowing it was Bobby, knowing that he wasn't calling for a replay of what they'd just done.

Pretended to do.

Sort of.

She didn't bother even to say hello. "Are you okay?"

He'd been so freaked out earlier that she'd made up an excuse to get off the phone, thinking he needed time alone to get his heart and lungs working again.

But now she was wondering if that hadn't been a mistake. Maybe what he'd really needed was to talk.

"I don't know," he answered her. "I'm trying to figure out which level of hell I'm going to be assigned to."

"He's able to make a joke," Colleen said. "Should I take that as a good sign?"

"I wasn't joking. Dammit, Colleen, I can't do that ever again. I can't. I shouldn't have even—"

"All right," she said. "Look, Guilt Man, let it go. I steamrolled over you. You didn't stand a chance. Besides, it's not as if it was real."

"No?" he said. "That's funny, because from this end, it sounded pretty authentic."

"Well, yeah," she said. "Sure. On a certain level it was. But the truth is, your participation was nice, but it wasn't necessary. All I ever really have to do is think about you. If you want to know the truth, this isn't the first time I've let my fantasies of you and me push me over the edge—"

"Oh, my God, don't tell me that!"

"Sorry." Colleen made herself stop talking. She was making this worse, telling him secrets that made her blush when she stopped to think about it. But his feelings of guilt were completely unwarranted.

"I've got to leave," he told her, his voice uncharacteristically unsteady. "I have to get out of here. I've decided— I'm going down to Little Creek early. I'll be back in a few days, with the rest of Alpha Squad."

With Wes.

One step forward, two steps back.

"I'd appreciate it if you didn't go into detail with my brother about—"

"I'm going to tell him that I didn't touch you. Much. But that I wanted to."

"Because it's not like I make a habit of doing that— phone sex, I mean. And since you obviously didn't like it, I'm not going to—"

"No," he interrupted her. "You know, if I'm Guilt Man, then you're Miss Low Self-Esteem. How could you even think I didn't like it? I loved it. Every excruciating minute. You are unbelievably hot, and you completely killed me. If you got one of those 900 numbers, you could make a fortune, but you damn well better not."

"You loved it, but you don't want to do it again?"

Bobby was silent on the other end of the line, and Colleen waited, heart in her throat.

"It's not enough," he finally said.

"Come over," she said, hearing her desire coat her voice. "Please. It's not too late to—"

"I can't."

"I don't understand why not. If you want me, and I want

you, *why* can't we get together? Why does this have to be so hard?"

"If we were a pair of rabbits, sure," Bobby said. "It would be simple. But we're not, and it's not. This attraction between us…it's all mixed up with what I want, which is *not* to get involved with someone who lives three thousand miles away from me, and with what I want for you, which is for you to live happily ever after with a good man who loves you, and children if you want them, and a career that makes you jump out of bed with pleasure and excitement every single morning for the rest of your life. And if that's not complicated enough, there's also what I know *Wes* wants for you—which is more than just a man who loves you, but someone who will take care of you, too. Someone who's not in the Teams, someone who's not even in the Navy. Someone who can buy you presents and vacations and houses and cars without having to get a bank loan. Someone who'll *be* there, every morning, without fail."

"He also wants to make sure that I don't have any fun at all, the hypocrite. Making noise about how I have to wait until I'm married, when he's out there getting it on with any and every woman he can."

"He loves you," Bobby told her. "He's scared you'll end up pregnant and hating your life. Abandoned by some loser. Or worse—tied to some loser forever."

"As if I'd sleep with a loser."

Bobby laughed softly. "Yeah, well, I think I might fall into Wes's definition of a loser, so yes, you would."

"Ho," Colleen said. "Who's Mr. Low Self-Esteem now?"

"*Wes's* definition," he said again. "Not necessarily mine."

"Or mine," she countered. "It's definitely not mine."

"So, okay," he told her. "We toss the fact that I want to make love to you for about seventy-two hours straight into that mess of what you want and I want and Wes wants. Boom. What happens upon impact? You get lucky, I get lucky, which would probably be transcendental—no, not probably, *definitely*. So that's great…or is it? Because all I can see, besides the immediate gratification of us both getting off, is a boatload of pain.

"I risk getting too…I don't know, *attached* to someone who lives three thousand miles away from me.

"I risk my relationship with your brother….

"You risk your relationship with your brother….

"You risk losing any opportunities that might be out there of actually meeting someone special, because you're messing around with me."

Maybe you're the special one. Colleen didn't dare say it aloud. He obviously didn't think so.

"I've got a flight into Norfolk that leaves Logan just after 1500 hours," he said quietly. "I'm going into the Relief Aid office in the morning. I've got a meeting set up at 1100 hours to talk about the security we're going to be providing in Tulgeria—and what we expect from your group in terms of following the rules we set up. I figured you'd want to sit in on that."

"Yeah," Colleen said. "I'll be there." And how weird was *that* going to be—meeting his eyes for the first time since they'd…since she'd… She took a deep breath. "I'll borrow a truck, after, and give you a lift to the airport."

"That's okay. I'll take the T." He spoke quickly.

"What, are you afraid I'm going to jump you, right there in the truck, in the airport's short-term parking lot?"

"No," he said. He laughed, but it was grim instead of amused. "I'm afraid I'm going to jump you. From here on in, Colleen, we don't go anywhere alone."

"But—"

"I'm sorry. I don't trust myself around you."

"Bobby—"

"Good night, Colleen."

"Wait," she said, but he'd already hung up.

One step forward, two steps back.

Okay. Okay. She just had to figure out a way to get him alone. Before 1500—3:00 p.m.—tomorrow.

How hard could *that* be?

THE RELIEF AID OFFICE was hushed and quiet when Bobby came in at 1055. The radio—which usually played classic rock at full volume—was off. No one was packing boxes of canned goods and other donations. People stood, talking quietly in small groups.

Rene pushed past him, making a beeline for the ladies' room, head down. She was crying.

What the…?

Bobby looked around, more carefully this time, but Colleen was nowhere in sight.

He saw Susan Fitzgerald, the group's leading volunteer, sitting at the row of desks on the other side of the room. She was on the phone, and as he watched, she hung up. She just sat there, then, rubbing her forehead and her eyes behind her glasses.

"What's going on?" he asked.

"Another quake hit Tulgeria this morning," she told him. "About 2 a.m., our time. I'm not sure how it happened, whether it was from a fire caused by downed power lines or from the actual shock waves, but one of the local terrorist cells had an ammunitions stockpile, and it went up in a big way. The Tulgerian government thought they were under attack and launched a counteroffensive."

Oh, God. Bobby could tell from the look on Susan's face that the worst news was coming. He braced himself.

"St. Christof's—our orphanage—sustained a direct hit from some sort of missile," Susan told him. "We lost at least half of the kids."

Oh, Christ. "Does Colleen know?"

Susan nodded. "She was here when the news came in. But she went home. Her little girl—the one she'd been writing to—was on the list of children who were killed."

Analena. Oh, God. Bobby closed his eyes.

"She was very upset," Susan told him. "Understandably."

He straightened up and started for the door. He knew damn well that Colleen's apartment was the last place he should go, but it was the one place in the world where he absolutely needed to be right now. To hell with his rules.

To hell with everything.

"Bobby," Susan called after him. "She told me you're leaving for Virginia in a few hours. Try to talk her into coming back here when you go. She really shouldn't be alone."

COLLEEN LET THE DOORBELL ring the same way she'd let the phone ring.

She didn't want to talk to anyone, didn't want to see anyone, didn't want to have to try to explain how a little girl she'd never met could have owned such an enormous piece of her heart.

She didn't want to do anything but lie here, on her bed, in her room, with the shades pulled down, and cry over the injustice of a world in which orphanages were bombed during a war that really didn't exist.

Yet, at the same time, the last thing she wanted was to be alone. Back when she was a kid, when her world fell apart and she needed a shoulder to cry on, she'd gone to her brother Ethan. He was closest in age to her—the one Skelly kid who didn't have that infamous knee-jerk temper and that smart-mouthed impatience.

She'd loved him, and he'd died, too. What was it with her…that made the people she loved disappear? She stared up at her ceiling, at the cracks and chips that she'd memorized through too many sleepless nights. She should have learned by now just to stop loving, to stop taking chances. Yeah, like that would ever happen. Maybe she was stupid, but that was one lesson she refused to learn.

Every single day, she fell in love over and over. When she walked past a little girl with a new puppy. When a baby stared at her unblinkingly on the trolley and then smiled, a big, drooly, gummy grin. When she saw an elderly couple out for a stroll, still holding hands. She lost her heart to them all.

Still, just once, she wanted more than to be a witness to other people's happy endings. She wanted to be part of one.

She wanted Bobby.

She didn't care when the doorbell stopped ringing and the phone started up again, knowing it was probably Bobby, and crying even harder because she'd pushed too hard and now he was leaving, too.

Because he didn't want her love, not in any format. Not even quick and easy and free—the way she'd offered it.

She just lay on her bed, head aching and face numb from the hours she'd already cried, but unable to stop.

But then she wasn't alone anymore. She didn't know how he got in. Her door was locked. She hadn't even heard his footsteps on the floor.

It was as if Bobby had just suddenly materialized, next to her bed.

He didn't hesitate, he just lay down right next to her and drew her into his arms. He didn't say a word, he just held her close, cradling her with his entire body.

His shirt was soft against her cheek. He smelled like clean clothes and coffee. The trace of cigarette smoke that usually lingered on his shirt and even in his hair had finally been washed away.

But it was late. If he was going to get to Logan in time to catch his flight to Norfolk… "You have to leave soon," she told him, trying to be strong, wiping her face and lifting her head to look into his eyes.

For a man who could make one mean war face when he wanted to, he had the softest, most gentle eyes. "No." He shook his head slightly. "I don't."

Colleen couldn't help it. Fresh tears welled, and she shook from trying so hard not to cry.

"It's okay," he told her. "Go on and cry. I've got you, sweet. I'm here. I'll be here for as long as you need me."

She clung to him.

And he just held her and held her and held her.

As she fell asleep, still held tightly in his arms, his fingers running gently through her hair, her last thought was to wonder hazily what he was going to say when he found out that she could well need him forever.

BOBBY WOKE UP SLOWLY. He knew even before he opened his eyes that, like Dorothy, he wasn't in Kansas anymore. Wherever he was, it wasn't his apartment on the base, and he most certainly wasn't alone.

It came to him in a flash. Massachusetts. Colleen Skelly.

She was lying against him, on top of him, beneath him, her leg thrown across his, his thigh pressed tight between her legs. Her head was on his shoulder, his arms beneath her and around her, the softness of her breasts against his chest, her hand tucked up alongside his neck.

They were both still fully dressed, but Bobby knew with an acceptance of his fate—it was actually quite calming and peaceful, all things considered—that after she awoke, they wouldn't keep their clothes on for long.

He'd had his chance for a clean escape, and he'd blown it. He was here, and there was no way in hell he was going to walk away now.

Wes was just going to have to kill him.

But, damn, it was going to be worth it. Bobby was going to die with a smile on his face.

His hand had slipped up underneath the edge of Colleen's T-shirt, and he took advantage of that, gliding his fingers across the smooth skin of her back, up all the way to the back strap of her bra, down to the waistband of her shorts. Up and back in an unending circle.

Man, he could lie here, just touching her lightly like this, for the rest of his life.

But Colleen stirred, and he waited, still caressing the softness of her skin, feeling her wake up and become as aware of him as he was of her.

She didn't move, didn't pull away from him.

And he didn't stop touching her.

"How long did I sleep?" she finally asked, her voice even huskier than usual.

"I don't know," he admitted. "I fell asleep, too." He glanced at the windows. The light was starting to weaken. "It's probably around 1900—seven o'clock."

"Thank you," she said. "For coming here."

"You want to talk about it?" Bobby asked. "About Analena?"

"No," she said. "Because when I say it out loud, it all sounds so stupid. I mean, what was I thinking? That I was going to bring her here, to live with me? I mean, come on—who was I kidding? I don't have room—look at this place. And I don't have money—I can barely pay my own bills. I couldn't live here without Ashley paying for half of everything. I had to sell my car to stay in law school. And that's *with* the school loans. And how am I supposed to take care of a kid while I'm going to school? I don't have time for an instant family—not now while I'm in law school. I don't have time for a husband, let alone a child. And yet…"

She shook her head. "When I saw her pictures and read her letters… Oh, Bobby, she was so alive. I didn't even get a chance to know her, but I wanted to—God, I wanted to!"

"If you had met her, you would have fallen completely in love with her." He smiled. "I know you pretty well. And she would've loved you, too. And you would have somehow made it work," he told her. "It wouldn't have been easy, but there are some things you just have to do, you know? So you do it, and it all works out. I'm sorry you won't get that chance with Analena."

She lifted her head to look at him. "You don't think I'm being ridiculous?"

"I would never think of you as ridiculous," he told her quietly. "Generous, yes. Warm. Giving. Loving, caring…"

Something shifted. There was a sudden something in her eyes that clued him in to the fact that, like him, she was suddenly acutely, intensely aware of every inch of him that was in contact with every inch of her.

"Sexy as hell," he whispered. "But never ridiculous."

Her gaze dropped to his mouth. He saw it coming. She was going to kiss him, and his fate would be sealed.

He met her halfway, wanting to take a proactive part in this, wanting to do more than simply be unable to resist the temptation.

Her lips were soft, her mouth almost unbearably sweet. It was a slow, languorous kiss—as if they both knew that from here on in, there was no turning back, no need to rush.

He kissed her again, longer this time, deeper—just in

case she had any last, lingering doubts about what was
going to happen next.

But before he could kiss her again, she pulled away.
There were tears in her eyes.

"I didn't want it to happen this way," she said.

He tried to understand what she was telling him, tried
to rein himself in. "Colleen, if you don't want me to
stay—"

"No," she said. "I do want you to stay. I want you. Too
much. See, I lay awake last night, figuring out ways to
get you back here. I was going to make something up,
try to trick you into coming here after the meeting and
then…"

Comprehension dawned. She'd gotten what she'd
wanted. He was here. But at what price? An earthquake
and a war. A body count that included people she'd
loved.

"No," he told her, not wanting her to believe that. "I
would've shown up here sooner or later. Even if I'd gotten
on that plane—and I'm not sure I would have been able
to—I would've called you from Little Creek tonight. I
wouldn't have been able to resist."

She wiped her eyes with the heel of her hands.
"Really?"

"The things you do to me with just a telephone… Man,
oh, man."

Tears still clung to her eyelashes, and her nose was
slightly pink. But she was laughing.

As he held her gaze, he remembered the things she said
to him last night and let her see that memory reflected in
his eyes. She blushed slightly.

"I've really never done that before," she told him. "I
mean, the phone part." She blushed again as she looked
away, embarrassed by what she'd just again admitted.

He needed her to know what merely thinking about

her—about that—did to him. He pulled her chin back so that she had to look into his eyes, as he answered her with just as much soul-baring honesty. "Maybe someday you'll let me watch."

Someday. The word hung between them. It implied that there was going to be more than just tonight.

"You don't do long-distance relationships," she reminded him.

"No," he corrected her. "I don't *want* to do it that way. I have in the past, and I've hated it. It's so hard to—"

"I don't want to be something that's hard," she told him. "I don't want to be an obligation that turns into something you dread dealing with."

He steeled himself, preparing to pull away from her, out of her arms. "Then maybe I should go, before—"

"Maybe we should just make love and not worry about tomorrow," she countered.

She kissed him, and it was dizzying. He kissed her back hungrily, possessively—all sense of laziness gone. He wanted her, now. He needed her.

Now.

Her hands were in his hair, freeing it completely from the ponytail that had already halfway fallen out. She kissed him even harder, angling her head to give him better access to her mouth—or maybe to give herself better access to *his* mouth.

Could she really do this?

Make love to him tonight and only tonight?

Her legs tightened around his thigh, and he stopped thinking. He kissed her again and again, loving the taste of her, the feel of her in his arms. He reached between them, sliding his hand up under her shirt to fill his hand with her breast.

She pulled back from him to tug at his T-shirt. She wanted it off, and it was easier simply to give up—temporarily—trying to kiss and touch as much of her as he possibly could, and take his shirt off himself. His shoulder was still stiff, and the only way he could get a T-shirt on or off was awkwardly. Painfully. One arm at a time.

Before he even got it off, she'd started on his shorts, her fingers cool against his stomach as she unfastened the button and then the zipper.

She had his shorts halfway down his legs by the time he tossed his shirt onto the floor.

He helped her, kicking his legs free, and then there he was. On her bed in only his briefs, while she was still fully clothed.

He reached for her, intending to rid her of her T-shirt and shorts as efficiently as she'd taken care of his, but she distracted him by kissing him. And then he distracted himself by touching her breasts beneath her shirt, by unfastening her bra and kissing her right through the cotton, by burying his face in the softness of her body.

It wasn't until he tried to push her shirt up over her breasts so that he could see her as well as touch and kiss, that he felt her tense.

And he remembered.

She was self-conscious about her body.

Probably because she wasn't stick thin like the alleged Hollywood ideal.

The hell with that—she was *his* ideal. She was curvaceous. Stacked. Voluptuous. She was perfection.

Man, if he were her, he would walk around in one of those little nonexistent tank tops that were so popular. She should wear one without a bra, and just watch all the men faint as she passed by.

Someday he'd get her one of those. She could wear it here, in the privacy of her room, if she didn't want to wear it in public. Man, he hadn't thought he could get any harder, any hotter, but just the thought of her wearing something like that, just because he liked it—just for him—heated him up another notch.

She would do it, too. After he made her realize that he truly worshiped her body, that he found her unbelievably beautiful and sexy, she would be just as adventurous about that as she was with everything else.

Phone sex. Sweet heaven.

Phone sex was all about words. About saying what he wanted, about saying how he felt.

He hadn't been very good at it—not like Colleen. Unlike her, words weren't his strong suit. But he had to do it again now. He had to use words to reassure her, to let her know just how beautiful he thought she was.

He could do it with body language, with his eyes, with his mouth and his hands. He could show her, by the way he made love to her, but even then, he knew she wouldn't completely believe him.

No, if he wanted to dissolve that edge of tension that tightened her shoulders, he had to do it with words.

Or did he? Maybe he could do a combination of both show *and* tell.

"I think you're spectacular," he told her. "You're incredible and gorgeous and..."

And he was doing this wrong. She wasn't buying any of it.

He touched her, reaching up beneath her shirt to caress her. He had the show part down. He wanted to taste her, and he realized with a flash that instead of trying to make up compliments filled with meaningless adjectives, he should just say what he wanted, say how he felt. He should just open his mouth and speak his very thoughts.

"I want to taste you right here," he told her as he touched her. "I want to feel you in my mouth."

He tugged her shirt up just a little, watching her face,

ready to take it even more slowly if she wanted him to. But she didn't tense up, so he drew it up a little more, exposing the underside of her breast, so pale and soft and perfect. And then he forgot to watch her eyes because there was her nipple, peeking out. He'd been holding his breath, he realized, and he let it out in a rush. "Oh, yeah."

She was already taut with desire, and he lowered his head to do just what he'd described. She made a sound that he liked, a sound that had nothing to do with being self-conscious and everything to do with pleasure.

He drew her shirt up then, up and over her head, and she sat up to help him.

And there she was.

As he pulled back to look at her, he opened his mouth and let his thoughts escape.

Unfortunately, his expression of sincere admiration was one of Wes's favorite, more colorful turns of phrase.

Fortunately, Colleen laughed. She looked at him, looked at the expression he knew was on his face, the pure pleasure he let shine from his eyes.

"You're so beautiful," he breathed. "I've died and gone to heaven."

"Gee," she said, "and I don't even have my pants off."

He grabbed her by the waist of her shorts, flipping her back onto the bed and, as she whooped in surprised laughter, he corrected that.

In five seconds flat she was naked and he was kissing her, touching, loving the feel of all that smooth, perfect skin against him. And when he pulled back to really look at her, there wasn't a bit of tension in the air.

But this talking thing was working so well, why stop?

"Do you know what you do to me?" he asked her as he touched, kissed, explored. He didn't give her time to answer. He just took one of her own exploring hands, and pressed it against him.

"You are *so* sexy, that happens to me every time I see you," he whispered, looking into her eyes to let her see the intense pleasure that shot through him at her touch. "Every time I *think* of you."

She was breathing hard, and he pulled her to him and kissed her again, reaching between them to help her rid him of his briefs.

Her fingers closed around him, and he would have told her how much he liked that, but words failed him, and all he could do was groan.

She seemed to understand and answered him in kind as he slipped his hand between her legs. She was so slick and soft and hot, he could feel himself teetering on the edge of his self-control. He needed a condom. *Now.*

But when he spoke, all he could manage to say was her name.

Again she understood. "Top drawer. Bedside table."

He lunged for it, found it. An unopened, cellophane-wrapped box. He both loved and hated the fact that the box was unopened. Growling with frustration, he tried to rip the damned thing in half.

Colleen took it from his hands and opened it quickly, laughing at the way he fumbled the little wrapped package, getting in the way, touching and kissing him as he tried to cover himself.

Slow down. She'd told him herself that she hadn't had much experience. He didn't want to be too rough, didn't want to hurt her or scare her or...

She pulled him back with her onto the bed in a move that Xena the Warrior Princess would have been in awe of. And she told him, in extremely precise language, exactly what she wanted.

How could he refuse?

Especially when she kissed him, when she lifted her hips and reached between them to find him and guide him and...

He entered her far less gently than he'd intended, but her moan was one of pure pleasure.

"Yes," she told him as he pushed himself even more deeply inside her. "Oh, Bobby, yes..."

He kissed her, touched her, stroked her, murmuring things that he couldn't believe were coming out of his mouth, things that he loved about her body, things he wanted to do to her, things she made him feel—things that made her laugh and gasp and murmur equally sexy things back to him, until he was damn near blind with passion and desire.

Gentle had long-gone right out the window. He was filling her, hard and fast, and she was right there with him, urging him on.

She told him when she began to climax—as if he wouldn't know from the sound of her voice. As if he couldn't feel her shatter around him. Still, he loved that she told him, and her breathless words helped push him over the edge.

And just like that he was flying, his release rocketing through him with so much power and force he had to shout her name, and even that wasn't enough.

He wanted to tell her how she made him feel, about the sheer, crystal perfection of the moment that seemed to surround him, shimmering and wonderful, filling his chest until it was hard to breathe, until he wanted to cry from its pure beauty.

But there were no words that could describe how he felt. To do it justice, he would have to invent a completely new vocabulary.

Bobby realized then that he was lying on top of her, crushing her, completely spent. His shoulder felt as if he'd just been shot all over again—funny, he hadn't felt even a twinge until now and—

Colleen was crying.

"Oh, my God," he said, shifting off her, pulling her so that she was in his arms. "Did I hurt you? Did I…?"

"No!" she said, kissing him. "No, it's just…that was so perfect, it doesn't seem fair. Why should I be so lucky to be able to share something so special with you?"

"I'm sorry," he said, kissing her hair, holding her close. He knew she was thinking about Analena.

"Will you stay with me?" she asked. "All night?"

"I'm right here," he said. "I'm not going anywhere."

"Thank you." Colleen closed her eyes, her head against his chest, her skin still damp from their lovemaking.

Bobby lay naked in Colleen's bed, holding her close, breathing in her sweet scent, desperately trying to fend off the harsh reality that was crashing down around him.

He'd just made love with Colleen Skelly.

No, he'd just had *sex* with Colleen Skelly. He'd just got it on with Wes's little sister. He'd put it to her. Nailed her. Scored. That was the way Wes was going to see it—not sweetly disguised with pretty words like *making love*.

Last night he'd had phone sex with Colleen. Tonight he'd done the real deal.

Just one night, she wanted. Just one time. Just to find out what it would be like.

Would she stick to that? Give him breakfast in the morning, shake his hand and thank him for the fun experience and send him on his way?

Bobby wasn't sure whether to hope so or hope not. He already wanted too much. He wanted— No, he couldn't even think it.

Maybe, if they only made love this once, Wes would understand that it was an attraction so powerful—more powerful than both of them—that couldn't be denied.

Bobby tried that on for size, tried to picture Wes's calm acceptance and rational understanding and—

Nah.

Wes was going to kill him. No doubt about that.

Bobby smiled, though, as he ran his hand down Colleen's incredible body. She snuggled against him, turning so that they were spooned together, her back to his front. He tucked his good arm around her, filling his hand with the weight of her breasts.

Oh, man.

Yeah, Wes was going to kill him.

But before he did, Bobby would ask them to put four words on his tombstone: It Was Worth It.

CHAPTER TWELVE

COLLEEN WOKE UP ALONE IN HER BED.

It was barely even dawn, and her first thought was that she'd dreamed it. All of it. Everything that had happened yesterday and last night—it was all one giant combination nightmare and raging hot fantasy.

But Bobby's T-shirt and briefs were still on her floor. Unless he'd left her apartment wearing only his shorts, he hadn't gone far.

She could smell coffee brewing, and she climbed out of bed.

Muscles she didn't even know existed protested— further proof that last night hadn't been a dream. It was a good ache, combined with a warmth that seemed to spread through her as she remembered Bobby's whispered words as he'd... As they'd...

Who knew that such a taciturn man would be able to express himself so eloquently?

But even more eloquent than his words was the expressiveness of his face, the depth of emotion and expressions of sheer pleasure he didn't try to hide from her as they made love.

They'd made love.

The thought didn't fill her with laughter and song as she'd imagined it would.

Yes, it had been great. Making love to Bobby had been more wonderful than she'd ever dared to dream. More special and soul shattering than she'd imagined. But it didn't begin to make up for the deaths of all those children. Nothing could do that.

She found her robe and pulled it on, sitting back on the edge of the bed, gathering her strength.

She didn't want to leave her room. She wanted to hide here for the rest of the week.

But life went on, and there were things that needed to be done for the children who'd survived. And in order to get them done, there were truths that had to be faced.

There were going to be tears shed when she went into the Relief Aid office. She was also going to have to break the news to the church youth group that had helped raise money for the trip. Those kids had exchanged letters and pictures with the children in Tulgeria. Telling them of the tragedy wasn't going to be easy.

And then there was Bobby.

He had to be faced, too. She'd lied to him. Telling him that she'd be content with only one night. Well, maybe it hadn't been a lie. At the time, she'd talked herself into believing it was possible.

But right now all she felt was foolish. Deceitful. Pathetic.

Desperate.

She wanted to make love to him again. And again. And again, and again.

Maybe he wanted her again, too. She'd read—extensively—that men liked sex. Morning, noon and night, according to some sources.

Well, it was morning, and she would never discover whether he was inclined to run away or to stay a little longer unless she stood up and walked out of this room.

She squared her shoulders and did just that. And after a quick pit stop in the bathroom—where she also made sure her hair wasn't making her look too much like the bride of Frankenstein—she went into the kitchen.

Bobby greeted her with a smile and an already-poured cup of coffee. "I hope I didn't wake you," he said, turning back to the stove where both oatmeal and eggs were cooking, "but I didn't have dinner last night, and I woke up pretty hungry."

As if on cue, her stomach growled.

He shot her another smile. "You, too, I guess."

God, he was gorgeous. He'd showered, and he was wearing only his cargo shorts, low on his hips. With his chest bare and his hair down loose around his shoulders, he looked as if he should be adorning the front of one of those romance novels where the kidnapped white girl finds powerful and lasting love with the exotically handsome Indian warrior.

The timer buzzed, and as Colleen watched, the Indian warrior look-alike in her kitchen used her pink-flowered oven mitts to pull something that looked remarkably like a coffee cake out of her oven.

It was. He'd baked a *coffee cake*. From scratch. He smiled at her again as he put it carefully on a cooling rack.

He'd set her kitchen table, too, poured her a glass of cranberry juice. She sat down as he served them both a generous helping of eggs and bowls of oatmeal.

It was delicious. All of it. She wasn't normally a fan of oatmeal, but somehow he'd made it light and flavorful instead of thick and gluey.

"What's on your schedule for today?" he asked, as if he normally sat across from her at breakfast and inquired about her day after a night of hot sex.

She had to think about it. "I have to drop a tuition check at the law school before noon. There's probably going to be some kind of memorial service for—"

She broke off abruptly.

"You okay?" he asked softly, concern in his eyes.

Colleen forced a smile. "Yeah," she told him. "Mostly. It's just…it'll take time." She took a deep breath. They'd been discussing her day. "I'll need to spend some time this afternoon spreading the word about the memorial service. And I should probably go into the Relief Aid office later, too. There's still a lot to do before we leave."

He stopped eating, his fork halfway to his mouth. "You're still planning on going…?" He didn't let her speak. He laughed and answered for her. "Of course you're still planning on going. What was I thinking?" He put down his fork. "Colleen, what do you want me to do? Do you want me to get down on my knees and beg you not to go?"

Before she could answer, he rubbed his forehead and swore. "I take that back," he continued. "I'm sorry. I shouldn't have said that. I'm a little…off balance today."

"Because…we made love last night?" she asked softly.

He looked at her, taking in her makeup-free face, her hair, the thin cotton of her robe that met with a deep vee between her breasts. "Yes," he admitted. "I'm a little nervous about what happens next."

She chose her words carefully. "What do you want to have happen next?"

Bobby shook his head. "I don't think what I want should particularly factor in. I don't even know what I want." He picked up his fork again. "So I'm just going to save my guilt for later and enjoy having breakfast with you—enjoy how beautiful you look in the morning."

He did just that, eating his eggs and oatmeal as he gazed at her. What he really liked was looking at her breasts—she knew that after last night. But he never just ogled her. Somehow, he managed to look at her inoffensively, respectfully, looking into her eyes as well, looking at her as a whole person, instead of just a female body.

She looked back at him, trying to see him the same way. He was darkly handsome, with bold features that told of his Native American heritage. He was handsome and smart and reliable. He was honest and sincere and funny and kind. And impossibly buff with a body that was at least a two thousand on a scale from one to ten.

"Why aren't you married?" she asked him. He was also ten years older than she was. It seemed impossible that some smart woman hadn't grabbed him up. Yet, here he was. Eating breakfast in her kitchen after spending the night in her bed. "Both you and Wes," she added, to make the question seem a little less as if she were wondering how to sign up for the role of *wife*.

He paused only slightly as he ate his oatmeal. "Marriage has never been part of my short-term plan. Wes's either. The responsibility of a wife and a family... It's pretty intense. We've both seen some of the guys really struggle with it." He smiled. "It's also hard to get married when the women you fall in love with don't fall in love with you." He laughed softly. "Harder still when they're married to someone else."

Colleen's heart was in her throat. "You're in love with someone who's married...?"

He glanced up at her, a flash of dark eyes. "No, I was thinking of...a friend." He made his voice lighter, teasing. "Hey, what kind of man do you think I am, anyway? If I could be in love with someone else while I messed around with you...?"

Relief made her giddy. "Well, I'm in love with Mel Gibson and *I* messed around with you last night."

He laughed, pushing his plate away from the edge of the table. He'd eaten both the pile of eggs and the mound of oatmeal and now he glanced over at the coffee cake, taking a sip of his cooling coffee.

"Is that really what we did last night?" Colleen asked

him. "Messed around?" She leaned forward and felt her robe gap farther open. Bobby's gaze flickered down, and the sudden heat in his eyes made her breathless. *He* may claim not to know what was going to happen next, but *she* did. And it didn't have anything to do with the coffee cake.

"Yeah," he said. "I guess so. Isn't it?"

"I don't know," she said honestly. "I don't have a lot of experience to compare it to. Can I ask you something?"

Bobby laughed again. "Why do I get the feeling I should brace myself?"

"Maybe you better," she said. "It's kind of a weird question, but it's something I need to know."

"Oh, man. Okay." He put down his mug, held on to the table with both hands.

"Okay." Colleen cleared her throat. "What I want to know is, are you really good in bed?"

Bobby laughed in genuine surprise. "Wow, I guess not," he said. "I mean, if you have to ask…"

"No," she said. "Don't be dumb. Last night was incredible. We both know that. But what I want to know is if you're some kind of amazing superlover, capable of heating up even the most frigid of women—"

"Whoa," he said. "Colleen, you are so completely the *farthest* thing from frigid that—"

"Yes," she said, "that's what I thought, too, but…"

"But someone told you that you were," he guessed correctly. "Damn!"

"My college boyfriend," she admitted. "Dan. The jerk."

"I feel this overpowering urge to kill him. What did he tell you?"

"It wasn't so much what he said, but more what he implied. He was my first lover," she admitted. "I was crazy about him, but when we—I never managed to— You know. And he quit after the third try. He told me he thought we should just be friends."

"Oh, God." Bobby winced.

"I thought it had to be my fault—that there was something wrong with me." Colleen had never told all of this to anyone. Not even Ashley, who had heard a decidedly watered-down version of the story. "I spent a few years doing the nun thing. And then, about a year and a half ago…" She couldn't believe she was actually telling him this, her very deepest secrets. But she wanted to. She needed him to understand. "I bought this book, a kind of a self-help guide for sexually challenged women—I guess that's a PC term for frigid these days. And I discovered fairly early on that the problem probably wasn't entirely mine."

"So, you haven't—" Bobby was looking at her as if he were trying to see inside her head. "I mean, between last night and the jerk, you haven't…?"

"There's been no one else. Just me and the book," she told him, wishing she could read his mind, too. Was this freaking him out, or did he like the fact that he'd essentially been her first real lover? "Trying desperately to learn how to be normal."

"Yeah, I don't know," Bobby shook his head. "It's probably hopeless. Because I *am* somewhat legendary. And it's a real shame, but if you want to have any kind of satisfying sex life, you're just going to have to spend the rest of your life making love to me."

Colleen stared at him.

"That was a joke," he said quickly. "I'm kidding. Colleen, last night I didn't do anything special. I mean, it was *all* special, but you were right there with me, the entire time. Except…"

"What?" She searched his face.

"Well, without having been there, it's hard to know for

sure, but...my guess is that you were—I don't know—
tense at the thought of getting naked, and the jerk was
a little quick on the trigger. He probably didn't give you
time to relax before it was all over. And in my book, that's
more his fault than yours."

"He was always telling me he thought I should lose
weight," Colleen remembered. "Not in so many words.
More like, 'Gee, if you lost ten pounds you'd look great in
that shirt.' And, 'Why don't you find out what kind of diet
Cindy Crawford is on and try that? Maybe that'll work.'
That kind of thing. And you're right, I hated taking off
my clothes in front of him."

Bobby just shook his head as he looked at her. God,
when he looked at her like that, he made her feel like the
most beautiful, most desirable woman in the world.

"I liked taking off my clothes for you," she told him
softly, and the heat in his eyes got even more intense.

"I'm glad," he whispered. "Because I liked it, too."

Time hung as she gazed into his eyes, as she lost herself
in the warmth of his soul. He still wanted her. He wanted
more, too.

But then he looked away, as if he were afraid of where
that look was taking them.

Guilt, he'd said before, and she knew if she didn't act
quickly, he was going to walk out of her apartment and
never come back. At least not without a chaperone.

"Don't move," she told him. She pushed her chair back
from the table and stood up. "Stay right there."

She was down the hall and in the bedroom in a flash,
grabbing what she needed.

Bobby turned to look at her as she came back into the
kitchen, still sitting where she'd commanded him to stay.
He quickly looked away from her, and she realized that
her robe had slipped open even farther—the deep vee now
extending all the way down to her waist.

She didn't adjust it, didn't pull it closed. She just moved closer, so that she was standing beside him. Close enough that she was invading his personal space.

But she didn't touch him. Didn't even speak. She just waited for him to turn his head and look up at her.

He did just that. Looked at her. Looked away again. Swallowed hard. "Colleen, I think—"

Now was definitely not the time for thinking. She sat on his lap, straddling him, forcing him to look at her. Her robe was completely open now, the belt having slipped its loose knot.

He was breathing hard—and trying not to. "I thought we decided this was going to be a one-night thing. Just to get it out of our systems."

"Am I out of your system?" she asked, knowing full well that she wasn't.

"No, and if I'm not careful, you're going to get under my skin," he admitted. "Colleen, please don't do this to me. I spent the night convincing myself that as long as we didn't make love again, I'd be okay. And I know it's a long shot, but even your brother might understand that something like this could happen between us—once."

His words would have swayed her—if he hadn't touched her, his hands on her thighs, just lightly, as if he couldn't stop himself, couldn't resist.

She shrugged her robe off her shoulders, and it fell to the floor behind her, and then there she was. Naked, in the middle of her kitchen, with daylight streaming in the windows, warming her skin, bathing her in golden sunshine.

Bobby's breath caught in his throat, and as he looked at her, she felt beautiful. She saw herself as if through his eyes, and she *was* beautiful.

It felt unbelievably good.

She shifted forward, pressing herself against him,

feeling him, large and hard beneath his shorts. No doubt about it. He still desired her. He made a sound, low in his throat. And then he kissed her.

His passion took her breath away. It was as if he'd suddenly exploded, as if he needed to kiss her to stay alive, to touch as much of her as he possibly could or else he'd die. His hands were everywhere, his mouth everywhere else.

It was intoxicating, addicting—to be wanted so desperately. It was almost as good as being loved.

She reached between them and unfastened his shorts as she kissed him, taking him into her hand, pressing him against her, letting him know that she wanted him desperately, too.

She still held the condom she'd taken from her bedroom, although the little paper wrapper was tightly scrunched in her hand. She tore it open, and Bobby took it from her, covering himself and then—oh, yes!—he was inside of her.

He tried, but he couldn't keep from groaning aloud, from holding her close and burying his face in her breasts. She moved slowly, stroking him with her body, filling herself completely with him.

Making love to Bobby Taylor was just as amazing in the daylight as it had been last night.

She pulled back slightly to watch him as she moved on top of him, and he held her gaze, his eyes sparking with heat beneath heavy eyelids.

She couldn't get enough of him. She pressed against him, wanting more, wanting forever, wanting him never to leave, wanting this moment never to end.

Wanting him to fall in love with her as completely as she'd fallen in love with him.

Oh, no, what had she done? She didn't love him. She couldn't love him.

She must've made some kind of noise of frustration and despair, because he stood up. He just lifted himself from the chair, with her in his arms, with his body still buried deeply inside her. Even deeper now that he was standing.

Colleen gasped, and then had to laugh as he carried her—effortlessly, as if she weighed nothing—across the room, her arms around his neck, her legs now locked around his waist. He didn't stop until he'd pressed her up against the wall by the refrigerator. The muscles in his chest and arms stood out, making him seem twice as big. Making her seem almost small.

Still… "Don't hurt your shoulder," she told him.

"What shoulder?" he asked hoarsely, and kissed her.

It was so impossibly macho, the way he held her, her back against the wall, the way he possessed her so completely with his mouth. His kiss was far from gentle, and that was so exciting, it was almost ridiculous. Still, there was no denying that she found it sexy beyond belief, to be pinned here, like this, as he kissed her so proprietarily.

She was expecting more roughness, expecting sex that was hard and fast and wild, but instead he began a long, lingering withdrawal, then an equally deliberate penetration that filled her maddeningly slowly.

It was sexier than she could have dreamed possible— this man holding her like this, taking his time to take her completely. On his terms.

He kissed her face, her throat, her neck as if he owned her.

And he did.

She felt her release begin before she was ready for it, before he'd even begun that slow, sensuous slide inside of her for the third heart-stopping time. She didn't want this to end, and she tried to stop herself, to hold him still for a moment, but she was powerless.

And she didn't mind.

Because she loved what he was doing. She loved his strength and his power, loved the fact that he was watching her with such intense desire in his eyes.

Loved that even though he was pretending to be in control, she knew that he wasn't. She owned him as absolutely as he owned her. More.

She held his gaze while she melted around him, while she flew apart from wave upon endless wave of pleasure.

He smiled, a fierce, proud, fairly obnoxious male grin. It would have made her roll her eyes a day or so ago, but today she found she loved it. She loved being pure female to his pure male. It didn't mean she was weaker. On the contrary. She was his perfect match, his opposite, his equal.

"I loved watching you do that last night," he murmured as he kissed her again. "And I love it even more this morning."

He was her first real lover in the physical sense of the word. And he was also the first man she'd ever known who liked who she was—not merely the promise of the person he could mold her into becoming.

"I want to do that to you again," he said. "Right now. Is that okay with you?"

Colleen just laughed.

He lifted her away from the wall and carried her down the hall to her bedroom, kicking the door shut behind them.

CHAPTER THIRTEEN

BOBBY WAS FLOATING.

He was in that place halfway between sleep and consciousness, his face buried in Colleen's sweet-smelling hair, his body still cradled between the softness of her legs.

So much for willpower. So much for resolving not to make love to her again. So much for hoping that Wes would forgive him for one little, single transgression.

Ah, but how he'd loved making love to her again. And no red-blooded, heterosexual man could've resisted the temptation of Colleen Skelly, naked, on his lap.

And really, deep in his heart, he knew it didn't matter. Wes was going to go ape over the fact that Bobby had slept with Colleen. Realistically, how much worse could it be to have slept with her twice? What difference could it possibly make?

To Wes? None. Probably. Hopefully.

But the difference it made to Bobby was enormous.

As enormous as the difference between heaven and hell.

Speaking of heaven, he was still inside of her, he realized, forcing himself to return to earth. Falling asleep immediately after sex was not a smart move when using condoms as the sole method of birth control. Because condoms could leak.

He should have pulled out of her twenty minutes ago.

And for that matter, he should also have been aware that he was still on top of her, crushing her.

But she hadn't protested. In fact, she still had her arms tightly wrapped around him.

He shifted his weight, pulling away from her and reaching between them to…

Uh-oh. "Uh, Colleen…?" Bobby sat up, suddenly fully, painfully, completely alert.

She stirred, stretched, sexy as hell, a distraction even now, when he should have been completely nondistractible.

"Don't leave yet, Bobby," she murmured, still half asleep. "Stay for a while, please?"

"Colleen, I think you better get up and take a shower." Condoms sometimes did something far worse than leak. "The condom broke."

She laughed as she opened her eyes. "Yeah, right." Her smile faded as she looked into his eyes. "Oh, no, you're not kidding are you?" She sat up.

Silently he shook his head.

Twenty minutes. She'd been lying on her back for at least twenty minutes after he'd unknowingly sent his sperm deep inside of her.

Was it possible she already was pregnant? How quickly could that happen?

Quickly. Instantly—if the timing was right. In a flash, a heartbeat.

In a burst of latex.

"Well," Colleen said, her eyes wide. "These past few days have certainly been full of first-time experiences for me, and this one's no exception. What do we do about this? Is a shower really going to help at this point?"

Count on Colleen not to have hysterics. Count on her to be upbeat and positive and proactive in trying to correct what could well be the biggest, most life-changing mistake either one of them had ever made.

"Probably not," he admitted. "Although…"

"I'll take one right now, if you want me to. I'm not sure where I am in my cycle. I've never really been regular." She was sitting there, unconcerned about her nakedness, looking to him for suggestions and options and his opinion, with complete and total trust.

That kind of trust was an incredible turn-on, and he felt his body respond. How could that be? The disbelief and cold fear that had surged through his veins at his discovery should have brought about an opposite physical response—more similar to the response one had from swimming in an icy lake.

And his mental reaction to a broken condom should have included not even *thinking* about having sex for the next three weeks without shaking with fear.

But there was Colleen, sitting next to him on her bed, all bare breasts and blue-green eyes and quiet, steadfast trust.

Right now she needed him to be honest about this. There was no quick fix. No miraculous solutions. "I think it's probably too late to do anything but pray."

She nodded. "That's what I figured."

"I'm sorry."

"It's not your fault," she said.

He shook his head. "It's not about fault—it's about responsibility, and I *am* responsible."

"Well, I am, too. You were coerced."

Bobby smiled, thinking of the way she'd sat on his lap, intending to seduce him, wondering if she had even the slightest clue that his last hope of resisting her had vanished the moment she'd appeared in the kitchen wearing only that robe.

"Yeah," he said, "as if that was really hard for you to do."

She smiled back at him, and his world shrank to a few square feet of her bed—to her eyes, her smile, her face and body.

"It was another one of those first-time endeavors for me," she told him. "I was proud of myself for not chickening out."

"You're a natural." His voice was husky. "But that's not what I meant. I meant it wasn't hard because when it comes to you, I'm a total pushover."

Just looking into her eyes like this made him want her again—badly enough that he wasn't able to keep it any kind of secret.

Colleen noticed and laughed softly. "Well now, *there's* an interesting, hedonistic approach to this problem." She crawled toward him, across the bed, her eyes gleaming and her smile filled with the very devil. "You know that old saying, when a door closes, somewhere a window opens? Well, how about, when a condom breaks, a window of opportunity opens?"

Bobby knew that wasn't necessarily true. He knew he should stop her, back away, stand up, do *any*thing but just sit there and wait for her to…

Too late.

COLLEEN SAT UP. "OH, MY GOD."

"Mmph," Bobby said, facedown on her bed.

It was 11:05. Fifty-five minutes to make it to her law school in the Fenway from Cambridge. Without a car, on the T. "Oh, my *God!*"

Bobby lifted his head. "What's the—"

She was already scrambling for the bathroom, climbing directly over him, inadvertently pushing his face back into the pillow.

"Mmmrph!"

"Sorry!"

Thanking the Lord—not for the first time today—that Ashley was still on the Vineyard, Colleen flew down the hallway stark naked and slapped on the bathroom light. One glance in the mirror and she knew she had to take a shower. Her hair was wild. And her face still held the satisfied look of a woman who'd kept her lover very busy all morning long.

She couldn't do anything about the face, but the hair she could fix with a fast shower.

She turned on the shower and climbed in before the water had a chance to heat up, singing a few operatic high notes in an attempt to counteract the cold.

"You all right?" Bobby had followed her in. Of course, she'd left the bathroom door wide open.

She peeked out from behind the shower curtain. He was as naked as she was, standing in front of the commode with that utterly masculine, wide-spread stance.

"I have to take a tuition check to my law school," she told him, quickly rinsing her hair, loving the fact that he was comfortable enough to be in the bathroom with her, feeling as if they'd crossed some kind of invisible, unspoken line. They were lovers now—not just two people who had given in to temptation and made love once. "The deadline's noon today, and like a total idiot, I pushed it off until the last minute." Literally.

"I'll come with you."

She turned off the water and pulled back the curtain, grabbing her towel and drying herself as she rushed back to her bedroom. "I can't wait for you," she called to him. "I'm literally forty-five seconds from walking out the door."

She stepped into clean underwear and pulled her blue dress—easy and loose fitting, perfect for days she was running dangerously late—over her head, even though she was still damp. Feet into sandals.

"What do you know," Bobby said. "A woman who can go wheels-up in less than three minutes." He laughed. "I feel as if I should drop to my knees right now and propose."

Colleen was reaching for the tuition check, which she'd hidden for safety in her complete collection of Shakespeare, and she didn't freeze, didn't faint, didn't gasp and spin to face him, didn't let herself react at all. He was teasing. He didn't have a clue that his lightly spoken words had sent a rush of excitement and longing through her that was so powerful she'd nearly fallen over.

Oh, she was so stupid. She actually wanted...the impossible. As if he really would marry her. He'd told her just hours ago that staying single was part of his career plan.

She made herself smile as she turned around, as she stuffed the check and a book to read into her knapsack, as she checked to make sure she had money for the T, then zipped her bag closed.

"It's going to take me at least a few hours," she said, brushing out her wet hair as she headed back into the kitchen to grab an apple from the fridge. He followed her, followed her to the door, still naked and completely comfortable about that.

Colleen could picture him trailing her all the way out to the street. Wouldn't *that* give little old Mrs. Gibaldi who lived downstairs an eyeful?

She turned to face him. "I'd love it if you were still here when I got back. Wearing just that." She kissed him, lowered her voice, gave him a smile designed to let him read her very thoughts. "And if you think getting dressed in three minutes is fast, just wait and see how long it takes me to get *un*dressed."

He kissed her, pulling her into his arms, his hand coming up to cup her breast as if he couldn't not touch her.

Colleen felt herself start to dissolve into a puddle of heat. What would happen if she didn't get that check to the office on time?

She might have to pay a penalty. Or she'd get bumped from the admissions list. There were so many students wait-listed, the admissions office could afford to play hardball. Reluctantly, she pulled back from Bobby.

"I'll hurry," she told him.

"Good," he said, still touching her, looking at her as if she were the one standing naked in front of him, lowering his head to kiss her breast before he let her go. "I'll be here."

He wasn't in love with her. He was in lust.

And that was exactly what she'd wanted, she reminded herself as she ran down the stairs.

Except, now that she had it, it wasn't enough.

THE PHONE WAS RINGING as Bobby stepped out of Colleen's shower.

He grabbed a towel and wrapped it around himself as he went dripping into the kitchen. "'Lo?"

He heard the sound of an open phone line, as if someone were there but silent. Then, "Bobby?"

It was Wes. No, not just "It was Wes," but "Oh, God, it was Wes."

"Hey!" Bobby said, trying desperately to sound normal—as opposed to sounding like a man who was standing nearly naked not two feet from the spot where mere hours earlier he'd pinned Wes's sister to the wall as they'd... As he'd...

"What are you doing at Colleen's place?" Wes sounded

funny. Or maybe Bobby just imagined it. Guilt had a way of doing that—making everyone sound suspicious.

"Um…" Bobby said. He was going to have to tell Wes about what was going on between him and Colleen, but the last thing he wanted was to break the news over the telephone. Still, he wasn't going to lie. Not to Wes. Never to Wes.

Fortunately—as usual—Wes didn't particularly want his question answered. "You are one hard man to get hold of," he continued. "I called your hotel room last night— late—and you were either AWOL or otherwise occupied, you lucky son of a bitch."

"Well," Bobby said, "yeah." He wasn't sure if Wes particularly cared what he was agreeing to, but the truth was he'd been AWOL, otherwise occupied *and* a lucky son of a bitch. "Where are you?"

"Little Creek. You need to get your butt down here, bro, pronto. We've got a meeting with Admiral Robinson at 1900 hours. There's a flight out of Logan that leaves in just under two hours. If you scramble, you can make it, easy. There'll be a ticket there, waiting for you."

Scrambling meant leaving before Colleen got back. Bobby looked at the kitchen clock and swore. Best-case scenario didn't get her back here for another ninety minutes. That's if she had no holdups—if the T ran like a dream.

"I'm not sure I can make it," he told Wes.

"Sure you can. Tell Colleen to drive you to the airport."

"Oh," Bobby said. Now, here was a secret he could divulge with no pain. "No. She can't—she sold her car."

"What?"

"She's been doing all this charity work—pro bono legal stuff, you know? Along with her usual volunteer work,"

Bobby told Wes. "She sold the Mustang because she was having trouble making ends meet."

Wes swore loudly. "I can't believe she sold that car. I would've lent her money. Why didn't she ask me for money?"

"I offered to do the same. She didn't want it from either one of us."

"That's stupid. Let me talk to the stupid girl, will you?"

"Actually," Bobby told Wes, "it's not stupid at all." And she wasn't a girl. She was a woman. A gorgeous, vibrant, independent, sexy woman. "She wants to do this her way. By herself. And then when she graduates, and passes the bar exam, she'll know—*she* did this. Herself. I don't blame her, man."

"Yeah, yeah, right, just put her on the phone."

Bobby took a deep breath, praying that Wes wouldn't think it was weird—him being in Colleen's apartment when she wasn't home. "She's not here. She had to go over to the law school for something and—"

"Leave her a message then. Tell her to call me." Wes rattled off a phone number that Bobby dutifully wrote on a scrap of paper. But he then folded it up, intending to put it into his pocket as soon as he was wearing something that had a pocket. No way was he going to risk Colleen calling Wes back before he himself had a chance to speak to him.

"Put it in gear," Wes ordered. "You're needed for this meeting. If Colleen's going to be stupid and insist on going to Tulgeria, we need to do this right. If you get down here tonight, we'll get started planning this op a full twelve hours earlier than if we wait to have this meeting in the morning. I want those extra twelve hours. This is Colleen's safety—her *life*—we're talking about here."

"I'm there," Bobby said. "I'll be on that flight."

"Thank you. Hey, I missed you, man. How's the shoulder? You been taking it easy?"

Not exactly, considering that for the past twenty-four hours he'd been engaged in almost nonstop, highly gymnastic sex. With Wes's precious little sister. Oh, God.

"I'm feeling much better," Bobby told the man who was the best friend he'd ever had in his life. Not a lie—it was true. The shoulder was still stiff and sore, and he still couldn't reach over his head without pain, but he was, without a doubt, feeling exceptionally good this morning.

Physically.

Emotionally was an entirely different story. Guilt. Doubt. Anxiety.

"Hey," Bobby said. "Will you do me a favor and pick me up in Norfolk alone? There's something we need to talk about."

"Uh-oh," Wes said. "Sounds heavy. You all right? God—you didn't get some girl pregnant did you? I didn't even know you were seeing anyone since you and Kyra split."

"I didn't get anyone..." Bobby started to deny, but then cut himself off. Oh, Lord, it was possible that he had indeed gotten Colleen pregnant just this morning. The thought still made him weak in the knees. "Just meet my flight, okay?"

"Ho," Wes said. "No way can you make hints that something dire is going down and then not tell me what the—"

"I'll tell you later," Bobby said, and hung up the phone.

CHAPTER FOURTEEN

WHEN COLLEEN GOT HOME, Clark and Kenneth were sitting in her living room, playing cards.

"Hey," Clark said. "Where's your TV?"

"I don't have a TV," she told him. "What are you doing here? Is Ashley back?"

"Nah. Mr. Platonic called us," Clark answered. "He didn't want you coming home to an empty apartment."

"He had to go someplace called Little Creek," Kenneth volunteered. "He left a note on your bed. I didn't let Clark read it."

Bobby had gone to Little Creek. He'd finally run away, leaving the two stooges behind as baby-sitters.

"Thanks," she said. "I'm home now. You don't have to hang here."

"We don't mind," Clark said. "You actually have food in your kitchen and—"

"Please, I need you to go," Colleen told them. "I'm sorry." She had no idea what Bobby had written in that note that was in her bedroom. She couldn't deal with reading it while they were in her living room.

And she couldn't deal with not reading it another second longer.

"It's cool," Clark said. "I was betting we wouldn't get the warmest welcome, since you're one of those liberated, I-can-take-care-of-myself babes and—"

She heard the door close as Kenneth dragged Clark out.

Colleen took her backpack into her bedroom. Bobby

had cleaned up the room. And made the bed, too. And left a note, right on her pillow.

"I got a call and had to run," it said in bold block letters—an attempt by someone with messy penmanship to write clearly. "Heading to Little Creek—to a meeting I can't miss. I'm sorry (more than I can say!) that I couldn't stick around to kiss you goodbye properly, but this is what it's like—being part of Alpha Squad. When I have to go, I go, whether I want to or not."

He'd then written something that he'd crossed out. Try as she might, Colleen couldn't see beneath the scribbled pen to the letters below. The first word looked as if it might be *maybe*. But she couldn't read the rest.

"Stay safe!" he wrote, both words underlined twice. "I'll call you from Little Creek." He'd signed it "Bobby." Not "Love, Bobby." Not "Passionately yours, Bobby." Just "Bobby."

Colleen lay back on her bed, trying not to overanalyze his note, wishing he hadn't had to go, trying not to wonder if he were ever coming back.

He'd come back if she were pregnant. Maybe she should wish she actually was. He'd insist that she marry him and...

The thought made her sit up, shocked at herself. What a terrible thing to wish for. She didn't want to be an obligation. A lifelong responsibility. A permanent mistake.

She wanted him to come back here because he liked being with her. And yes, okay—because he liked making love to her. She wasn't going to pretend their relationship wasn't based mostly on sex. Great sex. Incredible sex.

She knew that he liked making love to her. And so she would see him again, Colleen told herself. And when he called from Little Creek—if he called—she'd make herself sound relaxed. As if she wasn't a bundle of anxiety. As if she had no doubt that he would be back in her bed in a matter of a day or two. And as if her world wouldn't end if he didn't come back.

The phone rang, and she rolled to the edge of her bed, lying on her stomach to look at the caller ID box, hoping... *Yes.* It was Bobby. Had to be. The area code and exchange was from Little Creek. She knew those numbers well— Wes had been stationed there when he'd first joined the Navy. Back before he'd even met Bobby Taylor.

Bobby must've just arrived, and he was calling her first thing. Maybe this wasn't just about sex for him....

Colleen picked up the phone, keeping her voice light, even though her heart was in her throat. "Too bad you had to leave. I spent the entire T ride imagining all the different ways we were going to make love again this afternoon."

The words that came out of the phone were deafening and colorful. The voice wasn't Bobby's. It was her brother's. "I don't know who you think I am, Colleen, but you better tell me who you thought you were talking to so that I can kill him."

"Wes," she said weakly. Oh, no!

"This is great. This is just great. Just what I want to hear coming out of the mouth of my little sister."

Her temper sparked. "Excuse me, I'm *not* little. I haven't been little for a long time. I'm twenty-three years old, thank you very much, and yes, you want to know the truth? I'm in a relationship that's intensely physical and *enormously* satisfying. I spent last night and most of the morning having wild sex."

Wes shouted. "Oh, my *God!* Don't tell me that! I don't want to hear that!"

"If I were Sean or...or..." She didn't want to say Ethan. Mentioning their dead brother was like stomping with both feet on one of Wes's more sensitive buttons. "Or *Frank* you'd be *happy* for me!"

"Frank's a *priest!*"

"You know what I mean," Colleen countered. "If I were one of the guys in Alpha Squad, and I told you I just got lucky, you'd be slapping me on the back and congratulating me. I don't see the difference—"

"The difference is you're a girl!"

"No," she said, tightly. "I'm a *woman*. Maybe that's the basis of your relationship problems, Wes. Maybe until you stop seeing women as *girls,* until you treat them as *equals*—"

"Yeah, thanks a million, Dr. Freud. Like you even have a half a clue about my *problems*." He swore.

"I know you're unhappy," she said softly. "And angry almost all the time. I think you've got some unresolved issues that you've really got to deal with before—"

He refused to follow her out of this argument and into a more personal, private discussion. "Damn straight I've got unresolved issues—and they're all about this jackass you've been letting take advantage of you. You probably think he loves you, right? Is that what he told you?"

"No," Colleen said, stung by his implications. "As a matter of fact he hasn't. He likes me, though. And he respects me—which is more than I can say about *you*."

"What, is he some geeky lawyer?"

"That's not your business." Colleen closed her eyes. She couldn't let herself get mad and tell him it was Bobby. If Bobby wanted to tell him, fine. But her brother wasn't going to hear it first from her. No way. "Look, I have to go. You know, paint myself with body oil," she lied just to annoy him. "Get ready for tonight."

It got the response she'd expected, through gritted teeth. "Col*leen!*"

"I'm glad you're back safely."

"Wait," he said. "I'm calling for a reason."

"No kidding? A reason besides sibling harassment?"

"Yeah. I have to go pick up Bobby at the airport, but before I leave, I need info on your contacts in the Tulgerian government. Admiral Robinson is going to run a quick check on everyone involved." Wes paused. "Didn't you get my message to call me?" he asked. "When I spoke to Bobby just before noon, I told him to leave a message for you and—"

Silence.

Big, long silence.

Colleen could almost hear the wheels in Wes's head turning as he put two and two together.

Colleen had spent—in her own words—"most of the morning having wild sex" with her mysterious lover.

Her brother had spoken to Bobby earlier. In Colleen's apartment. Just before noon. As in the "just before noon" that occurred at the very end of a morning filled with wild sex.

"Tell me I'm wrong," Wes said very, very quietly— never a good sign. "Tell me it's not Bobby Taylor. Tell me my best friend didn't betray me."

Colleen couldn't keep quiet at that. "*Betray* you? Oh, my God, Wesley, that's absurd. What's between me and Bobby has nothing to do with you at all!"

"I'm right?" Wes lost it. "I *am* right! How could he *do* that, that son of a—I'm gonna kill him!"

Oh, *damn!* "Wes! Listen to me! It was *my* fault. I—"

But her brother had already hung up.

Oh, dear Lord, this was going to be bad. Wes was going to pick up Bobby from the airport and...

Colleen checked her caller-ID box and tried to call Wes back.

THE FLIGHT TO NORFOLK was just long enough to set Bobby completely on edge. He'd had enough time to buy a book at the airport store, but he stared at the words on the page, unable to concentrate on the bestselling story.

What was he going to say to Wes?

"So, hey, nice to see you. Yeah, Cambridge was great. I liked it a lot—especially when I was having sex with your sister."

Oh, man.

Thinking about his impending conversation with Wes was making him feel edgy and unsettled.

Thinking about Colleen was making him crazy.

A glance at his watch told him that she had surely come back to her apartment by now.

If he hadn't left, she'd be naked, just as she'd promised, and he'd be buried deep inside of her and—

He shifted in his seat. Coach wasn't built for some-one his size, and his knees were already pressed against the back of the seat in front of him. He was already un-comfortable as hell—thinking of Colleen wasn't going to help.

But as Bobby closed his eyes, he couldn't help but think of her.

It was probably good that he'd had to leave. If it had been left up to him, he never would have left. He would have just stayed there forever, in Colleen's bedroom, wait-ing for her to come and make love to him.

She had cast a spell over him, and he couldn't resist her. All she had to do was smile, and he was putty in her hands.

This way the spell was broken. Wasn't it? God, he hoped so. It would be just his luck to fall for another woman who didn't love him. Even better luck to fall for a woman who clearly only saw him as a sexual plaything. If he wasn't careful, his heart was going to get trashed.

Bobby tried to focus again on his book, tried to banish the image of Colleen, her eyes filled with laughter as she leaned forward to kiss him, as she pressed her body against him, as their legs tangled and…

Help.

He wanted her with every breath.

God, why couldn't he have felt this way about Kyra?

Because even back then, he was in love with Colleen.

Man, where had *that* thought come from? Love. God. This was already way too complicated without screwing it up by putting love into the picture.

In a matter of minutes Bobby was going to be hip deep in a conversation with Wes that he was dreading with every ounce of his being. And Wes was going to warn him away from Colleen. *Don't go near her any more.* He could hear the words already.

If he were smart, he'd heed his friend.

If he weren't smart, if he kept thinking with his body instead of his brain, he was going to get in too deep. Before he even blinked, he would find himself in a long-distance relationship, God help him. And then it would be a year from now, and he'd be on the phone with Colleen again, having to tell her—again—that he wasn't going to make it out for the weekend, and she would tell him that was okay—

again—but in truth, he'd know that she was trying not to cry.

He didn't want to make her cry—but that didn't mean he was in love with her.

And the fact that he wanted to be with her constantly, the fact that he missed her desperately even now, mere hours after having been in bed with her, well, that was just his body's healthy response to great sex. It was natural, having had some, to want more.

Bobby squeezed his eyes shut. Oh, God, he wanted more.

It wouldn't be too hard to talk Colleen into giving a

bicoastal relationship a try. She was adventurous and she liked him. And, of course, he'd never had a long-distance relationship with someone who liked phone sex....

Bobby felt himself start to smile. Yeah, who was he kidding? Pretending he had any choice at all? Pretending that he wasn't going to spend every waking hour working on ways to get back to Cambridge to see Colleen. The truth was, unless she flat-out refused to see him again, he was going to be raking up the frequent flyer miles, big-time.

He was already in too deep.

And, jeez, if Colleen were pregnant...

Oh, hell. As the plane approached the runway for a landing, Bobby tried to imagine Wes's reaction to *that* news.

"Hey, man! Not only did I do the nasty with your sister more times than I can remember, but the condom broke and I probably knocked her up, ruining her dreams of finishing law school, condemning her to a life with a husband she doesn't particularly love, who isn't even around all that often, anyway. And how was *your* week?"

BOBBY CAME OFF THE plane the way he'd gotten on. With no luggage, wearing the same cargo shorts and shirt he'd worn over to Colleen's nearly a full twenty-four hours ago.

Not that he'd been wearing them for that entire time. On the contrary.

As he came out of the walkway that connected the plane to the terminal, he scanned the crowd, searching for Wes's familiar face.

And then, there he was. Wes Skelly. He was leaning against the wall, arms crossed in front of his chest, looking more like a biker than a chief in the elite U.S. Navy SEALs. He was wearing baggy green cargo pants with lots of pockets and a white tank top that showed off his tan and revealed the barbwire tattoo on his upper arm. His hair was long and messy. The longer it got, the lighter it looked as it was bleached by the sun, as the reddish highlights were brought out.

Bobby and Wes had been virtually inseparable for nearly eleven years—even though they'd hated each other's guts at the outset of BUD/S training, when they'd been assigned together as swim buddies. That was something not many people knew. But Wes had earned Bobby's respect through the grueling training sessions—the same way Bobby earned Wes's. It took them a while, but once they recognized that they were made from the same unbreakable fabric, they'd started working together.

It was a case of one plus one equaling three. As a team, they were unstoppable. And so they became allies.

And when Wes's little brother Ethan had died, they'd taken their partnership a step forward and become friends. Real friends. Over the past decade that bond had strengthened to the point where it seemed indestructible.

But years of working with explosives had taught Bobby that indestructibility was a myth. There was no such thing.

And there was a very good chance that over the next few minutes, he was going to destroy ten years of friendship with just a few small words.

I slept with your sister.

"Hey," Wes said in greeting. "You look tired."

Bobby shrugged. "I'm okay. You?"

Wes pushed himself off the wall. "Please tell me you didn't check your luggage."

They started walking, following the stream of humanity away from the gate. "I didn't. I didn't bring it. There was no time to go back to the hotel. I just left it there."

"Bummer," Wes said. "Paying for a room when you don't even sleep there. That's pretty stupid."

"Yeah," Bobby agreed. *I slept with your sister.* How the hell was he supposed to say something like that? Just blurting it out seemed wrong, and yet there was no real graceful way to lead into a topic like that.

"How's Colleen?" Wes asked.

"She's—" Bobby hesitated. Beautiful. Heart-stoppingly sexy. Great in bed. Maybe carrying his baby. "Doing okay. Selling the car wasn't easy for her."

"Jeez, I can't believe she did that. Her Mustang... That's like selling a child."

"She got a good price. The buyer was a collector, and she was sure he'd take good care of it."

Wes pushed open a door that led toward the parking area. "Still..."

"Did Jake fill you in on the situation with this Tulgerian orphanage Colleen and her friends have been trying to move out of the war zone?" Bobby asked.

"Yeah, apparently the building was hit in some kind of skirmish a day or so ago. The place was pretty much destroyed, and the survivors were brought to a local hospital—but the place doesn't even have electricity or running water. We'll be going out there pretty much upon insertion in Tulgeria to move the kids back into the city."

"Good," Bobby said. "I'm glad the admiral's made that a priority. Wes, there's something you need to know..." The easy stuff first. "The little girl that Colleen was hoping to adopt was killed in that air strike."

Wes stared at him in the shadowy dimness of the parking garage. "Adopt?" he said, loud enough that his voice echoed. "She was going to *adopt* a kid? What, was she nuts? She's just a kid herself."

"No, she's not," Bobby said quietly. "She's a grown woman. And—" okay, here's where he had to say it "—I should know. I've...uh, been with her, Wes. Colleen. And me."

Wes stopped walking. "Aw, come on, Bobby, you can do better than that. You've *been* with her? You could say *slept with,* but of course you didn't sleep much, did you, dirt wad? How about…" He used the crudest possible expression. "Yeah, that works. *That's* what you did, huh? You *son* of a…" He was shouting now.

Bobby stood there. Stunned. Wes had known. Somehow he'd already known. And Bobby had been too self-absorbed to realize it.

"I sent you there to take *care* of her," Wes continued. "And *this* is what you do? How could you do this to me?"

"It wasn't about you," Bobby tried to explain. "It was about me and— Wes, I've been crazy about her for years."

"Oh, this is fine," Wes had gone beyond full volume and into overload. "For *years,* and this is the first I hear of it? What, were you just waiting for a chance to get her alone, scumbag?" He shoved Bobby, both hands against his chest.

Bobby let himself get shoved. He could have planted himself and absorbed it, but he didn't. "No. Believe me I tried to stay away from her, but…I couldn't do it. As weird as it sounds, she got it into her head that she wanted me, and hell, you know how she gets. I didn't stand a chance."

Wes was in his face. "You're ten years older than she is, and you're trying to tell me that *she* seduced *you?*"

"It's not that simple. You've got to believe—" Bobby cut himself off. "Look, you're right. It *is* my fault. I'm more experienced. She offered, and God, I wanted her, and I didn't do the right thing. For *you.*"

"Ho, *that's* great!" Wes was pacing now, a tightly wound bundle of energy, ready to blow. "Meaning you did the right thing for Colleen, is that what you're saying?

How right is it, Bobby, that she sits around and waits for you, that she'll have half a life, pretending to be okay, but really terrified, just waiting to get word that something's happened to you? And say you *don't* get your head blown off on some op. Say you do make it home. Retire from the teams in a few years. Then what? How right is it that she's the one who makes more money working as a lawyer? How's she supposed to have kids? Put 'em in day care? That's just great."

Kids…day care… Bobby was shocked. "Wes, whoa, I'm not going to marry her."

Wes stopped short, turning to stare with his mouth open, as if Bobby'd just announced his plan to detonate a nuclear warhead over New York City. "Then what the hell were you doing with her, dirt wad?"

Bobby shook his head, laughing slightly in disbelief. "Come on. She's twenty-three. She's just experimenting. She doesn't want to *marry* me."

In hindsight, it was probably the laughter that did it.

Wes exploded. "You *son* of a bitch. You went into this with completely dishonorable intentions!" He put his shoulder into a solid right jab, right in Bobby's face.

Bobby saw it coming. He didn't dodge it or block it. He just stood there, turning his head only slightly to deflect the force of the blow. It rocked him back on his heels, but he quickly regained his balance.

"Wes, don't do this." There were people around. Getting into and out of cars. It wouldn't be long until someone called a security team, who would call the police, who would haul their butts to jail.

Wes hit him again, harder this time, an ear-ringing blow, and again Bobby didn't defend himself.

"Fight back, you bastard," Wes snarled.

"No."

"*Damn* it!" Wes launched himself at Bobby, hitting

him in the exact place that would knock him over, take him down onto his back on the concrete. After years of training together, Wes knew his weak spots well.

"Hey!" The shout echoed against the concrete ceilings and walls as Wes hit him with a flurry of punches. "Hey, Skelly, back off!"

The voice belonged to Lucky O'Donlon. An SUV pulled up with a screech of tires, and O'Donlon and Crash Hawken were suddenly there, in the airport parking garage, pulling Wes off him.

And the three newest members of Alpha Squad, Rio Rosetti, Mike Lee and Thomas King climbed out of the back, helping Bobby to his feet.

"You okay, Chief?" Rio asked, his Italian street-punk attitude completely overridden by wide-eyed concern. The kid had some kind of hero worship thing going for both Bobby and Wes. If this little altercation didn't cure him of it forever, Bobby didn't know what would.

He nodded at Rio. "Yeah." His nose was bleeding. By some miracle it wasn't broken. It should have been. Wes had hit him hard enough.

"Here, Chief." Mike handed him a handkerchief.

"Thanks."

Crash and Lucky were both holding on tightly to Wes, who was sputtering—and ready to go another round if they released him.

"You want to explain what this is all about?" Crash was the senior officer present. He rarely used his officer voice—he rarely spoke at all—but when he did, he was obeyed instantly. To put it mildly.

But Wes wouldn't have listened to the president of the United States at this moment, and Bobby didn't want to explain any of this to anyone. "No, sir," he said stiffly, politely. "With all due respect, sir..."

"We got a call from your sister, Skelly," Lucky

O'Donlon said. "She was adamant we follow you down here to the airport. She said she had good reason to believe you were going to try to kick the hell out of Taylor, here, and she didn't want either of you guys to get arrested."

"Did she say *why* I was going to kick the hell out of Taylor?" Wes asked. "Did she tell you what that *good reason* was?"

It was obvious she hadn't.

Bobby took a step toward Wes. "What we were discussing is not public information. Show some respect to your sister."

Wes laughed in his face, looked up at Crash and Lucky. "You guys know what this *friend* of mine did?"

Bobby got large. "This is between you and me, Skelly. So help me God, if you breathe a single word of—"

Wes breathed four words. He told them all, quite loudly, in the foulest possible language what Bobby had done with his sister. "Apparently, she's doing some *experimenting* these days. All you have to do is go to Cambridge, Massachusetts, and look her up. Colleen Skelly. She's probably in the phone book. Anyone else want to give her a go?"

Wes Skelly was a dead man.

Bobby jumped on top of him with a roar. The hell with the fact that Wes was being held in place by Lucky and Crash. The hell with everything. No one had the right to talk about Colleen that way. *No* one.

He hit Wes in the face, harder than he'd ever hit him before, then he tackled him. It was enough to take them down to the concrete—Lucky and Crash with them.

He hit Wes again, wanting to make him bleed.

The other SEALs were on top of him then, grabbing his back and his arms, trying to pull him away, but they couldn't stop him. No one could stop him. Bobby yanked Wes up by the front of his shirt as he got to his feet, hauling him away from Lucky and Crash, with Rio, Mike and Thomas clinging to him like monkeys.

He pulled back his arm, ready to throw another brain-shaking punch when another voice, a new voice, rang out.

"Stop this. *Right. Now.*"

It was the senior chief.

Another truck had pulled up.

Bobby froze, and that was all the other SEALs needed. Lucky and Crash pulled Wes out of his grip and safely out of range, and then, God, Senior Chief Harvard Becker was there, standing in between him and Wes.

"Thank you for coming, Senior," Crash said quietly. He looked at Bobby. "I answered the phone when Colleen called. She didn't say as much, but I correctly guessed the cause of the, uh, tension between you and Skelly. I anticipated that the senior's presence would be helpful."

Wes's nose was broken, and as Bobby watched—not without some grim satisfaction—he leaned forward slightly, his face averted as he bled onto the concrete floor.

Lucky stepped closer to Harvard. He was speaking to him quietly, no doubt filling him in. Telling him that Bobby slept with Wes's sister.

God, this was so unfair to Colleen. She was going to Tulgeria with this very group of men. Who would all look at her differently, knowing that she and Bobby had...

Damn it, why couldn't Wes have agreed to talk this problem out...privately? Why had he turned this into a fist fight and, as a result, made Bobby's intimate relationship with Colleen public knowledge?

"So what do you want to do?" Harvard asked, hands on his hips as he looked from Bobby to Wes, his shaved head gleaming in the dim garage light. "You children want to move this somewhere so you can continue to beat the hell out of each other? Or you want to pretend to be grown-ups for a change and try working this out with a conversation?"

"Colleen doesn't sleep around," Bobby said, looking at Wes, willing him to meet his gaze. But Wes didn't look up, so he turned back to Harvard. "If he implies that again, Senior—or anything else even remotely disrespectful—I'll rip his head off." He used Wes's favorite adjective for emphasis.

Harvard nodded, his dark eyes narrowing slightly as he looked at Bobby. "Okay." He turned to Wes. "You hear that, Chief Skelly? Do you understand what this man is saying to you?"

"Yeah," Wes answered sullenly. "He'll rip my head off." He added his favorite adjective, too. "Let him try."

"No," Harvard said. "Those are the *words* he used, but the actual semantics—what he really means by saying those words—is that he cares a great deal for your sister. You fools are on the same side here. So what's it going to be? Talk or fight?"

"Talk," Bobby said.

"There's nothing to say," Wes countered. "Except from now on he better stay the hell away from her. If he so much as *talks* to her again, I'll rip *his* head off."

"Even if I wanted to do that," Bobby said quietly, "which I don't, I couldn't. I've got to talk to her again. There's more that you need to know, Skelly, but I'm not going to talk about it here in front of everyone."

Wes looked up, finally meeting Bobby's gaze, horror in his eyes. "Oh, my God," he said. "You got her pregnant."

"All right," Harvard commanded. "Let's take this someplace private. Taylor, in my truck. Rosetti, take Chief Skelly's keys, drive him to the base and escort him to my office. On the double."

"YOU'RE GOING TO have to marry her."

Bobby sat back in his chair, his breath all but knocked out of him. "What? Wes, that's insane."

Wes Skelly sat across the table from him in the conference room on base that Harvard had appropriated and made into a temporary office. He was still furious. Bobby had never seen him stay so angry for such a long time.

It was possible Wes was going to be angry at Bobby forever.

He leaned forward now, glaring. "What's *insane* is for you to go all the way to Cambridge to *help* me and end up messing around with my sister. What's *insane* is that we're even having this conversation in the first place— that you couldn't keep your pants zipped. You got yourself into this situation. You play the game—you pay when you lose. And you lost big-time, buddy, when that condom broke."

"And I'm willing to take responsibility if necessary—"

"If necessary?" Wes laughed. "*Now* who's insane? You really think Colleen's going to marry you if she *has* to? No way. Not Colleen. She's too stubborn, too much of an idealist. No, you have to go back to Boston tomorrow morning. First thing. And make her think you *want* to marry her. Get her to say yes *now*—before she does one of those home tests. Otherwise, she's going to be knocked up and refusing to take your phone calls. And boy, won't *that* be fun."

Bobby shook his head. It was aching, and his face was throbbing where Wes's fists had connected with it—which was just about everywhere. He suspected Wes's nose hurt far worse; yet, both of their physical pain combined was nothing compared to the apprehension that was starting to churn in his stomach. Ask Colleen to marry him. God.

"She's not going to agree to marry me. She wanted a fling, not a lifetime commitment."

"Well, too bad for her," Wes countered.

"Wes, she deserves—" Bobby rubbed his forehead and just said it "—she deserves better than me."

"Damn straight she does," Wes agreed. "I wanted her to marry a lawyer or a doctor. I didn't want this for her—to be a Navy wife, like my mother." He swore. "I wanted her to hook up with someone rich, not some poor, dumb Navy chief who'll have to work double shifts to buy her a washer and dryer. Damn, if she's going to marry Navy, she should at least have been smart enough to pick an officer."

This wasn't a surprise. Wes had voiced his wishes for Colleen often enough in the past. The surprise came from how bad Bobby felt hearing this. "I wanted that for her, too," he told Wes quietly.

"Here's what you do," Wes told him. "You go to Colleen's and you tell her we had a fight. You tell her that I wanted you to stay the hell away from her. You tell her that you told me that you wouldn't—that you want to marry her. And you tell her that I flat-out forbid it." He laughed, but there wasn't any humor in it. "She'll agree to marry you then."

"She's not going to ruin her life just to tick you off," Bobby argued.

"Wanna bet?" Wes stood up. "After the meeting I'll get you a seat on the next flight back to Boston."

"Are you ever going to forgive me?" Bobby asked.

"No." Wes didn't turn around as he went out the door.

CHAPTER FIFTEEN

COLLEEN CAME HOME FROM the Tulgerian children's memorial service at St. Margaret's to find Ashley home and no new messages on the answering machine. Bobby had called last night, while she was at a Relief Aid meeting, so at least she knew he'd survived his altercation with her brother. Still, she was dying to speak to him.

Dying to be with him again.

"Any calls?" she called to Ashley, who was in her room.

"No."

"When did you get back?" Colleen asked, going to her roommate's bedroom door and finding her...*packing?*

"I'm not back," Ashley said, wiping her eyes and her nose with her sleeve. She had been crying but she forced an overly bright smile. "I'm only here temporarily and I'm not telling you where I'm going because you might tell someone."

Colleen sighed. "I guess Brad found you."

"I guess you would be the person who told him where I was...?"

"I'm sorry, but he seemed sincerely broken up over your disappearing act."

"You mean broken up over losing his chances to inherit my share of DeWitt and Klein," Ashley countered, savagely throwing clothes into the open suitcase on her bed. "How could you even *think* I'd consider getting back together with him? My father hired him to be my husband, and he went along with it! Some things are unforgivable."

"People change when they fall in love."

"Not *that* much." She emptied her entire drawer of underwear into the suitcase. "I figured out how to get my father off my back. I'm dropping out of law school."

What? Colleen took another step into the room. "Ashley—"

"I'm going to go to bartending school and get a job dancing in some exotic bar like the women in that video we rented before I left for New York."

Colleen laughed in surprise. She quickly stopped when Ashley shot her a dark look.

"You don't think I'd be any good at it?"

"No," Colleen protested. "No, I think you'd be great. It's just… Isn't it a little late in your childhood to start sporting the career equivalent of—" she thought of Clark. "—of blue hair?"

"It's never too late," Ashley said. "And my father deserves all the blue hair—symbolic or other—that he gets." She closed her suitcase, locked it. "Look, I'm going to send for the rest of my things. And I'll pay my share of the rent until you find a new roommate."

"I don't want a new roommate!" Colleen followed her into the living room. "You're my best friend. I can't believe you're so mad at me that you're leaving!"

Ashley set her suitcase down. "I'm not leaving because I'm mad at you," she said. "I'm not really mad at you at all. I just…I did a lot of thinking, and… Colleen, I have to get out of here. Boston's too close to my father in New York. And you know, maybe Clark's right. Maybe I should go to one of those survival training schools. Learn to swim with sharks. See if I can grow a backbone—although I suspect it's a little late for that."

"You have a *great* backbone."

"No, *you* have a great backbone. I'm really good at borrowing yours when I need it," Ashley countered. She pushed her hair back from her face, attempting to put several escaped tendrils neatly back into place. "I have to do this, Colleen. I've got a cab waiting…."

Colleen hugged her friend. "Call me," she said, pulling back to look into Ashley's face. Her friend's normally perfect complexion was sallow, and she had dark circles beneath her eyes. This Brad thing had truly damaged her. "Whenever you get where you're going, when you've had a little more time to think about this—call me, Ash. You can always change your mind and come back. But if you don't—well, I'll come out to visit and cheer while you dance on the bar."

Ashley smiled even though her eyes filled with tears. "See, everything's okay with you. Why couldn't *you* be my father?"

Colleen had teared up, too, but she still had to laugh. "Aside from the obvious biological problems, I'm not ready to be anyone's parent. I'm having a tough enough time right now keeping my own life straightened out."

And yet, she could well be pregnant. Right now. Right this moment, a baby could be sparking to life inside her. In nine months she could be someone's mother. Someone very small who looked an awful lot like Bobby Taylor.

And somehow that thought wasn't quite so terrifying as she'd expected it to be.

She heard an echo of Bobby's deep voice, soft and rumbly, close to her ear. *There are some things you just have to do, you know? So you do it, and it all works out.*

If she were pregnant, despite what she'd just told Ashley, she would make it work out. Somehow.

She gave her friend one more hug. "You liked law

school," she told Ashley. "Don't cut off your nose to spite your face."

"Maybe I'll go back some day—anonymously."

"That'll look good on your diploma—Anonymous DeWitt."

"The lawyer with blue hair." Ashley smiled back at Colleen, wiping her eyes again before dragging her suitcase to the door.

The door buzzer rang.

"That's probably the cab driver," Ashley said, "wondering if I sneaked out the back door."

Colleen pushed the button for the intercom. "She'll be right down."

"Actually, I was hoping to come up." The voice over the ancient speaker was crackly but unmistakable, and Colleen's heart leaped.

Bobby.

"I thought you were the cab driver," she told him, leaning close to the microphone.

"You're not going anywhere, are you?" Did he sound worried? She hoped so.

"No," she said. "The cab's Ashley's."

She buzzed him into the lobby as Ashley opened the apartment door. From the sound of his footsteps, he took the stairs two at a time, and then there he was. Carrying *flowers?*

He was. He had what looked like a garden in his arms—an outrageous mix of lilies and daisies and big, bold, crazy-looking flowers for which she didn't know the names. He thrust them toward her as he quickly took the suitcase from Ashley's hands. "Let me get that for you."

"No, you don't need to—" But he was already down the stairs. Ashley looked helplessly at Colleen. "See? No backbone."

"Call me," Colleen said, and then Ashley was gone.

Leaving Colleen face-to-face with the flowers that Bobby had brought. For *her*.

She had to smile. It was silly and sweet and a complete surprise. She left the door ajar and went into the kitchen to find a vase. She was filling it with water when Bobby returned.

He looked nice, as if he'd taken special care with his appearance. He was wearing Dockers instead of his usual jeans, a polo shirt with a collar in a muted shade of green. His hair was neatly braided. Someone had helped him with that.

"Sorry I didn't call you last night. The meeting didn't end until well after midnight. And then I was up early, catching a flight back here."

He was nervous. She could see it in his eyes, in the tension in his shoulders—but only because she knew him so very well. Anyone else would see a completely re-laxed, easygoing man, standing in her kitchen, dwarfing the refrigerator.

"Thanks for the flowers," she said. "I love them."

He smiled. "Good. I didn't think you were the roses type, and they, well, they reminded me of you."

"What?" she said. "Big and flashy?"

His smile widened. "Yeah."

Colleen laughed as she turned to give him a disbeliev-ing look. Their eyes met and held, and just like that the heat was back, full force.

"I missed you," she whispered.

"I missed you, too."

"Kinda hard for you to take off my clothes when you're way over there."

He yanked his gaze away, cleared his throat. "Yeah, well. Hmmm. I think we need to talk before…" He cleared his throat. "You want to go out, take a walk? Get some coffee?"

She put the flowers into the water. "You're afraid if we stay here, we won't be able to keep from getting naked."

"Yes," he said. "Yes, I am."

Colleen laughed, opening the refrigerator. "How about we take a glass of iced tea to the roof?"

"Am I going to get the urge to jump you there?"

"Absolutely," she said as she poured the tea. "But unless you're an exhibitionist, you won't. There's a taller building right behind this one. There are about three floors of apartments that have a bird's-eye view of this roof."

She gave him one of the glasses and a kiss.

His mouth was soft and warm and wonderful, his body so solid and strong, and she felt herself melt against him.

She looked up at him. "You sure you don't want to…?"

"Roof," he said. "Please?"

Colleen led the way, up the main staircase, through the exit door and out into the bright sunshine. A long-departed former tenant had built a sundeck, complete with large pots of dirt in which she and Ashley had planted flowers last May. It wasn't luxurious, but it was a far cry from the peeling tar paper on the neighboring buildings' roofs.

There was even a bench, placed strategically in the shade provided by the larger building next door.

Colleen sat down. Bobby sat, too—about as far away from her as he could manage.

"So I guess I should ask about my brother," she said. "Is he in intensive care?"

"No." Bobby looked down into his iced tea. "We *did* fight, though."

She knew. She could see the shadows of bruises on his face. "It must've been awful," she said quietly.

He turned to gaze at her, and her heart moved up into her throat. He had such a way of looking at her, as if he could see inside her head, inside her very heart and soul, as if he saw her completely, as a whole, unique, special person.

"Marry me."

Colleen nearly dropped her glass. *What?*

But she'd heard him correctly. He reached into his pocket and took out a jeweler's box. A *ring* box. He opened it and handed it to her—it was a diamond in a gorgeously simple setting, perfect for accenting the size of the stone. Which was enormous. It had to have cost him three months' pay.

She couldn't breathe. She couldn't speak. She couldn't move. Bobby Taylor wanted to marry her.

"Please," he said quietly. "I should have said, *please* marry me."

The sky was remarkably blue, and the air was fresh and sweet. On the street below, a woman shouted for someone named Lenny. A car horn honked. A bus roared past.

Bobby Taylor wanted to *marry* her.

And yes, *yes,* she wanted to marry him, too. *Marry* him! The thought was dizzying, terrifying, but it came with a burst of happiness that was so strong, she laughed aloud.

Colleen looked up at him then, into the almost palpable warmth of his eyes. He was waiting for her answer.

But she was waiting, too, she realized. This was where he would tell her that he loved her.

Except he didn't. He didn't say anything. He just sat there, watching her, slightly nervous, slightly…detached? As if he were waiting for her to say no.

Colleen looked hard into his eyes. He was sitting there, waiting, as if he expected her to turn him down.

As if he didn't really want her to marry him.

As if…

Her happiness fizzled, and she handed him the ring

box. "Wes put you up to this, didn't he?" She saw the truth in his eyes. Oh, no, she was right. "Oh, Bobby."

"I'm not going to lie to you," he said quietly. "It *was* Wes's idea. But I wouldn't have asked if I didn't want to do it."

"Yeah," Colleen said, standing up and walking away so that her back was to him. She couldn't bear to let him see her disappointment. "Right. You look really enthusiastic. Grim is more like it. 'I'm here to be sentenced to life in prison, your honor.'"

"I'm scared. Can you blame me for that?" he countered. She heard the ice tinkling in his glass as he set it down, as he stood up and moved directly behind her. But he didn't touch her. He just stood there, impossible to ignore.

"This is a big step," he said quietly. "A major life decision for both of us. And I'm not sure marrying me is the right thing for *you* to do. I don't make a lot of money, Colleen, and my job takes me all over the world. Being a Navy wife sucks—I'm not sure I want to do that to you. I don't know if I could make you happy enough to ignore all the negatives of being married to me. And, yes, that scares me."

He took a deep breath. "But the fact is, you could be pregnant. With my child. That's not something I can ignore."

"I know," she whispered.

"If you *are* pregnant, you *will* marry me," he told her, his quiet voice leaving no room for argument. "Even if it's only just for a year or two, if that's how you want to play it."

Colleen nodded. "If I'm pregnant. But I'm probably not, so I'm not going to marry you." She shook her head. "I can't believe you would *marry* me, just because Wes told you to." She laughed, but her throat ached, and she knew she was dangerously close to crying. "I can't decide if that makes you a really good friend or a total chump."

She headed for the door to the stairs, praying she would make it into her apartment before her tears escaped. "I should get back to work."

God, she was a fool. If he'd been just a little more disingenuous, if he'd lied and told her he loved her, she would have given herself away. She would have thrown her arms around his neck and told him yes. Yes, she'd marry him, yes, she loved him, too.

She loved him so much...but there was no *too*.

"Colleen, wait."

Oh, damn, he was chasing her down the stairs. He caught her at her apartment door as she fumbled her key in the lock, as her vision blurred from her tears.

She pushed open the door, and he followed. She tried to turn away, but it was too late.

"I'm so sorry," he said hoarsely, engulfing her in his arms. "Please believe me—the last thing I wanted to do was upset you like this."

He was so solid, so huge, and his arms gave her the illusion of safety. Of being home.

He swore softly. "I didn't mean to make you cry, Colleen."

She just held him tightly, wanting them both just to pretend this hadn't happened. He hadn't asked her to marry him, she hadn't discovered just how much she truly loved him. Yeah, that would be easy to forget. He could return the ring to the jeweler's, but she didn't have a clue what she was going to do with her heart.

She did, however, know exactly what to do with her body. Yes, she was going to take advantage of every second she had with this man.

She pushed the door closed behind them and, wrapping her arms around his neck, pulled his head down for a kiss.

He hesitated—for about one-tenth of a second. Then, with a groan, he kissed her, too.

And Colleen stopped crying.

HOW THE HELL HAD *this* happened?

As Bobby awoke, he knew exactly where he was before he even opened his eyes.

He could smell the sweet scent of Colleen, feel her softness nestled against him.

Her windows were open, and a soft breeze from this perfect summer day caressed his naked behind. Colleen caressed him, too. She was running her fingers lightly up and down the arm he'd draped around her after she'd succeeded in completely wearing him out. Had they made love twice or three times?

How *had* that happened—even once? It didn't quite line up with him asking to marry her, and her getting angry because she saw clear through him, saw it had been Wesley's idea in the first place.

Except she hadn't been so much angry as *hurt,* and…

He lifted his face from her pillow to find her watching him. She smiled. "Hi."

He wanted her again. Just from one smile. Except it wasn't so much his body that reacted this time. It was his *heart* that expanded. He wanted to wake up to her smile every day. He wanted…

"You need to go," she said to him. "I have to pack for Tulgeria, and you're distracting me."

"I'll help you."

"Yeah, right." She laughed and leaned forward to kiss him. "Ten minutes of your *help,* you'll have me back in bed."

"Seriously, Colleen, I know exactly what you need to take. No bright colors, no white, either, otherwise you're setting yourself up as a potential sniper target. Think drabs—browns, greens, beiges. I also don't want you to bring anything clingy—wear loose overshirts, okay? Long sleeves, long skirts—and you know this already. Right." Bobby laughed, disgusted with himself. "Sorry."

She kissed him again. "I love that you care."

"I do," he said, holding her gaze, wishing there was some way to convey just how much.

But the door buzzer rang, and Colleen gently extracted herself from his arms. She slipped on her robe. Man, he loved that robe. He sat up. "Maybe you should let me get the door."

But she was already out of the room. "I've got it."

Whoever had buzzed had gotten past the building's security entrance and was now knocking directly on the door to Colleen's apartment.

Where *were* his shorts?

"Oh, my God," he heard Colleen say. "What are *you* doing here?"

"What, I can't visit my own sister?" Oh, damn! It was Wes. "Sleeping in today, huh? Late night last night?"

"No," she said flatly. "What do you want, Wes? I'm mad at you."

"I'm looking for Taylor. But he better not be here, with you dressed like that."

The hell with his shorts. Bobby grabbed his pants, pulling them on, tripping over his own feet in his haste and just barely keeping himself from doing a nosedive onto the floor. His recovery made an incriminating *thump*.

Wes swore—a steady stream of epithets that grew louder as he moved down the hall toward Colleen's bedroom.

Bobby was searching for his shirt among the sheets and blankets that spilled from the bed and onto the floor as Wes pushed the door open. He slowly straightened up, his hair wild around his shoulder, his feet bare and his shirt nowhere to be found.

Damn, there it was—over near Colleen's closet, near where he'd tossed his socks and shoes.

"Well, this is just beautiful," Wes said. His eyes were cold and hard—they were someone else's eyes. The Wes Skelly who'd been closer to him than a brother for years was gone. As Bobby watched, Wes turned to Colleen. "You're marrying this son of a bitch over my dead body."

Bobby knew Wes honestly thought that would make Colleen determined to marry him. "Wes—"

"You don't want me to marry him?" she asked innocently.

Wes crossed his arms. "Absolutely not."

"Okay," Colleen said blithely. "Sorry, Bobby, I can't marry you. Wes won't let me." She turned and went into the kitchen.

"What?" Wes followed, sputtering. "But you *have* to marry him. Especially now."

Bobby pulled on his shirt and grabbed his socks and shoes.

"I'm not marrying Bobby," Colleen repeated. "I don't *have* to marry Bobby. And there's nothing you can do to *make* me, thank you very much. I'm a grown woman, Wesley, who happens to be in a completely mutual, intimate relationship with a very attractive man. You either need to deal with that or get your negative opinions out of my apartment."

Wes was still sputtering. "But—"

She moved grandly from the kitchen to the door, opening it wide for him. "Leave."

Wes looked at Bobby. "No way am I leaving with him still here!"

"Then take him with you," Colleen said. "I have work to do." She pointed the way. "Go. Both of you."

Bobby moved, and Wes followed. But at the door Colleen stopped Bobby, kissed him. "Sorry about my brother the grouch. I had a lovely afternoon, thank you. I'll see you tonight."

If her intention was to infuriate her brother, she'd succeeded.

She closed the door behind them, with Bobby still holding his socks and shoes.

Wes gave him a scathing look. "What is *wrong* with you?"

How could he explain? He wasn't sure himself how it happened. Every time he turned around, he found himself in bed with Colleen. When it came to her, he—a man who'd set time-and-distance records for swimming underwater, a man who'd outlasted more physically fit SEAL candidates during BUD/S through sheer determination, a man who'd turned himself around from a huge man carrying quite a bit of extra weight into a solid, muscular monster—had no willpower.

Because being with her felt so right. It was *right.*

That thought came out of nowhere, blindsiding him, and he stood there for a moment just blinking at Wes.

"You were supposed to get her to marry you," Wes continued. "Instead you—"

"I tried. I was trying to—"

"That was *trying?*"

"If she's pregnant, she'll marry me. She agreed to that."

"Perfect," Wes said, "so naturally you feel inclined to keep trying to get her pregnant."

"Of course not. Wes, when I'm with her—"

"I don't want to hear it." Wes glared at him. "Just stay the hell away from her," he said, and clattered down the stairs. "And stay away from me, too."

CHAPTER SIXTEEN

THE EARLY-AFTERNOON MEETING between Alpha Squad and the members of Relief Aid who were going to Tulgeria tomorrow had gone well.

Colleen had been afraid that some of the more left-wing group members would be opposed to protection from the U.S. military, but with the recent outbreak of violence in the dangerous country, there wasn't a single protest.

She'd sat quietly, listening to the information presented by the SEALs. Bobby and the squad's commander, Captain Joe Catalanotto, sat up on a desk in the front of the room, feet swinging, extremely casual, dressed down in shorts and T-shirts—just a coupla guys. Who also happened to be members of *the* most elite military force in the world.

Bobby did most of the talking—a smart move, since he'd been working alongside most of the Relief Aid volunteers for the past few days. They knew and trusted him.

He warned them of the dangers they'd be encountering and the precautions and methods the SEALs would be taking to protect them, in his usual straightforward, quiet manner. And everything he said was taken very seriously.

The SEALs would maintain a low profile, blending in with the volunteers. Only a few would be obvious guards and carry obvious weapons.

After the meeting they'd mingled over iced tea and lemonade. She'd met many of the SEALs her brother had mentioned in his letters and emails down through the years. Joe Cat, Blue, Lucky, Cowboy, Crash. Some of the nicknames were pretty funny.

Spaceman. His real name was Jim Slade, and he was tall and good-looking in an earthy way, with craggy features and the kind of blue eyes that were perpetually amused. He'd followed her around for a while and had even invited her back to the hotel, to have dinner with him later.

Bobby had overheard that, and Colleen had expected him to step forward, to make some kind of proprietary move. But he hadn't. He'd just met Colleen's eyes briefly, then gone back to the conversation he'd been having with Relief Aid leader, Susan Fitzgerald.

And Colleen was bemused—more with her own reaction. It was stupid really. If Bobby had gotten all macho and possessive on her, she would have been annoyed. But since he hadn't, she found herself wondering why not. Didn't he *feel* possessive toward her? And wasn't *that* a stupid thing to wonder? She didn't want to be any man's possession.

She'd spoken to Bobby only briefly before he'd left for another meeting with his team, held back at the hotel. She'd stayed behind and helped discuss plans for TV news coverage of tonight's bon voyage party.

That meeting was brief, and Colleen was on the T, heading toward Cambridge before four o'clock. She was inside the lobby of Bobby's hotel by 4:15.

She used the lobby phone to dial his room.

Bobby answered on the first ring, and she knew right away that she'd woken him up.

"Sorry," she said.

"No, I was just catching a nap. Are you, um... Where are you?"

"Downstairs. Can I come up?"

Silence. She heard the rustle of sheets as he sat up. "How about you give me a few minutes to get dressed? I'll meet you in the bar."

"How about I come up?"

"Colleen—"

"Room 712, right? I'll be there in a sec."

"COLLEEN..." SHE'D HUNG UP.

Bobby dumped the phone's handset into the cradle and lay back in his bed.

What was the point in getting dressed? She was coming up here. In five minutes—ten tops—she'd have him out of his clothes.

He threw back the covers, anyway, got up and pulled on his pants and a T-shirt. If he was quick enough, he'd meet her in the hall, outside the elevators. He pulled on his sneakers, checked himself in the mirror to make sure his hair hadn't completely fallen out of its braid.

He opened the door, and Colleen was standing there, ready to knock.

"Hi," she said. "Good timing."

She swept past him, into the room.

No, it was bad timing. The last place they should be right now was here, alone in his hotel room. If Wes found out, he'd be furious.

Bobby had been shaken by what had happened this morning. He truly had not intended to take advantage of Colleen, but he honest-to-God could not stop himself from climbing into her bed and making love to her.

Even though she didn't want to marry him.

Was he turning into some kind of prude in his old age? So what if she didn't want to marry him. She wanted to do him, and that was what mattered.

Wasn't it?

"I have a favor to ask," she told him now.

God, she looked beautiful, in a blue-flowered sleeveless dress that flowed almost all the way to the floor. He'd been hyperaware of her all throughout the afternoon's meeting—aware of how easy it would be to get her out of that dress, with its single zipper down the back.

Bobby crossed the room and opened the curtains, letting in the bright late-afternoon sunshine. "Name it," he said.

"I know we don't officially need your protection until we enter Tulgeria," she told him, "but remember I told you about that bon voyage party? It's tonight at the VFW right down the street from St. Margaret's—the church where I had that car wash?"

Bobby nodded. "I know St. Margaret's." It was in that same crummy 'hood where the AIDS Center was creating a controversy among the locals.

Colleen put her backpack down and came to help as he attempted to make the bed. "We just found out that the local Fox affiliate is sending TV cameras tonight. That's great news—we could use all the public support we can get." Together they pulled up the bedspread. "But…"

"But the cameras are going to attract attention in the neighborhood." Bobby knew just where she was heading. "You're afraid John Morrison's going to show up. Crash your party."

She nodded. "It wouldn't surprise me one bit if he caused trouble, just to get the news camera pointed in his direction."

He took a deep breath. "There's something I should probably tell you. Don't be angry with me, but I checked up on John Morrison. I was worried about you, and I wanted to know how much of a wild card he was."

"There's not much to find out," Colleen countered. "I did the same thing right after he and I…met. He served in the army, did a tour in Vietnam. There's an ex-wife and a kid somewhere in New York. He inherited his bar from his father, who got it from *his* father. He's dating one of his waitresses—she shows up in the ER every now and then for some stitches. After I found *that* out, I started carrying one of those little spray cans of mace."

"Good plan. He's got the potential to be violent," Bobby told her. "Oh, I meant to tell you—I got a call right before I left the hotel. The woman who was attacked—Andrea Barker—she came out of her coma. Turns out it was her ex-husband who beat her up. He ignored a restraining order and…"

Colleen touched his arm. "Andrea's out of her coma—that's great news."

He stepped back slightly. "So is the fact that it wasn't Morrison who put her into the hospital. That fits with what I found out about him—that he never leaves his neighborhood. He rarely leaves his bar. In fact, his drinking pals are all still talking about the trips he made to New York—one about a year ago, the other just a few months back. I also found out he used to be a member of St. Margaret's but he stopped going to church about a year ago. I played out a hunch and called his ex in New York, and sure enough, a year ago was when he found out his son was dying of AIDS."

Colleen closed her eyes. "Oh, no."

"Yeah. John, Jr., died two months ago. He was living with Morrison's ex-wife in the Bronx. She's worried about John. According to her, he's angry and ashamed that even when his son was dying, he couldn't acknowledge the kid, couldn't bring himself to visit. God forbid anyone find out his son was gay, you know? And that's the thing, Colleen. No one up here knows anything. They don't even know that his kid is dead. He hasn't spoken to anyone about this. They still come into the bar and ask how Johnny's doing—if he's gotten that big break as an actor, if he's on Broadway yet."

Oh, God. "The poor man."

"Regardless of that, this *poor man* is responsible for putting cinder blocks through the center's windows. If he gets near you tonight, his health will be at risk."

"You'll be there?" she asked.

"Absolutely. I'll bring some of the guys, too. Rio, Thomas and Mike. And Jim Slade. He'll definitely come. What time does it start?"

"Eight. The camera crew's due to arrive at 7:30."

"We'll be there at seven."

"Thank you." Colleen sat down on his bed. "I liked meeting Rio, Thomas and Mike...Lee, right?" She smiled. "They really think the world of you. Make sure you tell them what you told me about John Morrison. If he shows up, let's try to treat him with compassion."

"We'll get him out of there as quickly—and compassionately—as possible," he promised. "I'm glad you had a chance to meet them—they're good men. All the guys in the squad are. Although some are definitely special. The senior chief—Harvard Becker. Did you meet him? I'd follow him into hell if he asked."

"Big black man, shaved head, great smile?" she asked.

"That's Harvard. Hey, whatdya think of Slade? Spaceman?" Bobby tried to ask the question casually, as if he was just talking, as if her answer didn't matter to him. The stupid thing was, he wasn't sure if he wanted her to tell him that she liked the man or hated him.

Colleen was gazing at him. "I thought he was nice. Why?"

"He's a lieutenant," Bobby told her. "An officer who's probably going to get out of the Teams pretty soon. He's having a tough time with his knees and... He's not sure what he's going to do. For a while he was thinking JAG—you know, going to law school, getting a degree, doing a stint in the regular Navy as a lawyer. I just thought you'd, um, you probably have a lot in common. You know, with you going to law school, too?"

Colleen shrugged. "Lawyers are boring."

"You're not. Slade's not, either."

She laughed. "Is there a reason you sound like you're trying to sell this guy to me?"

It was Bobby's turn to shrug. "He's a good man."

"You're a good man, too. A *very* good man."

She was gazing at him with that look in her eyes that made him crazy. And she smiled that smile that made his knees weak as she leaned back on her elbows. "So why are we talking about your friend? Why are we talking at all? Wouldn't you rather help me make Wes really mad—and spend the next half hour or so naked?"

Bobby was proud of himself. He didn't move toward her, didn't instantly strip off both his clothes and hers. "Colleen, I love being with you, you know that, but I don't want to be a pawn in this war you've got going with your brother."

She sat up, her smile instantly gone, wide-eyed. "Whoa—wait! Bobby, I was making a joke. I wasn't serious."

She wasn't serious. "That's part of the problem here," he told her quietly. "You and me, we're not serious, but Wes is. He doesn't want you messing around, not with a man that you don't have a serious shot at having a future with, you know? He thinks that's wrong and..." And Bobby was starting to think it was wrong, too.

It was one thing to have a casual sexual relationship with a woman who was older, someone his age, who lived near the Navy base, who'd maybe been through a nasty divorce and had no intention of repeating that mistake in the near future.

But with Colleen there were expectations.

Although, God help him, it sure seemed as if all the expectations were *his*.

"Wes thinks what we've got going is wrong? Well, what's *wrong*," Colleen countered hotly as she got to her feet, "is strong-arming your best friend into proposing marriage to your sister. What if I'd said yes? Would you have married me just because Wes told you to?"

"No," he said. He would have married her because he wanted to. Because unlike Colleen, this relationship was more to him than great sex. He turned away from her. "Look, maybe you should go."

She moved in front of him, forced him to look at her. "And do what?" she said sharply. "Have an early dinner with Jim Slade?"

He didn't nod, didn't say yes, but somehow the answer was written on his face. Slade was the kind of man she should be with. How could she meet men like him if she was wasting her time with Bobby?

"Oh, my God," she said. "You were, weren't you? You were trying to set me up with your friend." Her voice caught as she struggled not to cry, and as she gazed at him, she suddenly looked and sounded impossibly young and so very uncertain. "Bobby, what's going on? Don't you want me anymore?"

Oh, damn, he was going to cry, too. He wanted her more than he could ever say. He wanted her with every breath, with every beat of his heart. "I want to do what's right for you, Colleen. I need to—"

She kissed him.

God help him, she kissed him, and he was lost.

Again.

In truth, it was no ordinary kiss. It was fire and hunger

and need. It was passion and fury, with a whole lot of anger and hurt thrown in. It consumed him completely, until doing the right thing was no longer an option but an impossibility. Sure, he'd do the right thing—if the right thing meant sweeping her into his arms and carrying her to his bed. If the right thing meant nearly ripping her dress in his haste to get it off her, of pushing down his pants and covering himself and thrusting, hard, inside of her as she clung to him, as she begged him for more.

More.

He was ready to give her all he had to give—body, heart and soul, and he did, disguising it as near-mindless sex, hard and rough and fast.

She called out his name as she climaxed, shaking around him, and he joined her in a hot rush of pleasure so intense it was almost pain.

And then there he was again. Back from that place of insanity and passion, back to this extremely familiar real world that was filled with rumpled bedclothes and mind-numbing guilt.

He swore. "I'm sorry," he whispered as he rolled off her.

She sat up on the edge of the bed instead of snuggling against him, and he realized she was getting dressed. Bra, dress, sandals. Her panties had been torn—damn, he'd done that—and she threw them in the garbage.

She ran her fingers through her hair, picked up her pack. "I'm sorry that you're sorry," she said quietly, "but... I'm a fool—I still want to see you later tonight. Will you come to my place after the thing at the VFW?"

Bobby didn't answer right away, and she looked at him. "Please?"

"Yes," he whispered, and she let herself out the door.

THE ELEVATOR DOOR OPENED, and Colleen found herself face-to-face with Wes.

He was getting off on this floor, Bobby's floor, followed by the trio of young SEALs she was starting to think of as The Mod Squad. Pete, Link and Mike Lee.

Wes's expression was grim, and Colleen knew that she looked like a woman who'd just been with a man. She should have taken more time, should have gone into the bathroom and splashed water on her still-flushed face.

Except then she would have been in Bobby's room when Wes knocked on the door.

She went into the elevator, her head held high as her brother glared at her. "Don't worry," she told him. "You win. I'm not going to see him again after tonight."

They were leaving for Tulgeria in the morning. While they were there, she would be sharing a room with Susan and Rene, and Bobby would be in with one or two of the SEALs for the week. There would be no place to be alone, no time, either. Bobby would have no trouble avoiding her.

And after they got back to the States, he'd head for California with the rest of Alpha Squad.

He wasn't interested in a long-distance relationship.

She wasn't interested in one that created limitless amounts of anguish and guilt.

There was no way their relationship could work out. This was what he'd tried to tell her in his room. That was why he'd tried to spark her interest in his stupid friend.

What they'd shared—a few days of truly great sex— was almost over. It *was* over, and they both knew it in their hearts. It was just taking their bodies a little bit longer to catch up.

The elevator door closed, and Colleen put on her sunglasses, afraid of who else she'd run into on the way to the lobby, and unwilling to let them see her cry.

BOBBY DIDN'T ANSWER THE DOOR.

He knew from the weight of the knock that it was Wes—the last person in the world he wanted to see.

No, Wes was the *second* to last person Bobby wanted to see right now. The first was Colleen. God forbid she see him and know that he'd been crying.

Man, he'd screwed this up, big-time. He should have stayed away from her. He should have taken the T to Logan and hopped the next flight to Australia. He should have hung up the phone that first night she'd called him. He should have—

"Open the damn door, Taylor. I know you're in there!"

Wes was the one person he should have been able to run to, the one person who could have helped him sort this out, to figure out what to do now that he'd completely messed it up by falling in love.

"I love her." Bobby said it aloud, to the door, knowing Wes couldn't hear him over the sound of his own knocking. "I'm in love with Colleen."

Still, it was a shock to speak the words, to admit these powerful feelings that he'd worked overtime to deny right from the very start.

Right from her nineteenth birthday, when he and Wes had taken Colleen and a group of her girlfriends from college to Busch Gardens. Bobby hadn't seen her in a few years, and suddenly there she was. All grown up. He'd gotten into an argument with her about some political issue, and she was so well-informed and so well-spoken, she'd convinced him that he was backing the wrong party. He'd fallen for her then—a girl-woman who wasn't afraid to tell a man that he was wrong.

Yeah, he'd loved her for years, but it wasn't until this past week, until they became lovers, that his love for her had deepened and grown into this complete, everlasting force. It was bigger than he was. It was all-consuming and powerful. He'd never felt anything like it in his entire life, and it scared the hell out of him.

"I can't say no to her," Bobby said to Wes, through the door. "She wants me to meet her tonight, and I'm going to be there, because, damn it, I can't stay away from her. It's tearing me up, because I know this isn't what you want for her. I know you wanted better. But if she came to me and told me she loved me, too, and that she wanted to marry me, I'd do it. Tonight. I'd take her to Vegas before she changed her mind. Yeah, I'd do it, even though I know what a mistake it would be for her.

"But she doesn't want to marry me." Bobby wiped his face, his eyes. "She only wants to sleep with me. I don't have to worry about her waking up seven years from now and hating her life. I only have to worry about spending the rest of *my* life wanting someone I can't have."

Bobby sat on the edge of the hotel room bed, right where Colleen had sat just a short time ago.

"God, I want her in my life," he said aloud. "What am I going to do, Wes?"

No one answered.

Wes had stopped knocking on the door. He was gone.

And Bobby was alone.

AS THE TV NEWS CAMERAS arrived, Colleen glanced at her watch. It was about 7:20.

Bobby and his friends were already there, already in place—Thomas and Jim Slade seemingly casually hanging out on the sidewalk in front of the church parking lot, Rio and Mike up near the truck that held the camera.

Bobby was sticking close to her in the crowd.

"There's a good chance if Morrison's going to try anything, he's going to target you," he explained. He was dressed in jeans and a white button-down shirt with a jacket over it, despite the heat.

"Are you wearing a jacket because you've got on a gun under there?" She had to ask.

He laughed. "I'm wearing a jacket because I'm here posing as a member of Relief Aid, and I wanted to look nice."

Oh. "You do," she said. "You look very nice."

"So do you." His gaze skimmed appreciatively down her denim skirt, taking in the yellow daisies that adorned her blouse. "You always do."

Time hung for a moment, as she fell into the bottomless depths of his eyes. But then he looked away.

"I'm sorry," Colleen said. "About this afternoon."

"No." He glanced at her. "I was the one who was—"

"No," she said. "You weren't."

His eyes were apologetic. "I can't come over tonight. I'm sorry, but…"

She nodded. Had to ask. "Are you sure?"

"No." He met her gaze again, smiled ruefully. "I mean, five minutes ago, yeah, I was sure. But here you are and…" He shook his head.

"Well, if you change your mind, I'll be home." Colleen tried to sound casual, tried to sound as if sharing this one last night with him didn't mean so much to her. She cleared her throat. "I should probably go inside pretty soon. If John Morrison were coming, he'd probably be here by now."

Famous last words.

"Hey! Hey, hippie chick! Nice party you're throwing here. What are we celebrating? The fact that you're going away and won't be around to annoy us for a whole week?"

It was John Morrison, and he was drunk, holding a bottle wrapped in a paper bag.

As Bobby stepped in front of her, he seemed to expand, and Colleen realized that a baseball bat was dangling from Morrison's other hand.

"How about we let those cameras cover some real news?" Morrison asked loudly—loudly enough for heads to turn in his direction.

Loudly enough for the other SEALs to move toward them. But the crowd was thick, and they were having trouble getting through the crush. As were the police officers who'd been assigned to keep traffic moving.

"I'm going down the street," Morrison continued, "just a block or so over, to that AIDS Center they're building down there. I'm going to break the windows in protest. We don't want it in our neighborhood. We don't want *you* in our neighborhood."

He pointed at Colleen with the baseball bat, swinging it up toward her, and just like that, it was over.

She barely saw Bobby move. Yet somehow he'd taken the bat away from Morrison and had the man down on the ground before she even blinked.

The other SEALs made the scene a few seconds before the police.

Bobby lifted Morrison to his feet, handed the man to Spaceman. "Take him inside. There are some empty rooms upstairs." He turned to Rio. "Find Father Timothy. Tell him it has to do with that matter I discussed with him earlier this week." He looked at Colleen. "You okay?"

She watched as Spaceman hustled Morrison inside. "Yeah. I don't think he was going to hurt me."

"What's going on here?" the police officer—a big, ruddy-cheeked beat cop named Danny O'Sullivan—planted himself in front of them.

Bobby touched her arm and lowered his voice. "You want to press charges? Lifting the bat like that could be considered assault. At the least, we could get him for drunk and disorderly."

She met his gaze. "No." Not if Father Timothy was getting involved. Bobby had talked to Timothy earlier in the week, he'd said.

Be compassionate, she'd told him, just that afternoon. Obviously, he hadn't needed the reminder.

"Just a little outburst from a friend who had too much to drink," Bobby told O'Sullivan. He squeezed Colleen's arm. "You want to take it from here? I want to go inside to talk to Morrison."

She nodded, and he pulled Thomas King over. "Don't let Colleen out of your sight."

"Aye, aye, Chief."

The crowd parted for Bobby as Colleen turned back to the cop. "Really, Dan," she said. "Everything's fine. We'll see John gets home safely."

O'Sullivan looked at the bat that Mike Lee had picked up through narrowed eyes. "What, did Johnny want to get a game going or something?"

"Or something," Colleen agreed.

"Sometimes it does a body more harm than good to be protected by friends," O'Sullivan said.

"He's had a recent tragedy in his family," she told him. "He doesn't need a night in jail, Dan. He needs to talk to his parish priest."

O'Sullivan smiled as he shook his head. "I wish I were twenty-something and still believed I could save the world, one poor loser at a time. Good luck on your trip to Tulgeria." He nodded to Thomas, who was still standing beside her.

She glanced at Thomas, too. "Let's go inside."

BOBBY WAS IN AN upstairs storage room, talking to John Morrison about Vietnam. He was much too young to have been there, but he must've been something of a historian, because he knew the names of the rivers and the towns and the battles in which Morrison had fought.

John Morrison was drunk, but not as drunk as Colleen had first thought. His speech was slightly slurred, but he was following the conversation easily.

As she listened, lingering with Thomas King just outside the door, the two men talked about Admiral Jake Robinson, who'd also served in 'Nam. Morrison knew of the man and was impressed that Bobby thought of him as a friend. They talked about Bobby's career in the SEAL units. They talked about Morrison's bar, and his father who'd served in a tank division in World War II—who had died just two years ago after a long struggle with cancer. They talked about elderly parents, about loss, about death.

And suddenly they were talking about Wes.

"My best friend is still jammed up from his little brother's death," Bobby told Morrison. "It happened ten years ago, and he still won't talk about it. It's like he pretends the kid never existed." He paused. "Kind of like what you're doing with John Jr."

Silence.

"I'm sorry for your loss," she heard Bobby say quietly. "But you've got to find a way to vent your anger besides taking out the windows at the AIDS Center. Someone's going to end up hurt, and that will make my friend Colleen Skelly—and you know who she is—unhappy. And if you make Colleen unhappy, if you hurt someone, if you hurt *her,* then I'm going to have to come back here and hurt *you.* This is not a threat, John, it's a promise."

His friend. She was his *friend* Colleen—not his lover, not his girlfriend.

And Colleen knew the truth. He'd told her right from

the start—he wanted to be friends. And that's all they were, all they ever would be. Friends who had hot sex.

Despite his promise to hurt John Morrison, Bobby was, without a doubt, the kindest, most sensitive man she'd ever met. He was too kind to tell her again that he didn't love her, that he would never love her.

The sex they had was great, but he was the kind of man who would want more in a relationship than great sex.

She could hear Father Timothy coming, puffing his way up the stairs to talk to John Morrison, to try to set him on a path that would lead him out of the darkness into which he'd fallen.

The cynic in her knew that a talk with his priest probably wouldn't change anything. Morrison needed serious help. Chances were when he sobered up he'd be embarrassed and angry that the secret about his son's death had slipped out. Maybe he'd be angry enough to burn down the center.

Or maybe he'd go to grief counseling. She could almost hear Bobby's gentle voice telling her that maybe John Morrison would find peace and stop hating the world—and hating himself.

Father Timothy had almost reached the landing.

Colleen stepped closer to Thomas King, lowered her voice. "I need you to do me a favor and give Bobby a message for me."

Thomas nodded, his face serious to the point of grimness. That was his default expression. He was very black, very serious, very intense. He now turned that intensity directly upon her.

"Please tell him that I thought he probably shouldn't come to my place tonight." Good Lord, could she sound any more equivocal? "Tell him I'm sorry, but I don't want him to come over."

An expression outside of his serious and grim

repertoire—one of disbelief—flashed across Thomas King's face and he suddenly looked his actual, rather tender age. "Maybe that's something you should tell Chief Taylor yourself."

"Please," she said. "Just give him the message."

Father Timothy had cleared the top of the stairs, and she went down, as swiftly as she could, before she changed her mind.

CHAPTER SEVENTEEN

THEY'D WON.

Well, they weren't going to be able to bring the orphans back to the United States at the end of the week, but no one had really expected that. The Tulgerian government *had* given the Relief Aid volunteers permission to move the children to a location near the American Embassy. Paid for, of course, with American dollars.

The other good news was that the government was making it possible for American citizens to travel to the capital city, Tulibek, to petition to adopt. The older children in particular would be allowed to leave, for exorbitant adoption fees.

It *was* a victory—although it was a bittersweet one for Colleen. She was sitting, looking out the window, her forehead against the glass, as the bus moved steadily north, into the even more dangerous war zone.

Bobby watched her, well aware of what she was thinking. In a matter of minutes they would arrive at the hospital where the children had been taken after the orphanage had been destroyed. As they went inside, Analena wouldn't be among the children who rushed to greet her.

Yes, it was a bittersweet victory for Colleen.

It was a city bus—this vehicle they were in. Some of the hard plastic seats faced forward, some faced the center of the bus. There was space for people to stand, bars and straps to hold on to.

Colleen was facing forward, and the seat next to her

was empty. He sat down beside her, wishing for the privacy that came with seats that had high backs. He lowered his voice instead. "You okay?"

She wiped her eyes, forced a smile. "I'm great."

Yeah, sure she was. He wanted to hold her hand, but he didn't dare touch her. "The past few days have been crazy, huh?"

She gave him another smile. "Yeah, I've been glad many times over that you and Alpha Squad are here."

God, he'd missed her. When Thomas King had given him her message—don't come over—he'd known that it was over between them. Right up until then he'd harbored hope. Maybe if he went to her and told her that he loved her... Maybe if he begged, she'd agree to keep seeing him. And maybe someday she'd fall in love with him, too.

"You and Wes are on friendlier terms again," she noted. "I mean, at least you seem to be talking."

Bobby nodded, even though that was far from the truth. The final insult in this whole messed-up situation was the damage he'd done to his decade of friendship with Wes. It seemed irreparable.

Wes was talking to him, sure—but it was only an exchange of information. They weren't sharing their thoughts, not the way they used to. When he looked at Wes, he could no longer read the man's mind.

How much of that was his own fault, his own sense of guilt? He didn't know.

"Life goes on, huh?" Colleen said. "Despite all the disappointments and tragedies. There's always good news happening somewhere." She gestured to the bus, to the four other Relief Aid volunteers who sat quietly talking in the back of the bus. "This is good news—the fact that we're going to bring those children back to a safer location. And, oh, here's some good news for you—I'm not pregnant. I got my period this morning. So you can stop worrying about Wes coming after you with a shotgun, huh?"

She wasn't pregnant.

Colleen tried to smile, but just managed to look... almost wistful? "You know, it's stupid, but I imagined if I was, you know, pregnant, the baby would be a boy who would look just like you."

She was kidding, wasn't she? Bobby tried to make a joke. "Poor kid."

"Lucky kid." She *wasn't* kidding. The look she was giving him was fierce. "You're the most beautiful man I've ever known, Bobby. Both inside and out."

He didn't know what to say. He didn't know what to think.

And Colleen went back to looking out the window. "Funny, isn't it, how one person's good news can be some-one else's disappointment?"

"You're disappointed? About..." He had to search for the words. "You wanted to have a baby? But, Colleen, you said—"

"Not just any baby." When she looked at him, the tears were back in her eyes. "I wanted Analena. And I wanted *your* baby. I'd make a terrible mother, wouldn't I? I'm already playing favorites."

"Colleen. I'm..." Speechless.

"I had this stupid fantasy going," she said in a very small voice, almost as if she were talking to herself, not to him, "that I'd be pregnant, and you'd have to marry me. And then, after we were married, I'd somehow make you love me, too. But real life doesn't work that way. People who have to get married usually end up resenting each other, and I'd hate it if you ever resented me."

Make you. Love me. Too. Bobby wasn't sure, but he thought it was possible he was having a heart attack. His chest was tight and his brain felt numb. "Colleen, are you telling me—"

"Heads up, Taylor. We're getting close," Senior Chief Harvard Becker's voice cut through. "I need your eyes and ears with me right now."

Damn.

Colleen had turned her attention back to the drab scenery flashing past, outside the window.

Bobby stood up, shouldering his weapon, using every ounce of training he'd ever had to get his head back in place, to focus on the mission.

Rio Rosetti was nearby, and he caught Bobby's eye. "You okay, Chief? Your shoulder all right?"

His shoulder? "I'm fine," he said shortly. Dammit, he needed to talk to Wes. Just because Colleen loved him—and she only *maybe* loved him, he didn't know it for sure—didn't mean that gave him the right to go and ruin her life by marrying her. Did it?

"Okay, listen up," Captain Joe Catalanotto said for the benefit of the Relief Aid volunteers, the bus driver and the Tulgerian guard who was leading them down the unmarked roads to the hospital.

All of the SEALs knew precisely how this was going to go down. Swiftly and efficiently.

"We sent a small team in early, to do surveillance," Joe Cat continued. "One of those men will meet us on the road about a mile from the hospital, tell us if there's anything unusual to watch out for. If it's all clear, we'll pull up right outside the hospital doors, but everyone will stay in their seats. Another team will go in to check the place out, join forces with the rest of the surveillance team. Only when they secure entrances and give the all-clear do any of you get off this bus. Is that understood?"

A murmur of voices. Yes, sir.

"At that point," Joe Cat said even though they'd already

gone over it dozens of times, "you'll move from the bus to the building as quickly as possible. Once inside, you will stay close. You do not wander off under any circumstances."

"You all right?"

Bobby turned to see Wes right behind him.

"The bus driver will stay in the vehicle," Joe Cat continued. "The plan is to return to the bus with the children and nuns as quickly—"

"Your head's not here," Wes said quietly. "Come on, Bobby. Now's not the time to screw around."

"I'm in love with your sister."

"Ah, jeez, perfect timing," Wes muttered.

"I think she loves me, too."

"No kidding, genius. You're just figuring that out now?"

"If she'll have me, I'm going to marry her." Damn it, he was as good as any doctor or lawyer out there. He'd figure out a way to make money, to buy her the things she deserved. When she was with him, he could do *any*thing. "I'm sorry, Wes."

"What are you crazy? You're *sorry?*" Wes stared at him. "You're apologizing for something I'd sell my left nut to have. If it were me in love with your sister, Bobby, you better believe I would have told you to flip off days ago." He shook his head in disgust.

"But you said…"

"Marry her," Wes said. "All right? Just don't do it right this second if you don't flipping mind. We're all a little busy, making sure these tourists stay alive—in case you haven't noticed?"

These tourists—including Colleen.

"I'll forgive you for damn near anything," Wes continued, "but if you get Colleen killed, I swear to God, you're a dead man."

Colleen. Killed.

Wham.

Just like that, Bobby's head was together. He was back and ready—200 percent ready—for this op, for keeping Colleen and the others safe.

"Yeah, that's more like it," Wes said, glancing up at him as he checked his weapon. "You're all here now."

Bobby leaned over to look out the windows, to scan the desolate countryside. "I love you, man. Do you really forgive me?"

"If you hug me," Wes said, "I'll kill you."

There was nothing out the window. Just rocks and dust. "I missed you, Wesley."

"Yeah," Wes said, heading toward the front of the bus. "I'm going to miss you, too."

SOMETHING WAS WRONG.

Colleen shifted in her seat, trying to see the men having a discussion at the front of the bus.

They'd stopped, supposedly to pick up one of the SEALs who'd been sent ahead on surveillance.

But instead of picking him up and driving the last mile to the hospital at the outskirts of the small town, they'd all but parked here at the side of the road.

The SEAL had come onto the bus—it looked like the man who was nicknamed Lucky, allegedly from his past exploits with women. Yeah, that perfect nose was unmistakable despite the layers of dust and cam ouflage greasepaint. He was talking to the captain and the SEAL who, according to Wes, had actually gone to Harvard University—the senior chief who was almost as tall as Bobby. The other men were listening intently.

Susan came forward a few seats to sit behind Colleen. "Do you know what's going on?" she whispered.

Colleen shook her head. Whatever they were saying,

their voices were too low. Please, God, don't let there be trouble.

"All right," the captain finally said. "We have a situation at the hospital. For a place that's supposedly staffed by a single doctor and four nuns, we've got twelve men inside, wearing surgical scrubs and long white coats—the better to hide their Uzis.

"We've ID'd them as members of two particularly nasty local terrorist cells. We're actually surprised they haven't blown each other to pieces by now—but apparently their goal of taking out a bus-load of hated Americans is more than enough to overcome their natural distaste for each other."

Colleen flashed hot and then cold. Terrorists. In the hospital with the nuns and the children. "Oh, my God," she breathed.

Behind her, she heard Rene start to cry. Susan moved back to sit with her.

Captain Catalanotto held up his hand. "We're going in there," he told them. "Covertly—that means secretly, without them knowing we're there. Lieutenant O'Donlon's report indicates these are amateur soldiers we're up against. We can take them out quickly. And we will.

"We're leaving Lieutenant Slade and Chiefs Taylor and Skelly here with you on the bus. They are in command, if there's an emergency, you will do as they say. I considered sending the bus back into Tulibek…"

He held up his hand again as there was a murmur of voices. It was amazing, really, how effective that was.

"But I made a command decision. I think you'll be safer right here until we secure the hospital. Once we have possession of that building, the bus will approach, but you will *not* leave the vehicle. We'll be going over the hospital inch by inch, making sure the terrorists didn't leave any booby traps or other nasty surprises. Our priority will be to check the children and get them out of there and onto the bus.

"Are there any questions?"

Susan Fitzgerald, head of Relief Aid, stood up. "Yes, sir. You've just basically told us that you and your men are going to sneak into a building where there are twelve terrorists with twelve machine guns waiting for you. I'm just curious, sir. Does your wife know about the danger you're going to be in this afternoon?"

For a moment there was complete silence on the bus. No one moved, no one breathed.

But then Captain Catalanotto exchanged a look with his executive officer, Lieutenant Commander McCoy. They both wore wedding rings. In fact, many of the men in Alpha Squad were married.

Colleen looked up and found Bobby watching her. As she met his eyes, he smiled very slightly. Ruefully. His mouth moved as he spoke to her silently from across the bus. "This is what we do. This is what it's like."

"Yeah, Dr. Fitzgerald," Captain Catalanotto finally said. "My wife knows. And God bless her for staying with me, anyway."

"I don't care," Colleen mouthed back, but Bobby had already looked away.

COLLEEN SAT ON THE bus in silence.

Wes and Jim Slade both paced. Bobby stood, across the aisle from her. He was still, but he was on the balls of his feet—as if he were ready to leap into action at the slightest provocation.

Colleen tried not to look at him. God forbid she distract him. Still, he was standing close, as if he wanted to be near her, too.

"How much longer?" Susan Fitzgerald finally asked.

"We don't know, ma'am," Wes answered from the back

of the bus. He touched his radio headset. "They'll open a
channel we can receive at this distance only after they've
got the place secure. Not until then."

"Will we hear gunshots?" one of the men, Kurt Freid-
richson, asked.

"No, sir," Wes told him. "Because there'll be no weapons discharged. Alpha Squad will take them down without
a struggle. I can guarantee that as much as I can guarantee
anything in this world."

"This isn't the time for conversation," Bobby said
quietly.

And once again there was silence.

"Jackpot," Wes said, into his radio headset. "Affirma-
tive, sir. We copy that." He made an adjustment to his
lip microphone. "We've been given the order to move
toward the hospital. The building has been secured with
no casualties."

"Oh, thank God," Colleen breathed. It was over. They
were all safe—children, nuns, SEALs.

"Let's move it out," Spaceman—Jim Slade—said to
the bus driver.

"No!" Wes shouted from the back of the bus.
"Bobby!"

Colleen barely looked up, she barely had time to think,
let alone react.

But the Tulgerian guard, the man who'd been hired by
the bus driver to guide them to the hospital, had pulled
a gun out of nowhere. He was sitting three rows up and
across the aisle. She was the closest to him.

The closest target.

But Colleen got only a glimpse of the bottomless dark
hole of the gun's barrel before Bobby was on top of her,
covering her, pushing her down.

The noise was tremendous. A gunshot. Was that really
what it sounded like? It was deafening. Terrifying.

A second one, and then a third. But Colleen couldn't see. She could only hear. Screaming. Was that her voice? Wes, cursing a blue storm. Spaceman. Shouting. For a helo. Man down.

Man down? Oh, God.

"Bobby?"

"Are we clear?" That was Bobby's voice. Colleen could feel it rumbling in his chest.

But then she felt something else. Something wet and warm and…

"We're clear." Wes. "Jeezus!"

"Are you all right?" Bobby pulled back, off her and, thank God, she *was*. But she was covered with blood.

His blood.

"Oh, my God," Colleen said, starting to shake. "Don't die. Don't you dare die on me!"

Bobby had been shot. Right now, right this minute, he was bleeding his life away onto the floor of the bus.

"Of all the *stupid* things you've done," she said, "stepping in front of a loaded gun again—again—has to take the cake."

"I'm okay," he said. He touched her face, forced her to look into his eyes. They were still brown, still calm, still Bobby's eyes. "Breathe," he ordered her. "Stay with me, Colleen. Because I'm okay."

She breathed because he wanted her to breathe, but she couldn't keep her tears from spilling over. "You're bleeding." Maybe he didn't know.

He didn't. He looked down, looked amazed. "Oh, man."

Wes was there, helping him into the seat next to Colleen, already working to try to stop the flow. "God *damn,* you've got a lot of blood. Bobby, I can't get this to stop."

Bobby squeezed Colleen's hand. "You should get out of here." His voice was tight. "Because you know, it didn't hurt at first—probably from adrenaline, but God, oh my God, now it does, and you don't need to be here to see this. I don't want you here, Colleen. Please."

"I love you," she said, "and if you think I'm going anywhere right now—besides with you to a hospital—then you don't know me very well."

"He wants to marry you," Wes told her.

"Oh, wonderful timing," Bobby said, gritting his teeth. "Like this is the most romantic moment of my life."

"Yeah?" Colleen said, trying to help Wes by keeping Bobby still, by holding him tightly. "Well, too bad, because I'm marrying you whether you ask me or not."

"She said that she loved you," Wes countered.

"Don't die," Colleen begged him. She looked at her brother. "Don't you dare let him die!"

"How could I die?" Bobby asked. "I'm surrounded by Skellys. Death couldn't get a word in edgewise."

Wes shouted toward the driver. "Can we move this bus a little faster? I need a hospital corpsman and I need him *now!*"

CHAPTER EIGHTEEN

BOBBY WOKE UP IN a U.S. Military hospital.

Someone was sitting beside his bed, holding his hand, and it took him a few fuzzy seconds to focus on...

Wes.

He squeezed his best friend's fingers because his throat was too dry to speak.

"Hey." Wes was on his feet almost immediately. "Welcome back."

He grabbed a cup, aimed the straw for Bobby's mouth. Hadn't they just done this a few months ago?

"The news is good," Wes told him. "You're going to be okay. No permanent damage."

"Colleen?" Bobby managed to say.

"She's here." Wes gave him another sip of water. "She went to get some coffee. Do you remember getting moved out of ICU?"

Bobby shook his head. He remembered...

Colleen. Tears in her beautiful eyes. *I love you....*

Had she really said that? Please, God, let it be true.

"You had us scared for a while there, but when they moved you into this room, you surfaced for a while. I was pretty sure you were zoned out on painkillers, but Colleen got a lot of mileage out of hearing your voice. She slept after that—first time in more than seventy-two hours. She really loves you, man."

Bobby looked into his best friend's eyes. He didn't say anything. He didn't have to. Wes always did enough talking for both of them.

"And you know, I love you, too," Wes told him. "And you know how I mean that, so no making any stupid jokes. I'm glad Colleen's not here right now, because I need to tell you that I know I was wrong. She doesn't need a doctor or a lawyer. That's garbage. She doesn't need an officer. She doesn't need money. Of all the women in the world, Colleen doesn't give a damn about money.

"What she needs, bro, is a man who loves her more than life itself. She needs you."

I love her. Bobby didn't have to say the words aloud. He knew Wes knew.

"The really stupid thing is," Wes continued, "that I probably knew that right from the start. You and Colleen. I mean, she was made for you, man. And you're going to make her really happy. She's been crazy about you forever.

"See, my big problem is that I'm scared," Wes admitted. "When I found out that you and she had—" He shook his head. "I knew right at that moment that you were going to marry her, and that things would never be the same. Because you'd be one of the guys who'd found what they were looking for, and I'd still be here, on the outside. Searching.

"You know, on that training op that you missed because of your shoulder, because you were in Cambridge—it was just me and a bunch of mostly married men. After the op, we had a night to kill before our flight back, and everyone went to bed early. Even Spaceman—he had to ice his knees, he's really hurting these days. Thomas King—he's worse than some of the married guys. He just goes and locks himself in his room. And Mike Lee's got a girl somewhere. So that leaves Rio Rosetti. Can you picture me and Rosetti, out on the town?"

Actually, Bobby could.

"Yeah, well, believe me, it sucked. He went home with

some sweet young tourist that he should've stayed far away from, and I'm thinking about how that's me ten years ago, and how I'm looking for something different now. Something *you* managed to find.

"Scared and jealous—it's not a good combination. I hope someday you'll forgive me for the things I said."

"You know I already do," Bobby whispered.

"So marry her," Wes said. "If you don't, I'll beat you senseless."

"Oh, this is just perfect." Colleen. "Threatening to beat up the man who just saved your sister's life." She swept into the room, and everything was heightened. It was suddenly brighter, suddenly sharper, clearer. She smelled great. She looked gorgeous.

"I'm just telling him to marry you," Wes said.

Bobby used every ounce of available energy to lift his hand and point to Wes and then to the door. "Privacy," he whispered.

"Attaboy," Wes said, as he went out the door.

Colleen sat beside him. Took his hand. Her fingers were cool and strong.

"Colleen—"

"Shhh. We have plenty of time. You don't need to—"

It was such an effort to speak. "I want...now..."

"Bobby Taylor, will you marry me?" she asked. "Will you help me find a law school near San Diego, so I can transfer and be with you for the rest of my life?"

Bobby smiled. It was much easier to let a Skelly do the talking. "Yes."

"I love you," she said. "And I know you love me."

"Yes."

She kissed him, her mouth so sweet and cool against his.

"When you're feeling better, do you want to..." She leaned forward and whispered into his ear.

Absolutely. Every day, for the rest of their lives. "Yes," Bobby whispered, knowing from her beautiful smile that she knew damn well what he was thinking, glad that Wes wasn't the only Skelly who could read his mind.

EPILOGUE

"WHAT TIME DOES THE MOVIE START?" Bobby asked as
he cleared the Chinese food containers off the kitchen
table.

"Seven thirty-five. We have to leave in ten minutes."
Colleen was going through the mail, opening today's responses to the wedding invitations. She looked tired—
she'd been getting up early to meet with the administrators
of a local San Diego women's shelter who were in the
process of buying a big old house. She was handling tomorrow morning's closing—pro bono, of course.

"Are you sure you want to go?" he asked.

She looked up. Smiled. "Yes. Absolutely. You've wanted
to see this movie for weeks. If we don't go tonight…"

"We'll go another night," he told her. They were getting
married. They had a lifetime to see movies together. The
thought still made him a little dizzy. She loved him….

"No," she said. "I definitely want to go tonight."

Aside from her legal work, there were a million things
to do, what with finding a new apartment big enough for
the two of them and all the wedding plans.

They were getting married in four weeks, in Colleen's
mother's hometown in Oklahoma. It was where the Skellys
had settled after her dad had retired from the Navy. Colleen had only lived there her last few years of high school,
but her grandparents and a whole pack of cousins were
there. Besides, softhearted Colleen knew how important it

was to her mother to see her daughter married in the same church in which she'd taken her own wedding vows.

But it made planning this wedding a real juggling act.

And no way was Bobby willingly going to let Colleen head back to Oklahoma for the next four weeks. No, he'd gotten real used to having her around, real fast. They were just going to have to get good at juggling.

She frowned down at the reply card she'd just opened. "Spaceman's not coming to the wedding?"

"No, he told me he's going in for surgery on his knees."

"Oh, rats!"

Bobby tried to sound casual. "Is it really that big a deal?"

Colleen looked up at him. "Are you jealous?"

"No."

"You are." She laughed as she stood up and came toward him. "What, do you think I want him there so I can change my mind at the last minute and marry him instead of you?" She wrapped her arms around his neck as she twinkled her eyes at him.

Something tightened in his chest and he pulled her more tightly to him. "Just try it."

"I was going to try to set him up with Ashley."

Ashley? And Jim Slade? Bobby didn't laugh. At least not aloud.

"Ashley DeWitt," Colleen said. "My roommate from Boston?"

"I know who she is. And...I don't think so, Colleen." He tried to be tactful. "She's not exactly his type. You know, icy blonde?"

"Ash is very warm."

"Yeah, well..."

She narrowed her eyes at him. "Her warmth has nothing

to do with it. What you really mean is that she's too skinny. She's not stacked enough for Spaceman, is that what you're trying to say?"

"Yes. Don't you hate him now? Thank God he's not coming to the wedding."

She laughed and his chest got even tighter. He wanted to kiss her, but that would mean that he'd have to stop looking at her, and he loved looking at her.

"Didn't he have that friend who started that camp—you know, mock SEAL training for corporate executives?" she asked. "Kind of an Outward Bound program for business geeks? Someone—Rio, I think—was telling me about it."

"Yeah," Bobby said, settling on sliding his hand up beneath the edge of her T-shirt and running his fingers across the smooth skin of her back. "Randy Something—former SEAL from Team Two. Down in Florida. He's doing really well—he's constantly understaffed."

"Ashley wants to do something like that," Colleen told him. "Can you find out Randy's phone number so I can give it to her?"

Ashley DeWitt, in her designer suits, would last about ten minutes in the kind of program Randy ran. But Bobby kept his mouth shut because, who knows? Maybe he was wrong. Maybe she'd kick butt.

"Sure," he said. "I'll call Spaceman first thing tomorrow."

Colleen touched his face. "Thank you," she said. And he knew she wasn't talking about his promise to call Spaceman. She'd read his mind, and was thanking him for not discounting Ashley. "I love you so much."

And that feeling in his chest got tighter than ever.

"I love you, too," he told her. He'd started telling her that whenever he got this feeling. Not that it necessarily made his chest any less tight, but it made her eyes soften, made her smile, made her kiss him.

She kissed him now, and he closed his eyes as he kissed her back, losing himself in her sweetness, pulling her closer, igniting the fire he knew he'd feel for her until the end of time.

"We'll be late for the movie," she whispered, but then whooped as he swung her up into his arms and carried her down the hall to the bedroom.

"What movie?" Bobby asked, and kicked the bedroom door closed.

* * * * *

REQUEST YOUR FREE BOOKS!

2 FREE NOVELS
FROM THE ROMANCE COLLECTION
PLUS 2 FREE GIFTS!

YES! Please send me 2 FREE novels from the Romance Collection and my 2 FREE gifts (gifts are worth about $10). After receiving them, if I don't wish to receive any more books, I can return the shipping statement marked "cancel." If I don't cancel, I will receive 4 brand-new novels every month and be billed just $5.74 per book in the U.S. or $6.24 per book in Canada. That's a saving of at least 28% off the cover price. It's quite a bargain! Shipping and handling is just 50¢ per book in the U.S. and 75¢ per book in Canada.* I understand that accepting the 2 free books and gifts places me under no obligation to buy anything. I can always return a shipment and cancel at any time. Even if I never buy another book, the two free books and gifts are mine to keep forever.

194/394 MDN FDC5

Name	(PLEASE PRINT)	
Address		Apt. #
City	State/Prov.	Zip/Postal Code

Signature (if under 18, a parent or guardian must sign)

Mail to the **Reader Service:**
IN U.S.A.: P.O. Box 1867, Buffalo, NY 14240-1867
IN CANADA: P.O. Box 609, Fort Erie, Ontario L2A 5X3

Not valid for current subscribers to the Romance Collection
or the Romance/Suspense Collection.

Want to try two free books from another line?
Call 1-800-873-8635 or visit www.ReaderService.com.

* Terms and prices subject to change without notice. Prices do not include applicable taxes. Sales tax applicable in N.Y. Canadian residents will be charged applicable taxes. Offer not valid in Quebec. This offer is limited to one order per household. All orders subject to credit approval. Credit or debit balances in a customer's account(s) may be offset by any other outstanding balance owed by or to the customer. Please allow 4 to 6 weeks for delivery. Offer available while quantities last.

Your Privacy—The Reader Service is committed to protecting your privacy. Our Privacy Policy is available online at www.ReaderService.com or upon request from the Reader Service.

We make a portion of our mailing list available to reputable third parties that offer products we believe may interest you. If you prefer that we not exchange your name with third parties, or if you wish to clarify or modify your communication preferences, please visit us at www.ReaderService.com/consumerschoice or write to us at Reader Service Preference Service, P.O. Box 9062, Buffalo, NY 14269. Include your complete name and address.

SUZANNE BROCKMANN

77624	TALL, DARK AND DARING	___ $7.99 U.S.	___ $9.99 CAN.
77518	TALL, DARK AND DEVASTATING	___ $7.99 U.S.	___ $9.99 CAN.
77517	TALL, DARK AND FEARLESS	___ $7.99 U.S.	___ $9.99 CAN.
77516	TALL, DARK AND DANGEROUS	___ $7.99 U.S.	___ $9.99 CAN.

(limited quantities available)

TOTAL AMOUNT	$ _____
POSTAGE & HANDLING	$ _____
($1.00 FOR 1 BOOK, 50¢ for each additional)	
APPLICABLE TAXES*	$ _____
TOTAL PAYABLE	$ _____

(check or money order—please do not send cash)

To order, complete this form and send it, along with a check or money order for the total above, payable to HQN Books, to: **In the U.S.:** 3010 Walden Avenue, P.O. Box 9077, Buffalo, NY 14269-9077; **In Canada:** P.O. Box 636, Fort Erie, Ontario, L2A 5X3.

Name: _____
Address: _____ City: _____
State/Prov.: _____ Zip/Postal Code: _____
Account Number (if applicable): _____

075 CSAS

*New York residents remit applicable sales taxes.
*Canadian residents remit applicable GST and provincial taxes.

HQN™ | **HARLEQUIN**®
™ www.Harlequin.com

PHSB0511BL